THE HAVEN ◀ TEN ▶

Amber Bayley

The Haven Ten

ISBN: 978-1-7394998-2-2 (paperback)

ISBN: 978-1-7394998-0-8 (eBook)

Cover design by Amber Bayley © 2023

Edited by Sophie Claypole

First five chapters also edited by Bryony Leah

CONTENTS

Content Warnings   1

Dedications   3

1. Existing   5

2. Wilting   15

3. Unknown   23

4. Something's Out There   33

5. Strangers   51

6. Decisions   61

7. Shadow Man   73

8. Special   85

9. The Stream   93

10. The Journey   103

11. Destination   119

12. Clash   135

13. The Rules   149

14. Run   163

15. The Wolves   177

16. Awaiting Darkness   191

17. Time To Think   205

18. Underwater   217

19. Sabotage   233

20. Goodnight   245

21. Week Two   259

22. Spiralling   273

23. A Thimble   287

24. Try Me   299

25. The Truth   313

26. Halo   329

27. See The Light   347

28. Bullet To The Head   363

29. Debrief   383

30. Secret   401

31. Clean Slate   419

Epilogue   437

Stay Connected!   443

Author's Note   445

Acknowledgements   447

About the Author   449

CONTENT WARNINGS

The Haven Ten is an adult sci-fi romance that contains strong language and content some might find distressing, including kidnapping, violence, death/murder, classism, homelessness, mentions of suicide, strangulation, stalking, mentions of alcohol and substance abuse, depression and dissociation, mentions of childhood emotional and physical abuse by a parent, drowning, body insecurity and self-contempt, attempted rape (assumed, non-graphic), mentions of infant death, and sexual themes.

In loving memory of my big sister, Tammy.

Writing this book helped me to cope with your loss. But I still miss your larger-than-life presence every day.

And for my dear friend James.

You were one of only three people in my life who took the time to read the first draft. You were the kindest man I've ever known, and the world without your hilarious stories and impressions is a much duller place.

Chapter 1

As usual, judgement looms above all; it casts an intimidating shadow.

'Excuse me, Miss,' a gruff male voice utters from behind me.

I pivot to face a bulbous-nosed supermarket security guard and force a gracious smile. His dull, grey eyes narrow in suspicion as he glares at me.

'Yes? Can I help you?' I ask in a polite voice, all innocence, my English accent instantly posher than normal.

'Can you open your jacket, please?' he requests, his hands firmly on his hips.

'That's a bit forward. Don't you think I'm too young for you?' I reply sardonically, folding my arms across my chest.

Is thirty considered young? Probably not. But this guy has at least a decade on me.

The security guard frowns. 'Miss, I suspect that you're attempting to steal from this supermarket. I believe you have something under your jacket. If you won't open your jacket, I'll have to call the police.'

Masking my nerves, I scoff at him before unzipping my black hoodie, revealing only a threadbare, white T-shirt underneath. His disdainful frown lifts to a look of surprise. I spin to show him that there's nothing concealed in the back of my jeans, either. I even flash him my tummy.

The security guard clears his throat, his ruddy cheeks glowing brighter.

'See? Now, are you going to stop harassing me, or are you going to continue making me strip off in public?' I snap, zipping my jacket back up sharply. I hate talking to people. I've managed not to interact with anyone for a full five days this week. This knob has tarnished my record.

'Sorry, Miss, I—I thought I saw you take something. My mistake,' the security guard says, backing away. He turns and scurries down another aisle, trying and failing to appear nonchalant.

Biting my lip to conceal a smirk, I leave the supermarket, my hands dangling loosely at my sides, away from my pockets.

Once I'm down the road and around a corner, I whip out the cheese and onion pasty from my bra. 'Always trust your gut,' I mumble, opening the packet to take my first bite of food in two days.

Walking back to my alleyway, I struggle to ignore my pangs of sympathy for the clueless security guard.

I've had worse interactions with security over the years. He was actually quite polite given the circumstances. I guess he's just an average bloke in his fifties, probably living alone and working all hours to afford his extortionate London rent. He's likely got a shitty studio flat and the only thing he has to look forward to after work is a cold beer in front of his TV.

I hurry past a group of youths loitering outside a corner shop and keep my distance, not glancing back. My hands are firmly in my pockets, my head down to avoid eye contact, and my hood is up.

You're the suspicious one here, Ruby, I remind myself, wanting to laugh. I'm the one who's just committed a crime—no matter how much I try to justify it with my aching hunger.

My thoughts drift back to the sad, pathetic security guard: the poor guy was only doing his job. To be fair, I'd be lucky to even be in his shitty position in life. At least he *has* a position. I cringe at myself. I'm jealous of a twatty supermarket security guard now; I'm the sad, pathetic one.

Sensing eyes on the back of my head, I look over my shoulder to check no one is pursuing me. I've been more paranoid than usual in recent months. I keep getting this niggling feeling that someone is following me. Or at least watching me. At the chilling thought, all the hairs on the back of my neck stand up.

There have been numerous occasions (usually on days I haven't eaten much), where money or packages of food have miraculously crossed my path.

Last week, there was a rolled-up twenty-pound note on my favourite bench in St. James's Park. That might not have been suspicious if I hadn't found another rolled-up twenty there the week before.

That's why, last night, when I discovered the sealed egg mayonnaise sandwich, untouched, in the bin I raid every evening in my preferred alleyway, I ignored it and went hungry. Again, I wouldn't have suspected anything if it hadn't happened the week before, and the week before that. Untouched sandwiches sitting pretty at the top of the bin, as if they were waiting for me. Just thinking about it makes me shudder.

My tingling spine stiffens at the cold caress of the wind. I breathe moist, hot air onto my balled-up fists, walking faster to warm myself up.

Prepare yourself for another cold night, I tell myself glumly. I jam my hands back into my pockets, the sleepless nights I've suffered through this week replaying in my mind. The phantom sounds of my body shivering violently against my cardboard boxes and the clatter of my chattering teeth fill my ears.

Please, *not tonight*, I beg the universe, knowing I won't be heard.

I never am.

Bitterness is all I know now—it's all I have left. It consumes me sometimes, when I allow it. It keeps the fire alive in my belly. However, that fire isn't keeping me warm tonight.

The bitter cold nips mercilessly at my fingers and toes. I almost can't stand it. It doesn't matter how snuggled I am in my sleeping bag—the extremities always suffer the worst of it. I'd prefer the numbness that follows winter's searing bite. The autumn evenings force me to feel all those little bones slowly chilling to the core.

It leaves me brittle.

I make a mental note: steal a pair of socks to make into mittens. It's only August, but the summer weather hasn't been too summery recently.

My head rests on a stack of flattened cardboard boxes beside a recycling bin, behind a dingy Italian restaurant. At least this alleyway doesn't have an overwhelming smell of urine; the odour here is more rotting food than human waste. Although I'm used to those pungent smells by now. This has become *my* alleyway. I always seem to come back to it when I run out of options.

Options—that makes it sound as though I have the luxury of choice. Choosing a pissy alleyway over another pissier alleyway isn't exactly a choice.

I pull my legs up into my stomach and squeeze my icy hands between my thighs. I'd stuff my head into the sleeping bag too, but I must remain vigilant. I need to keep one eye on the streets. I can't let my guard down. Especially when I'm unconscious, as that's when I'm most likely to be attacked or mugged, despite having nothing of worth anymore. My sandwich stalker pops into my head, and another shudder forces its way down my rigid spine.

Everything I own now—all three things—are essential for my survival: my pack of provisions, my sleeping bag, and the clothes on my back.

I guess if I lost my pack, it wouldn't *kill* me. I could last a day or two without food and water until I nicked some more. Despite my run-in with the security guard today, it's possible to swipe food from big, chain supermarkets without much trouble. My sleeping bag, on the other hand, may have rips here and there, but it's better than nothing. If I didn't have it tonight, I'd surely freeze to death. Too many people I've known from the streets have gone out that way—hypothermia. We're only provided emergency shelter when the temperature is below zero. Too late for some.

Wistfully, I reminisce on the years I was lucky enough to own a small tent. A full-time camper sounds far better than *rough sleeper* or *homeless*. It doesn't have as many negative connotations attached. Unfortunately, my tent was seized by police earlier in the year. Being homeless is practically a criminal offence now. Anyway, I'm saving the pennies for a new one. Well, second-hand or third-hand even, as long as it's waterproof.

My days of squatting in derelict houses have also been and gone—too many drug addicts clogging them up.

At present, a concrete bed is what I make do with.

Last week, I had more clothes and supplies. I hid my pack under a bridge one evening before collecting hot food from a charity point. Then, when I came to collect it later, the bloody thing was empty. That was a bit of a kick when I was—*am* already down. So down that the up is a tiny pinprick of unreachable light in the endless dark.

All I have to wear are my grubby, weathered jeans, a plain whitish T-shirt, and a black hoodie. I don't even have a coat to my name. I must return to that charity point to get hold of one before winter really sets in. I also need new trainers because these soles are *extremely* well-worn; I'm practically walking on my socks now. If you can still call them socks. They're more like a bunch of loose cotton threads which coil around my toes.

I add another pair of socks to my mental list.

Fortunately, I've learnt valuable lessons since becoming homeless. The first seven or so years after I escaped from home at eighteen, I was in and out of B&Bs and bedsits. After that, I rented a tiny box room in an old woman's house for six hundred a month—way over half my wages—and even that 'bedroom' was cheap at the time. Her name was Hettie. She always smelled like a wet dog. I hated that smell, and she hated me.

Back then, I was working as a waitress. The last restaurant I worked in made me redundant before I could find another job that wasn't a zero-hour contract. As a result, I couldn't afford my rent that month. Hettie threw me out without hesitation—the old cow. Then I had to start frequenting grimy hostels and shelters since no one gave a shit—no friends willing to let me sofa surf for more than a couple of nights here and there, begrudgingly—heartless bastards.

Desperate, I attempted to secure another permanent job anywhere I could, but once I didn't have a fixed address, I didn't stand a chance. I'm fairly intelligent—I did well at school. Although that never seemed to help me in the real world. I knew I couldn't afford university fees and living costs on part-time wages. And even if I could, a degree doesn't mean much these days. Many of my so-called friends became overqualified sales assistants after university due to the recession. I didn't bother wasting my time or money. I only wanted to leave home as soon as I could support myself.

It turned out to be a lot harder to leave home for my doomed generation.

The government implemented austerity, so people like me—the working poor—were the worst off. Rent and the cost of living skyrocketed while everything else came crumbling down. I went from the working poor to just plain poor. I hadn't popped out any kids, so I didn't receive much support from the council. I was simply placed on waiting list after waiting list until, eventually, I gave up asking for help from the government altogether. Or anyone else for that matter.

Homelessness has soared in the past decade, and before I realised what had happened, I was out in the cold with the rest of them, only hoping to survive from one day to the next. My hoodie is the only thing that has my back.

In the past, I ignorantly assumed homeless people did it to themselves—that it was *their* fault they were destitute. I didn't know how wrong I was until it happened to me, too easily and too quickly. It's as if I was thrown into a hundred-foot-deep muddy pit in the middle of nowhere, and I was desperately trying to climb out. Yet the mud made me slide back down, over and over. I was screaming for help, but nobody heard me.

Shelters and hostels are fine... if it's snowing outside and there's a chance I could freeze to death. Options, right? Still, if I can avoid them, I do. Especially being a woman. In a shared room, sleep is always a struggle to slip into; I worry there's someone who will either rob me or rape me—or both. A few hostel-goers I've met in the past fed into the homeless stereotype, which frustrated me. Some were drunk, looking to score drugs, or had turned to a life of crime. Those things have never been my style. I don't need those defences to cope out here on my own. That being said, I don't blame the people that do. They're also trying to escape the muddy pit. I'm more afraid of 'normal' people and what they would do to keep their precious society in order.

Admittedly, I'm a bit of a hypocrite. Sometimes, I'll resort to stealing from supermarkets to get by—only when I'm too hungry or thirsty to function. Despite that, I don't see myself as a criminal. Those chains waste so much food that they don't even notice, and they *absolutely* deserve it. Even the restaurant I used to work in made us spray-paint the food we couldn't sell before we chucked it away, so the homeless wouldn't raid our bins. Back then, I thought it was cruel. Now, I see it for what it truly is: inhuman.

I never steal from small businesses or individuals—I do have *some* morals. The streets haven't taken all of them from me... yet.

Most days, I'm forced to either buy the supplies I need and have a hot meal or pay for a hostel bed. My tummy usually wins that war. Sleeping rough might sound a lot worse, and most of the time it is, especially when it's colder like tonight. On the upside, I feel more secure when I isolate myself—hiding from people and their narrow-minded judgement.

To survive, I only have myself to rely on. I've learnt the hard way that you can't trust anyone else. Ever. No matter how much they pretend to care.

Stop thinking about the past and go to sleep, I order myself, sighing. I'll forget the cold if I sleep. I'll forget the bitterness, forget the emptiness of my hollow bones, and I'll forget that I'm even existing.

As that's all I ever do now: I just exist.

Chapter 2

WILTING

I'm dreaming I'm on a bed of roses. The chilling ripple of the scarlet petals envelops my body inch by inch. Their sweet scent sends me home. I breathe it in and I'm as light as their touch. I remember my garden in the summer—a place I once loved.

My mother planted a rose bush the spring before the incident. She liked spending those days in the garden with a glass of wine and a book. She said she could relax in nature, that if we spent enough time outside with the grass between our toes we could feel it breathing. 'I'm feeling life,' she'd say.

She spent most of that spring nurturing that rose bush to bloom. Those roses were the last living thing I had of her. I would run to the garden that summer, as soon as I woke up, and lie next to them with my eyes shut. I imagined her reading her book aloud to me like she used to. Her voice would grow fainter each day.

After that summer, I grew up, and I started to despise the sight of roses. I never wanted to be reminded—to lay my gaze upon the blood-red prison of petals and that stem of jagged thorns which could sting me without a touch. They couldn't comfort me any longer, and I could never find solace in that garden again. The more time I spent outside, feeling the grass between my toes, the more I felt it dying.

The wilting of my mother's rose bush was her irrevocable death.

I open my eyes.

Groggy, I have to blink a few times. It's painful. My pupils take a while to adjust to the radiant sun beating down on me. I'm lying face up, just as when I fell asleep, but something is different. Something is off.

My back doesn't hurt. I don't sense the cold, unyielding concrete beneath me anymore. The odour has also disappeared—replaced by fresh meadow air.

I lift a heavy hand to shield my watering eyes and I recoil when something tickles the sensitive pad of my other palm. Has a maggot wriggled out of the bin? I whip my head down to see what it is.

It's a blade of grass.

There's lush grass all around me. A vivid green sea. There's no restaurant anymore—no alleyway, no buildings, and no streets. Only rolling hills of open space against a blazing blue sky. *This is definitely not where you rested your head last night*, I remind myself, unpleasantly mystified.

My stomach turns, bile rising to my throat. I swallow it down then focus on my oxygen intake to quell this dizzying fever dream. *This can't be real... This can't be real...* I repeat in my mind as I survey my surroundings, attempting to absorb the scene and make sense of it.

I sit up stiffly. My body has a tingling numbness around its edges. This can't be a dream. Somebody must have moved me. But I'm usually a light sleeper. How could anyone have moved me so far without waking me up? This is fucking unreal. I swear I'm more dazed the more awake I get.

I search my body for any sign of injury or vulnerability. Then it dawns on me:

Where the fuck are my possessions?!

Blood drains from my face. The essentials that keep me alive are nowhere to be seen—no pack, no sleeping bag. I have nothing except what I'm wearing. The pins and needles prickling my skin have me grimacing. This can't be happening. Nobody can be this unlucky.

I'm screwed. No—worse. I'm dead.

It feels as though I've walked for hundreds of miles in this enduring heat. My body stings with the effort as if I'm being repeatedly stabbed with jagged shards of glass.

These hills seem infinite. I trek up one mound to be met with two more. It's endless valley after valley. There's nothing here—no tall trees to climb up and no bodies of water. Nothing besides the monotony of sprouting blades of green.

My mouth aches with dryness. Swallowing is an increasingly torturous task. My tongue seems to have doubled in size, and its roughness rubs on the roof of my mouth like sandpaper. I swirl it over my gums to get some saliva going as I reach the top of another ridiculously huge hill.

Please. Please let there be a vantage point on this one.

Each sharp step is accompanied by a jolt of pain which makes my head swim. Why couldn't this bastard have dropped me off somewhere flat? The more I think about it, the angrier I become. I would throw something if I *had* something to bloody throw.

Ironically, I trip up on a stone, landing hard on my left knee. I wince when the impact ripples through my body, sending more pain bolting up and down my legs.

I can't move. It hurts too much. I'm weak. I'm broken. *I give up*! Fuck it, I'll just roll over and let the sun cook me. What's the alternative? I'm completely lost in this hellhole. I don't have any food or water. I'm already dehydrated, and I'm almost certain I have heatstroke. The usually peachy skin on my chest has burnt to a tender shade of meaty pink. I'm lost out here, dried up and withered, like a discarded bag of bones. What's the point in carrying on anyway?

Nobody would miss you, Ruby. Nobody would even notice you're gone, I acknowledge, wallowing in self-pity. Although I know it's all true.

Slowly, I drag my exhausted body, one agonising metre at a time, up the rest of the hill. I'm so close now. One more pull from my trembling arms should do it.

With that goal in mind, I will my weather-beaten body to cooperate. I collect desperate breaths and plead with a God I don't believe in to grant me some relief from this place. Even just a hint at which direction to go in.

Finally, I make it to the top despite my body shaking uncontrollably. When I peer over the hill, my heart sinks to my toes. There's nothing aside from more peaks and valleys. No sign of civilisation and no provisions.

There's no chance.

I could fucking cry. But I don't. I can't remember the last time I cried.

Instead, I flop onto my back, resting my pounding head on the soft grass. My eyes close against the harsh sun, leaving an orangey glow behind my eyelids. I could fall asleep here and never wake up. Would it make things easier? *Probably*, I admit.

I've been waiting to finally give up on the increasingly gruelling task of merely trying. I've been pursuing this feeling of hopelessness for years. Hope is a wondrous thing for most people—it has its own life force, and I've been drawing from it since my mother died.

If you can make it through one more night on the street, in the freezing cold, you will find somewhere safer and warmer tomorrow. I fooled myself into believing that every time I felt low. Though, usually, I did find something in the end. That one night when things were a little better would get me through the rest of the shitty week. It would keep me fighting to survive each hunger pain and every shiver.

At least I had a choice of shops to steal water from in London. At least I had the whole city to rifle through to survive. I have nothing here—it's a scenic wasteland.

But I knew this was coming. Part of me wanted to welcome it with open arms. I'd imagined a wave of tranquillity would flow through me and I'd finally be unburdened, able to let go of it all and float away into a calming mist.

Now, I'm sure I've reached my limit. I don't want to try anymore because I'm too tired of falling—of spiralling down to a bottomless chasm of doom and gloom. This time, I don't have the strength to claw my way back up. I'm just relieved it's been on my terms; I'm not being stabbed by a drug-fuelled miscreant in a public toilet somewhere or having my sleeping bag set on fire by a bunch of yobs.

I'm choosing to lie down here, on this hopeless hill, and finally accept the fate I've been running from for most of my life.

My weighted body sinks into the ground, limbs leaden, chest tight, and ears ringing. This valley can swallow me up for all I care. I inhale a few deep breaths in quick succession, which encourages the drowsiness; my head spins and whirls.

What do you want your last thought to be if you don't wake up? I muse to regain some semblance of calm.

My mother's face instantly surfaces in my mind: her kind face, framed by short chestnut curls that had highlights of caramel in the sun. She had eyes as green as a forest, like my eyes, although hers were a much nicer shade. Mine are more moss-coloured. Hers were bigger, brighter, and full of life—the opposite of mine.

Her name was April, an old ladies' name. She never got to see old age, though. I also have an old ladies' name: Ruby. She told me it was because I was her special little gem.

Tears begin to accumulate in the corners of my eyes, so I attempt to push her image back down into the dark recesses of my brain. It's too painful for a last thought. I want my last thought to settle me, to prepare me for whatever comes next. If there *is* a next. I don't mind if it is merely blackness I float into. I wouldn't know if everything suddenly stopped anyway.

Perhaps that would be the kindest thing death could grant us: an absolute end. The best night's sleep you'd never wake up from.

Out of nowhere, the unrelenting light is swept away by a shadow.

A velvety male voice coats the silence I've been enjoying. 'Excuse me, are you dead or just sunbathing?'

Startled, I fling my eyes open to see a man standing over me, blocking the sun's stifling reach. The outline of his body seems to glow because of this, as if he's been sent down from the heavens to escort me to the afterlife.

Am I dead?

I squint up at him in my dazed state while he continues to stare down at me with worry. His messy black hair caresses the whisperings of the wind, its strands engaging in a slow dance with the sweeping air. It's a complete contrast to his creamy skin, yet it complements it well.

His concerned eyes pierce through me, right to the core of my being. They're crystal blue—the kind of eyes that could gleam even in the dark.

A sudden jolt electrifies my heart awake.

'Are you lost, too?' he queries, offering me his hand and that glimmer of hope.

Chapter 3

Unknown

Taking the stranger's hand, I accept the termination of my termination plan.

His pale skin is noticeably cleaner than mine. Suddenly, embarrassment scorches, my sun-induced flush cold in comparison. I cringe at the thought of how I must look.

It's not only my hands that are dirty; I haven't been able to shower in two days, and my only set of clothes is so filthy a moth wouldn't want a nibble. Plus, I'm grimy and sweaty from the hiking I've been forced to do. Luckily, I don't smell too bad as I had a wet wipe wash last night before bed.

I may be homeless, but I manage to keep myself reasonably clean. I'm not too proud to accept charity, especially when they have hot showers on offer. I always prioritise hygiene products with the limited money I have. They're harder to steal than food.

My long, curly—well, matted—brown mane can't be tamed, though. Despite my best attempts at tying it back in a bun, the wisps of my fringe stick to my forehead.

Why do you care how you look to him? That shouldn't be your priority right now.

It shouldn't, but there's just something about him that chases all my other thoughts away. Something I recognise deep within myself.

The guy pulls me up onto my aching feet, snapping me out of my warm daze. My legs are dangerously wobbly. Flustered, I stare down at the grass I've come to loathe, avoiding his gaze. I can feel his eyes on me, awareness prickling over my already itchy skin. I'm uncomfortable with being stared at.

'Are you all right? You look a bit... hazy,' the man says hesitantly, obviously not wanting to offend.

'Erm, yeah, I'm fine. Just tired. I've been walking around for hours, hoping to find someone... or something,' I mutter faintly, clearing my throat between sentences and trying not to sound as weak as I am.

'Here—I've got water.' He reaches for the clear plastic bottle stuffed into his jean pocket and hands it to me.

I try not to snatch it out of his hands and guzzle it down like I desperately want to. Instead, I casually unscrew the top and attempt to sip it. My throat is so tight that I can barely swallow a mouthful. It takes a few strained sips to push the dry lump down my throat.

'Thank you,' I express more strongly this time, meeting his eyes for a brief moment when I offer the bottle back. They're intense and narrow as he observes me. I flinch away.

'Drink the rest—seriously. You look like you need it more than I do.' He refuses to take it back and motions for me to carry on.

I hesitate, knowing it would be selfish of me to continue.

'Go on,' he insists.

Gratefully, I oblige, bringing the bottle back to my chapped lips. The water is miraculously icy and refreshing. Gulping down the rest, I start to feel human again. My hands and legs are noticeably less shaky. I drain the bottle quickly, then draw in a deep, steadying breath. My head clears.

The man in front of me finally comes into focus. He appears youthful, although I'd guess he's in his late twenties. He has high cheekbones, a straight, slightly rounded nose, and faint dimples, which must deepen when he smiles. His black, wavy hair is the perfect length: the ends flick over his ears and sweep across his forehead. He's of medium build, wearing an outfit similar to mine: Converse, dark jeans, a white T-shirt, and a black unbuttoned shirt. His clothes are much cleaner than mine—newer and brighter. He probably got his with actual money: a normal person not needing to beg, borrow, and steal to acquire anything and everything like me.

'Thanks. I did have some water in my backpack, but someone stole all my stuff and dumped me out here while I was asleep,' I inform him. Saying it out loud causes my face to heat with a sudden rush of burning rage. To control it, I clamp my jaw shut to the point of pain.

'I also woke up here with nothing. I found that bottle whilst travelling. I'm assuming this is some sick joke. Someone could be watching,' he remarks, surveying the expansive yet empty landscape.

Whilst? This guy must be comfortably middle class, if not upper. There's a subtle cadence that most would miss. I'm more conscious of the differences. I bet he's one of those champagne socialists who pretend to slum it by hiding how well-spoken they are around the less-fortunate.

'That's weird. Can't be only one person doing this, then. To kidnap the both of us, you'd need at least two, maybe more,' I mutter, paranoia matching his.

'Possibly. I was in my flat, so they must have broken in when I was asleep. Where were you when they took you?' he questions, his eyes darting to mine before I can look away.

How can I say 'I was sleeping next to a bin in a pissy alleyway' without it sounding bad? People look at you differently when they know you're homeless. Less like a person and more like a dirty rat. Therefore, I have to lie.

'Erm, I—I was also in my flat,' I mumble, concentrating on my hands as they fiddle with the bottle top. I hate unnecessary lies. I feel more guilty because he's being so nice to me. Nevertheless, I don't want him to know I'm the dirt on society's shoe. I want him to see me as a woman. A typical thirty-year-old woman who lives in a flat, sleeps in a regular bed—one that isn't surrounded by bins—and owns soap. Or at least has a hairbrush to her name.

'I'm Logan West,' he introduces himself, offering me his hand to shake.

Panicking, I quickly wipe my hand on my dirty jeans, making no difference to them at all. 'Ruby Hayes.' I reluctantly shake his hand and break off contact as quickly as possible.

You shouldn't have given him your full name, you twit, I think, suddenly worried.

Why am I trusting this stranger so quickly? I'm never usually this trusting with anyone. Especially someone I've just met under suspicious circumstances. He could be an axe murderer. He could be the guy who kidnapped me, for all I know.

'Can you walk? We must be close to somewhere by now. There aren't many rural places like this near London. We're bound to come across something soon.' He glances at me with concern-soaked eyes again. Concern over my continuing weakness, or the flimsy hope we'll stumble across civilisation soon? I can't tell.

Surely he wouldn't be bothered about your welfare if he meant you harm, I reason, trusting my sense of calm around him, if nothing else. My instincts tell me his worry is no act, and he hasn't given me a reason to doubt him thus far. Regardless, I still need to keep my wits about me. We're stuck in this situation together, in the middle of God knows where.

'Unless we're not near London,' I blurt out.

My stomach swooshes, a cold wave of dread crashing into my senses. It was meant as an offhand comment, but I have a terrifying suspicion it's true.

Dragging myself through this hopeless place is torturous. But at least I'm not alone anymore. With Logan here, the monotonous backdrop may as well be invisible. Although I imagine his presence in any setting draws the eye.

I gradually grow bolder in the hour that ticks by. I manage to make eye contact with Logan for three whole seconds when he talks about his favourite food: a Spanish omelette with chorizo. I agree with his choice despite not knowing what a Spanish omelette involves (apart from eggs, of course). He tells me his mum often made the traditional Spanish dish for breakfast after they took a trip to Barcelona when he was twelve.

'What's your favourite food?' Logan enquires as we start trudging up another steep hill.

'Hmm... what's my favourite?' I stall, attempting to think of something more interesting than an egg mayonnaise sandwich. 'Well, I think my favourite has to be... spaghetti bolognese.' The last time I had spaghetti bolognese was about five years ago. From what I remember, it was decent.

I don't know why I'm lying so much. Usually, I don't care what people think of me. I must want to impress him, and I can't do that with my awfully mundane personality. My father used to drum that into me often enough.

I've never been a very likeable or noteworthy person, judging by the absence of any real friends at school. And it only got worse when my mum died; I crawled back into my shell and never came out again.

I'm a shadow. A transparent object in the background. The ghost of a person whose potential was lost when the life was sucked out of them by another's death.

We finally reach the top of the hill and I sneak another peek at Logan's face while his heavily lashed eyes are focused on the landscape.

He's annoyingly attractive, although not in a glaring way; his looks are more subtle and gently pleasing to the eye. Undeniable in any sense. What's really striking about him is the combination of ebony hair, light blue irises like an early morning sky, and porcelain skin. His beauty is almost otherworldly.

And the dimples...

'What the hell?' Logan gasps, shielding his eyes from the sun's harassing glare.

'What's wrong with spaghetti bolognese?' I ask, my face falling.

'No—look,' he instructs, pointing to something beyond the hill.

I follow his instruction and instantly regret it.

In the distance, the green sea finally ends. But it's not what I had hoped for. There's no civilisation. If anything, it's worse than these valleys. Ahead of us is something which fills me with sickening dread.

My breath catches at the unlikely sight.

A forest.

No, that's a massive understatement. A bloody huge forest! A horizon of wilderness as far as the eye can see. It would be an awe-inspiring view if I weren't so afraid of it. It's the opposite of what should be there. If we were still in London, that is.

We've definitely surpassed lost now. We're heading towards the utterly unfathomable, and fucking ridiculous, unknown.

It takes us another twenty minutes to reach the edge of the dense forest. As we approach, we see how immense it really is. It's a jungle compared to the forests I've visited in the British countryside. The trees are leafy giants, overpowering our view ahead. It's intimidating. I was already struggling to breathe in that rolling green sea of valleys; I had no idea that I was wading towards this more perilous ocean of infinite trees.

'Maybe we should turn back,' I suggest, not hiding my unease.

'It's taken us nearly all afternoon to reach this point. If we journey back the way we came, we'll be walking in the dark only to end up where we started—with no water, no shelter, and no food. At least in there, we have a chance to find those things,' Logan counters, trying to make his disagreement sound reassuring.

But there can be no reassuring me at this point.

I thought living on the streets was bad enough. For me, I assumed circumstances couldn't get much worse. Obviously, I was very, *very* wrong. The only plus is that I have Logan here. I've never had anyone in the gutter. I'm surrounded by thousands of people every day in London, yet I can't remember the last time I actually spoke to someone, let alone had a conversation.

The supermarket security guard pops into my head. Does that count as a conversation? I doubt it. It was more of an altercation.

'Shall we brave it, Ruby? I'll leave the choice up to you,' Logan says with a shrug. He smiles at me with no hint of trepidation, his cute dimples more pronounced. 'I've been wild camping loads of times. I can keep us safe for the night.' His handsome face is open and kind. Still, I don't trust it.

Logan's attention returns to the forest, but I'm sure he can see me in his peripheral vision scowling at him. His lips quirk up at the corners. He's aware of me watching—assessing. His expression seems relaxed compared to mine, as if he's not worried in the slightest. I assume he wants me to believe he can take care of us. He doesn't know I've never needed anyone to look after me because I've always done a better job myself. People only let you down.

'Fine. I guess I have no other choice, as per usual. This is just typical. Great. Fucking fantastic,' I huff in a dry tone, then inwardly chastise myself for sounding so negative. Pessimism and sarcasm are simply my default settings. It happens when nothing in life tends to go right. I'm more than used to it.

Logan's smirk widens into a dimpled grin, and he struggles to hide a chuckle with a cough. Why is he finding this so amusing? Or is he laughing *at* me?

Blood pounds in my ears. I don't want to concede control to him. I want to decide my own fate, even if my unwise decisions leave me dead. Call it stubbornness, but at least I'll know that if something happens to me it's my own fucking fault. I refuse to be a mindless sheep thoughtlessly following other mindless sheep to the slaughter.

I refuse to be someone's victim again.

I'm probably deluded to think I have any dominion over my life, being homeless. The sense of freedom I have, though—not answering to anyone other than myself—is my way of coping with the danger at every turn. The streets of London are familiar now—I've made them my home. It's a screwed-up, unwelcoming home, but I've grown accustomed to it.

In contrast, I've been dumped out here, in the middle of nowhere, by some sick, twisted bastard—or bastards—who've managed to make a homeless woman even more vulnerable. Props to them.

Whatever we do, this foreign place can't be controlled—no matter how familiar it becomes. No amount of camping experience can comfort me as we move forwards, and I don't care how smug Logan is about it.

That being said, I do have to consider what's best for me right now. Stumbling up and down more hills all night, heading back to the place where we started, wasting this entire day in the vain hope dehydration won't kill us...

Or... trusting Logan?

Damn it. The phrase 'out of the frying pan, into the fire' rings in my head, over and over, as I take my first step into the wild.

Chapter 4

Something's Out There

Trudging through this nightmarish forest is crushing my already down-trodden soul.

I despised the valleys, but at least they didn't have fallen trees to climb over and hidden roots tripping me up with every step. This forest is a death trap.

Being surrounded by these leafy giants is triggering my claustrophobia. It's as if I've landed in a Tolkien novel. I live in London, where buildings are packed together and crowds of people are always rushing and pushing, so I'm not sure why these trees are so unsettling. Maybe it's because I'm not used to a place that's so alive and inhuman.

Up ahead, strobes of golden sunlight sneak in through the gaps in the canopy, larger than those we've passed so far.

'Logan, I think there's a clearing over there,' I say, pointing to the sun-soaked patches of grass.

He nods his agreement with a relieved smile.

We reach the clearing. It's only small. Still, it's a relief to find some open space. Immediately, I drop to the warm grass, sitting with my back pressed uncomfortably against a tree stump. With my eyes closed, I draw in deep, relaxing breaths.

Now I'm at rest, the overwhelming thirst creeps back in. And knowing there will be no water to drink tonight is more than frustrating—it's infuriating. I'm annoyed at myself for drinking that whole bottle of water earlier. Not only due to my sandpaper tongue: but because Logan must be feeling ten times worse than I do. He gave me the water he found without drinking any himself.

My guilt suddenly outweighs my thirst.

Logan sitting down beside me snaps me out of my thoughts. His back is also against the stump, and his side presses against my left arm. I'm very conscious of the skin-to-skin contact. We've both tied our long-sleeved outer layers around our waists, so our arms are exposed. The tickle of his skin as it skims mine has something sparking—my whole body heats from that innocuous contact.

Stop being such a simping mess. You've only just met the guy.

I swallow hard, shrugging off the intrusive thoughts.

'I know things aren't looking great, but I'm confident we'll get through this together. There's no need to worry,' Logan voices in a soothing tone, his eyes seeking mine. His smugness has evaporated into something genuine, as he clearly senses my distress.

Nevertheless, I won't put my trust in him simply because he has nice eyes, cute dimples, and says sweet things to put me at ease. His reassurance is doing the opposite, if anything. So, shirking his gaze, I stare at my hands, a blank mask slipping over my gloomy expression.

Generally, I'm a pessimist, although I shouldn't show it as much as I have been. I need to pretend to be positive, even if I'm not handling this change of scenery well. I don't want Logan to think he has to take care of me—of both of us—alone. I must adapt—as I did all those years ago when I first fell into the muddy pit of homelessness.

'I'm not worried. We'll take a break for ten minutes, and then we can gather stuff for a shelter,' I announce, planning to aim a forced smile at him.

I abort when I realise how close our faces would be if I turned. Heart seizing, I focus on the forest in front but continue sneaking furtive glances his way.

Logan's eyes reflect the sky as he admires it. He sighs. 'Do you think your loved ones will be looking for you?'

Loved ones? How am I supposed to answer that question? No one alive cares for me.

His smile to me is shy and coaxing. I assume he's trying to encourage me out of my shell, but my reaction is pure panic. My insides squirm again.

Snapping to my feet, I slap dirt off the back of my jeans. 'Break's over. I'll go collect some wood,' I mumble, hurrying away.

Logan watches me leave, his face unreadable.

Enjoying my reprieve from the pressure of Logan's attention, I collect a small pile of long branches that we can string together to make a buffer against the wind. I'm used to making my own shelters: cardboard boxes, discarded fabric, or newspapers work well enough. I'll miss my sleeping bag tonight, though. I doubt a pile of leaves will make a great substitute.

Now, I only have to bring all these branches back without fainting from the effort.

When I've finally chosen which branches to carry, I exhale tension, relaxing against a tree.

I need another break before I trek back to the clearing anyway. Part of me doesn't want to go back. If I do, Logan will try to get to know me, and I don't want to lie to him again. *But you don't want him to get to know you, so you will have to lie*, I reason, groaning in my head.

Or I could ask him a load of questions about himself to distract him from asking me any... but then I risk getting to know him, too. I can already tell I might like what I learn, and I can't let that happen. I'd rather not speak at all, get through tonight, and then go our separate ways tomorrow. That is, if we do finally find a way out of this savage greenery.

It's been so long since anyone was kind to me. And I haven't had a chance to feel anything remotely romantic since my early twenties. It's not often that I'm looked at for more than a passing second. If I ever am noticed, it's either disgusted cringes or sympathetic glances. Not how Logan has been looking at me. Like I'm a woman. Like I'm real and I matter.

Be that as it may, I can't fool myself into thinking anything might happen. Even friendship is unattainable. As soon as he finds out what I am, I'll become invisible again. Or worse, he'll detest me as I do myself.

Maybe that would be best for both of us. I should tell him the truth to keep him away.

On the streets, I count myself lucky that I'm mostly invisible. An angry woman covered in dirt isn't exactly appealing. And if anyone *does* look at me in that way, I run. The alternative is danger, in all its forms. I've evaded that situation many times. Men are usually the enemy, the obvious threat to avoid at night. They're the reason I make my bed behind bins, keep one eye open while I'm asleep, and hide a screwdriver in my sleeping bag.

Despite that, I'm not scared of being alone with Logan tonight. He seems different to the men I've met in my life. He's genuinely kind. I doubt it's to push his own agenda.

Last year, a guy offered to buy me a burger in exchange for a sexual favour. He didn't expect a swift kick there instead. That was the highlight of my week. I don't think he or his little friend would agree.

Logan, on the other hand, probably has a mother who teaches him to respect women: to treat them as equals, not objects to be discarded. I wish my mum had been around to teach my big brother that. Things could have turned out differently for both of us.

My brother, Jack, was one of the reasons I ended up homeless. We were so close when we were kids. Then my mum died, and everything changed. Thinking about what happened still gives me chills. I try not to reminisce about those times. Life was harder then than it ever was on the streets.

Don't think about it.

Needing to release this unwelcome emotion, I snap a branch in two. The sharp sound is satisfying. For an extra thrill, I snap another, throwing its remains onto the pile.

I'm growing aware again of my unfamiliar surroundings. *That's enough wood, Ruby. You can't spend any more time out here alone—it's starting to get dark.*

I hastily begin gathering my pile of wood.

Barely a minute later, a rustling sound catches my attention—the crunch of dried leaves and twigs. My eyes dart around, though I can't see much between the thickness of the trees.

The sound disrupts the silence again, closer and sharper this time, and I freeze. It could be an animal ready to pounce.

Stop being so irrational, I tell myself, trying to regulate my growing fear. I struggle to regain my composure. In Britain, what's the worst it could be? A fox? It's not as if I could be eaten by a fox. With how hungry I am, it should be worried about me eating it.

In case anything does spring out, I snatch up a branch to use as a weapon.

Twigs break nearby with a small crackle, followed by faint footsteps that sound as if they're approaching. That's when I remember that someone put me here. That someone could still be around, watching me.

'Logan! Logan!' I call out frantically. I cling to the tree I'm still flush against.

Whoever is out there must have been put off by my outburst, because I hear them running away, the forest swallowing their retreating footsteps.

Heart thumping, I remind myself to breathe. My head spins as I hyperventilate. I blink rapidly, fighting off the mist glazing over my eyes, and try to steady myself. The tunnel vision soon subsides. I finally remember how to move again, just as Logan comes bounding out of the trees, startling me.

'What's the matter? Are you hurt?' he enquires, a deep frown etched on his face.

'Something's out there. I—I think it was a person. They ran away when I called you,' I babble breathlessly.

Logan spends a minute searching the forest around us. When he returns his attention to me, he says, 'They're gone now, whoever they were. Maybe we shouldn't separate again.' Tenderly, he places a hand on my shoulder, and I forget my worry. He continues, his breathing as uneven as mine. 'I'm glad you're all right. When you called out like that, I thought you were hurt. You scared me.' His smile is coy, and I realise I've maintained eye contact this entire time.

More flustered than frightened now, I shrug off Logan's hand, then reach down for some wood. 'We'd better head back and make a shelter before it gets too dark.' I grab some branches while I talk so I don't have to look at him.

The atmosphere thickens with awkwardness.

Logan finally answers, thinning the air. 'Sure. I'll take the rest. There's more at camp, too.' He scoops up an armful of branches, moving past my sudden brush-off.

We journey back to the clearing, scanning the forest every few steps. We both keep our eyes peeled for a threat which could be lurking behind every tree.

We unload the branches onto the pile Logan collected. It's bigger than mine. Part of me is impressed, and the other, competitive part, is secretly annoyed.

'We have enough to build a den—or shall we call it a snug, as that's what it will be? We can collect some leaves and other soft foliage to make a mattress inside. We don't have time to make a fire tonight, unfortunately. We can think about that in the morning,' Logan says, stripping some bark with his clean, well-maintained fingernails.

Agitated by the prospect of staying here longer than necessary, I snap back with, 'I thought we were finding a way out of here tomorrow. Why would we need a fire?'

Logan hesitates, turning his branch to strip the other side. 'Well, aren't you thirsty? We can't walk for another day in this forest dehydrated. There's bound to be a stream around here somewhere. And earlier, when I was looking for wood, I found this metal container we could use to boil water. When we've had a drink, we can be on our way. To be honest, I'm so thirsty I don't know if I can last another day out here,' he confesses, ripping off more bark.

As soon as Logan admits to his thirst, I back down. My guilt for being selfish with his water rears again. It's my fault he feels as though he can't go on, and I shouldn't push him. Anyway, it's not like I can survive another day without water, either. If I could, I'd be quick to leave him and continue on my own again. Even though I suspect I need Logan's help more than I first thought. I have no idea how to start a fire from scratch or navigate without any landmarks.

'Okay, yeah... sorry. We'll make a fire and find water tomorrow. First thing,' I mumble, my cheeks hot.

Mirroring Logan, I pick up a branch to start peeling it. I hope I can do it as well as he does. My rope might turn out a bit ropey.

'No need to apologise. I haven't shown just how weak I'm feeling. But I guess there's no need for pride in a place like this,' Logan expresses earnestly as he plaits together the strips of bark to make a rope. 'We have to start trusting each other if we're going to make it out of here.'

'When it comes to showing weakness, you're not the only one. Before, when you met me on that hill, I was about ready to roll over and die.'

Instantly, I regret my admission. My eyes widen in horror at my candour. I don't know why I told him. It just slipped out. Hopefully, he thinks I'm joking.

Logan stops plaiting to glance over at me, and my gaze whips down to the branch in my hands.

'It's lucky I found you, then. If I hadn't, I'd be feeling the same right about now,' he responds, focusing his attention on plaiting again.

Logan's admission makes me feel better about my own. I suppress an involuntary smile and lift my head instead, grabbing another branch. As I do, there's a snap behind me in the bushes.

Startled, I jump towards Logan, who's already reaching for me.

He pushes me behind him, then shouts, 'Who's there? Come out!'

There's no reply.

'It was probably a rabbit,' I say, mentally pleading for it to be true.

Logan turns to me. 'I'll go check it out. You stay here. You'll be okay,' he states, rubbing my arms as if he's comforting a frightened child.

This sends a jolt through me for two reasons. The first: because he's touching me, and it makes my tummy twirl. And the second is the opposite: I don't want to be comforted like that. I'm no defenceless damsel in distress who needs to wait for a man to save her. I'm more than capable of saving myself. I've done so many times before. I want to smack his hands away, but his touch is quickly becoming an addiction.

Oh, God. What's going on with me? When those bastards stole me, they must have hit my head on something; I've not felt fully myself since I woke up here. These emotional flare-ups are mortifying. I never thought a man could have this effect on me.

Maybe that's because you've steered clear of them for so long.

This is so confusing.

'No. We'll both go check it out. It caught me off-guard, that's all,' I announce, attempting to cover any fear or schoolgirl giddiness.

Logan raises his eyebrows, a smile creeping at the corners of his mouth as if he's impressed, not sceptical. That's what I hope it means, anyway.

'Come on,' I demand, not waiting for an answer.

Determined, I step out from behind Logan, starting in the direction of the noise. I'm relieved when he follows closely behind because, as I'm trying to appear brave, my nerves spike and my heart begins to twitch.

Palpitations—I seem to be getting them a lot today.

Logan catches up to me, so we're side by side when we reach the edge of the clearing. Before stepping through the trees together, we share a glance full of trepidation.

41

We walk at a slower pace, constantly scanning our surroundings. My lungs seem to have forgotten their normal rhythm.

'Hello?' I echo out through the trees, hoping no one answers.

The forest is eerily silent. The emerging darkness cascades towards us as we tentatively venture outwards. If we wander too far from the clearing, finding our way back will be a struggle.

'They won't show themselves. We should head back and throw together a shelter before we lose the light completely,' I suggest, losing my nerve.

'We might have to take turns sleeping tonight.'

'I don't think either of us will be able to sleep tonight,' I point out flatly.

As I'm about to pivot on my heel, a fragment of light glints off something twenty yards ahead of us.

'What the hell is that on the ground?' I ask in a hushed tone, pointing it out to Logan.

'Shall we check it out?' he whispers, looking to me to make the first move.

Suddenly doubting this whole endeavour, I hesitate. Another twenty yards seems like a mile. The bushes are thick around here, too. It could be a trap. Although if our kidnappers wanted to hurt us, they would have done so already. They've had plenty of chances. I was alone for most of the day—if they wanted to recapture either of us, surely they wouldn't do it now, while we're together.

Logan closes the distance between us, offering me his hand. I blink at him, surprised by the gesture. But this time, I don't brush him off. I think we both need a hand, so I enclose his in mine. My heart was already pounding in fear, but now that Logan is this close to me, I can't breathe.

His palm is soft and warm against the rough frostiness of mine. That contrasting detail pulls my focus, and for a moment, my fear is an afterthought.

As we cautiously approach the glinting light, I can just make out a shape. It's a small, clear object. Then I realise what it is: a plastic bottle. Water glistens inside. I'm instantly suspicious: did someone leave it here for us? Something about the way it's placed—standing upright on the root of a tree... I have the creeping suspicion we're being watched. The thought produces a shudder.

Maybe my sandwich stalker kidnapped us. This is giving off the same vibes.

'Should we take it?' Logan whispers in my ear. And when his breath tingles hot on my skin, my tummy coils tightly. I'm not sure my reaction is from fear alone. With my adrenaline surging, I repress the desire to lean into him.

Concentrate, Ruby, I instruct myself, shaking my head. 'That bottle you found in the valleys—the same person must have left it. I drank it, and I feel fine, so it's probably not poisonous,' I speculate, noticing my sudden optimism. I imagine it's purely my intense thirst talking.

Logan bends to pick up the bottle. As he does, he finds it isn't the only thing left for us—behind the root is a black backpack.

'This is beyond creepy,' Logan comments, presenting me with the backpack.

'Yep, you can say that again. I want to get back to the clearing. We can open the pack there,' I declare, not caring if I sound scared. I can't stand being out here for another minute.

Logan slips the backpack over his shoulder and grabs my hand again, as if it's routine. We hurry back, throwing paranoid glances behind us like knives.

A minute or two later, we both plonk down by our stump in the clearing so that our backs are protected. Our heavy breaths synchronise.

'Open it,' I urge, a tight knot forming in my stomach.

Logan shrugs off the backpack and unzips the main compartment. He slowly separates the sides to reveal its contents. First, he takes out some thin yet sturdy-looking rope. It's knotted together to save space. He hands it to me while his other hand dives back into the backpack. Next, he pulls out a fire-starting kit.

'I guess we won't need to make a bow drill now,' he says with some relief.

The next item he lifts out of the backpack makes me gasp. It's an army knife in a brown leather sheath. Logan slowly draws the knife out, and a chill inches its way down my spine like a spider.

'Why would someone leave us a knife?' I ask. Whoever it was must not think we'll use it against them—or they're just incredibly dense.

'They must not mean us any harm. Whoever it is, they're helping us now,' Logan speculates, inspecting the knife.

'Yeah, we should be really thankful they kidnapped us and left us out here—wherever *here* is. They obviously just want to be friends,' I retort, rolling my eyes at him. The mystery kidnappers' motives are bewildering; it's giving me a headache.

Logan smirks as he slides the knife back into the scabbard, the metal zinging. 'Maybe they're as scared of you as you are of them.' He passes me the knife. 'You are quite intimidating, Ruby. In a good way,' he adds, his expression softening when he faces me.

As we make eye contact, he wets his lips. Then his gaze flickers down to my mouth.

A flash flood of heat hits me. Swallowing, I look away, resisting the sudden pull towards him. Logan confuses me nearly as much as our kidnappers. 'I'm not intimidating. You're just easily intimidat*ed*,' I reply, only half joking.

A rumbling belly laugh erupts from Logan. He nods. 'You could be right about that.'

It takes everything in me not to laugh along. It's unfortunate that everything about him seems to draw me in. The fact that he's not afraid to laugh at my jokes is another plus I have to ignore.

Logan's attention returns to the backpack. He fishes out a large metal flask we can use for water. After that comes something intriguing: a compass.

'Why would our kidnappers supply us with a tool that could lead us out of here?'

'Wait—there's something else in here,' Logan says, digging into the bottom of the backpack. He lifts out a piece of folded paper.

As he unfolds it, I realise it's not ordinary paper: it's a map.

'It's a map of the forest,' he murmurs, studying its contents.

'Let's see.'

Intrigued, I move closer to Logan, peering over his shoulder at the map. It's old and worn in places. Printed at the top is 'Arkinwood Forest'. In the centre, there's a black hand-drawn cross with 'Destination' scrawled beneath.

'Look—that's where we are. They've marked us here.' Logan draws my attention to the southwest corner of the map, which has 'You' scribbled on it in small writing. The rest of the map is vague and difficult to decipher.

Frowning, I shake my head. 'I don't like this. Anything could be at this destination. It could be some torture chamber for all we know.' The knot in my stomach turns to stone at the thought.

'Hmm. Yeah, we'd have to think and act carefully. It's a decision we can sleep on. At least we have some provisions now. We can drink this water, make a quick shelter, and then start a fire to keep us warm. We can decide in the morning,' Logan suggests. For safekeeping, he folds the map and returns it to the backpack.

Trying to appear casual, Logan yawns before leaning back, our shoulders brushing. His gleaming eyes lock onto mine when he turns his head. Then, his attention drifts slowly down to my lips again, as if the first look wasn't enough for him. My breath hitches, anticipation lighting a fire inside me. Unable to handle the tension, I whip my face away and frown as though in deep thought.

'Okay, we'll weigh up our options in the morning,' I reply unevenly.

I chew on my bottom lip as nervous energy buzzes through me. I hadn't realised how close I moved towards him in my eagerness to view the map.

Logan snickers at my reaction. 'Come on—let's make our snug for the night.'

He stands and offers me his hand. When I accept it, he pulls me up to him, our bodies nearly flush. A boyish smile plays on his lips as he brushes a leaf out of my hair. As my heart trips in my chest, a tight smile holds my mouth firm.

I know there's an obvious threat out there. But at present, the real danger is standing opposite me. A danger that, if I'm not careful, I will start to crave.

The shelter takes us about an hour to assemble. We use both the bark rope and the rope we were provided to secure the branch and brush roof.

With all the green cushioning inside, it's rather cosy. It's an achievement to make something out of nothing. I'm proud of it.

When the 'snug' is finished, I crawl inside, lie down on my back, and soak in the comfort of soft leaves beneath me while Logan tends to the fire. It only took us ten minutes to coax a flame, and now, I can feel my fingers and toes again.

I close my eyes, sigh deeply, and relax my tense, tired muscles. I'm drowsy already. This day has felt like a lifetime. Logan said earlier that he'll take the first watch, so I can drift off now without feeling guilty. I decide to wait, though, just to say goodnight to him. It would be rude not to.

An ugly thought crosses my mind. When it's Logan's turn to sleep, nothing would stop me from swiping the supplies and running off. I wouldn't need him anymore, equipped with a fire-starting kit and compass. Part of me is tempted to be on my own again, like I'm used to, but I don't think I'm ruthless enough to leave him here without supplies. My selfishness could kill him. Grumbling, I push the thought away.

For now.

'Is it comfy in there, Ruby?' Logan asks, crouching down to peer inside.

Rubbing my face to wake myself up, I confess, 'Yep. I nearly fell straight to sleep.'

'Let me test it out, then.' Logan squeezes in and lies down, face up, beside me. There's not much space, so our sides touch, and my pulse accelerates. I try to keep my breathing under control. 'It is comfy. I'd go as far as to say this is better than my bed,' he tells me, a smile in his voice. And without warning, he flips onto his side, propping himself up on one elbow to look down at me. 'My bed is cold and empty. At least in here, I have you.' His tone is velvety smooth.

My heart fumbles on a few beats while my tummy rearranges itself. Grappling with the sudden urge to jump up and escape, my eyes dart from his face to the snug's entrance. I haven't felt this vulnerable in years. I want to move away, yet I'm frozen in place by his magnetic stare.

My flushed face must be glowing. Will he notice the change in colour? This thought only makes my cheeks burn hotter.

'I'm really glad you're here with me. I don't know what I'd have done without you. I wouldn't have been motivated to do anything like this,' he continues in that low, purring voice, the vibrations rippling through me, making my skin tingle.

Unable to control my lungs any longer, I pant in shallow bursts, swallowing thickly between them. My mouth is suddenly drier than it's been all day. I'm not sure how to respond to all this. It's too overwhelming—too overstimulating.

'Ruby?' Logan prompts with a twitch of a smile. Does he know what he's doing to me?

Blinking, I hum a small noise of acknowledgement. I've lost the ability to speak.

Logan's dimples appear with a fully formed grin. 'It might get cold tonight. It's probably wise to use each other's body heat to keep warm,' he murmurs, huskier—more sensual. 'How do you feel about that?'

Does he want to snuggle?

I'm taken aback by the proposition. A thrill zigzags down my spine at the idea, and I break out in tiny, tingling bumps all over my body.

While Logan waits for my answer, his gaze roams my face—assessing. My breath snags on a sharp inhale when his eyes electrify as they drop to my lips. I lick them instinctively, my heart hammering in my chest as if it's trying to reach him. Is he going to kiss me? Do I even want him to? Panic and desire course through my veins as I imagine what his mouth would taste like.

The tension peaks in the silence, but it's broken by a roaring crash in the near distance. We both jump, Logan hitting his head on our low branch roof.

'Help!' a loud, deep voice rings out, shattering the silence and resounding through the forest in echoes.

Instinctively, I scramble to my hands and knees, remembering that we left the knife in the backpack by the fire. Logan braces himself in front of me. He's ready to defend us if need be. No one has ever been so willing to protect me, except for my mum.

When I was seven, a neighbour's dog escaped its home one afternoon. I was kicking a ball around outside while April was gardening. The enormous dog charged through our gate and started growling at me. I was petrified. But within seconds, my mum had positioned herself between us. It bit her, tearing a chunk out of her leg. That dog would have killed me if she hadn't been there. Yet all I recall feeling was guilt. My loving mother was hurt protecting me. I swore to myself that I wouldn't let anyone put themselves in harm's way for me again.

'Is anyone here? We need help!' The voice sounds desperate.

Cautiously, I crawl forwards. Logan reaches out to stop me, but I motion for him to stand down.

With warning bells ringing in my ears, I peek out of the entrance to our shelter. What I see has my mouth falling open in shock.

Next to our fire, lit by its flickering glow, stands a well-built copper-skinned man. His light blue shirt is torn and his jeans are muddy. He's carrying a dainty, pale, red-headed woman in a dirty green sundress. She's limp and lifeless in his arms.

'Please, help us,' the man mutters faintly, falling to his knees. He shoots me one more pained look before he closes his eyes and slams to the ground.

Chapter 5

STRANGERS

A gasp burns my throat as it swiftly exits. Without thinking, I rush out of the shelter towards the unconscious strangers, my heart fluttering wildly against my ribcage like a trapped bird desperate to flee its confinement.

'Ruby, wait!' Logan calls after me, but I don't listen.

A moment later, I reach the two strangers. Logan is right behind me. 'Check her pulse!' I order him, crouching to assess the unconscious man's injuries.

The man has minor scratches over his exposed skin. I press two fingers into his jugular to check his pulse. It's still strong. Exhaustion is the likely cause of his unconsciousness.

'She has a pulse, but it's weak,' Logan informs me, lifting his hand away from the woman's neck to rest it on her forehead. 'She hasn't got a temperature. In fact, she's cold. Our fire should warm her up.'

'All seems fine with this guy. He must have just tired himself out carrying her,' I assume, watching sweat drip from the man's face. His expression is peaceful, yet I suspect the sharp lines of his angular features would be intimidating if he weren't unconscious. The scratches don't detract from the beauty of his glowing skin. His hair is closely shaven, shorter than the shadowed stubble on his defined jaw. I reckon he's slightly older than Logan and me—perhaps mid-thirties.

'What should we do with them?' Logan asks in a hushed tone.

'We can't do much except try to get some water into them. We can't leave them like this. Anyway, I don't think they're much of a threat. They were looking for help,' I answer, hoping I'm right.

Logan fetches the water from our backpack while I move to inspect the woman. She has long, silky red hair that shimmers in the firelight. Her features are dainty and her ivory skin is like fine china, with faint freckles scattered over her pale cheeks. The scratches on her face make her look like a broken doll. I'd guess she's a few years younger than the rest of us: or perhaps it's her doll-like quality that makes her appear that way.

'Help me feed her some water,' Logan requests, kneeling on the other side of the woman.

Gently, I raise her head while Logan lowers the bottle to her lips. He drips the water into her mouth, taking care not to drown the poor woman.

Despite my fear of strangers, I hope they wake up soon so I can find out what they know. Presently, I can only wonder what's happened to them—why they're here, who they are, and if they're part of the group that kidnapped us. I doubt the latter is true because they're in worse shape than we are. Judging by their outfits, neither intended to go hiking in the woods. A fancy shirt and a sundress don't exactly scream 'the great outdoors', especially as they haven't brought supplies with them. I can only deduce they're in the same boat: dumped out here, too.

Of course, a small part of me is still wary. Even if they aren't in the best shape to take us on, you never know what desperate people are capable of.

I decide to voice my concerns to Logan. 'They don't seem to have provisions like we do, so I think it's safe to assume they've been dumped here with us. Unless they're working with our kidnappers... Maybe they're here planning a party and we just missed the invite,' I say dryly, flicking the woman's dress away from my knee.

Logan withdraws the bottle from the woman's lips, and I carefully lower her head back to the ground.

A faint, gravelly voice behind me replies, 'Aye, I brought us all here to have a rave, like. You should'a worn summat more appropriate for the occasion.'

Logan and I shoot up, whirling to face the man. He's still lying on his back where we left him, but he's fully conscious now. Straining, he inclines his head to look us over.

'Believe you me, I'm not that hardcore. Not now I'm in me thirties anyway. No more raving for me. You know how it goes,' he quips, attempting to sit up.

I shift back a little, wary of him. The man notices my unease.

'Don't worry yourself, love—we're no threat. I promise you. It sounds like we're in the same predicament.' He winces, then settles on propping himself up on his elbow. He has a Northern accent. It's not too strong, but it's enough to make me listen carefully so I understand every word.

'What happened to you?' I ask, slowly edging over to the man. Can I trust him?

My curiosity outweighing my doubt, I offer him a hand.

Logan follows my lead, striding over. The man accepts our help. We lean him against the tree stump before both crouching down in front of him. Logan seems tense and fidgety, as if something's bothering him. He must distrust the man more than I do.

Huh. Strange. When did I become the trusting kind? My gut is telling me that this man's claim is the truth, like something inside me has already connected to him in a weird, unexplainable way. These extreme circumstances must be heightening everything. This feeling was even more powerful when I met Logan on that hill this morning.

'Before we get into things, how's Freya doing?' the man asks worriedly. His wide-set, walnut-brown eyes fix on where she lays, his heavy brows knitting together.

'She's cold, and her pulse isn't as strong as it should be, but it doesn't look to be too serious,' Logan reports.

The man's expression softens in relief before he focuses his attention back on us. 'Good one. I thought she were a goner for a minute there. What's your name?' he enquires, offering Logan his hand.

'I'm Logan West. This is Ruby Hayes.' Logan shakes his hand first and I tentatively follow. Usually, I don't like touching people I've just met. I don't like touching people, full stop.

'Benjamin Mendel. Call me Ben. I would say it's nice to meet you, but not in these circumstances, like,' he says, letting out a jagged sigh.

'So, what's your story, Ben?' I pry, settling on the ground to hear the man out.

'Well, what can I tell you? This morning, I woke up in a valley, on me own, with nowt. After walking for fuck knows how long, I came across Freya over there. Same story—woke up here like me. We travelled together the rest of the afternoon and then found this forest,' Ben explains, wincing here and there between words.

'Sounds exactly like what we've experienced thus far,' Logan interjects, joining us on the ground.

Ben continues, 'We were exploring the forest when we came across some camping equi—'

'Were you left some provisions? Did you have a map and compass in yours as well?' My questions come out in an excited rush.

For a moment, Ben's mouth gapes. 'Aye. Hold on a sec—someone left them for us? On purpose?' His shock morphs into disturbed confusion. 'Yeah, we were left a backpack and a bottle of water. I heard someone out in the forest possibly following us. So... it wasn't you two?' I put to Ben cautiously. My expression must convey suspicion because his face falls into a scowl.

'Course not. We didn't even know anyone else was out here. I was running with Freya in me arms for twenty minutes before I spotted your fire. I left our provisions back at the accident,' he declares, offended by the implied accusation.

'Accident?' Logan hunches forward in interest. 'What accident?'

'We were making our own fire when we heard a loud crack. Out of nowhere, a huge branch fell from a tree and landed on us, like. It whacked Freya on the head—knocked her out. I heard another creak, so I picked her up and legged it. I was searching for help, but I didn't think I'd find it,' Ben recalls, the lines on his forehead deep.

'Why do you think the branch fell?' I ask. 'There hasn't been bad weather. Hardly any wind.'

A weight hits the pit of my stomach as an outlandish suspicion creeps up on me. Maybe the falling branch wasn't natural. I don't want to come out with my presumption of foul play yet, though. Without anything solid to back it up, my baseless theory would sound absurd.

Get a grip, Ruby. It was probably just the wind or a really chunky squirrel.

'I dunno. The trees are old. Maybe it came loose, and we were in the wrong place at the wrong time... Shit happens. It was weird, though. And with everything else... Pfft. Who knows?' Ben responds. I sense that he may be leaning towards my line of thinking—that it was no accident.

'Would you like some water?' Logan breaks the silence, offering Ben the bottle. He accepts it.

'Cheers, mate.' Ben swigs from the bottle and then rolls his shoulders. 'Do you think Freya will wake up soon?' He shoots her another worried glance.

'The branch must have hit her hard. She may have a concussion, although I doubt she'll be out for much longer,' Logan assures him as he reaches over to check her pulse again. 'Yeah, it feels stronger already. She'll be fine. We'll keep her by the fire so she stays warm.'

Ben nods in gratitude. 'What do you think about all this, then? What's the point in kidnapping a bunch of strangers and ditching them in a forest?' A flash of anger crosses his face, and I have to look away from him, intimidated by his harsh expression although it's not aimed at me. The peaceful expression he wore while unconscious erases itself from my mind.

'Whoever they are, they gave us what we need to survive. Plus, there's that map to consider.' Logan scans the forest while he talks.

Ben shifts his weight with a sharp intake of painful breath. He straightens. 'Do you think we should head to that destination place, then?'

'After hearing your story, I'm in no rush to check it out. I'd rather try to find a way out of here,' I put forward, having no interest in doing what the kidnappers want. Actually, I want to do the exact opposite, purely to spite them.

'We only have half a bottle of water left between us, and we have nothing to eat. Hopefully, this destination has more supplies. It could take us days to find a way out of this place. I think it's worth the risk, especially now there's four of us,' Logan argues, running a hand through his wavy coal-black hair.

Part of me wants to throw a rock at him for making so much sense. I manage to resist the urge.

'I dunno. I wanna see what Freya thinks when she wakes up,' Ben says, staring at Freya as if willing her eyes open.

Out of nowhere, a low hum of movement reverberates through the forest. We snap into silence. Logan and I stand, our stances defensive.

We hear it again, although it's impossible to determine its source over the loud crackling of our fire.

'Where's the knife?' I whisper to Logan.

Logan doesn't answer. Instead, he retrieves the backpack, and then carefully removes the sheathed army knife. Now armed, he moves back to me with the knife pressed firmly to his hip.

A crunch and snap sound from somewhere in the ominous dark, outside of the clearing. It doesn't sound too close, yet there's undoubtedly someone—or some*thing*—out there, closing in.

'We could run,' I suggest to Logan, panic rising in my chest with each breath.

'Don't you think we should wait to see what it is first? It could be anything,' he replies, trying his hardest to peer through the opaque forest.

Under my breath, I mutter, 'Yeah, that's what I'm worried about.'

'What about Ben and Freya? They can't run,' Logan reminds me, and guilt rushes in for considering leaving them behind.

Another crunch. This time, closer.

'I think it was to the left of us,' Ben estimates as he attempts to stand. He's still a little shaky, so I give him a hand to pull him to his feet.

'Look—can you see that? Those lights.' Logan speaks in a hushed tone, pointing out two faint lights between the trees.

A handful of seconds later, muffled scuffles on the forest floor indicate approaching footsteps. Without realising, we've drifted closer to each other, the two men on either side of me. Whatever happens next, I know that despite barely knowing one another, we'll attempt to protect this little group we've formed.

The lights and the footsteps creep closer to the edge of the shadowed trees. Our breaths come faster and harder. The anticipation is boiling over and our bodies are rigid with tension.

Skin prickling, I swallow down bile. My tummy apparently disagrees with the idea of staying still and waiting—it's all over the place.

Logan slides his free hand into mine. I don't look. I simply accept it. He squeezes my hand gently, still focused on the lights. None of us can afford to take our eyes off them. They could be dangerous, and they're heading straight for us. It's fight or flight, and with the way I feel, if there's trouble, there's no running this time.

As the lights draw nearer, they flicker like flames. Two little dancing balls of fire are only a few feet away from the edge of the clearing. Any minute now, we'll know.

My lungs stall.

After an agonising beat, a young man emerges from the shadows, illuminated by our firelight. He holds a flaming branch—a makeshift torch. He's tall and slender with shiny bronze hair and a boyishly cute face—impish. He wears a dark green jumper, burgundy jeans, and tan brogues. He's not dressed for this forest, either.

He stops when he spots us staring at him. The tension is palpable. We stand there facing each other for what seems like an eternity.

All at once, the tension dissolves when the young man breaks into a friendly grin and chuckles. 'Friend or foe?' he asks sheepishly, holding his hands up as if we're about to shoot him. 'Guys. Guys. Am I that terrifying?' He laughs again, this one rattling with nerves.

Logan, Ben, and I exchange a narrow-eyed look.

'Zoe, you were correct: there are people here, but it appears that they want to murder us,' the young man says to the other light several feet behind him—the one still concealed in darkness. His tone is surprisingly cheery. His eyebrows lift high. 'Well, this is rather awkward, isn't it?'

He offers us a clenched smile. And I finally exhale.

Chapter 6

DECISIONS

'Seriously, guys. I have to say, you're rather intimidating. All that stoic tension you have going on... Somebody say something. *Please*,' the young man urges, his cheeky grin faltering.

So far, the young man seems well-spoken—posher than the three of us—though I suspect Logan also comes from a place of privilege. I think he's good at masking it. He lives in central London without a million roommates: that screams 'I come from money.' Also, Logan just stands straighter, his head held higher than Ben and me as though he's been bred to look down on people. He hasn't done so... yet. If he finds out I'm homeless, that will probably change.

I only assume Ben and Freya are working class because most people are, but I could be wrong. It's too early to judge. Technically, as I'm not working anymore, I'm part of the dreaded and socially shunned underclass.

I may be a poverty-stricken vagabond, but my mum used to encourage me to speak 'proper' English. She was from a wealthier background than my dad, who was a typical cockney lad. I've tried not to get lazy with my pronunciation over the years—mainly to stop myself from sounding like him.

My mum's family were of Jewish descent, hence the curly hair. I never met any of them. They're distant relatives, some of whom are still alive, but most are scattered across Europe. My mum lost touch with them when she married my dad. They didn't approve because he wasn't of the Jewish faith. Although that should have been the least of their concerns, considering his other more *unsavoury* qualities. Unfortunately, both sets of grandparents died before I was born.

The fire pops, the sound startling us all. The young man yelps then laughs at himself.

The young man, who appears to be in his early twenties, reminds me of a cartoon character I loved as a kid—Peter Pan. He doesn't seem like much of a threat, either.

Going with my gut, I step forwards. 'Hi, sorry. We thought you might be dangerous,' I tell him, not moving too far from Logan and Ben. I'm still cautious of the second torch holder, the one who hasn't revealed themselves yet—someone he called *Zoe*.

'Then you took one look at me and thought, no, certainly not dangerous. Devilishly handsome, yet would struggle even killing a fly,' the young man jokes, his grin returning.

'What about your skulking mate over there? When are we gonna get a look at her?' Ben questions, showing no sign of a smile.

Silence.

I glance back at Logan and Ben: both are rigid, glaring harshly at the young man and his unknown companion.

The young man turns to the person hidden in the shadows. 'Come on, Zoe. You *cannot* leave me hanging here,' he implores, gesturing her out.

'Tell that guy to put the knife down first,' the woman's voice calls out, kind of squeaky.

The young man clicks his tongue. 'They're not going to harm us. I'm sure they're very... friendly, once they stop staring like that,' he quips again, striving to defuse the situation.

Deciding to help him out, I relax my posture and force my mouth to return a welcoming smile. 'Logan, you can put the knife down.'

Ben interjects. 'Don't be daft. She could have a weapon on her that we can't see. Don't put it down. We should clock her first to make sure.'

I understand the point Ben is making, but it's not going to help the situation.

The woman's flame flickers. 'There's a fucking dead girl right next to you, and you want me to come in there when you're armed? Please, I'm not fucking thick!' she exclaims defiantly.

'Oh, yes, so there is. I did not notice that,' the young man says casually, spotting Freya on the ground.

'She's not dead. She and Ben only found us half an hour ago. A branch fell on them in the forest and Ben ran here with her, searching for help,' I relay earnestly.

I'm met with another awkward silence.

I continue, regardless. 'Let me guess: you both woke up here with nothing and no clue as to what the hell is going on.' Risking it, I inch towards them. I don't need to look back at Logan to tell he doesn't like it, because I hear him take a step closer to me.

'Oh, it's happened to you, too? Brilliant.' The young man claps his hand on his thigh. 'At least we're not the only ones. I was worried I'd be stuck with *her* the entire time,' he remarks with a teasing snicker, thumb pointing towards Zoe.

I like him already.

'Logan, put the knife down,' I instruct with less patience. He complies immediately, as if he was waiting for me to be sure. Ben doesn't look too pleased about it, though.

63

'Fine, I'll come out,' the woman relents, clearly aggravated.

With a moody pout on her lips, Zoe finally steps into the clearing. Her hair is mid-length and blonde, waving just past her shoulders. It's a little clumpy and matted: a twig even pokes out from the top, like she lost a fight with a bush. Her face is small and pixie-like, ending in a point at her chin—heart-shaped, like mine. She's suffered through some sunburn as well—her nose and cheeks are red and look sore. My pinkish tan isn't as bad in comparison. Both her black trousers and white shirt are splattered with mud. Her patent black shoes are also caked in dirt. Her look towards me is sour.

'I'm Ruby. That's Logan, and that's Ben. The unconscious woman is Freya,' I say, introducing us all. Stepping up to the young man and moody woman, I offer them my hand to shake, trying to be polite and welcoming.

'It's a pleasure to meet you, Ruby. I'm Charles, but I prefer to go by Charlie.' Charlie shakes my hand eagerly. He smiles kindly, his warm hazel eyes smiling, too.

Next, I outstretch a hand in Zoe's direction. She glares at me in disgust, then stomps past in a huff. In response, I snort a derisive laugh, my hand dropping back to my side.

'I apologise on Zoe's behalf. I've only known her for half a day, but trust me, that's enough time to gather she's going to be a difficult one,' Charlie says with a small shake of his head.

Over my shoulder, I watch Zoe stride up to our campfire. She plants herself down on the log, ignoring everyone else's presence. She rubs her torch out in the dirt, drops it on the ground right beside poor Freya, and then folds her arms.

Ben shoots me a withering look. And, shaking his head, he paces away from us to hunker down next to Freya. He chucks Zoe's discarded torch further away from camp.

Logan approaches Charlie and me with a more forgiving smile.

'I'm sorry if we weren't very welcoming. It's been a strange day,' Logan says, shaking Charlie's hand in greeting.

Charlie scoffs. 'Yes, to say the least.'

Drama over, we all make our way to the warmth of the fire.

Those of us who are conscious are circled around the fire, perched on logs. The flames, crackling and popping, mask the awkward silence. We all sheepishly glance at one another, waiting for someone to speak first.

Logan clears his throat and bites the bullet. 'I think we started off on the wrong foot. We all seem to be stuck in the same boat here. And in my opinion, we should stick together,' he finishes, leaning back and opening his hands, inviting the group to discuss. 'Does anyone disagree?'

'I do,' Zoe interjects, mockingly raising her hand above her head and waving it like a kid in a classroom. 'No offence, but I don't know or like any of you, so why would I want to stick around?'

'Hmm, maybe because there are some nutters lurking about? You know, the ones who kidnapped all of us?' I counter, unable to hold my tongue.

Zoe completely ignores me, like I don't exist to her.

'There is safety in numbers,' Logan adds, shrugging. 'It's the more pragmatic option.'

Zoe dramatically rolls her eyes. This girl is really starting to piss me off.

'I don't care. Come tomorrow, we'll be gone. I don't see anything here which makes me want to stay,' she declares, turning her nose up at us.

'Who's we? I'm staying with these guys. They have that terrifying stare thing working in their favour,' Charlie returns lightly. 'I imagine we'll all be great friends by this time tomorrow.'

Hearing that, the urge to reach out and pat Charlie on the back is strong. I think I'm going to get on with this guy.

'Charles! You'd let me go out there on my own? What kind of man are you?!' Zoe shouts across the fire at him. He blinks rapidly, shocked by her outburst.

That's it, I've had enough of her.

I lean forwards to bite back with, 'Hey! Just because you lack common sense, doesn't mean Charlie has to.'

Whipping her head in my direction, Zoe glowers, her blue-green eyes attempting to intimidate me, but I stare her down. Despite the hostility, she disregards my threat and points a finger at Charlie. 'You've known these people for five minutes, and you're ready to stay with *them* over *me*?!' she screeches in disgust, as if she doesn't believe he'll dare try it.

'Zoe, I didn't mean it that way. Of course, I wouldn't wish for you to go out there alone. With that being said, I believe grouping together is what's best, for the both of us,' Charlie clarifies, holding his hands up in defence. 'We were struggling before now. It makes sense to stay with them.'

'You're a pathetic coward.' Zoe spits the words out, and Charlie lowers his gaze to the ground. 'Never mind. I didn't like you much anyway.'

I shoot to my feet, with the desire to rage at her. I'm about to explode when Logan steps in. He stands in front of me, shielding her from my wrath.

'Right, let's cool this down before things get too heated. You're all free to do what you want. There's no point arguing about it,' Logan mediates, placing a hand on my shoulder to calm me. He offers me an understanding smile when our eyes meet.

Loudly expelling a breath, I drop back down onto the log, still feeling like I want to fight her. I guess I should abstain for the time being. There's still the rest of the night to get through.

'Zoe, you may not like being around us, but I think you'll dislike being out there on your own a lot more. We can protect each other—extra eyes watching out for any threats. Also, searching for food and water as a team will be far easier. It's your best option and you know it. Things can work out if you give them a chance. Don't let your feelings cloud your judgement,' Logan sums up calmly and diplomatically. It's something I've never done well, especially with someone as self-centred and pig-headed as Zoe.

Charlie stares blankly at the hissing flames as he nervously twiddles his thumbs. Beside him, Ben appears completely uninterested in this conversation. He's watching Freya breathe. I turn back to Zoe, who seems like she's contemplating her next words carefully. We only make eye contact for a split second, yet it's evident that she loathes me. The feeling is mutual.

'Whatever,' Zoe finally replies, dismissing us with a wave of her hand. She shifts herself away from us, folding her arms again.

I would rather have seen her go, but Logan was too good at convincing her to stay. He has a way with words—a good peacemaker.

Logan returns to his seat in the circle and sighs. 'We also have a few decisions to make on tomorrow's plans,' he reminds us, continuing to lead the group conversation. 'After we find water, and hopefully something edible, we could check this destination place ou––'

Ben cuts him off. 'Nah, mate, I told you, I'm not gonna decide on the map 'til Freya wakes up.'

'You have a map, too?' Charlie chimes in. His head lifts again, along with his spirits.

Logan rolls his neck, relieving tension. 'Sure... okay. We'll wait until Freya's awake to discuss that. However, there are still the issues of sleeping arrangements, water shortage, and the absence of food to confront. Anyone have any ideas?'

'Why don't we all just sleep here, around the fire? It's warm, and I'll feel better knowing we're grouped together in case anyone stumbles upon us in the dark,' I add to the conversation. The thought of the shelter I was so proud of going to waste jolts me with disappointment.

As if she reads my mind, Zoe pipes up, 'I'll sleep in that crappy little stick thing, then.'

She's looking at my perfect shelter like it's some pile of rubbish. The temptation to strike out at her rears up again. Instead, I clench my fists and bite the inside of my mouth, so I don't shout obscenities at her.

'Fine, you can sleep in the shelter. The rest of us will stay here,' Logan allows, looking equally as disappointed about our snug going to waste. I'd rather it goes unused than have Zoe sleep in it. I'm childish like that.

With the go-ahead from Logan, Zoe hurries, heavy-footed, to the shelter and crawls in without any parting words. Not that I'm complaining.

'*Anyway...*' Charlie emphasises, flashing his light brown eyebrows. He stretches like he's pushing away the tension from his long limbs before relaxing again. We can all relax now *she's* gone.

Charlie swivels to me, smiling warmly. I return the gesture. It seems cruel to repress it. We then exchange a look of disbelief at Zoe's cantankerous behaviour.

I don't know why, but I feel an instant friendship forming with Charlie, despite knowing him for less than an hour. He seems so jovial and sincere—very likeable. It's also easier to hold Charlie's gaze than Logan's. That could be down to what I feel when Logan and I make eye contact. There's a lot more pressure under that magnetic-blue stare. Charlie's eyes, on the other hand, are warm pools of praline with chocolate flecks.

'What about food and water?' Logan asks, directing the conversation before it can veer off.

Logan must like to know what he's doing and where he stands at all times. I'm more spontaneous—living minute to minute without much thought to the future—without much care. I guess I have the streets to thank for that bleak outlook.

'Water... Oh, yes, I forgot to mention: we came across a stream, about an hour's walk back.' Charlie reels off this information casually, pointing in the direction he and Zoe came from.

'*Forgot to mention?*' Ben throws Charlie a dirty look. I don't like it. If Ben isn't careful, I'll confront him next.

'I'm so very sorry. It kind of slipped my mind. You guys were pointing a knife at me when we first met, remember?' Charlie points out, but Ben only stares at him with an indignant frown. Charlie awkwardly purses his lips together in a tighter smile.

'Well then, at least that's sorted. First thing tomorrow, we'll follow Charlie down to the stream to collect enough water for the day,' Logan carries on, ignoring the tension.

'Did you see any berries or anything to eat on your travels, Charlie?' I ask politely, chucking Ben a disapproving glare from across the fire.

Ben rotates away, back to Freya. I suspect his shortness and hostility towards Charlie are due to his frustration at Freya's state. Nonetheless, I won't let him take it out on someone as vulnerable as Charlie, who seems too fragile to handle misplaced anger.

'No, unfortunately not. I'm famished,' Charlie replies, somehow remaining cheerful.

'None of us has eaten all day,' I inform him, suddenly aware of the gnawing hunger attacking my stomach. My throat senses some stomach acid crawling up from the emptiness inside me and swallows pre-emptively.

'Yeah, and it's been a long old day,' Logan mutters, rubbing his face.

Noticing how red and worn everyone's eyes look, I stand up. 'We can sort the rest out tomorrow. I think we all need some sleep. We could cut some greenery from those softer bushes over there to use as mattresses,' I suggest, pointing to the same bushes Logan and I cut cushioning from earlier.

'Fine by me, love.' Ben perks up a bit, probably happy to end this exhausting conversation.

'Yes! Good thinking, Batman,' Charlie says with a quick pat on my back and a thankful grin. I grin back, his enthusiasm contagious.

In my peripheral vision, I catch Logan scowling at us before he drags his gaze away. I gather he didn't take well to that friendly exchange.

'Charlie, get your knife out. We don't have all night. Ben, you can use mine when I'm done,' Logan states abruptly, striding away to retrieve our knife from where he dropped it.

We each follow at our own pace, reluctant to do any strenuous work before bed.

It's taken us about twenty minutes of tiring work, but we now have four thin beds lined up in a row. Mine is between Charlie's and Logan's. Ben gathered a larger pile of green materials for him to share with Freya, who still hasn't woken up. It's clear that Ben is growing more concerned about her as time wears on. He remained silent throughout making the beds.

Ben lies down on his back next to Freya, shutting his eyes immediately.

Logan is already in his bed, resting his head on his arms. He watches me while I put the finishing touches on mine. He hasn't talked much since the look he threw Charlie and me at the start of our task. I don't understand why the friendly exchange bothered him so much. Maybe it's wishful thinking from me. He's probably just tired.

On my other side, Charlie slumps down onto his bed. 'If you get cold, Ruby, I'm a great snuggler,' he says, smiling in mock innocence. I shake my head at him in equally mocking disapproval, knowing he's only kidding. 'I assure you, you'll be missing out.'

Scoffing, Logan rolls his eyes.

Charlie smirks. 'Would you like to snuggle, Logan? I can switch beds with Ruby. I don't mind,' he offers, and I can't help but laugh at the image.

Logan tuts, but he can't hide the upward twitch of his lips. It's hard to resist Charlie's boyish charm.

'Well?' Charlie prompts, feigned hope in his voice.

Logan flips over to lie on his front. 'Sleep well, everyone.'

Charlie and I snicker at Logan's avoidance.

Just before Logan closes his eyes, he winks at me. The only thing I manage to offer in return is an awkwardly clenched, almost grimacing, smile. I can't remember how to flirt. It's been too long. Anyway, I think all these signals he's giving me are simply amplified in my head. *He's only trying to put you at ease, Ruby. Don't get too excited.*

'Goodnight, guys,' Charlie says through a yawn. He shuts his eyes, nodding off almost instantly.

Finally, I lie back on my makeshift mattress. As soon as I do, the burning ache in my limbs and the throbbing at my temples remind me how exhausted I am. Closing my eyes for a minute, the heavy blanket of sleep hovers, ready to engulf me fully. The soft roar of the fire is surprisingly soothing, like a dangerously wild lullaby. It's also comforting to have Logan and Charlie on either side of me. I feel safer. It's strange, because I'm so used to being a lone wolf—not needing anyone else. It's nice to have some backup for once in my life. This is the most relaxed I've felt at bedtime since I became homeless, and that's despite the perilous situation we've found ourselves in.

At this moment, I don't care that I'm in a forest with mysterious kidnappers lurking somewhere out there. All I want to do is rest.

Before sleep can sweep me under, I whisper, 'Until morning light.' It's what my mum used to reply when I told her goodnight.

As I allow my consciousness to melt away into slumber, I vaguely notice a faint, tickling caress. Someone is tracing feather-light circles onto the back of my hand. I don't know who it is, but the pleasant sensation helps me drift off into complete, fulfilling darkness.

Chapter 7

SHADOW MAN

I'm back in my alleyway in London.

The gloomy dark is a familiar friend. It must still be the middle of the night. It's deadly quiet. Too quiet. The typical London noises are noticeably absent—no cars zooming, no loud drunks passing by.

Something isn't right.

Anxiously, I tiptoe down the narrow gap towards the road, then slowly peek around the corner. The street is empty. There's no signs of life—there aren't any lights illuminating windows, and the still, heavy silence is crushing. Unease halts my steps, as if my body can sense that it's walking into a trap.

A flicker of movement at the top of the street draws my attention: a human-shaped shadow, hovering. It slinks around the street corner and rests against a wall. It can't be a shadow. It must be a person. And, from its build, I would guess a man.

A shiver rattles me.

'Hello?' I call out to him, my voice hollow in my throat. My words evaporate off my tongue.

The shadow man doesn't answer. He leans against the wall, not looking my way. It's too dark for me to see his face. He's an obscured silhouette.

A woman sweeps around the same corner, past the shadow man. She's too busy staring down at her feet to notice him. Her hands are jammed in her jacket pockets. When she finally raises her chin, my breath hitches. I recognise her.

The woman is me.

My body goes rigid, my jaw dropping in shock. This can't be real. I'm watching myself. I must be dreaming.

The other me is wearing dark, nondescript clothing, her hair up in my usual, loose, curly bun, the fringe sweeping and framing her face—my face.

As she strolls along, unaware, the ominous shadow man follows behind her. I attempt to call out a warning, but I can't—no sound comes out of my mouth. I want to move, yet my feet seem to stick to the pavement, not budging an inch. Frantic, I fight against my invisible restraints, thrashing wildly. But I soon tire—my body is numb and weak.

Fruitlessly, I scream. The silence is an encompassing hum. All I can do is watch the shadow man catch up to the other me.

Out of nowhere, a second man appears across the street opposite me, as if he materialised out of nothing. A man whose presence tugs at my memory. It's too dark to make out his features.

When he notices the other me, a creeping smile spreads across his face. Not a kind smile.

A tremor of pure fear quakes through me. Something about this is vaguely familiar. My mind is as foggy as this street, though, and I can't quite grasp what's happening.

The other me clocks the man heading in her direction. She pauses briefly, turns, and then crosses to the other side of the road. The shadow man, who's skulking behind her, hangs back, hiding between two buildings.

She reaches the other side and continues walking, faster than before. The second man makes a U-turn and crosses the road behind her. He's following her, too. Shit. The shadow man slips back out of the gap he found and slowly drifts closer on the opposite walkway.

I still can't move. I'm literally trapped in silence. Something bad is going to happen to the other me, and I can't stop it. My heart sinks at the realisation and then starts pounding with panic.

As an unwilling bystander, I watch the other me glance behind her to find that the man has followed her. She quickens her pace again, a fissure of fear flashing in her guarded eyes. A stronger pang of recognition jolts through me—this has happened before.

As the second man draws near, his face becomes clearer. He has long, greasy blond hair and a scraggly beard. His soulless eyes are locked on the other me, his expression menacing. I remember that look.

This isn't real. It can't be, I tell myself, the rational part of me taking over. *However, deep down, I'm aware that this isn't merely a vivid dream—it's a memory.*

The second man is rapidly approaching the other me. She glances over her shoulder again and wisely decides it's time to run. There's undiluted terror in her eyes now—my eyes. He chases after her.

They're almost upon me. If I can reach out and grab him when they run past, I might be able to save her.

Before I have the chance to intervene, the second man seizes her and shoves her against a wall. She cries out soundlessly in pain, winded. He pounces on her, wrestling her to the ground. Then he proceeds to drag her by the hair towards me. She's obviously screaming—her mouth wide open, her face scrunched in anguish—but I can't hear anything. I'm powerless to stop him, just as she is—or was. This is my *memory after all.*

Horrified at the sight of myself in danger, I cover my face with my hands.

I can recall this moment now: how terrified I was. I thought I was going to be raped and murdered. Yet I can't quite remember what happened next. Needing to know, I peek through my trembling fingers.

Without warning, the shadow man strikes, tackling the second man off the other me. I'd forgotten about him. His silhouette is clearer up close—he's dressed in all black, his heavy hood masking his face. He punches the second man to the ground.

The other me scrambles to her feet and takes off—running away from the scuffle. She races right past, not seeing me. She looks a bit younger than I am now, with shorter hair. This must have occurred a few years ago.

The shadow man has the attacker in a headlock. The second man struggles against the hold, yet can't escape from the shadow man's grasp. It's not long before he loses consciousness.

The shadow man straightens. Hood still up, he moves around the man on the ground, bends down, and grabs both of his arms. He starts dragging him towards me.

He's so close now. A couple more feet and I'll be able to see his face.

'Ruby?' A faint voice echoes through the street. I wonder where it's coming from. There's no one else around.

My vision blurs, then blacks out completely.

'Ruby, wake up,' the voice instructs. There's an unmistakable draw to this more tangible reality.

When I open my eyes, I'm surprised to find so much light. I'm forced to squint.

Logan's face hovers over mine. Behind him, I can make out the soft blue of the morning sky, matching his eyes. The rich, mossy smell of the forest floor hits my nostrils. The rustling of wind through dry trees is grounding. *This isn't a dream. You're awake now,* I tell myself, blinking several times to adjust.

'Morning. You were tossing and turning. I think you were having a nightmare,' Logan informs me, his tone betraying his worry.

Rubbing my eyes, I sit up slowly, still a bit disorientated. The details of what I experienced seem to slip from my mind now that I'm conscious. I need to remember it—to keep the memory that was somehow lost to me. How do I not recall being attacked?

You were attacked, and someone—a hooded man in black—saved you. I'm sure of it. Maybe not exactly like the dream depicted—the silence, the dead street. But it was definitely a memory. *It happened to you. It wasn't merely a bad dream*, I drum into myself, determined to not let it fade away again.

As he studies my face, Logan's eyebrows draw together. 'Are you okay?'

'Yeah, only a bad dream,' I lie, hunching my shoulders.

He doesn't need to know that I have dark memories rattling around my head that even I have kept secret from myself. *He doesn't need to know anything about you, and that's how it has to stay.*

'Everyone's still asleep. It's quite early. I thought I'd let them get some more rest before we start another tough day,' Logan says in a hushed tone, sitting back on his leafy bed.

More awake now, I survey our camp. Charlie is lying on his side, facing me. He must have shifted closer in his sleep because he's nearly in my bed. His mouth is ajar, and his breaths are deep and rhythmic. He looks peaceful. Cute, like a puppy.

Next, I check on Ben and Freya. Freya hasn't moved since last night, and Ben is lying on his front beside her. I can't see his face, though his body seems tense even at rest.

Satisfied everyone is still in one piece, my attention returns to Logan. Our fire, behind him, has died down to smouldering embers, the greyish smoke wafting high. The taste of ash lingers on my tongue, the pleasant scent of burning wood mingling with the fresh forest air.

'Any idea what time it is?' I ask, rubbing the thin coating of soot from my face.

'From the sun's position, I'd say it's about 6 a.m. You can get more sleep if you want? I'll wake everyone up in about an hour,' he replies, running a hand over his hair to brush away the ash settled on top.

Out of nowhere, the urge to reach up and sweep a rogue strand away from his face comes over me. Thankfully, I resist. That would be weird.

'I won't be able to go back to sleep now. I don't mind lying down for a bit longer, though. I ache all over,' I admit, carefully lowering my stiff, burning body back to my makeshift bed.

It would be nice to relax before I have to exert myself again. Nonetheless, quenching my thirst as soon as possible takes priority. My mouth is bone-dry, barely able to swallow what's left of my saliva. Both mine and Logan's voices have a sharp raspiness to them.

'You relax. I'll go for a quick walk to find something for breakfast,' Logan tells me, rising to his feet.

Fear springs up in my chest. 'You shouldn't wander about the forest on your own. You could get hurt.'

'Don't worry, I'll take the knife. I promise I won't go far. If trouble finds me, I'll call,' he reassures me, smirking. He's clearly amused by me fussing over him.

Logan strides over to our backpack to pluck out the sheathed knife. He slides it under the waistband of his jeans. I catch a glimpse of his lightly toned stomach and my body warms, driving out the chill from the morning air. *Why are you finding this inane action so sexy?* I ask myself, rubbing my face to disperse the heat.

'Be careful,' I warn him, my voice tight.

Logan chuckles lightly as he creeps out of the clearing. As soon as he disappears through the trees, a dull ache in my chest warns me of my growing attachment.

How can I miss Logan already? He's only been gone a minute.

Stop it, I chastise myself, rubbing the ache away. *You can't let him in. You have to keep your distance.*

Sighing, I gaze up at the pale, sunless sky. How can Logan guess the sun's position if the trees obscure our view? I need to learn this stuff in case I'm ever lost on my own. *Ask him later*, I think, relaxing back onto my bed.

There's no point dwelling on the memory-dream now. It was in the past. Something I obviously made myself forget.

With my anxiety still weighing on my chest, I close my eyes for a long minute to focus on my breathing. I can't let myself fall asleep. I'd run the risk of reliving that memory again. However, there's a part of me that wants to go back, purely so I can see the shadow man's face. I must have seen him before I ran away. It's surely buried in my subconscious somewhere. I simply couldn't reach it before Logan woke me up.

Charlie stirs next to me. My eyes flick open to witness one of his long arms draping itself across my middle. He's still asleep. And I've apparently become a cuddly toy to him. His hot breath tickles the delicate skin below my ear. I want to reclaim my space, but he looks so serene that I force myself to accept it.

I haven't been held like this since I was a child. After my mum died, I used to creep into my brother's bed and ask him to cuddle me like she used to. I knew he didn't really enjoy it. He only did it to comfort me. Perhaps I can do that for Charlie.

'I told you I was a good snuggler,' Charlie whispers in my ear.

With a start, I flinch away, and he snickers.

'You've been awake this whole time?!' I accuse him, trying not to laugh along. I should be annoyed, but somehow I'm not. Playfully, I shove him back onto his own bed.

Charlie's mischievous giggles subside. 'Of course. I wanted to see how you'd react. At first, I was expecting a swift kick in the goolies, but then you *relaxed*,' he teases me, rolling over with a smug grin plastered across his face. 'Next time, I'm the little spoon.' He winks.

'You're the boy who never grew up, aren't you? Like Peter Pan. You've got the hair for it, and the arrogance.' I lightly elbow him.

'I'd say it's more boyish charm than arrogance. Although that's significantly better than some of the things I was called at boarding school,' Charlie admits, shrugging. We both sit up in our beds. He notices Logan's empty one. 'Where did that handsome chap scamper off to at this early hour?'

'He went out in search of food. He took the knife, just in case,' I reply, stretching. My back gives a satisfying click.

Yawning, Charlie stretches his arms above his head. 'He likes to lead and take care of things, doesn't he? Not that I'm complaining. I wouldn't like to do it myself.'

'Yeah, me neither. I prefer to stay in the background,' I mumble, catching his yawn.

'That's not what you were doing last night. I thought *you* were the leader. You're a natural, I assure you,' he remarks, giving me an encouraging smile.

I snort incredulously. 'Um, I don't think so. I'm not really used to the whole *group* thing. I only like to make decisions that concern myself, not others.'

There's absolutely no planet where I'd fancy myself a leader of anything. I don't want the role or the responsibility. Leading would mean I'd have to care what happens to these people, and I'm trying not to become attached to them. I should be trying harder to separate myself emotionally. Conversely, I'm learning that it's difficult to not form bonds with people in an extreme situation—forced to work together to survive. I already feel like I've known Logan and Charlie much longer than a day.

On the street, if anyone had attempted to hold my hand or cuddle me, I probably would have punched them. Yet the human contact I've received this last day has been a comfort. I've enjoyed the company despite the circumstances.

'Is Zoe still in the shelter?' Charlie asks.

Shit. I'd forgotten about her. 'I think so. I haven't seen her come out yet,' I answer, hoping she doesn't anytime soon. And, judging by the look on Charlie's face, he feels the same way.

'What's the time?' Ben murmurs, raising his head from the nook of his arm.

'Logan thought it was about 6 a.m. Did you have a good sleep?' I ask politely, attempting to figure out his mood today.

'Nah, mate. Sleeping on leaves is fucking shite. I was hoping I'd wake up back in me bed,' Ben replies dimly.

Not a good mood, then. I should warn Charlie not to push Ben's buttons today, so that he's not the target of any more death stares.

Ben doesn't get up. He slams his head back into the nook of his arm with a rumbling groan. Definitely not a good mood. Charlie's look suggests that he knows not to push him today.

'I cannot wait to find that stream,' Charlie proclaims, opening and closing his mouth like he can absorb even a microscopic droplet of moisture from the air. 'I've never been thirstier, and that includes when I went to that Little Mix concert in my desperate teenage years.'

In a dramatic show, his eyes roll back, and he sticks out his dry tongue, panting like a dying dog. I shake my head at his silly display despite the smile tugging on the corners of my lips.

It's refreshing to be around someone as light-hearted as Charlie—even in this stressful situation. Because, if I weren't smiling right now, I'd be wanting to throw things and scream in frustration. I've never considered myself a humorous or cheerful person. Still, I can appreciate people who are. And Charlie has made me smile more than I have in years.

'You seem in high spirits today, given our circumstances,' Charlie observes, and his evaluation takes me by surprise. Am I smiling *too* much? 'I'm happy you're here. If everyone was as serious as Zoe and Ben, I'd want to off myself,' he continues in a whisper.

'Oi, I heard that, mate,' Ben mumbles, not harshly. His mood must not be as bad as I anticipated.

'My sincere apologies. I only meant it about sixty per cent,' Charlie jokes, winking at me with an exaggerated smile on his impish face.

'You know, it's strange you think that, because I'm usually deadly serious about *everything*. Maybe this place has finally broken me,' I suggest, only half joking. This strange experience has taken me out of my comfort zone, chucked me in with a bunch of strangers, and has yet to reveal its secrets. If anything was going to drive me up the wall, it would be that.

Yesterday was hell. More so than usual. First, I wanted to curl up and die. Then, I thought I was going to be murdered by some creepy lurker. Our kidnappers could have been hiding behind every tree, which only encouraged my fighting spirit.

This morning, however, I feel different—lighter. I'm not as frightened as I was yesterday. The reasons elude me. Maybe Charlie's cheerfulness actually *has* rubbed off on me.

'Or... I'm so hilarious that you can't help it. *I've* broken you. Or most likely fixed you,' Charlie jests, aiming a toothy grin at me.

I pick up a stick and throw it at him. He ducks, but it hits him anyway, snagging in his bronze hair. We both burst out laughing. I can't remember the last time I really laughed like this. It fills my chest with warmth.

Charlie looks past me at something. 'Zoe?'

Twisting around, I catch Zoe storming into the clearing. She doesn't acknowledge us. Instead, she scrambles back into the shelter as quickly as possible.

I frown in bewilderment. 'She's been out in the forest this whole time?' I hadn't seen or heard her come out of the shelter since Logan woke me up.

'Perhaps she saw Logan out there and came running back,' Charlie guesses, shrugging a shoulder.

Half a minute drags on in silence, then crunching footsteps sound from the direction Zoe just emerged from. Charlie and I are both watching—waiting.

Logan trudges into view. He spots us and waves awkwardly. 'I didn't find anything, unfortunately,' he says, walking up to what remains of our fire.

'Did you see Zoe out there?' I ask him.

Logan's features turn down and tighten. 'No, why? Is she not in the shelter?'

'She only came back into camp a minute ago. She must have left before any of us woke up. Charlie and I have been awake since you went off.' I already disliked Zoe, but I'm now growing more suspicious of her.

'Maybe she thought to leave then changed her mind,' Logan suggests, shrugging apathetically. He perches on the log opposite us.

'Ben is awake too, by the way,' Charlie informs him.

Ben waves a hand back at us without lifting his head from his bed.

'He's not ready to get up yet, though. Lazy really. Unacceptable,' Charlie continues, smiling cheekily. He's obviously testing the waters with Ben.

Ben lifts a hand again. This time, his middle finger is up too. We all snicker in response.

I'm just as reluctant as Ben to start another gruelling day. I wish I could sit here long into the afternoon, wallowing, avoiding, withdrawing. I'm too exhausted—both mentally and physically.

On the other hand, I can't imagine giving up now, unlike yesterday. I *will* find a way out of here. This forest will *not* beat me. Not now that I have people who I want to rescue from here.

I've tried to stay distant. I've tried not to like them or become emotionally attached. Yet I suspect I've already failed in that.

Miserably.

Chapter 8

SPECIAL

Rising from my makeshift bed is the first hurdle. It takes some mental preparation.

Forcing myself to my feet, with every muscle in my body resisting, is not a good start to the day. In addition, we'll have to walk for an hour to find this stream. Simply imagining the task has my muscles spasming. I'm glad to see I'm not the only one whose body is fighting them: Ben and Charlie also groan when they attempt to stand.

Appearing equally as weary, Zoe crawls out of the shelter. When she sees me staring, her glare sharpens. I ignore the impulse to ask her what her problem is. Instead, I pivot to Charlie, who's also watching her.

'Safe to say she's not your biggest fan,' he observes, offering me an empathetic smile. 'And there was me thinking I was special.'

'Yeah, I can't believe you managed to survive a whole afternoon with her.' With a flash of my eyebrows, I walk away. Charlie follows closely behind. It seems we're on the same page: both preferring to keep a healthy distance from Zoe. Nonetheless, I'm sure she'll hit us with her eye daggers throughout the day.

Ben is half-focused on stretching while Logan talks over plans with him. Charlie and I approach them, intrigued.

'I think we should pack everything up and make a new camp by the stream today,' Logan suggests.

'Aye, I'm gonna be carrying Freya all the way there, so I'd prefer not to trek back here with her after,' Ben reminds him, rolling his shoulders. He's likely still suffering from last night's trek with her weight in his arms.

'You don't have to carry her all the way. I'll help. I can take over when you tire,' Logan offers kindly.

Ben nods in agreement, although I doubt he'll take him up on it. He appears to have really bonded with Freya already. He's constantly checking her pulse and watching her breathe. There's no way he'd allow Logan to take over caring for her.

'Ready to go?' I ask. I don't really want to leave the clearing, despite knowing that our water situation is beyond desperate.

The clearing feels like a safe space now. It's more open—nothing can sneak up on me here. As soon as we walk back into that mysterious mass of trees, I'll have to be on high alert, unwilling—no, un*able*—to relax for a second.

'Yeah, let's go. Stay close,' Logan announces, moving to take the lead.

Ben bends to scoop Freya up. However, before he even touches her, her eyes spring open, and she sits bolt upright with a yelping gasp. Ben stumbles back in shock, his arse landing in the mud. We all stare, open-mouthed, at Freya in silent suspense.

Slowly, Freya comprehends our presence with her eyebrows drawn. 'What's going on?' she demands. Her baby blue eyes find Ben, who regains his balance and composure.

'Freya! How are you? I was proper worried, like,' Ben exclaims, crouching down to her.

Freya adjusts the straps of her sundress. 'I have a mild headache, but other than that, I'm fine.'

Her assessing eyes thoroughly scan Charlie and me. They flicker briefly to Logan, skip over Zoe altogether, and then fall back to Ben.

To him, she whispers, 'Who are they?'

'Don't worry. They're sound. They're mates,' Ben says matter-of-factly, and I can't fight the smile that spreads across my face.

As we journey through the forest, we fill Freya in on what happened to her. Logan relays the story of finding the supplies left out for us. And, while she does express concern over a mysterious lurker leaving us little 'gifts', she shares Logan's assumption that our kidnappers must not wish us harm. I seem to be the only person who's afraid that some guy with a chainsaw will leap out of the bushes to hack us all to pieces. I guess I've seen one too many horror films.

Ben has been sticking close to Freya, shadowing her steps as if he expects her to keel over again. Every five minutes, he asks her if she's okay or if she needs a break. She seems strong enough, though, especially for someone who's been unconscious for hours. From the shrewd look in her eyes, I can tell she's no pushover. She's definitely not as fragile and dainty as she appears.

We're closing in on where Charlie claims he saw the stream. He's been leading the way for the last hour, following a trail of trees he marked on the way to our clearing. It's clear that he's not comfortable in a position of leadership, unlike Logan. 'It must be around here somewhere,'

Charlie keeps saying, or 'That tree certainly looks familiar'. He's clearly doubting himself. I understand how he's feeling. I couldn't handle the pressure of guiding our thirsty group in search of water, either. At least he hasn't completely fallen apart. He is sweating, though, and often mumbles 'Good grief' and 'For heaven's sake' under his breath.

We take a break in a small clearing with a fallen tree we use as a seat. We pass around the last drops of water from the bottle Logan and I found. By the time it reaches me, there's no point even expending the energy it will take to lift it to my lips. I offer the last sips to Charlie because I feel sorry for him.

He thanks me, drinking the rest and unaware that I skipped my turn. It probably didn't help much, but it's the least I can do.

Charlie wipes the sweat off his forehead, then runs his fingers through his shimmering, bronze hair. He's oddly quiet while he taps his heel against the ground. I bet he's worrying that the stream was some cruel mirage and he's led us all on a wild goose chase.

'It's okay, Charlie. We'll find it,' I assure him, patting his knee to stop it from shaking.

'What if it was a figment of my imagination? It *was* dark. I—I swear I heard water rushing, though... and Zoe confirmed it. I made sure to mark the trees with my knife. I simply need to locate the first tree. How hard can that be?' Charlie mutters, planting his face in his hands. He groans.

I peer down the line at everyone else. They all look just as exhausted and dejected. No wonder Charlie is panicking. They're so fed up with walking around aimlessly that any of them could snap at any moment.

I stare down at the dirt beneath my feet, also starting to doubt Charlie's sense of direction. I need to lift the mood somehow, to give Charlie a chance to remember, but my mind is firing blanks. Dehydration is slowly killing my brain cells.

Heaving a sigh, I shuffle back on the tree trunk, struggling to think how to distract the group. *This is so fucking frustrating*! I groan internally, kicking my heel back against the trunk. The little thunk isn't as satisfying as I had hoped. I woke up in a relatively good mood, as well. Not anymore. This whole situation makes me want to scream.

Scream... hmm. Now that's an idea.

Without second-guessing, I snap to my feet, squeeze my eyes shut, and let out a fierce yell, throwing all of my anger and frustration into it. When I run out of air, I open my eyes and pant my breaths, feeling a hell of a lot better already.

Peeking over my shoulder, I find the others staring at me in total shock. My cheeks burn from the attention. But I force myself to say, 'Go on. Try it.'

They glance uncertainly at each other. For a moment, I worry that I humiliated myself for no reason. Then, just as I'm about to sit back down and shut up for the rest of the day, Logan springs up, throws his head back, and yells to the sky with all his might. When he's finished, our eyes meet, and we share a knowing smile. That sounded as good as I expect it felt.

Logan jerks his chin, silently telling me to get ready for round two. I nod, sucking in a huge breath. Logan does the same, rubbing his hands together in anticipation. When our lungs are filled, we let loose: our screams harmonising, our broken song tearing through the trees and soaring through the sky, carried by the winding wind.

Midway through our wild melody, Ben joins with his deeper, more powerful tone, jumping up from his seat between Logan and me. Charlie and Freya decide to take part, too. Freya's scream hits notes inaccessible to the rest of us. My throat is way too dry to reach those heights.

We keep going, cursing the heavens until our lungs are as raw as our vocal cords. Ben even hops on top of the tree trunk and beats his chest like Tarzan. It makes us all laugh until our sides hurt. Our screams turn to shouts, then to howls. It's like we're a pack of excitable huskies, imitating their more ferocious cousins.

The only person not partaking in this chaotic game is Zoe. She has her fingers in her ears, sitting as far away from us as possible, at the other end of the fallen tree.

Completely spent, our howling laughs taper off. And with heavy, rasping breaths, we all fall back onto our tree seats to recover. Looking at them, it's obvious our screaming match worked wonders on our collective mood. The only eyes that haven't brightened are Zoe's.

I rest my elbows on my knees to catch my breath. The pitfalls of my spontaneous therapy session are now presenting themselves. My physical symptoms are much worse—my throat kills and I'm fucking exhausted. On the other hand, mentally I'm energised and ready to tackle the day. The contrast is staggering.

It seems the others are in the same war between bodies and minds. The lingering smiles on their faces are a good sign, though. Hopefully, they don't regret our screams. Because I certainly don't, despite the consequences.

Peering down at the bark between my thighs, I spot a deep, straight gash and run my fingers along it, wondering what could have made a mark so uniform. Then it clicks. I shift to the side. 'Charlie, could this be your first tree?' I ask, drawing his attention to the sliced line.

Charlie leans closer to inspect the mark. His face lights up. 'Yes! That's it! I knew it was around here somewhere,' he exclaims, jumping up in excitement. 'It must have fallen in the night.'

'That's strange. What do you think uprooted it? Because it doesn't appear as though it's been chopped down,' I say, growing increasingly paranoid about this forest. But maybe I'm being overly suspicious and this 'Arkinwood Forest' is merely old and falling down, one tree at a time.

'The *what* doesn't matter. All that matters is that we've found the *where*,' Charlie pronounces happily.

'Right, so where now, posh boy?' Ben asks impatiently, his voice cracking with dryness.

Guilt circulates. *That's your fault, Ruby. You made things worse.*

Charlie's frown of concentration returns for a moment, and then his expression relaxes. He points to the east of us. 'That way. Down a hill. Five minutes, tops.'

'Great. Lead the way then, mate,' Ben replies, slapping Charlie's shoulder in a friendly gesture, although it nearly knocks him forward.

Charlie grins in response but I detect nerves hidden underneath.

Charlie leads in the direction he suggested. We all follow behind him in single file. Charlie, Ben, Freya, and Zoe are all ahead of me. I try to keep pace but, as soon as I step out of the clearing, my foot snags on something in the undergrowth and my left trainer slips off. Shit.

Retrieving my rogue shoe, I hang back, needing to retie my laces before I travel through this natural assault course. I plonk my arse on the ground to loosen the first knot. Logan steps around me and crouches to undo my other lace while I work on the first.

With our heads close, he murmurs, 'Ruby, what you inspired back there was truly breathtaking—in every sense of the word.'

Sliding my toes back into my trainers, I lift my eyes to his face. 'It probably caused more harm than good.'

'No. We needed it. Charlie needed it,' Logan insists, tightening the bow he's tied. 'I also saw you give him your share of the water.' He catches me staring. Flustered, I lower my gaze back to my feet. His fingers slide under my chin to raise it so that I'm forced to meet his eyes. 'That was kind of you,' he continues once our eyes are locked again. My pulse thunders in my ears as my breaths thin to shallow puffs.

Kind? I'm far from kind. Selfish is what I am.

Shrugging Logan's undeserved praise off, I revert to the task at hand. When I try bending my leg to reach my lace, his hand rests on top of mine to stop me. His touch is a static pulse. I jolt.

'Stand up. I'll do it.' The offer of assistance is more like a command. His lower tone pushes my belly into a backwards roll.

I rise to my feet, letting Logan take over. 'Erm... thanks,' I mumble when he finishes the second knot.

Still on one knee, Logan looks up at me and smiles. My lips twitch up shyly in return. 'I knew you were special the moment I saw you,' he breathes, his pupils expanding.

With my face flaming, I step back and look away, pretending to search for the others even though I can see them waiting for us. 'We shouldn't keep them waiting,' I force out, scratching the back of my flushed neck.

'You don't like compliments. I should have guessed,' Logan says, amused by my reaction. He rises and narrows the distance again. 'You'll get used to them. Trust me, you'll be getting more and more.' His tone isn't mocking. He believes this is true.

Frowning, I hurry towards the others, but I can feel Logan's eyes on the back of my head: the tiny hairs on my nape prickle, hyper-sensitive to the phantom touch of his gaze.

It's impossible for me to accept Logan's flattery. I don't think I've inspired anyone in my whole life. That ridiculous screaming idea was merely a distraction. I didn't intend for it to mean more. I didn't expect it to be such a bonding experience for us as a group.

He's right about one thing, though: I can't handle words of praise. And compliments make me uncomfortable because I know they can't be true.

Despite what Logan says, there's nothing special about me. I'm the most unextraordinary woman he'll ever meet.

Chapter 9

THE STREAM

My ears detect the faint trickle of water as we make our way downhill. Even the sound of its rippling has my throat aching. We all move faster down the hill towards the source of the noise. The rushing melody of liquid over stone becomes more apparent with every step. The terrain evens out, revealing the treeline. My heart leaps when I catch sight of the sun's glorious reflection twinkling off the clear stream. We're here at last and it's more beautiful than I could have imagined.

The stream is paradise compared to the forest. Smooth, round pebbles line the banks, and miniature waterfalls break up the coursing water every few meters. It's sprinkled with large, flat boulders, covered in spongy moss, overhanging the water's edge. The sun's rays shine down in strobes through the trees, lighting the water with a celestial glow.

'Thank heavens!' Charlie exclaims. He sprints to the stream, cups some water in his hands, and then splashes his sweat-soaked face. The rest of the group follows suit.

When I reach the bank, I'm so excited that I can't stop myself from wading into the stream. I just need to get in there and really *feel* it.

The cool flow tempts me further in, swirling around my legs. My jeans absorb water like a sponge. The temperature change relieves my hot, sticky skin, so I sink in deeper. The current of the stream isn't strong enough to worry about.

Reaching the middle, about waist-high, I crash down into the water, enjoying the rushing wave I create as it washes over the rest of my body. The refreshing spray cleans my dirt-covered face. I whirl to face the rest of the group. They smile back at me—except for Zoe, of course.

Charlie is the first to follow me in, but the others are only a second behind. They wade in after me, smiling and laughing as they dive into the fresh, crisp water. The tension of the forest washes away in these precious moments. The pleasure and relief on everyone's faces, while we bask in the oasis we've found here, is unmistakable.

With my limited means, I try not to take anything for granted. Water is something I treasure. A hot shower and a refreshing beverage are hard to come by when you're homeless: but I've never felt more thankful for water than at this moment. I swig a mouthful to eradicate the drought in my body.

'Don't swallow any water. We need to boil it first,' Logan calls out to us through the splashing.

Heeding his warning, I spit out the mouthful I've collected. It did its job, though; I can sense my throat opening up again, and my lips can move without fear of cracking.

Charlie splashes me and I splash him back. The others join us in our new game. Everyone who isn't Zoe, I mean. She's hanging back closer to the bank, watching us with a sour look. Underneath it all, I imagine she wants to join in, yet her pride is getting the better of her. Or maybe she does simply despise us.

Once the frenzied spray of disrupted water settles, we disperse, breathless from laughing. Logan drifts closer to me, his body submerged in the stream up to his neck. He must be kneeling as he's much taller than I am: the water only reaches my breasts. I'm five foot three. I reckon he's at least five ten.

'Feeling refreshed?' he enquires, the direct sunlight warming the icy blue of his irises.

'Yep, nice and cool now,' I reply nervously, staring down at the water lapping at my torso. Our weirdly intimate moment while tying my shoelaces is still at the forefront of my mind.

Logan bobs a little with the current. 'Charlie got you good. You're soaked,' he observes, his gaze lifting to the soggy strands of my fringe, which are now plastered to my forehead.

Suddenly self-conscious, I ruffle the water out of it. 'We'll all dry off quickly in this weather.'

'You look good all wet, though,' Logan drawls, the timbre of his voice lowering suggestively. A cheeky, one-dimpled grin forms on his face as he witnesses my damp cheeks heat. I'm surprised the droplets lingering on my skin aren't sizzling off.

My eyes wide and lips parted, I rigidly inhale, trapping the air in my lungs. My mind grasps for a verbal response as this physical one is mortifying. 'Erm, I—I like water,' I splutter out, this insistent heat spreading down my neck and chest, travelling lower still.

Logan breathes a soft chuckle, his attention averting to allow me to compose myself. 'I like water, too. I also like most of *them* so far. What about you?' He gestures to the others with a jerk of his perfect, square chin. He's even got another dimple there.

'Yeah, they seem all right. Except for Zoe maybe.' Glancing in her direction, I find that she's watching Logan and me from the pebbled bank. She's too far away to hear our conversation, but her narrow-eyed glare tells me she doesn't need to.

Wanting to hide from Zoe's scrutiny, I sink lower, bending my knees so I'm on Logan's level. His head blocks my view of her. The water cools my growing flush.

'Ignore her. She's obviously not the type to make the best out of a bad situation,' he comments with a dismissive wave of his wet hand. Clear drops of liquid fling off his fingers like diamonds, the light catching them before they re-join the stream.

I'm not the type, either, I retort in my head. Being homeless is not a situation with any redeeming factors, believe me. I've certainly never made the best of it, if that's even possible. It's something which only gets worse as time goes on. It leaves me more bitter and hopeless with each endlessly empty day that passes.

Logan tentatively moves closer, rings of water growing around us, rippling outwards. Focusing on them seems safer than lifting my eyes to meet his right now. I don't know what I might find in that gleaming gaze. His flirtatious energy is hard to handle. It's also dangerous. He has no idea who I am. And, if I'm honest, neither do I.

Standing up straight again, I nonchalantly angle my body away from him to alleviate this sudden pressure building between us. This halts his advance, his ebony eyebrows pinching a little. I suppose I wasn't as subtle as I had hoped.

Clearing my throat, I take a step towards the others.

A rogue pebble dislodges under my foot, causing me to lose my balance. Logan's wet hands reach out before my stumble submerges me. He directs me into his waiting arms instead, water sloshing over our shoulders. A gasp tumbles from my lips as I realise how close our faces are to each other—how my breasts are cushioning between our bodies. Our eyes widen when they connect, both of our breaths hitching at the unexpected contact.

Logan's hold tightens as the current sways us. His hands are splayed on the top and bottom of my back, the press of his fingers deepening. All my insides go molten. In contrast, all my muscles lock in place—frozen in a mixture of fear and longing.

'I've got you,' Logan murmurs, his voice surprisingly tender, yet also filled with a sensual smoke. His heavy lashes shadow his already-darkening gaze as he maintains eye contact.

Goosebumps awaken on my skin, and I suppress a shiver. 'Thanks, but you can let go of me now,' I utter, abruptly disengaging.

As soon as Logan's grip loosens, I push off his chest, righting my footing so I can make my escape.

Without looking back at him, I hastily wade over to the group, needing to put as much space between us as possible. The others will be a good buffer after that strangely pleasurable misstep.

Logan only caught you to stop you from making a fool of yourself. There's no need to read into it, I tell myself, ignoring the fluttering in my stomach.

It takes me several minutes to calm my charging pulse. I spend that time fastidiously rubbing dirt out of my T-shirt. Logan has also re-joined the group, slotting himself between Charlie and Ben. I hope my pretence of indifference fools him into thinking that interaction didn't affect me. From the sly, darting glances I've snuck, he seems just as unaffected as I wish I could be.

Beside me, Freya jumps on top of Ben, pushing him playfully under the water. He emerges, grabs her legs, and carries her through the water on his back. Her arms are wound around his neck and they're both grinning broadly, giggling like naughty school kids. I think they're creeping over the 'just friends' line into something more. If I'm right, they'll make a cute couple.

The sharp barb of jealousy stings me as I observe them together. I've never had that, and I doubt I ever will.

Mostly because I refuse to let myself cross that line.

After about ten minutes of floating around and rejuvenating in the stream, we return to the bank to dry off. We lounge on one of the large boulders to bathe in the sun's warm rays.

Finally fresh and clean, and a lot more relaxed, I massage the excess tension out of my thighs. It's a relief to get the clingy grime of the forest off me, for a while at least. I let my hair down and allow it to dry naturally into my soft, springy, chestnut curls.

With the fire-starting kit in hand, Logan is attempting to generate an ember. We only have a small bundle of tinder and a few twigs we picked up earlier. As soon as a flame ignites, we'll have to scramble to find some more. Though currently, we're all too comfortable to care.

'Now that we've found water, we can start planning our next move. Maybe vote on it?' Logan suggests, while he conjures up multiple sparks that don't take.

Ugh, we're back to this again. I can't be bothered to voice my opinion yet. *Wait to see what everyone else says first*, I think, cracking my neck.

'We should really check this destination out. I'm curious to see what's waiting for us there, and I'm sure they would've hurt us already if that was their intention,' Freya pronounces matter-of-factly, her eyes drifting shut as she leans back, allowing the sun to dry her face.

I thought she'd say something like that. She's shown that she's direct and unafraid to voice her opinions. I'm curious to see if Ben agrees with her. I think his initial stance was similar to mine. Has it changed now that Freya is awake?

Nobody offers an alternative. A minute rolls on in silent, dragging tension.

Ben finally pipes up at last. 'Aye, admittedly part of me is curious about this place, too. But why the hell would we plod along with this kidnapper's plan? I'd rather try and find our own way out, like.'

Exactly!

I'm glad Ben said what I was thinking. I could tell, from the silence, that he wasn't sure if he should express his disagreement or simply go with the flow, waiting until everyone else had finished before speaking, like I'm planning to do.

'We have no clue where we are. It could take us days to get out of this forest. Then potentially longer to find our way out of those dreadful valleys. All with a few bottles of water between us and no food. Rest assured, I don't want to play into their hands, either. But the alternative is no better. It could very well be worse,' Freya states. Her frustration is evident. Logan nods in agreement. She continues, 'It's only rational to at least scope the place out.'

'Where is everyone from, by the way? Or... where were you kidnapped? I was taken from my bed in West Sussex,' Charlie interjects.

I, for one, am glad for the distraction. Logan's exasperated demeanour suggests the opposite. It's obvious he wants a decision on this as soon as possible because he's been pushing for it since we found the map.

'I was taken from London and so was Ruby,' Logan answers, attempting to hurry things along. 'We were both asleep in our flats. Separately, of course.'

A slither of guilt worms around my gut at the lie I told him, which he's now repeating to the others.

'I live up near Manchester. I was... er... napping on a train platform,' Ben discloses, folding his arms protectively over his chest. I'm not sure why.

'I think I fell asleep on the sofa when I was flat-sitting for a friend in Edinburgh. I'm obviously not Scottish, though. I'm a southern lass,' Freya mentions, turning her attention back to sunbathing.

'Zoe, what about you?' Logan asks courteously. She hasn't spoken a word to us all day. She's not even sitting nearby.

Zoe rolls her eyes like this conversation isn't worth her time or effort. 'Urgh. Fine. If you must know, I stayed late to finish some work at my shitty office job in Bristol. I must have dozed off because I woke up in this nightmare,' she whines in a monotone voice.

She hasn't got much of a West Country accent, I note. I wonder where she's really from.

'It seems as though we were taken from random places. What we appear to have in common is that it happened when we were asleep,' Logan summarises, taking a break from attempting to produce a spark.

'The strange thing is, when I went to bed, I wasn't wearing these clothes. Someone must have dressed me in this,' Charlie remarks, shuddering, as if the mere thought of it creeps him out. I'm thankful that I'm still wearing the clothes I fell asleep in. The idea of someone dressing me while I was unconscious turns my stomach.

'Yeah, this whole situation is weird. I'd rather not dwell on it,' Freya says dismissively, shrugging it off. 'Let's move on and come up with a plan of action instead.'

'Okay, Ruby... what do you think *our* best option is?' Logan throws the question at me, gesturing to the group as a whole.

All eyes fall on me, and I swiftly avert mine to the stream, my face filling with heat. I'm annoyed at Logan for springing such a direct question on me before I've heard what Charlie and Zoe have to say. But I can't wriggle out of it now. Surely I made myself clear on this last night. Logan already knows my opinion. Why did he have to call me out in front of everyone when the others have only spoken up when they wanted to?

Not hiding my agitation, I scowl. Thinking over Logan's question—how he worded it—only irritates me more. He didn't ask 'What do you think?' He asked what I thought *our* best option is, which is harder for me to answer honestly. Because, at heart, I know that our best option is to check this place out. I just don't want to do it.

Gritting my teeth, I do the decent thing. 'Honestly, if I were on my own, I'd be trying my best to stay clear of it, as Ben said. But, since you asked what *our* best option is, as a group—it would be selfish of me to agree with him,' I admit, already hating my decision. 'I would love to keep as far away from that place as humanly possible, purely to spite them. However, logically speaking, Freya's right,' I conclude, sheepishly peeking back at them. Logan is smiling proudly, happy with my answer. Ben, not so much.

'Charlie?' Logan prompts expectantly.

'Well, I'm still hoping that this is some wild stitch-up—that all of you are Oscar-worthy actors and this is some sort of reality prank show. I assume we'll walk into this place, a camera crew will pop out, and everyone will laugh at how gullible I am,' Charlie jokes, though we barely offer him a smile in response. There's a beat of uncomfortable silence before he caves. 'Anyway... Yes, I agree with Ruby.' He waves the awkwardness off.

'I don't care what we do anymore. The quicker I leave this fucking forest, the better. And if that means going along with this whole *thing*, then so be it,' Zoe announces, obviously annoyed that nobody has asked for her opinion yet.

'Wow, everyone's suddenly so agreeable. I guess there's no need for a vote really, is there?' Ben comments, his brow heavy. He chucks me an '*I thought you had my back*' sort of look and my tummy chews on guilt. I know that Charlie would have agreed with him, if Logan hadn't asked me that tricky question.

'We'll have a drink, rest for an hour, then set off. As long as we stick together, we'll be fine. I'm sure of it,' Logan reassures us, finally producing a spark that catches. The tinder smokes.

Everyone scrambles up to gather firewood as Logan blows on it, breathing life into the flame. While they're distracted, I slip away, needing time alone to process my racing thoughts.

Successfully sneaking off through a patch of bushes, I find a thick tree to hide behind, away from the prying eyes of the group.

Once I'm comfortable, my back pressed up against the rough bark, I bury my head in my hands, trying not to panic about the decision I've made.

I may have unwittingly convinced everyone to walk into a trap.

Chapter 10

THE JOURNEY

'Hey, I was wondering where you'd scampered off to,' Charlie says, approaching me with a smile as I rest against a tree, enjoying my time alone.

For a brief beat, annoyance prickles me. I barely got five minutes to myself, but I can't reject Charlie and that boyish grin. 'I needed some time to think.'

'I understand. This whole situation is incredibly stressful. I don't know what to do with myself,' he shares, sitting down beside me. 'Are you feeling a tad downhearted?' His head tilts sympathetically. Usually, I hate when people look at me like that, although I believe Charlie's concern is genuine.

'I don't know. I'm more... overwhelmed, I think. This whole destination thing... I'm worried I've made a massive mistake by saying we should go,' I divulge, hoping he agrees with me—thus permitting me to change my mind.

'You were right. We could die either way, so I won't blame you if we are chopped up into little pieces. The others won't forgive you, though,' he teases. 'But at least you know *I* won't haunt you from the beyond.'

In response, I shake my head at him, trying to quash my smile. 'All right, Peter Pan. Are you always this annoyingly perky?' I mock, playfully ruffling his bronze hair.

'Actually, I have no idea why I'm being so chirpy. I'm rarely able to joke around at home. Probably because I have no one to joke around *with*,' Charlie admits, shrugging. His grin falters and a hint of pain flickers.

'What about family? Friends?' I enquire softly, too intrigued not to pry.

'Hmm. Well, in all honesty, I don't really have any.'

'Why not?'

Charlie rakes a hand through his hair before leaning his back against the tree beside me. He sighs. 'My parents died in a car accident when I was thirteen. Being an only child, I solely inherited their estate. And, because I was so young, I had to have a guardian and a trustee until I was eighteen—my grandmother, Margaret. She's passed now, too, unfortunately.' He frowns, staring off with glazed eyes.

A moment later, he continues. 'Friend-wise, I never had many. Those that hung around weren't real friends. They were only interested in me because I had money. For the last few years, I've been pottering around the Winshaw estate, alone. Money is great. I'm very privileged in that regard. However, despite its usefulness, it can't keep me company or laugh at my silly jokes, like you do.' He offers me a tight smile.

I smile back in the same way, unsure of how to respond. He's opened up to me, but I'm not ready to reciprocate. *You can reassure him*, I allow myself, as he must be telling me this for a reason.

'Well, *I'm* your friend,' I state softly. 'You're the first person I've said that to in a long time.' I don't divulge any more.

It's funny how removed our lives are from one another. I'm a penniless rough sleeper and he's apparently *Ritchie Rich*, with an inherited '*estate*'. Yet our loneliness ties us. We connect on a level I couldn't have imagined, given our differing backgrounds. We're unhappy in the same way—both missing the love and support that other people take for granted.

Charlie scans my face, seemingly trying to suss out if I'm only humouring him or if I meant what I said. He must decide it's the latter because his smile widens. I'm glad his demeanour isn't expectant—that I don't need to expose my past in all its ugliness. His eyes are softly rounded and full of warmth—a look reserved for a friend.

'Brilliant. And, as my friend, you're obliged to keep laughing at my jokes, obviously. Also, you have to give me back massages whenever I request one,' he jests. I elbow him, and he snickers.

'What are you two doing?' Logan's low voice rings out from behind us and we jump.

Charlie and I twist to see Logan stop a few feet away, his arms tightly folded and eyes narrowed.

'Nothing. We were only taking a break. Is that a crime?' I bite back, not liking his tone.

My attitude throws Logan off. His eyebrows shoot up and he unfolds his arms to shrug. 'No, but I was worried someone had taken you. You shouldn't wander off and hide from us like that,' he chastises me. His hands move to his hips.

'We're not hiding. If someone had called us, we would've come back. We're only sitting here, talking,' I argue, crossing my arms under my bust. I'm annoyed that he's annoyed. Charlie is quiet between us, sheepishly fiddling with his shoelaces.

'Fine. Go ahead. Talk. Relax. But when you're ready to rejoin the group, and drink the water we're working hard to purify, make sure you bring some wood back. Everyone else has collected their fair share.'

With that remark thickening the air, Logan coldly turns his back on us and strides away.

For a minute, Charlie and I stew in silence, watching Logan leave. It's obvious he wanted to make us feel guilty, and it's worked. We've been chilling here having a good old chin wag while everyone else worked to gather wood for the fire. But I suspect there was something more contributing to his attitude. It emerges when he sees Charlie and me bonding. Maybe he *is* jealous and I'm not just wishfully thinking. I can't imagine why he's threatened by Charlie, though. Charlie is a Labrador puppy—completely harmless.

'Perhaps we should collect some wood. I feel awful now,' Charlie says, mirroring my thoughts.

'Yeah, I guess we should.'

After we push to our feet, we half-heartedly shuffle away from our hiding place.

I miss being selfish. Now, I have to consider a whole group of people—all their actions, needs, and emotions. It's becoming too much for me to manage.

Apparently, I'm no longer allowed to have five minutes to think, away from the group, without being made to feel guilty about it. *Is it worth it?* I ask myself, rubbing my temple. Tension is building there. All this stress of being around people, caring about their welfare: it's so unfamiliar to me. And Logan keeps acting as though he's worried about me. Do I actually have people who care about *my* welfare now, too? That's all the more unfamiliar. Alien, even.

Before we rejoin the group, Charlie and I collect an armful of wood each.

They're gathered around the fire by the overhanging boulder. Resting on a flat stone inside the flames is the metal container that Logan found. Charlie and I unload our wood onto the pile they've collected.

'Water's nearly boiled. I don't know about you lot, but the anticipation alone is killing me,' Freya announces, balling her fists in excitement. Ben eyes her adoringly.

'Ah, about time. Have you guys been slacking?' Charlie quips cheekily. The group receive it well, cracking smiles. Zoe and Logan are the two who roll their eyes.

Logan is mindlessly poking at the fire with a stick. He hasn't acknowledged Charlie and me since our return. I imagine he'll be frosty with us for the rest of the day, if this is any indication. We've only known each other for twenty-four hours and he's already acting like he owns me. I don't like it one bit.

It's not solely stubbornness or that I hate being told what to do. It stems from something much deeper within me, from the fraught childhood I suffered through after my mum's death. I prefer to repress those memories—the memories of what my dad did to my brother and me when he'd come home drunk and angry at the world.

When I'm being contained or controlled in any way, I'm reminded of those painful memories, where I felt more like property than a person—a worthless object, broken and discarded.

I was a punching bag through most of my teenage years. It left me covered in tiny cracks which have never fully healed. Nobody owns me now, though. And nobody ever will again. I promised myself that after I finally escaped my dad's clutches.

The water hisses, producing small steaming bubbles which rise to the surface. Everyone gazes at the container longingly. We're all subconsciously licking our lips.

'Now, we only have to wait until it cools down,' Logan says dismally, and we give a collective sigh.

I've never felt so impatient in my life.

After an hour of boiling, cooling, sharing water, boiling, cooling, sharing water, our effort has finally paid off; we're all rehydrated. Plus, we've filled our flasks and bottles in preparation for the journey. Everyone seems in higher spirits: even Zoe isn't scowling as much.

Logan still hasn't made eye contact with me and I refuse to talk to him first. I'm avoiding him as much as I can while we share the same space.

Draining my last sip of the water, I pass the container back to Ben, who packs it in the bag. Everyone is up and moving, ready for our dreaded journey to the mysterious kidnapper's lair. Rightly or wrongly—we'll soon find out.

Since I contributed to this decision, a nest of ants has taken up residence in my stomach. Although, at present, it's not my own safety I'm most concerned with. I'm worried for the others. It will be *my* fault if they're hurt. I'm pretty sure that I can take care of myself in a fight. But if something bad *does* happen at this place... I know I can't protect everyone.

Logan is busy studying the map. I walk past him to grab our backpack.

Without taking his attention off the map, he addresses me. 'Ruby, can you come here for a second, please? I could use your opinion.'

For a heartbeat, I hesitate, my stubbornness prodding me to refuse him. Resisting that spiteful urge, I oblige, throwing the backpack over my shoulder before I approach him.

Logan presents the map to me. 'Now that we've found the stream, the map makes much more sense.' He points to the dots weaving up the deep crease of the map. 'I reckon it was purposefully obtuse, so we'd still have to work to find the stream. Anyway, we could go straight up north from here. Although that could be the obvious route. If we want to be stealthier, we could approach from the west.' He traces a route with his finger while he talks. 'What do you think?'

'To be honest, I don't think it will make much of a difference. They're already expecting us,' I answer, not looking directly at him. I catch his furtive sideways glances at me, though. Things are still awkward between us and we're both acutely aware of it.

'Hmm. Yeah, you're probably right... Also, I want to apologise for how I talked to you earlier. I'm not your father. You can wander off all you like,' he offers, examining the map and trying to act casual.

The unexpected mention of my dad stings, but I recover quickly. *Logan is definitely not your father, Ruby, and you shouldn't hold a grudge. He was only worried about you. Maybe even a little jealous of Charlie,* I tell myself. *He's no monster.*

'All I wanted was a few minutes to myself. But then Charlie found me and we started talking about his family... Ugh, I'm sorry, too. I don't know, sometimes... I'm too defensive and bite back when I probably shouldn't,' I blurt out. I'm not very good at apologies. I don't have to make them very often. Nonetheless, I want to convey my regret to him the best I can. And to my surprise, I *am* sorry. Usually, I don't care enough to feel regret.

'Don't worry. I think we were all in a bad mood. Now we're sufficiently hydrated, I'm sure tensions will ease,' Logan points out, folding the map and sliding it into his pocket.

I chaff. 'Yeah, if we forget that we could all be walking into a trap soon.'

Logan raises his eyebrows, a slight smirk forming. 'We have to find out what's going on sooner or later,' he responds, cocking his head. 'Aren't you curious at all?'

'We all know what happened to the cat,' I retort, walking away from him. The lightness of his laugh follows me. The fact that he responds well to my little comebacks inflates my practically non-existent ego.

Despite my stubbornness earlier, I'm glad we've cleared the air. If we were in the real world, I wouldn't have bothered as we probably would have never seen each other again. But, because we're stuck in this situation together, I'm trying to approach things differently. I can't stand the tension and I really didn't like feeling a possible rift forming between us. I guess I'm just not used to having friends.

I've had spats with fellow homeless people in the past: over places to sleep, hostel beds, or begging territory. None of them were ever people I cared about. It never mattered what they thought of me, despite knowing some of them for years.

It's tough to pinpoint why, but I feel closer to these people—strangers I've only known a day. I want them to like me. Saying that, I doubt it's possible. *I* don't even like me.

We decide to follow the stream up north as it brings us right to the edge of the destination marked on the map. Packing in tightly together, we start the journey.

I hope it's not our last.

We trail the stream for over an hour, barely speaking. Charlie attempts to crack jokes but the rest of us don't seem as keen to make any unnecessary noise, so he gives up after a while.

We're a close-knit group, only ever drifting a few feet apart. Logan is out in front with Freya and Ben, while Charlie and I are in the middle. Zoe brings up the rear. Every so often, we hear a tut or huff from her when we slow our pace.

Pausing, Logan checks the map and compass. 'We're heading too far east. We need to leave the stream and follow north, through the forest,' he claims, holding up the compass as proof.

My stomach flips over at the news. I was hoping we didn't have to trek deeper into the forest until we were nearing the end. My nerves have been soothed in the last hour by how open the stream is. The compact forest whips my anxiety into a frenzy, especially as we close in on this destination.

'We'll just have to be extra vigilant. We'll be fine if we stick together. There's safety in numbers,' Freya says optimistically, stroking Ben's arm in comfort.

It's no secret that Ben is the most unwilling to make this journey upstream. His arms are crossed, a deep frown marks his face, and he's chewing on his lips in anxious thought. I don't think it's the forest that scares him: it's the lack of control. I understand completely. Following this map feels like we're already accepting defeat.

'Right, let's just get on with it, then,' Ben mutters despondently, rolling up his jeans in preparation to cross the shallow part of the stream.

Great. Just great. This fucking forest can do one.

For half an hour, we hike through the forest. The tension is mounting. It's impossible to regulate my growing fear. I'm hyper-alert to every noise or movement. My own footsteps put me on edge. My breaths are heavy and burning. I'm clamming up, my whole body rigid in anticipation—ready to run at a moment's notice.

Ben is in the same fragile state I am. His nerves must be shot, because his eyes are darting all over the place. I'm surprised his sharp neck turns at the slightest sound haven't given him whiplash. The noise is always caused by one of us, though. The forest itself is suspiciously peaceful.

The rest of the group look relaxed compared Ben and me. I want them to be as restless as we are. I don't understand how they can be so blasé about walking to our potential deaths. In my mind, it's feeling more and more like a certainty.

The trees are thinning as we head north, which should make me feel better because the forest is less dense—not as easy for a kidnapper to hide. Yet it only intensifies my claustrophobia. The forest feels as though it's closing in on me despite the extra space, which my anxious mind disregards. I can't keep this up for much longer. My head is swimming, and I've developed a persistent stitch which has been tearing at my ribcage for the last ten minutes. At first, I barely noticed because everything was hurting. But now, it's all I can think about. If we *did* stop, I'm not sure I'd be able to start back up again.

'For fuck's sake, I wish we'd get to this bloody place already,' Zoe grumbles behind me. She lets out a frustrated groan.

For once, I understand where she's coming from. No matter what I imagine this place could be, I'd rather get there now and be done with it. Hiking through this forest, in heightened anticipation, is torture.

'It shouldn't take much longer. We're close, according to the map,' Logan says, loudly enough for us all to hear without shouting.

When did he become such a map expert? Shame he didn't have that skill this morning, when we were in search of the stream.

Nobody bothers to add anything. We're all too tired and fed up, so we continue marching through the rough terrain in aggravated silence.

Out of nowhere, a creaking sound creeps through the trees. We all pause, our eyes darting around for the source of the menacing disturbance. Without realising, we've formed a protective circle, our backs against each other. The creaking grows louder, transforming into splintering snaps.

'I know that sound.' Ben scans the tops of the trees, his eyes widening in horror. 'Leg it! Run!' he yells, just as something right above us cracks with a deafening snap.

We all scramble away. Charlie is a second behind, so I grab at his sleeve to yank him along with me.

A moment later, a large tree crashes down behind us. The vibrating boom spurs us on.

Creaks and loud cracks echo from all sides. The direction of the danger is indecipherable now. All we can do is keep running while the forest around us falls apart. The chaotic rumble beneath us is a sinister curse.

Logan allows Ben and Freya to overtake him. He falls beside Charlie and me, grabbing my hand to pull me along faster. I reach out for Charlie's, too, not wanting him to lag behind.

Glancing back, I see Zoe is struggling to catch up. Another tree trunk tears to our right, like it's being crushed by an invisible force. It's leaning our way and, if we're not quick enough, it could land right on top of us. Fear stabs at my chest as air is trapped in my throat.

Zoe follows my wide-eyed gaze, spotting the looming tree for herself. She squeals... and the break in concentration trips her up. She face-plants the ground a second later.

'Zoe!' I pull away from Logan and scramble back to her.

Logan and Charlie turn back, too. And when I reach Zoe, who's still lying flat on the ground, the trees' thick shadow falls upon us in warning.

Time slows, freezing both Zoe and me in our terror.

'Come on!' Logan shouts, tugging me to my feet.

Charlie grabs Zoe and pulls her up, too, and together, they drag us out of harm's way in the nick of time. The tree slams into the ground, right where we were mere seconds ago. The vibrations rocket up my legs like an earthquake, shaking me to the core. Yet Logan persists in forcing me along with him.

We race on, straight through the frightening display of Mother Nature's power and ambivalence. Losing sight of Ben and Freya, I panic at the thought of them bleeding out, trapped under a tree somewhere in this natural war zone.

I run faster than I ever thought I could. My lungs revolt, tired of inflating and deflating so rapidly. Logan's tight grip on my wrist won't loosen. He's not letting me break away again. Charlie and Zoe are beside us, managing to keep up with our pace.

A handful of minutes later, the booming fades into the background. We slow our pace when we realise we haven't heard or felt a crash in a while.

When we reach a break in the trees, we all collapse in heaps on the ground, desperately trying to recover our lost oxygen.

Every sharp intake of air scalds my throat so much that I'm close to vomiting. The forest falls silent again. Our gasping breaths are the only sounds. I collapse on my back, my muscles seizing and spasming. The intense pain makes me wince and groan. The shock has yet to leave me, either. I'm struggling to process this recent, mind-boggling incident.

'Is anyone hurt?' Logan asks between strained gasps.

'Hurt? My fucking skull was nearly crushed back there!' Zoe screeches. 'That wasn't supposed to happen!'

Logan pushes himself up on his knees to face her. 'No, you're right. Trees don't fall like that naturally. I don't know what the hell is happening here,' he replies, striving to regain control of his lungs.

Mine are still working too hard for me to speak. The tightness in my chest heightens my panic. It's like someone is squeezing my heart and lungs in the palm of their hand. My head is spinning so chaotically that blurry red and black stars start flashing in my vision.

'Ben and Freya?' Charlie manages to puff out.

'I saw them run on ahead of us. They should be fine. The trees were only falling back there,' Logan claims. 'Our path looks clear moving forwards.'

A warm hand rests on my arm. 'Ruby, are you okay?' Logan enquires, moving closer to check on me.

'No... I can't... breathe,' I pant out through raw, insufficient gulps of air.

'Sit up. You're panicking and lying flat on your back isn't giving your lungs enough room to expand,' he instructs, helping me sit upright. 'Come here.'

Logan drags me to him, positioning my back against his chest. He slots my head into the crook of his neck. Taking my hand, he places it palm-down onto my chest.

'Slow your breathing with deeper breaths. Match mine and try to focus more on the feel of your palm than the pain.' His voice is soothing.

Mind still reeling, I strive to copy Logan's movements. When he takes a deep breath in, I puff out my chest, too.

'Hold it,' he orders, and I obey. 'Now let it go.' He slowly blows the air out of his lungs, and I follow. 'Good, keep going.'

My head clears a little, so I repeat his movements for the next minute, until my lungs aren't as tight.

Charlie shuffles closer. He's watching me, a worried frown on his red, sweat-damp face. Zoe isn't interested. She's sitting with her back to us.

Logan's hand breaks away from the top of mine. He places it directly on my chest to check my heartbeat is slowing. I'm acutely aware that his palm is now resting above my left breast, skin-to-skin, his fingertips inches from my nipple... which is fucking hardening. What the fuck is wrong with me?!

'You're okay, Ruby. You're over the worst of it. It was only a panic attack. You're fine. You're safe,' Logan murmurs, his heavy, rough breaths warming the shell of my ear. 'You're doing so well.' His face angles inwards, his cheek brushing mine. 'That's it.' The whisper of his lips sensitises my skin. His fingers twitch on my chest.

Despite Logan working to calm me, it's not having the desired effect. As my mind and body return to their normal rhythm, I'm comprehending the position I'm in—sitting between his legs, leaning on him, with his hand on my chest—*palming my cleavage*. It's lucky my face is already burning through exertion. Otherwise, the evidence of my embarrassment would be humiliating.

Yeah, embarrassment. That's all this is.

'I'm okay. I can breathe now.' I swipe Logan's hand away from my chest and lift my weight from his torso. My lower half tingles and a strange pulsing in my abdomen is disconcerting. The unfamiliar internal pull is dragging low, gathering something hot and heavy. 'Thanks,' I add quickly, sounding a bit hoarse.

Logan moves out from behind to kneel next to me instead. He lays a hand on my shoulder in case I fall back. 'No problem. Keep focusing on the rhythm,' he says softly, studying me.

Why are his eyes so black? That could either be from fear or...

No. Surely not.

'Really, I'm fine now,' I repeat more curtly, not wanting any more fuss.

'Yeah, stop being so dramatic, Logan. She's fine,' Zoe snaps, not bothering to look around at us. 'She's just doing it for attention.'

Exasperated, I roll my eyes, but internally I worry they might believe her. I purposely avoid attention where I can. I hope Logan doesn't think I was milking it to coax that reaction from him.

Charlie sighs in relief, seeing that I'm better. 'Well, thank God that's over with.' He brushes moist hair out of his eyes. 'Now we only have to find the rest of our party.' He pushes himself up to stretch. 'Wherefore art thou, Benny boy?' he calls in jest.

'I'm here, you muppet,' Ben answers, his voice seeming to come from thin air.

Our heads swivel in search of him.

Ben and Freya trudge out from behind a thick knot of trees. Thankfully, they appear unhurt. 'And I'm not the only one.' He shifts to the side, unveiling two new faces behind him.

The two strangers stare down at me, unsmiling.

Chapter 11

DESTINATION

The first stranger is a stocky man with deep brown skin. His body is compact yet sturdy. I'd guess he's around Logan's age. His expression is a hard frown; his square jaw and arched eyebrows enhance this. He's wearing olive green combat trousers, a black T-shirt, and military-style, lace-up boots.

The second is an attractive woman. She's not as hard-faced as the man but her expression is stony. She has smooth, Amber-tanned skin and big hazel eyes, set behind thick lashes. She has natural tight curls of golden brown, which frame her oval face nicely. She's wearing ripped jeans, a dark grey T-shirt, and white trainers. She appears to be a similar age to me. She's petite, though more svelte in stature—athletic. Unlike Zoe and me, who are more mid-sized.

'Hello there,' Charlie says, waving at them.

They don't return the greeting.

'On our leisurely little jog, we came across these two. They're also on their way to the map's destination, apparently,' Freya informs us, breaking the tension.

'We heard the commotion and came to check it out. We didn't expect to find more people,' the woman says, her voice flat and suspicious. She must not trust us. I can't blame her. I wouldn't trust a large group of strangers out here, either, given the circumstances.

Logan stands up and steps forward. 'Hi, I'm Logan. That's Ruby, Charlie, and Zoe,' he introduces, pointing us out to them.

The new man and woman's guarded gazes roam over us. Their expressions don't change. They stay where they are, rigid like statues.

The man finally speaks. 'I'm Eli. That's Sasha.' His voice is deep and abrupt.

'What direction have you travelled from?' Logan enquires.

'Northwest. Ben said you've come from the south,' Eli answers, his voice also rife with suspicion.

We might have a tough time persuading them to cooperate with us. But then again, I'm sure this is how Logan, Ben, and I appeared to Charlie and Zoe when we first met them. It's difficult to tell who you can trust in a situation like this.

'We've not had the time to discuss much but I tried to fill 'em in on the basics, you know—kidnapped, nearly crushed. The usual,' Ben jokes, his dark humour loosening the atmosphere.

Nobody has moved in a while. It's awkward sitting on the ground when everyone else is standing around me. Although I doubt my body will work upright just yet. I'm still feeling the effects of the run too acutely. My system is in a complete state of shock, both physically and mentally.

As if she can read my thoughts, Sasha surveys me under a frown and says, 'I'd stay sitting if I were you. You don't look too good.'

'Ruby had a panic attack,' Logan relays.

'I'm fine!' I snap, a bit *too* loudly. I don't appreciate Logan telling everyone, making them think I'm weak.

For an instant, Sasha's firm expression slips. She smiles briefly at my response, then switches to serious again.

'So... what do we do now? We still need to locate this destination place,' Charlie chimes in. He purses his lips, glancing to me as if I'll make the decision.

The rest of us automatically look to Logan for the answer, while Logan is focused on Eli and Sasha.

'We've already found it,' Eli reveals hesitantly, shifting his weight, understandably in two minds on whether to trust us with this information.

His words push my stomach off a cliff. We must be awfully close. A sliver of panic returns to accelerate my heart again.

'You found it? Where?' Ben challenges them, likely annoyed they didn't mention this to him before.

'It's a five-minute walk away. We were scoping the place out from afar when we heard the trees falling,' Sasha informs us.

'Can you show us the way? We'll be more of a force standing together,' Logan says, his expression open and trusting.

Sasha and Eli share an unspoken look of indecision.

'Or more of a target, like,' Ben remarks in a dry tone.

Sasha shrugs at Eli, offering him the decision. She scans each of us again, her eyes lingering on me. I look away but her attention presses on me. Not that her look is menacing. She's only studying me. If anything, she seems more concerned for my welfare.

'Fine. We'll lead the way,' Eli finally replies in a tone that indicates his displeasure. Sasha simply nods in affirmation, a hint of a smile on her face.

'Wait, what's actually at this destination?' I demand. I'm not going anywhere with them without knowing what they've already seen. Trust should go both ways.

Eli and Sasha tense at my question, exchanging another glance before they address me.

'A cabin,' Eli discloses in his deep, penetrating voice.

I shudder as an unnerving chill crawls down my spine, like a hungry spider descending from its web, hunting for prey.

After a minute or two, the dizziness dissipates, and I'm able to stand.

Charlie and Logan are positioned on either side of me, in case my body fails as we follow Sasha and Eli towards this destination.

'Did you see inside the cabin?' Ben asks them.

'No, we weren't close enough. From afar, all we could see was a big log cabin with a lake beside it, and there was a rowing boat tied to the dock. The place is sitting out in the open but the forest surrounds it. Some mountains were to the east. It could mean we're in the Scottish Highlands. I don't know where else would have mountains and a forest like this,' Sasha speculates as she walks on ahead.

It sounds plausible to me. Although I've never been to Scotland, so my opinion wouldn't hold much weight. The only time I've left the southeast of England was when my mum took me and my brother to Devon the summer before she died.

I'm nearly thirty-one years old and I've never been on a foreign holiday. *You're pathetic, Ruby.*

'I'm familiar with Edinburgh, but I haven't visited the highlands, so I won't be much help. But someone must live at this cabin if they've left a boat tied up. Hopefully, we'll find out what's going on when we get there,' Freya guesses, not sounding too worried.

Hopefully?

Hopefully, Freya is wrong. *Hopefully*, we'll get to this cabin, find nothing there, then make our own way out of here. *Hopefully*, not through the mountains because I'm not much of a hiker. I'm not used to exercise in general.

If we *do* come across a person in there... I don't know how we'll handle it. I can't imagine the mysterious kidnappers coming out and saying, 'Hi, we're your kidnappers, nice to meet you. Who wants dinner?' I doubt that very much. They may have left supplies for us in the woods, but that doesn't mean their intention isn't to harm us. Once we're enclosed and trapped like fish in a barrel, it would be easy to pick us off. Nothing good can come from meeting them. Things will likely kick off in a big way. I'll be the first in there with my fists raised.

I'd rather leave here not knowing who kidnapped us because I don't trust myself in the same room as them. The only thing driving me towards this cabin is the chance that there's more supplies for us. It's purely for the good of the group.

The trees are thinning up ahead, allowing more light to illuminate the forest around us.

'We're here,' Sasha whispers ominously.

The anxious knot in my stomach reties itself. After I swallow down the lump in my throat, I suck in a deeper breath to steady my nerves.

'Anyone have a plan? Because I've got nowt,' Ben asks in a hushed tone when we begin to slow our pace.

As we steadily close in, the space past the treeline opens up. I can scarcely make out the cabin in the distance. Beside it, the lake is about sixty meters wide and double the length. There's a small wooden dock on the cabin side. An old rowing boat is tied to it, swaying in the damp breeze. The air is fresher here, crisp and sweet.

We come to a stop by the treeline and sink low to the ground, behind some bushes.

'Could someone not go look through the window while the rest of us wait here?' Freya suggests, peering down the line of faces. 'If it's clear, they could wave us down.'

What I hear is: 'Just in case it's a trap, we'll wait here and send in some live bait—a person who walks in there expecting they may never walk back out again.'

We don't have much time to mull over the idea before Eli nods. 'That could be a good plan, if we had a willing volunteer?' He stares expectantly at each of us in turn.

There's no way I'm volunteering for this. You'd have to be a complete––

'I'll go.' Logan jumps to his feet, pulling the knife from the waistband of his jeans.

Why am I not surprised Logan would offer himself up as live bait. Him and his ridiculous hero complex.

Looking skyward, I exhale my frustration. And when no one else offers, I match his senselessness. 'I'll go with you,' I blurt out. *Shit. You can't take it back now.* I groan internally as I stand up to join him.

Some of our group are surprised I volunteered, especially Charlie, whose forehead crinkles in worry. I also notice a few impressed looks that follow. Logan struggles to suppress a grin.

'You don't need to accompany him, Ruby. He'll be fine. Won't you, Logan?' Charlie prompts, slapping a hand on Logan's chest and trying to force his agreement.

'Yeah, I don't mind doing this solo. No need for both of us to walk into a trap. It's safer for you to stay here and wait with everyone else. You didn't even want to come here,' Logan points out, offering me a chance to change my mind.

'I can't let you go in there on your own.' I hold my hand out, palm open. 'Someone hand me a knife. Let's get this shit over with.'

Eli passes me his knife without question. I'm amazed he trusts me with it already.

'I could come along as well? I'm certainly no fighter but I can undoubtedly talk people to death,' Charlie says in a small voice. Despite the brave offer, his fear is as clear as day. He's only willing to put himself forward because I'm his friend.

Adamantly, I shake my head. 'No, you stay here with Ben and Freya. Protect them. We don't really know Sasha or Eli yet. I'm not sure we can trust them,' I whisper to him, exaggerating my own fear to make him stay.

I may not know Eli and Sasha as well as the others, but I also don't think they're lying, and I doubt they mean us harm. Mostly because they're outnumbered. Plus, Eli willingly handed over his weapon. If Charlie came along and ended up hurt because of me, I couldn't bear that guilt.

'All right. But if you're not out of that cabin in five minutes, I'm coming in after you,' Charlie vows, resting a shaky hand on my shoulder. He's not joking anymore. His brow creases again and the urge to hug him is overwhelming.

'I'll be fine, Charlie. We'll be back soon,' I promise, wanting to reassure him. We fake a smile at each other, neither believing a word of it.

Stepping away from Charlie, I join Logan, who's waiting patiently for me.

'Erm... take care. We'll be watching so, you know, if anything happens... we won't mess about. We'll rock up and drag you both outta there fast,' Ben declares with a resigned shrug.

'Nah, if anything happens, run away,' I tell him firmly. I don't need them attempting to rescue us to only get caught up themselves. We don't all have to be martyrs in this. 'Make sure Charlie doesn't come after us, either,' I add under my breath, so Charlie doesn't hear.

'That's the whole point of only two of us entering. It's so the rest of you can stay safe,' Logan insists, before he swallows down some water. When he's finished, he passes me the bottle and I take a swig to flush away my sudden dehydration.

It's clear that Ben is in two minds about this. First and foremost, he wants to keep himself and Freya safe, for obvious reasons. On the other hand, I'm sure he feels a sense of duty to us now, too, like we're a team.

'Be careful,' Freya says, her features soft.

To my surprise, she leans in to hug me, and I clam up, standing rigid. Thankfully, she breaks off contact quickly, sensing my discomfort. It's a sweet gesture, but I'm still not used to that much affection. As a consolation, I offer her a tight-lipped smile, awkwardly nodding.

A few metres away, Sasha and Eli are watching our goodbyes. Eli appears confused at our apparent closeness as a group. Unlike Sasha, who is trying to dampen her grin. She must be warming to us.

Zoe is sitting away from the group, her elbows resting on her knees, her jaw cupped in her palms. She's gazing out to the lake, lost in her own world. I can't guess her mood. She's not scowling or throwing me dirty looks anymore. It seems as though she's no longer present in this situation. I wish I could be like that. I'm more than present now—I'm participating. I've literally volunteered myself for the slaughter.

You've turned into that mindless fucking sheep, Ruby.

'Stay on this side of the cabin so we can see you,' Ben instructs us.

We nod in acknowledgement, ready to roll. Logan sets a quick pace out of the trees into the wide expanse of complete vulnerability. I steal another second to inhale a lungful of air before I venture out behind him.

My heart pounds against my ribcage as soon as I leave the coverage of the trees. We're completely exposed. Someone could be watching us from the cabin—or from *anywhere* around here. We won't know until it's too late.

Our speed dwindles when we reach the side of the cabin without windows. Regardless, we try to keep a low profile. Up close, the cabin is a lot bigger than I thought. It's more like a two-storey house. It has decking at the front, with four wooden chairs positioned around a small, rustic table.

With our backs pressed to the outside wall of the cabin, we creep up to the corner of it. Like usual, Logan is leading. He peers around the side to scan the door of the dwelling.

He turns back to me. 'The door's shut. I can't see anything from where we are. There's a window around here. I could go peek in?'

'We'll go together. Crawl,' I instruct him, motioning for him to lower to the ground. He does as I ask, getting on his hands and knees. I do the same.

We crawl around the corner of the cabin, then stop below a rectangular window. Logan faces me, and I nod my approval.

Slowly, he raises his head, and my breathing accelerates.

When Logan is high enough to peek over the window frame, he hovers there, watching for a minute. All the while, my gaze roams the huge clearing, searching for any hint of a threat. But all I see is greenery and all I hear—besides our heavy breathing—is the boat knocking lightly against the dock. The setting is actually quite peaceful and picturesque.

Logan lowers his head. 'It's empty downstairs. There's furniture but no sign of life.' He checks again. 'I think we should just go in there,' he suggests breezily. 'To hell with it.'

'Well, I think we should watch for a few more minutes at least. There could be someone hiding upstairs,' I argue, not liking the idea of boldly marching in when we haven't thoroughly checked the place out first.

'It's okay. I'll go in. You can keep a lookout from here,' he says, standing up.

Grabbing Logan's forearm, I pull him back to his knees. 'Have you completely lost it? No, I won't wait here. I think we've already established that I'm not letting you go in on your own.'

Logan smirks. 'Wow, aren't you a stubborn little thing?'

Offended, I glower at him. 'Me?! *You're* the stubborn one,' I retort, poking him in the chest, and he simply chuckles. The delightful sound calms me.

Keeping our backs bent, we hurry towards the entrance of the cabin. Logan positions himself to the left of the door and I stay on the right. He grabs the rusty brass handle and slowly turns it. A small click releases the door and it inches open.

Hesitant, I throw a glance back up to the trees, in the direction we came from. The others aren't visible but I'm sure they're watching. They're probably wondering what the hell we're thinking—bowling into this place without properly vetting it.

A burning lump forms in the back of my throat at the thought of not seeing them again. I swallow it down, focusing back on the door. Logan holds it in place, ready to release it.

'Ready?' he asks, our gazes interlocking.

We're so close behind this door that his warm, sweet-smelling breath coats my face. His eyes are intense, the irises like circular bolts of electricity. Spellbound, I forget for a moment what I should be ready for.

'No, but go for it,' I finally reply, holding my breath.

Logan releases the door with a nudge. It creaks open wide. Then, after a moment of silent anticipation, we're brave enough to step in.

Beyond the threshold is a living room. It's dark and dusty with two long, dark green fabric sofas opposite each other. A wood-burning fireplace, surrounded by stone, is centred on the far wall. There are also two checked armchairs in each corner, and a small, old-fashioned television is sitting atop a mahogany cabinet. A huge, antique Persian rug takes up nearly the whole floor. There's a wooden staircase on the left-hand side. But straight in front of us is a door. A kitchen, perhaps?

'A kitchen, perhaps?' Logan echoes as if he's read my mind. We slowly make our way to it. Without a moment's hesitation, he opens it.

There's nobody inside. Logan was right—it is the kitchen. It's an open-plan country kitchen, the cabinets sage green. On the right, there's a long, walnut dining table with ten matching chairs around it.

The cabin is much larger inside than I had imagined. It has the typical, rustic, log cabin interior. Though thankfully, it seems that it's been unoccupied for a while.

'We should explore upstairs as well,' Logan says, casually strolling back through the living room, towards the stairs.

'We don't have much time. Charlie said if we're longer than five minutes, he's coming in.'

'Then I guess we'll have to breeze through it. If anyone was here they would have heard us by now,' he replies with an easy shrug.

Logan makes his way up the stairs, not being too quiet as he does. I do admire his boldness. Being with him has steadied my nerves. I'm not as scared as I thought I would be, coming in. *Maybe you're braver than you give yourself credit for*, I say to myself, following him up the stairs.

At the top, a long landing cuts straight through the middle of the wooden floor, with three doors on each side, totalling six unexplored rooms. They're positioned directly opposite each other. *Great, more fucking doors to open*, I think sardonically, huffing.

'One door at a time,' Logan responds to my unspoken thought, walking up to the first door on his left. I'm right behind him, feeling safer with him nearby.

Logan twists the brass knob and pushes the door wide. Inside are two single beds between a window. There's a small bedside table with a lamp resting on it, a pine wardrobe to our right, and a matching dresser behind the door. The bedroom is small yet cosy, decorated with clean white linens and curtains. The blankets on the end of the beds are light blue.

Logan backs out. 'Right, next one.'

He strides to the room opposite, then swings the door open. Another bedroom. It has the same set-up as the first—twin beds, wardrobe, dresser, bedside table, lamp, blankets.

Forgetting my fear, I place my palm on the next doorknob and turn it. Logan comes to stand close behind me. *Very* close. His chest expands against my back when he breathes in. My arse grazes his crotch, the intimate contact sending a searing shockwave right through me.

Distracted, I fling the door open with too much force. Inside this bedroom is a man and woman kissing passionately in just their underwear.

Hearing the door knock against the wall, they freeze. Their heads slowly turn to us. We stare, wide-eyed, at each other for a tense beat before we all start screaming.

I stumble back, knocking into Logan, who slams into the hallway wall with me. The man and woman grab onto each other at first, but then scramble for their clothes. It's all happening so quickly, I don't have time to react.

'What the hell is wrong with you?! Ever heard of knocking?' the man shouts at us in annoyance, yanking on his jeans.

Logan is rubbing the back of his head where it hit the wall. I'm clutching my chest because my heart is trying to claw out of me in fright.

'Who are you?!' I shout back in return, breathless.

I feel like a bit of a voyeur, watching them dress, but I can't risk taking my eyes off them. Logan's attention drops to the wooden floor, allowing them the privacy I can't afford to give.

I'm able to see them better, now I'm over the shock of it all.

The man is tall, but isn't as slender as Charlie. His features are Mediterranean, with a tanned glow and mahogany brown hair that falls to his shoulders. He's good looking in a pretty, boy-band sort of way. I'd guess he's in his mid-twenties.

The woman is around the same age. She has long, almost black hair, and a cute round face with bright, sapphire eyes, a contrast against her fawn skin. She's not as pale as Logan, her eyes not as light, but she could pass for his sister, sharing similar distinctions in their appearance. She's slightly taller than me. I'm basically a Hobbit so most people are taller than me. She has a similar build to me, though. I'd describe myself as podgy, whereas she's curvy in all the right places.

Both of them are wearing black jeans and plain white vest tops. Well, that's all they've managed to put back on anyway. I spot a red checked shirt and a navy jumper, scrunched up on the bed. They notice my questioning look.

The man clears his throat. 'We were just... changing into new clothes,' he explains, cheeks reddening. He smooths his hair behind his ears.

We stand there awkwardly, measuring each other up.

'Are you the people that led us here?' I demand, my fists clenching, prepared to fight.

Logan rests a hand on my shoulder. Whether it's to hold me back or calm me, I'm not sure.

'Led you here? No! Did *you* lead *us* here?' the woman returns, struggling to match my harsh, accusatory tone. Her Irish accent is too soft and sweet to sound intimidating. The man's accent is the same as mine, southern English, not too posh. So far, only this woman, Ben, and Charlie buck the trend.

Full of suspicion, my eyes narrow on them. 'No. We thought the kidnappers might be here waiting for us,' I answer, toning down the volume of my voice.

'Oh man, you've been kidnapped, too?' the man asks, his eyes wide.

'Yeah, and we're not the only ones. The rest are waiting for us to tell them the coast is clear,' Logan clarifies for him.

Lips thinning, the man looks to the woman, who simply shrugs.

'How long have you been here?' I quiz them, still cautious.

'A couple hours, maybe. When we found the map, we decided to come straight here. We thought we'd find answers, but the place was empty,' the man discloses. He drops down onto the bed, a breath whooshing out of him. 'This is so trippy, man. I can't believe we're all out here, surviving in this wilderness. Forced together like this. Not that it's a bad thing. The more the merrier. Right?'

After a brief pause, Logan enquires, 'Are there any supplies?'

'We found fishing equipment and there's tinned food in the kitchen cupboards. Also, the taps are running fresh water, hot and cold,' the woman informs us, picking out a new jumper from the wardrobe.

Logan and I glance at each other, wondering what to do next.

The woman interrupts our silent communication. 'I'm Dawn, by the way,' she introduces herself with a sweet smile, hand on her heart.

'I'm Alex,' the man throws in with a quick wave.

'Ruby, Logan,' I mutter absentmindedly, and the two of them smile awkwardly at us.

Logan's mouth is close to my ear when he asks, 'Should we call the others in?' He's leaving the decision with me.

Why do I have to be the one to make it? These people look innocent enough and it didn't seem as though they were expecting us. But it's still a risk.

'How many of you are there?' Dawn requests, her tone timid.

'Including the two of you, we make ten,' Logan answers honestly.

Ten. There's ten of us now, I repeat to myself, something sparking in my mind. 'Ten people—ten dining room chairs,' I mumble, lost in thought.

'There's also five bedrooms, with two beds in each. Only one frigging bathroom, though,' Alex interjects, adding to my list.

A fierce silence roars into the room. My body locks in tension while I search my mind for the answer—the reason we've been led to this place. I push down the horrid thought that's clawing its way up. I'm unsuccessful in my attempts at casting it away. I hate what I'm about to say, but as soon as the thought enters my head, I'm sure it's correct.

'They expect us to stay here,' I whisper, mortified. Dread in its purest form has me in its cold clutches, so sickening that I nearly vomit.

Clearly our kidnapper's plan is for all of us to live here—together.

But for how long?

I'm not sure I want to learn the answer to that question.

Chapter 12

CLASH

Reluctantly accepting that we're not in immediate danger—the kidnappers intend for us to *live* here for an extended period—I decide it's safe to signal the others over to meet Dawn and Alex, so we can figure out a plan of action together. Besides, I need some fresh air in an open space. This unwanted revelation has made my head spin.

I'm all the more confused as to why we've been kidnapped and brought out here. If it's not to murder or torture us, then what's the point? Why would anyone want to bring ten strangers to a cabin in the middle of nowhere to live for... however long we're supposed to live here? What do we or the kidnappers gain? We may have answered one question, but it's only left us with a hundred more.

After we agree that my guess was likely accurate, we make our way downstairs to gather the others. It's a wonder that no one else seems as troubled as I am.

Maybe they're in shock, Ruby. Not everyone is as used to doom and gloom as you are.

Moving into the living space, I ask, 'Is no one else worried about why we've been brought to stay here? Or wondering how long this will go on for?'

'From the look of things, it's just a cabin with enough supplies for a few days. I'm sure we'll find out what's going on soon enough,' Logan replies, shrugging as though he thinks my worries are irrational. 'It's not like it's some torture chamber, Ruby.'

Blood hurtles to my head and pounds behind my ears.

'It depends on what you consider torture. I, for one, don't want to hang around here long enough to find out what's going on. I—I can't believe you!' I exclaim, practically stomping my foot.

Looking bewildered, Logan holds up his hands in defence. 'Wh—What? What have I done?'

'You've already given up, that's what,' I throw back, storming out of the front door onto the decking.

Logan doesn't immediately follow so I peek over my shoulder to observe his reaction through the open doorway. He stands where I left him, eyebrows raised, lips pressed together. Dawn and Alex creep out of the cabin to join me, maintaining an awkward silence.

Teeth grinding, Logan exhales loudly through his nose, and shakes his head in disbelief. He exits the cabin, maintaining his distance from me. He walks straight past us to the edge of the decking and starts waving his hands—the signal for the others to come out of hiding.

As soon as I realise I'm about to see them again, my heart lurches. I'm aching to be reunited with Ben, Freya, and Charlie especially. It surprises me that I'm so attached to them already. It's not a good sign. I shouldn't feel like this. I don't want to care this much, because I know something bad will happen. It always does.

I'm afraid that, if I continue to develop these bonds, when I eventually break them, it will tear me apart. And when we resume our lives beyond this forest, I don't see how my friendships with them could last. Someone in Charlie's position in society couldn't be seen with a degenerate like me. But now that Charlie has crossed my mind, I can't wait to see his little lost boy face again. We've only been separated for *ten minutes*.

God. It's pathetic how desperate for friendship I am.

As an antisocial introvert, analysing myself is an obsessive compulsion. Self-awareness is an important attribute for anyone. Personally, it helps me to survive the vagrant 'lifestyle'. I must be aware of both my surroundings and my reactions to them.

Thinking back to my actions today—attempting to lift the others' spirits with scream therapy, voting to find the cabin for the good of the group, risking my life to go back for Zoe, and then thoughtlessly volunteering to potentially bowl into my gruesome death with Logan—I notice that I'm not acting like my usual self. I don't hate that, despite knowing I probably *should* be worried.

Normally, I'm quite a selfish person: a loner who avoids conventional human relationships. I've been this way for years. But I'm opposing that here—changing, at least a little. I'm consciously making decisions which are beneficial to the group, to protect them. I'm also experiencing these *urges* to reach out and touch people—even *hug* them. That's really unlike me. That's more like the old me, before life threw me into the muddy pit of homelessness. I hate change; it unsettles my stomach and overwhelms my brain. Especially when it's completely out of my control. Yet I can't seem to stop myself now.

Do I regret any of my actions? Would it have been better for me to have gone solo in the forest and leave the group? Probably not. No. My answer is no to both questions. I like that I'm a part of this group.

'Ruby!' Charlie calls out.

Lifting my head, I spot him and his gangly legs sprinting down the hill. My heart swells. Just seeing him and knowing he's safe overpowers me. I don't realise it at first, but I'm automatically running towards him. Ben, Freya, and the others follow behind him. I'm galloping towards them, filled with absolute joy.

Charlie and I collide. His arms wrap around my waist, then lift me off my feet. He twirls me around.

'Peter Pan, I'm flying,' I joke as the world spins. Closing my eyes, I let myself enjoy the whirling sensation.

Also giggling, Charlie finally stops spinning us. He plants my feet back on solid ground. Ben and Freya catch up. All of us are breathing heavily from exhilaration. They join the embrace for a moment before we all break apart, grinning broadly.

Ben places a hand on my shoulder and squeezes it affectionately. 'You know, love, I thought we weren't gonna see you again for a minute there.'

'Me too,' I reply, catching my breath. I can't remember the last time I've felt this much relief and pleasure all mixed into one moment. I'm genuinely happy to be reunited with them after only *ten minutes* apart. It's ridiculous yet undeniable.

Happiness isn't an emotion I'm used to. I hope I can experience more of it. I'd forgotten how good it feels.

'I was so worried that I pulled out clumps of my hair—my beautiful hair!' Charlie gives me one final squeeze before releasing me. 'Don't do that to me again.'

I finally remember why people hug each other: it's comforting.

With a smile on my face, I glance over my shoulder to see Logan watching us, still on the decking. His expression is impassive. However, judging from his body language—his folded arms and tense posture—it's clear something is troubling him. His mild expression isn't fooling me.

My smile fades.

After we introduce everyone to Dawn and Alex, we make a beeline for the kitchen to rifle through the cupboards. We gather all the tins and place them together on the dining table. There's about thirty in total, including beans, fruits, soups, and some pasta meals. Between the ten of us, they would only last two days maximum. That's only if we decide to stay here. Which, at present, is something I'm unwilling to do.

Hopefully, I can convince everyone to risk the forest again, taking the food and the few bottles we have, filled with fresh water. That will enable us to survive a day or two of travel. I'm reasonably confident that most of them will agree with me, even if I don't have Logan's full support.

When I explain my theory to the others, I'm pleased to discover that Ben and Charlie are as disturbed as I am by the prospect of staying here. At first, Eli is unreadable, but then a deep frown forms. He's standing rigidly to the side, staring out of the window, deep in thought. The others don't offer their opinions. I assume they would rather focus on lunch. Their hunger is more pressing.

There are ten tins of fruit in front of us. We each pick one to eat. I'm saddled with the tinned peaches as I waited until last to choose. Luckily, Logan chose the pear halves over the peaches, before me. I hate pears, but if I had been stuck with them, I would have forced them down anyway. That's how hungry I am. The angry rumbling of my stomach wouldn't have let me forgo another meal, even if the only choice left was dog food. The taste of peaches isn't a strong memory, seeing as I can't remember the last time I ate one. I can only imagine how gloriously sweet they will be.

My mouth begins to salivate when I peel the lid back by the ring pull. The sliced fruit is soaked in a thin syrup.

Plucking out a slice, I let the syrup drip off a little, then pop it into my mouth. The succulent sweetness startles me as my back teeth, unused to sugar, ache when I bite down.

After a few rounds of chewing, I grow used to the tang and come to enjoy the taste. I carry on stuffing my mouth full of peaches, placating the hungry beast growling in my stomach.

The others are busy doing the same. We're all silent as we concentrate on our small, savoured meals.

Charlie grins at me, his mouth stuffed full of pineapple rings. This is the quietest I've seen him, apart from asleep. Even then, he sometimes snores and sleep talks, as I discovered last night.

'Guys, the oven works. We have electricity,' Freya mentions, inspecting the integrated oven. She fiddles with the dials, testing the heat.

'That means we can cook a meal tonight. We have fishing equipment now, so some of us can take the boat out onto the lake before it gets dark. Catch something for dinner,' Logan suggests, finishing those disgusting-looking grainy pears. He throws the empty tin in the bin.

'Why is no one asking the important question: why does a cabin in the middle of nowhere have electricity and running water? Where's it coming from? I don't see any towers or solar panels anywhere,' I interject, agitation creeping into my voice.

'There could be generators somewhere. A microgrid could be hidden in the forest. Who knows? Why does that matter when we have more important things to worry about?' Logan replies in an exasperated tone. My negative attitude is clearly grating on him.

A well-thought-out response eludes me. 'Because... because it's really... *weird*. This whole situation we're stuck in is unbelievable. It's fucking unreal. I can't understand why you're casually planning to fish and have dinner here like we're at some holiday camp. If we stay here, we're willing participants in whatever these unknown kidnappers have planned for us. We're offering ourselves up as fucking prisoners,' I rant at him, raising my voice.

Logan rubs his forehead as though he's dealing with an annoying child. 'Ruby, I'm not suggesting we give up and live here forever. All I'm proposing is that we take a break here, just for a day or two, to *recover*, before we race off and get lost in the forest again. Do you really think it's best to take all this food and head straight back out there a few hours before sunset? With all those trees crashing down without warning? Does no one deserve a hot shower or a good night's sleep first?'

We're standing at opposite ends of the large kitchen, though the gap feels minuscule as the tension fills the space between us.

Gritting my teeth, I allow his words to sink in before I bite back. I can see where he's coming from. It will be dark soon and those suspiciously brittle trees are a huge safety concern. Still, I'd hate to back down now.

Yes, I'm being stubborn on this, but if we *do* stay here, even for one night, it's letting the kidnappers win. And I can't allow that.

My mind is made up: I don't trust this place.

'I don't give a shit. I'm not staying here. End of. You can all do what you want but I'm filling up my bottle, packing some food, then fucking off. When I *do* find help, I'll direct them here to retrieve your bodies.' My words spit out like venom. It was harsh but hopefully it snaps them back to reality—pushes them to join me. Because, really, the last thing I want is to leave any of them behind. Including Zoe.

'I'm with you, love, I am. I don't wanna sleep here, either. But we don't have to leave straight away. Do we?' Ben asks, leaning back against the counter. I throw him a confused look and he shrugs. 'I'm knackered. I could do with a nap first, like.'

I can't believe Ben isn't running out the door at the first opportunity. The heat of betrayal singes the skin around my face. This is probably how he felt at the stream when I didn't back him up.

'I also plan on joining you, Ruby. But... would it be terrible of me to shower first? I realise I'll just get dirty again the second we step foot in the forest. Still... I do hate feeling this sticky,' Charlie says timidly, as if he doesn't want to be shouted at—as if I'm acting like some sort of tyrant.

I glance around, noticing that most of them are avoiding eye contact with me.

'Who's the bitch now?' Zoe whispers to me, walking past to chuck her empty tin in the bin. Her comment stings. Guilt also nips at me.

Shifting my weight, I sigh. I hate to admit it, but Zoe is probably right. That's what they're all thinking: that I'm unreasonable and hot-headed. This is exactly why I didn't want to lead the decision-making. If I had it my way, we'll all leave right now. Maybe that's selfish of me to ask. Should I allow people a rest before I expect them to journey into the forest again? I should at least let them shower first. *A shower would be nice*, I admit to myself, my face continuing to burn even as my blood cools.

Allowing myself to give in to these small comforts will inevitably test my resolve. It's a slippery slope, especially for someone like me, who hasn't known comfort in years.

'Fine, I'll wait until we're all showered and prepared. But I'm leaving today no matter what. I don't care if I have to sleep in the forest on my own in the pitch black. I'm not staying here,' I conclude in a calm yet firm tone.

Logan is measuring me through narrowed eyes. I can't stay in this room any longer with everyone looking at me like that. I need to get out.

Without another word, I spin on my heel and march out of the kitchen, straight towards the front door.

Once I step outside, the tension immediately releases my muscles, and the cool breeze soothes my sizzling skin. I lean against the wooden railing of the decking, drawing in fresh, crisp air to clear my thoughts. When my heartbeats slow, I'm calm enough to reflect on the heated exchange.

The reason I'm so frustrated with Logan is because, in my eyes, he's letting the kidnappers have their own way with us—he's eating from the palms of their hands. It seems ridiculous to me that we'd happily do what they want us to. We should be doing the exact opposite. I already compromised once, by agreeing to come here in the first place. To stay here because we're too afraid or too tired to try anything else is nonsensical.

Yet I probably could have handled it better. I shouldn't have been so vicious and petty. I guess there's no real urgency to leave. We should take some time to prepare. Perhaps I was a bit hasty in my anger. I am feeling a little guilty for my behaviour, especially seeing Charlie acting sheepish with me. Making people feel like they have to walk on eggshells around me was not my intention. I may be mouthy at times, but I'm not an aggressive person.

I'm not my dad.

The creaking of the wooden floor in the living room makes me straighten up.

'I'm glad you didn't cave in back there,' Sasha says, stepping out of the cabin. She rests her back against the pillar beside me.

Gripping onto the railing, I blow out another breath. 'Yeah, but I should still apologise to everyone,' I mutter, staring out to the lake. 'I was a bit of a bitch about it.'

'You were only standing your ground on what you thought was right. You shouldn't have to apologise for voicing your opinion. You're a strong-minded woman. If you were a man, you wouldn't be called a bitch for that. They'd say you were being assertive,' she astutely points out.

Trying to be discreet, I study Sasha in my peripheral, amazed that she's taking my side on this. She leans over the railing, her focus on the lake. Her comment about me being strong-minded fills me with a sense of pride.

Yeah, I shouldn't have to apologise for voicing my opinion even if people disagree with it. I wasn't being overly aggressive. Logan and I were both turning up the volume in there. No one called *him* a bitch.

'I bet Logan hates me now, though,' I blurt out without thinking. I hadn't realised how concerned I was with his perception of me until that fell out of my mouth. Usually, how I come across to people is the least of my concerns. But for some reason, I don't want these people to misjudge me. Especially Logan.

'Hmm, I don't think you need to stress about that. I've been watching the way he looks at you. Most men like it when a woman challenges them. It would be boring if you agreed with everything he says. Who doesn't enjoy a little drama every once in a while? You kept me pretty entertained in there,' she tells me, amusement lighting her face. I smile along with her.

I want to ask more about how Logan has been looking at me, but I don't want to appear as though I care too much about it. I'm starting to warm to Sasha. I want to get to know her better. She's not as intimidating when she smiles freely. Thankfully, the stony mask she wore on our first meeting has quickly crumbled. Unlike mine. It was only last night that Logan mentioned how intimidating *I* was.

'Where were you taken from?' I ask, not really knowing where to start.

'Norwich. I was staying with my sister, Saroyce, and my little nephew,' Sasha answers, her eyes filling with affection.

'What's his name?'

'Darwin. He's too cute to be real. He's a handful, though, now that he's a toddler. Babies are a lot easier to look after I think. Not that I really know.' Sadness drags her features down for a brief moment, but then she smiles again. 'Apparently, all you have to do is feed, change, and cuddle babies for the first year. Sounds easy enough to me.' She shrugs. That melancholy still lingers behind her eyes.

'I doubt new parents would agree. They'd probably slap you for saying that,' I remark, and we both snicker.

'What about you? Do you have any brothers or sisters?' Sasha asks, carrying on the polite conversation.

With my heart seizing, I fix my gaze on the rocking boat by the dock. 'Yeah, erm, an older brother—Jack.'

'Are you two close?'

'We were when we were kids but I... I haven't seen him for a long time,' I disclose, growing increasingly uncomfortable with the direction this conversation is heading. Delving into my past is not something I desire to do with anyone, no matter how much I like them. I haven't even gotten this personal with Charlie and he's the one I've connected to the most out here. I might have said that about Logan before the argument.

Sasha must sense my discomfort because she doesn't push me for more information. I'm thankful for it. I wouldn't want to be rude in refusing to answer her other questions. I like her more for that.

'I think Eli and I will come with you when you leave. I can sense his discomfort at the idea of staying here, too. He's a man of few words so you have to read his body language. He's stressed out—on edge. It would be nice to have a good night's sleep in a real bed. But... I wouldn't en-courage Eli to stay here if he doesn't want to,' Sasha expresses, a resigned smile on her face.

We continue chatting for a while, keeping the conversation light. Sasha talks more about her sister and nephew. She doesn't mention other family members, which gives me the impression Saroyce and Darwin may be it for her, family-wise.

As she opens up, I get more of a sense of who Sasha really is. Before this conversation, I thought she and Eli were the same—a bit intense, aloof, unapproachable. Similar to myself, before this experience started. But now I see that I've judged her too harshly. She's the first woman here who I've connected with on a deeper level.

I like Freya, but I know we're very different people. She's a lot more confident than I am—outgoing and direct. Our conversations today have been slightly one-sided.

Dawn, on the other hand, seems a little too sweet and naïve. And like Freya, I imagine she'd think me too negative and closed-off. I'm not sure what we'll have in common. She might surprise me. I haven't had a one-to-one conversation with her yet.

After only ten minutes of speaking with Sasha, it becomes apparent that we're on the same wavelength. It's been that way with Charlie and Ben, too. A sense of familiarity—an invisible tether. Somehow, we instantly understand each other. Maybe it's because I see similarities in a few aspects of our personalities. They mask their pain as I do. Charlie through humour, Ben through defensiveness, Sasha and I by brushing past troubles and moving on. I can relate to them better than the others. But it's only been a day, I guess. I shouldn't write people off simply because we're different.

In terms of friendship, Logan is where I struggle to make up my mind. Sometimes, I feel so close to him, as if I've known him for years. Then, at other times, we clash like we're speaking different languages—like we're not even on the same planet.

All I know is that the idea of leaving here without him makes me ache. I wish that, when we do eventually brave the forest, he comes with us, because I'm afraid I may change my mind about leaving if he doesn't.

'I don't know if it's purely my suspicious nature making me paranoid, but I have a funny feeling about this place. Like something isn't right. I mean, other than being kidnapped and dumped out here,' I mutter to Sasha, who nods slowly in understanding, her forehead crinkling. 'Maybe I'm being stubborn, but I have to at least *try*. I can't just go with the flow like Logan seems to want me to. I can't roll over and submit myself to this. Whatever *this* is. I also don't want to leave anybody behind.' Tired of thinking, I heave a sigh. A good night's sleep is so temping right about now. Yet I doubt I could sleep one wink here in this accommodating prison. 'I don't know. Maybe... if we *did* stay one night, people would be more willing--'

Sasha cuts me off before I can finish that sentence. 'I like that you're not willing to just roll over and go along with what someone else has planned for you. To me, that's one hell of an admirable quality, Ruby. There are some people in there who can only handle the easiest option presented to them. You're different, though, I can tell. You're a survivor, a fighter. You seem to know your own mind. You don't have to change that about yourself to do right by others. If they make the wrong decision then that's on them, not you. Don't go against what your gut is telling you simply because you're worried they won't follow you. They will, you'll see,' she declares, winking at me before she strides back into the cabin.

Soaking in Sasha's words of encouragement, I smile to myself. She's right. I need to stay strong on this because I know I'm not wrong. There's something off about this place and we should try to escape as soon as possible. I have to trust my instincts. *If people stay behind and get hurt then that's not your fault: you tried your best to convince them*, I console myself, still unable to evade this gnawing fear of loss.

Will I have to say goodbye to any of these strangers I'm quickly considering friends? Will I have to say goodbye to Logan?

My tummy tight with unease, I turn to walk back inside when something on the wooden table catches my eye. I do a double-take.

There's a white envelope positioned under a rock at the centre of the table.

That envelope wasn't there when we came in.

A forceful chill sweeps over my entire body, causing all the tiny hairs on my arms to stand on end.

Someone has put that there—*recently*.

Someone has left us a letter.

Chapter 13

THE RULES

Cautiously, I inch towards the table while scanning my surroundings for any movement.

There's no one visible.

They must have left the envelope here when we were all inside raiding the cupboards. They could be watching me from the forest somewhere, hidden.

Another shudder rakes down my spine.

I almost want to rip it up and throw it into the lake before the others see it. I'm determined to spite the kidnappers. But my curiosity is more pressing than the venom stored inside me.

The need to read is a heavy weight inside my chest.

I push aside the rock and pick up the sealed letter. On the front, in neat scroll writing, the envelope is addressed to 'Candidates'.

'What's that?' a voice behind me asks.

Startled, I spin to find Charlie peeking his head around the front door.

'Our thoughtful kidnappers have been kind enough to leave a love letter.'

Charlie's eyes widen and he practically stumbles out. 'What does it say?'

'I haven't opened it yet. Let's gather the others first,' I suggest. It's only right to read it with the whole group present.

Merely holding it in my hand is making me sick to my stomach. The thought of having to open it and read the words aloud—*nope*. A piece of paper has never felt more dangerous. It's like I've picked up a loaded gun.

I ask Charlie to gather everyone in the living room because I assume the kidnappers are still somewhere outside, spying on us. Once inside, I draw the curtains closed and shut the cabin door. It relieves a fraction of the anxiety that's clawing at my insides.

The group shuffles in from the kitchen. Logan is the first to march over to me as if he's completely forgotten our disagreement.

'What's happened?' he asks, concern pinching his features.

'We've been left this.' I hold up the envelope. 'I found it on the table outside. I haven't opened it yet. I was hoping someone else could.' I offer it to Logan.

He accepts it without hesitation. 'Okay, I'll do it. I'll read it out loud. But let me get through the whole thing without interrupting. We can discuss what it says after.'

Everyone nods along, despite their evident confusion.

They all appear just as curious as I am about what the letter could entail. We all soundlessly watch Logan in tense anticipation.

Logan carefully rips open the envelope to retrieve the typed letter inside, then hastily scans over the single page. His inspection only takes seconds, though it feels like an hour. The room is achingly silent while we wait to hear what's written for us.

Logan grips the paper in both hands, clears his throat, then begins to read aloud in a steady voice. 'Congratulations, candidates. Each of you has been selected for the primary stage of our prestigious training programme. We understand that you may be experiencing some confusion or frustration due to the unexpected nature of this situation. We can only apologise for the manner in which we have extracted you from your lives. Rest assured that you are in no danger. We are a confidential government organisation tasked with the recruitment of special people, like yourselves, into our employment. More information on the specifics of what we do and who we are will be provided at the conclusion of the initial evaluation period. This experience has been designed to test your survival and team-building skills. Thus far, you have all done exceptionally well, considering the limited information and resources with which you have been supplied. Over a two-week period, we will monitor your progression in this cabin environment. Our findings will assist us in assessing and determining your suitability for the next stage of the programme. At that point, you may each decide if you wish to progress onto higher prospects within our organisation or revert to your normal lives. Nonetheless, this stage of training is compulsory. All ten candidates must live in the cabin together for the full fourteen days.'

Logan's hands have started to shake a little. He collects a breath before he continues. 'The rules of the cabin are as follows...

1. All candidates must sleep in their assigned bedrooms, in the mixed-sex pair they were matched with on arrival. The assigned pairs are—

Room one: Sasha Reed and Elijah Conteh.
Room two: Ruby Hayes and Logan West.
Room three: Freya Clark and Benjamin Mendel.
Room four: Zoe Morgan and Charles Winshaw.
Room five: Dawn Kennedy and Alexander Costello.

2. Candidates must not harm each other or themselves during their stay. We will only provide emergency medical assistance if deemed necessary.

3. For safety reasons, all candidates must stay within the confines of the cabin between sunset and sunrise.

4. Candidates must not damage any structures, fixtures, or fittings provided for group or individual use.

5. Candidates will be supplied with rations, which are to be evenly distributed between group members.

6. Candidates are permitted to explore the surrounding forest during daytime hours and are encouraged to use the boat and fishing equipment provided, on the lake, in groups of no fewer than two and no more than four.'

'Candidates are reminded that this stage of training is compulsory, and any rule-breaking or non-compliance will result in strict punishment. We emphasise that more information will be provided to you once mandatory participation is complete. Thank you for your patience. We apologise for any inconvenience. We sincerely hope you enjoy your stay.'

When Logan finishes the letter, he looks up to absorb our reactions. We all seem to be trapped in a state of stunned silence.

I'm trying to process what Logan has read to us, but I'm having trouble accepting what I've heard. Training programme... candidates... government organisation... two weeks... compulsory. My brain has been fried. I don't know how to react. I'm also too flabbergasted for my anger to take root. I should be screaming, tearing up the letter, kicking down doors, and crashing through this place. Instead, I'm simply standing with my mouth agape, the same as the others, chewing on this information and struggling to digest it.

'The government is behind all this? This is some sort of test? I don't understand why they can't just tell us what's going on,' Eli says, confusion contorting his face.

'It's probably a top-secret organisation, like MI5 or something,' Alex speculates, scratching his jaw.

'What's the reasoning? I mean, I don't think I've ever applied for some secret MI5 operation. They could have swiped my CV from Pizza Hut, but I doubt it,' Dawn jokes unevenly, wringing her hands.

'Yes, good point. What's so special about us? The only talent I have is doing the worm dance. Although only when I'm incredibly intoxicated,' Charlie comments with a shaky laugh, running a nervous hand over his hair.

'Nowt, this is just some bleeding stunt to mess about with our heads. Some twisted git is sitting in the forest somewhere, laughing at how gullible we all are, like,' Ben interjects solemnly.

'But if it's not the government, then who is it? And what would their purpose be? What would some weirdo get out of this if it were simply a random kidnapping? At least this theory makes *some* sense. You can imagine a top-secret government agency doing something like this—to recruit people. All covert and mysterious. What would anyone else gain from this?' Freya poses the questions, challenging Ben. He shrugs, as confused as the rest of us.

'Why explain in a typed letter, though? Why not come to us in person, or show us a video on the TV or something? It's suspiciously old-fashioned,' Eli comments, his eyes narrow under his arched frown.

'Anonymity, perhaps? To keep us in the dark,' Sasha guesses.

'To keep us scared,' I amend. 'Too scared to venture out in search of escape. Placing the letter on the table was a statement: telling us they're watching. That they're out there... *evaluating*.' My insides twist with renewed dread.

Right now, I don't know what to think. It's hard to believe that this ridiculous setup is some government-sponsored trial, designed to test and recruit us. On the other hand, this whole situation is hard to believe, no matter the culprit or intention. I've been drugged, moved to this mysterious and remote forest, and forced to survive with nine strangers for no apparent reason. This is definitely not a typical Tuesday. So I'm not denying it's a possibility. The question which is demanding my attention, though, is: why me?

Why would they want someone like me for a government programme? I'm just some unexceptional, unfit homeless woman, who can't even hold down a waitressing job. What's so special about me? *Nothing.* That's why this explanation is so unimaginable. Ben is probably right: some warped twat must be messing with our heads for a laugh.

It doesn't matter whether I trust the information that the letter provided. I'm still ploughing ahead with my plan to leave this cabin. I don't care about the rules forbidding me from escaping. If anything, it makes me even more determined.

'What do we do now?' Alex asks, fiddling with his floppy hair.

The room sinks into silence again as we think on it. So, sensing the opportunity to sway their decision, I uncharacteristically decide to step up and take control of the situation. 'We leave. We pack the supplies and head north.'

'What about the rules? They said we'd be punished if we break them,' Alex responds, worry flickering across his features. He glances across to Logan as if hoping that he'll challenge me so Alex won't have to.

'What can they do? If they are who they say they are, they can't torture or kill us. What do we really have to lose? We're already stuck in this hellhole with basic rations. What's the worst they can do to us?' I reason, trying to seem blasé. If they're going to follow me, I have to act cocky. I have to act like I'm sure—like I'm solid in my resolve.

'Ruby's right. If anything, this could be a test to see what they'll do. Perhaps if we push them, we can find out more,' Logan contributes, surprising me.

I turn to him, unsure why he's finally agreeing with me. When he sees my expression, his mouth tilts up.

'Yes, Ruby. I'm won't fight you on this anymore. You take the lead. I trust you.' One of his full-blown grins—which reveal those beautiful dimples—starts spreading further across his face and my tummy flutters.

My cheeks heat as I reflect on his comment. He wants me to take the lead because he trusts me. *I* don't even trust me. My casual confidence has worked a bit *too* well, it seems.

It's hard to believe we're not descending into another argument on this issue.

'Aye, screw the rules. I don't care what this letter says. I don't care if they are a bleeding government organisation. I'm getting the hell outta here,' Ben declares defiantly.

'They can't steal us away from our lives like this, without our permission, and then expect us to follow their rules without telling us why. Where's the respect?' Eli remarks in a gruff voice, clearly worked up.

I'm not used to hearing Eli speak so passionately. I'm not used to hearing him speak, full stop. Sasha, with her eyes downcast and forehead furrowed, strokes Eli's shoulder, which immediately relaxes his tense posture.

'They call us candidates but then they say the two weeks here is compulsory. So we're not candidates, we're fucking prisoners,' Ben adds just as passionately, feeding off Eli's aggravated energy.

'Well, I'm staying. You can all leave. Honestly, it would be a relief,' Zoe retorts, slumping down onto the sofa and making herself comfortable.

I roll my eyes. The only time she pipes up is to say something venomous. I'm grateful that none of us retaliate.

'So, apart from Logan, Eli, and Ben, who's coming with me?' Anxiety ties knots in my belly while I wait with forced patience for their responses. I'm worried that I haven't made my case as strongly as I could have. But it's now or never. I'm hoping I don't have to leave anyone behind—bar Zoe, who, to me, isn't part of the group anyway.

'You know I'm in, of course. And besides, if I stayed, there's a high chance that Zoe will finish me off with those deadly eye daggers of hers,' Charlie says light-heartedly, but Zoe still shoots him a hateful scowl, her lip curling.

The rest of us try to hide our amusement, to no avail. Logan and Eli are the only two who manage to keep their expressions respectfully blank.

'I'm coming with you,' Sasha confirms, flashing me a quick grin.

'I hate the idea of going back into that forest again, after what happened with the trees. I think it's way too dangerous. But if you're all going... Ugh, I will, too,' Freya mutters in a sullen tone, folding her arms.

Ben wraps a comforting arm around Freya, yet he can't hide the triumphant shine in his dark eyes. It's brave of her to decide to come with us after she was knocked unconscious before. I need to stop assuming that pretty, feminine girls aren't as tough and capable as I am. Freya is just as brave as anyone. Internalised misogyny be damned.

For someone who hates being judged on first impressions, I'm too quick to fall into the same trap myself. There's a lot of society's bullshit I still have to unlearn.

Fuck stereotypes: they only feed prejudice in all its nefarious forms.

'Yeah, man, I don't mind either way,' Alex concedes with a relaxed shrug.

'I'll come, too,' Dawn adds, raising her hand in our little count.

Relief floods me, releasing the knots in my stomach. Everyone, apart from Zoe, is coming with us. I don't have to say goodbye to any of them. Also, they seem more certain about joining me than they were earlier. Maybe that's because, last time, we voted amidst a heated argument and Logan's opposition. This time, he was the first to support me.

My gaze flicks over to Logan to find him already watching me. He offers me a small smile which I reciprocate. Warmth blankets my heart, momentarily filling that void in my chest. I'm proud that I've convinced the majority to follow me. I guess I'm better at leading than I thought. The pressure is on now, though.

'All right, then. Okay. So... prepare to leave in about an hour. Get showered, pack the food, and steal a few blankets to use in the forest tonight. In the meantime, we'll try to keep a low profile so they don't realise what we're planning to do. Then we make a break for it,' I assert, acting casual to mask my nerves.

They all nod in agreement, some more satisfied than others. Sasha winks at me with a proud smirk on her face. She was right. She predicted this outcome in our conversation on the decking earlier.

Hopefully, I deliver on this and it's worth the risk.

After I help pack the tins of food into bags and fill all the water containers, I trudge upstairs to the bathroom at the end of the hall.

Everyone else managed to have speedy showers. I'm the last to freshen up before we venture back out into the wilderness. I'm looking forward to being all fresh and clean again, even if it's short-lived.

Dawn and Alex, when they first checked the bedrooms, discovered new clothes hanging in the wardrobes for each of us. That means I'll finally have a change of clothes. It's the only benefit I'm gaining from this experience—a new outfit.

The bathroom is already warm and misty from the shower Charlie had before me. It's tiled in sandstone with white and silver accessories. The shower cubicle has various soaps and shampoos lined up on a rack inside. There's one remaining clean towel left for me on the rail in the corner.

Shutting the door behind me, I make sure to lock it. I might take a few extra minutes in here, since there's no one waiting for me to finish. I cherish hot showers when and where I can get them. They're a luxury for me, given my circumstances. Hostel and shelter bathrooms aren't nearly as nice as this one. They're usually dirty, with lukewarm water and low-pressure shower heads. Also, I have to hold my nose the whole time and make sure not to tread on anything sharp.

Paranoid that there could be cameras, I step into the cubicle still in my underwear, then turn on the water. It's already at the perfect temperature, so I dip my head under the warm spray, allowing it to wash away the forest and my fears about returning to it, if only for the next ten minutes.

While I'm finishing my luxurious soak in the shower, I think over the letter.

Putting aside the alleged reason we're here, the rules are a different game entirely. Some of them I can understand, like not hurting anyone or breaking anything. They're reasonable. Even the one about staying inside the cabin after dark is a sensible rule. What's really puzzling to me is the one regarding the sleeping arrangements—we're required to share our room with the partner they assigned us when we first arrived in the valley—mixed-sex pairs. Logan is mine. He was the first person I bumped into. That must mean we were each placed close enough to find each other before meeting anyone else.

But why? I ask myself, scratching my shampoo-foamed head. If this is a team-building exercise, then why force us to form a stronger bond with a certain individual? Obviously, Zoe and Charlie didn't work well as a pair. Still, it's plain to see that the rest of us have a deeper connection with the partners we had before entering into this group dynamic.

It could be designed to ease us into a group mentality. I know that if I woke up with nine strangers around me, I without a doubt would have tried to escape on my own immediately. I would have been too overwhelmed by people that I didn't know or trust. Getting used to being around Logan first—learning to trust him, and then slowly being introduced to new pairs—it's a clever tactic to forming the group, I'd say. We haven't really turned on each other. None of us have fractured off... yet. We've learnt to accept one another with each new pair and have developed relationships in a relatively short space of time. I suspect none of us are used to this.

In the real world, I reckon most of us are rubbish in social situations. Even Freya and Dawn (who both seem chatty and friendly—normal-*ish* by comparison), told me, while we were waiting downstairs, that they don't have many real friends to speak of. And then there's the rest of us, whom I imagine are the people permanently scowling at the back of a party. The intense, quiet, scary ones. Except for Charlie. I can see him being a wallflower. Behind his sometimes-questionable humour is a lost boy; a big kid who lacks confidence.

I'm more of a weed than a flower, I think, hopping out of the shower. I encase myself in the towel, then stealthily remove my soggy underwear.

I guess that's why they're training us in this environment—this 'team building' experiment. They want us to learn how to work well with others. They're manipulating us into changing our typical behaviours. And it's working *too* well. Especially on me. I've irrefutably felt a change within me today. They've taken society's rejects to mould us into something useful to them. For what purpose? I still have no clue.

There must be a reason why we were chosen. Out of all the people they could have picked in the whole of the United Kingdom, who were probably smarter, stronger, and better qualified for some sort of government programme, why did *we* make the cut? There must be something we have in common—something which sets us apart.

To check the coast is clear, I peek out before dashing towards my assigned bedroom, clutching the towel tightly to my body. I spend the next five minutes racking my brain while I dry off.

Logan's and my wardrobe is packed full of new clothes. They're all hanging neatly on a rail. One half is meant for Logan and the second half is obviously meant for me. My side has a range of outfits to suit different purposes. There are a couple of pairs of jeans, a number of different coloured T-shirts, and jumpers. Although, at the end of the rail, there are a few less practical items.

A wine-red, beaded dress stands out, compared to the other casual outfits. When will I ever wear a dress here? I haven't worn a dress in over a decade. Evidently, they don't know me very well. They've even provided heeled sandals in my size at the bottom of the wardrobe, along with some Converse, boots, and trainers, which are much more my style.

Not wanting to stand around in only a towel, I select a pair of soft denim jeans, a white vest, and a checked shirt, to go with the new pair of lace-up boots I've chosen. I haven't worn real leather in a long time. They should be fairly comfortable to hike in.

I dress under the duvet, then swiftly leave the alluring comfort of the bed behind. The fresh material of my chosen outfit is soft against my clean skin.

My reflection in the long mirror by the door catches my eye. I look completely different to what I imagined. For once, I look relatively normal—not like a poor street rat.

My dark, damp hair flicks and falls past my breasts in loose curls. It's usually springier when dry. I rarely let my curls stay down for long, although they frame my face nicely now. I used to cut my curls short so they wouldn't bother me in summer. But I couldn't be bothered to do anything with my hair this year. I need to trim my fringe again, though: the straighter strands hang heavy on my eyelashes.

I wouldn't say I'm pretty. I've always been plain, unless I cake on makeup. Plus, I've never had a 'good' figure by societal standards. Eating mostly pre-packed meal deals and greasy burgers from fast food chains isn't the healthiest, but it *is* the cheapest. It's not like I can afford a gym membership, either; nonetheless, I should be more confident in my own skin. That's something nobody can take away from me. I might have nothing, and I might feel like the entire world is against me sometimes, but I've always owned my body. It's my sanctuary. It's the only place I've ever truly felt safe. Even if it's a bit rough around the edges.

My body may not be the thinnest or the most attractive, but it's my home. The only one I have.

Snapping myself out of this tangent of thought, I hurry back downstairs, eagerly prepared to leave this place. Admittedly it's been nice to shower and change my clothes. Still, I'm acutely aware that I can't get too comfortable here. I refuse to allow myself to fall into their trap. They won't manipulate me anymore. I'm my own person.

I decide my own rules.

Chapter 14

RUN

Most of the others have gathered in the living room. Logan and Ben are the only ones missing.

'You look nice.' Charlie compliments me as I approach. He's sitting on the sofa with Dawn and Alex. Sasha and Eli are standing by the window, peering out anxiously. Zoe is slumped in an armchair away from everyone else, playing with her damp hair.

Still unable to accept compliments, I pretend I didn't hear him. 'You were right about the shower. I feel better now I'm clean. Although I reckon we'll be dirty again in less than ten minutes.' The sofa opposite him is empty, so I claim it. It's the first time I've sat down since I've been here. It's surprisingly comfortable; its dishevelled appearance is unimportant to me. 'What are Ben and Logan doing?'

'They're peeping out of the back window to see if they can spot anyone before we leave,' Alex answers.

'We should make a move soon. Half of us leave through the front door and half through the kitchen window. We'll meet back up when we have cover in the forest.' I'm reciting the plan we made earlier before we all showered.

Zoe scoffs. 'You seriously think that will work? You haven't considered that maybe they can hear everything you say?'

Indeed, that sinister worry has plagued my mind more than once since entering. Of course our kidnappers could be listening to us inside this enclosed space. Our first step before planning was checking for cameras and audio recorders. We couldn't find any sign of them. That still didn't reassure me enough to shower fully nude. A recording device may be hidden somewhere unexpected. They may already be aware of our plans. Even so, we can use this opportunity to test their strength for our next escape attempt.

'It doesn't make much difference to you, does it? You're staying here like a good little prisoner,' I retort, matching her mocking tone.

'You really believe they'll let you go? With everything they've done so far, you think you can all run off through the forest without being noticed? They've said they're monitoring you. They'll find you and punish you. But you'll keep pissing them off, so much so that they'll end up wiping you away like the shit you are. Which, I guess, wouldn't bother me in the slightest. So, yeah... carry on. I, on the other hand, am not wasting my energy acting up for them. Anyway, I'm bored with this show now. I'm changing channels,' she taunts with a disdainful sneer, turning her back on me.

My body is trembling to launch itself at her, but I trap my anger deep inside and hold myself back. She wants that reaction from me.

'I'd rather try and fail through my own choices than be used like some puppet—allowing them to dictate what I do. Handing power to them without a fight... I can't. At least this way, I have a chance. I have some hope of escape,' I reply, my voice rising a little yet staying steady.

'Choice is an illusion, just like freedom, democracy, and yes—hope. None of you have control over your pathetic little lives. The people that *do* have control feed you lies so you can keep pretending things will work out one day—that you have a *choice*. That there's *hope*. All they do is twist and manipulate you into doing what they want anyway, without you even realising it. And there's nothing you can do about it. So there's no point in fighting it. Just give up. Because nothing ever works out the way you want, no matter how much you hope it does. You still end up crushed in the end. That's life,' Zoe concludes, a hint of sadness in her shrill voice.

I withhold the biting retort I was planning. Her rant is surprising. It's not about either of us or the situation: it's her perspective on life as she knows it. She's the pessimist in this confrontation, which makes me the optimist. I really *have* changed.

I used to agree with her views: thinking my choices were pointless and the only control I had over my life was deciding which alleyway to sleep in. Even that was dependent on which one smelt the least offensive that night.

Zoe's rant makes me wonder if she's simply projecting her hopelessness onto me. All this time, I've seen her as simply a nasty, bitter troll, who makes herself feel better by bringing others down. I've never stopped to ask myself *why* she's acting that way. There must be a reason.

Bitter—that's what I was before I was stuck in this situation. I always treated strangers I met on the street with cold hostility. That was my defence mechanism. Zoe is me, back in the real world. That's probably why I don't like her. She reminds me too much of the dark parts of myself—the parts that took over when my mum died.

I stare down at the patterned rug, unseeing: lost in a rare moment of clarity. 'You're probably right. But this is my way of coping. Even if I'm naively pretending that I have any choices. It doesn't matter because it provides me with enough strength to carry on—to know I'm doing all I can. I won't roll over without a fight. There's always hope, even when the odds are stacked against you. You let that chance slip away when you give up. Every time I've wanted to give up in the past, something happened to stop me.' Taking a breath, I shrug. 'Or maybe it's just not in my nature. I wish it were because it would make things a hell of a lot easier: having no responsibility, no decisions, no thoughts. But I think, if it *were* that easy to give up—to stop fighting—then we'd all be dead. There's no life without struggle.'

Coming back to myself, I look up to see everyone staring at me. Ben and Logan have quietly come in from the kitchen and are also listening intently. They all seem mesmerised by my words. Zoe's face has lost its malice. Her eyes trail away, emotionless.

The soft scrutiny of the collective gaze flusters me. Eye contact is something I'm slowly becoming used to. Even so, I'm not comfortable with people staring at me.

My face hot, I clear my throat. 'Anyway, we should get moving,' I mutter, darting towards the front door. The others finally avert their eyes and prepare to leave.

'Who's going where?' Ben enquires.

Somehow, I've found myself in charge of this whole operation and everyone is looking to me to lead them. *You better not fuck it up, Ruby.*

I need to split the group into two. Yet I don't like the thought of anyone I'm close to not being in my group, where I can keep an eye on them. Nevertheless, I must make sure I have a few strong leaders whom I trust in the other group.

'Charlie, Logan, Dawn, and Alex are with me—out the front door. The rest of you... be careful climbing out the back. We'll find you in the forest to the north. Remember to mark the trees. You have your compasses. We'll go first and hang around outside to distract anyone watching, while you lot climb out of the kitchen window. All okay?' My voice is surprisingly even, despite my heightened nerves.

I chose Charlie and Logan for obvious reasons. And, if I were being selfish, I would have also picked Ben and Freya. Putting my biases aside, I know they'll make a formidable team with Sasha and Eli. The weakest, in my eyes, are Dawn and Alex. They both seem a little lost most of the time, relying on others to lead them. They're too nice and agreeable for their own good.

Maybe that's too harsh a judgement to make after only a couple of hours. I suppose I'm used to equating kindness with weakness. There's no place for sweetness on the streets. You must be ruthless with tough skin to survive. I see that in some of the others, like Ben, Freya, Sasha, and Eli. That's why I'm sure the other group will be fine without me there.

'Right,' Ben says, clapping his hands together. He grips my shoulder reassuringly, clearly noticing my concerned expression. 'We'll see you in ten minutes, love.' With that, he releases me, leading his team out to the kitchen.

On her way out, Sasha throws me a flighty smile. 'See you soon.'

The kitchen door clicks softly when she shuts it behind her.

Zoe slovenly rises from her chair in the corner to lie down on one of the sofas. She draws a deep, tired breath. 'Good luck. You'll need it,' she mutters, her eyes already closed as though she's planning to nap through our ordeal. I can't tell if she's being sarcastic or not, so I ignore her.

Rigidly, I stand by the front door, mentally preparing myself to open it. Charlie and Logan are on either side of me, with Dawn and Alex behind us.

'Logan and I will walk out first. If anyone is watching, they'll see us casually milling about, chatting. Then after a minute, Charlie will join us. That's when he'll slam the door, which is the signal for the others to leave through the window. After another minute, Dawn and Alex will open the door and come out. We'll fake laugh and joke around, but as soon as I say run, do it. Once we have tree cover, we can search for each other,' I tell them in an authoritative voice that surprises even me. They nod in approval of the plan.

My blotchy hands are shaking as I clutch the door handle. My sweaty palms slide slightly across the cool brass in my grip. I have to put this foolhardy plan into action before anyone notices my tremor. With that in mind, I suck in a steely breath as I open the door and step out into the fading light. Logan follows closely behind me. We leave the decking and walk across to the edge of the lake. The sour, mossy scent of it carries across the breeze, only worsening the churning sickness in my stomach.

'This is a solid plan. You're a natural leader, Ruby. Everyone can see it now—except you, of course,' Logan comes out with as we inconspicuously scan the area.

'We don't know if it will work yet. They could have bugs in that cabin, hearing everything we've said.' Swallowing down my unease, I pick up a stone and chuck it into the lake.

Logan mimics my actions, collecting a handful of stones of his own. 'It's better than the idea I had: to stroll casually into the forest in our pairs. We'd be too vulnerable if we were that fractured, and it would have taken too long. At least this way, it's quick and simple, whatever happens,' he encourages me, throwing a stone. It skims the surface of the water before sinking into the murky depths. 'Hopefully, it takes them by surprise, so we have enough of a head start.'

Charlie exits the cabin, slamming the door shut behind him. That's the signal for the others to creep out the back. Logan and I greet Charlie with matching smiles, attempting to keep up pretences if anyone *is* watching us. Charlie ambles over, his boyish grin fixed in place.

'Dawn is a tad anxious. Although I'm sure she'll be fine once they're out here with us,' Charlie mentions. There's a hint of nerves in his voice, too.

Charlie slides his arm around my shoulder, then brings my head to his chest. Logan glances at us with a flash of annoyance in his expression. Swiftly, his hardened stare flicks back to the lake.

Forcing a laugh, I ask, 'What are you doing?'

'Acting casual. We need to appear as though we're happy and carefree. I know being wrapped up in my arms brings you tremendous joy and excitement but play it down a bit. We don't want it to seem too over the top,' Charlie jokes, ruffling my hair with his free hand. We both genuinely laugh when I playfully elbow him in the side.

It's funny that I wouldn't let anyone else be so tactile with me. When it comes to Charlie, he's just so bloody cute that I don't feel uncomfortable. He's like an annoying little brother you can't stay angry at.

Logan has his back to us as he lobs more stones into the lake. These don't skim the surface: they beat the water before they forcefully plunge down deep.

Dawn and Alex open the cabin door and shuffle out timidly. Waving them over, I casually move towards them with Charlie and Logan on my tail. We meet in the middle.

'I feel bad leaving Zoe behind on her own,' Dawn whispers. Her forehead furrows as her eyes dart around and she lifts a hand to her mouth to chew on her thumbnail.

She couldn't look more suspicious if she tried.

'She made her choice. But don't worry. When we get out of here, we'll tell the emergency services to come straight back for her,' I promise, attempting to calm Dawn's nerves. She nods in response. However, her anxiety-ridden demeanour doesn't improve.

Alex, on the other hand, seems relatively calm compared with Dawn. 'All this stealth business has worked up my appetite. When can we have dinner?' he queries, rubbing his stomach.

'When we're far away from this place,' I reply, my tone dry.

'So... not anytime soon, then? Can we eat as we go? I'm sure I can shovel some hot dogs into my mouth whilst we traipse about in search of the others,' Alex suggests, stretching his arms out while subtly scoping the area.

'Well, you've got a big enough mouth, mophead. The whole tin could probably fit in there,' Logan teases with a friendly smirk.

'Har har, you're so funny, Logs. No hot dogs for you,' Alex responds, pinching Logan's cheek. Logan bats his hand away, chuckling.

They're quite chummy already, I note, smiling at their exchange. I hadn't noticed them bonding enough to give each other nicknames. But I guess I've also made some instant friendships here. I called Charlie 'Peter Pan' earlier. That's what the kidnappers want. The situation they've dropped us in is heightening the need for fast friendships. Their team-building training is working like a dream. The stubborn part of me wants to rebel against it—to cast aside these new friendships purely to spite our captors. Though, in reality, I'd only be spiting myself.

It's been a few minutes: enough time for the others to have made it out, I think to myself. *It's now or never.* 'Okay, everyone ready?' I whisper, drawing their attention. They all look to me expectantly. 'Run!'

With urgency, my legs listen to my brain for once and pound through the dirt, away from the cabin. My adrenaline begins to pump more forcefully—supercharging my body.

As a unit, we sprint towards the trees north of the glade; a place we've yet to explore. Hopefully, it leads out of this place.

Logan is running beside me, keeping close. The rest are only a step behind. Alex, with his long legs, would likely be the fastest. Except he's alongside Dawn at the rear. I imagine he doesn't want to leave her side. It's similar to Logan with me.

I'm the worst to set the pace. I can't sprint for shit. We'll absolutely be caught if they all stay behind me.

It's then I realise the kidnapper's pair strategy has also worked well on us. When I was making my decision on who to separate into groups, I hadn't noticed until now that I had kept the initial pairs intact. Apart from Charlie and Zoe. I don't think the rest of us would have liked being separated from our valley partners. Especially Dawn and Alex, because their bond is more romantic, judging by the scene Logan and I stumbled upon when we first met them in the bedroom. Ben and Freya seem to be heading in that direction, too.

After we reach the forest border, we keep running through the trees for an extra minute before we take a breather. My legs and chest are already burning with tight spasms. I'm so unfit.

'Did anyone spot anything? Someone coming after us?' I question between sharp gasps of much-needed air.

'Nope, don't think so. I kept looking behind me to check—nothing,' Alex answers, swiping the hair out of his eyes.

Dawn is massaging a stitch out of her side as she says, 'Maybe they weren't watching us after all.'

'We'll soon see. Come on—let's find the others. They should be around here somewhere already,' I assert, continuing through the trees.

They follow my lead.

After ten minutes of fruitlessly searching the forest for the other group, the physical symptoms of my panic-activated adrenaline are starting to affect my balance. The thought of them captured or hurt makes my stomach roil with concern. If we can't find them, I don't know what we'll do. Turning back is still not an option for me. Continuing without them is also unthinkable.

My body shaking, I'm forced to rest, leaning against a tree trunk for support. I try to pass it off as though I only need another breather due to a stitch. The others also pause, waiting for me.

I huff. 'This was a terrible idea. We should have all stayed together. This is the world's shittest plan. And I'm a fucking prat,' I rant, then groan in frustration. With a deep scowl, I kick the tree trunk. Pain shoots up my toes, making me wince.

Logan grips my shoulders to pull me away from the tree so I can't do any more damage to my feet. 'I'm sure they're fine. They probably just ran deeper into the forest than we did.' He tries to comfort me by rubbing the tops of my arms, but it's not working.

'They said there would be strict punishments if we weren't compliant. I could've been wrong. They could be hurt, all because of my bloody stubbornness. It will be *my* fault,' I stress, angry at myself. Needing more pain to ground me, I kick a stone hard enough to stub my toe. Another groan rattles my throat. '*Fuck*! Why did anyone listen to me? I don't know what I'm doing. I'm no leader. I'm no one!'

Logan cups my head in his hands, twisting me to face him as he steps closer. He stoops down so we're eye-to-eye. 'Don't do that! Don't say that about yourself. None of this is your fault.' With his thumb, he tenderly strokes my cheek. The sensation is oddly calming, but it also makes my tummy flip. 'You're doing your best. We can all see that. No one will be hurt... they wouldn't—it wouldn't make sense to hurt us,' he maintains, trying to sound sure.

His crystalline irises are illuminated and warmed by the retreating light as the sun continues to disappear behind the shadowed mountains. His eyes are always stunning, but they're even more mesmerising in this twilight. My body stops shaking as I lose myself in his gaze, completely under his spell. I swallow hard, my heart thumping loudly in my ears, my breathing shallower.

I can only maintain eye contact with Logan for an extended beat before it becomes too intense. I break away, releasing myself from his magnetism. Sighing deeply, I slump against the tree again, trying my hardest to believe him.

'Okay, we'll go deeper. We'll search for another ten minutes. But if we still can't find them, we'll have to make a hard decision,' I concede, depressing myself with the thought of having to choose whether to leave them behind—without knowing if they're all right—or give up on the plan altogether and retreat. The latter, honestly, is not a choice I'd willingly make.

I remember what I said to Zoe back at the cabin: I don't think it's in my nature to give up, even if I want to. I'm worried it won't be such a hard decision at all. Perhaps the kidnappers expect me to go back for them, like a normal, empathetic person would. If this situation doesn't make me want to turn back, I don't see what else could.

I guess I haven't changed as much as I thought. I'm still a selfish, apathetic loner, willing to be ruthless to save myself. In truth, it's not purely self-preservation which is hardening my resolve.

Another, pettier, reason is stoking my stubbornness...

I can't let our kidnappers win.

Ten minutes tick by too fast. There's still no sign of the other group—no tracks and no markings on any trees. Ben, Freya, Sasha, and Eli are nowhere to be seen. They obviously never made it to the forest. Surely we'd have seen or heard them by now. They can't have gotten this lost. I even resort to calling out for them, risking revealing our location to the kidnappers because I can't stand what I've been thinking to myself—imagining them hurt or worse. All the while I've known I won't find out because I'll leave them behind to plough on, regardless.

Right. It's time to address the rest of my team and get this over with. They'll be disgusted with me, especially Logan, as he thinks I'm some noble leader. Nonetheless, I suspect it's what Ben would do. It's possibly what Sasha and Eli would do, too. If I were captured, I hope the others would push on, sending help back when they reach safety. Of course, a big part of me also wishes they *wouldn't* abandon me to save themselves. That's impossible to deny.

With my head down to avoid witnessing their reactions, I pivot around to explain my weak reasoning for abandoning the others. I have to force these treacherous words out with the hope they don't hate me for them. 'Erm... I think we should––'

Interrupting my sentence, a long, eerie howl erupts in the distance, to the west of us. It sweeps through the trees like a winter wind, chilling everything in its path. My stomach drops and a cold ripple travels down my spine at the sound, causing prickling goosebumps to form on my arms. I shudder before my eyes snap to the others. They appear just as frozen to their cores as I am.

An answering howl rings out from the mountains on the other side. Our heads whip in that direction. It sounds closer than the first one. My shallow breaths begin to quicken as my heart twitches in fear. A third ghostly howl pierces through the darkening sky, to the north. That's the direction we were heading. This time, it's as if the sound pulsates through the air around us—too close for comfort.

My wide eyes drift back to my group. Dawn is a deer in the headlights, much like me. Alex places a protective arm around her. Charlie is busy scanning the forest apprehensively. His cute, lost boy face is tight with fear. Beside him, Logan is observing me under a worried frown. His body is rigid, like he's ready to be our shield. When our eyes connect, I intuitively know what he's thinking.

The only animals that can make those sounds are wolves.

And we will have to run.

We will have to run back to the cabin.

Chapter 15

The Wolves

They're all looking to me to make the call. The seconds tick by slowly while the cogs in my head turn. I know the choice I have to make—if we don't turn back now, we'll be surrounded by a pack of wolves in the pitch black.

It's not really a choice at all.

A surrounding howl echoes, boxing us in. This time, the direction isn't so obvious. It could be coming from anywhere, yet its proximity is undeniable.

'We have to go back,' I whisper. The words burn my throat on the way out—the words of defeat.

Despite my statement, we remain petrified to the spot. I consciously make the effort to lift my feet and creep towards my group. We're all still searching the forest with worried eyes. Hopefully, we can scurry away without the animals realising we're here. As soon as I think this, I realise it's a ridiculous notion as, even if they miraculously haven't heard us trudging around already, they've almost certainly picked up our scent.

'Everyone stay close. We'll walk back quickly and quietly,' Logan instructs, his tone measured and soothing.

I reach for Charlie and move him to the front, ahead of me. He tries to hang back, but I nudge him forwards again. 'Go. I'll stay in the back. I have the knife,' I reveal, retrieving the sheathed knife from the waistband of my jeans to show him.

'You took it out of my backpack? When?' Logan demands in a harsh whisper behind me.

With a grimace, I swivel to face him. 'Erm, I took it out when you were in the shower. I thought it was best if I had it on my person. You know, in case I needed it,' I answer sheepishly.

Logan's harsh frown communicates his annoyance. And his sharp look says he thinks I've been a sneaky little thief without needing to open his mouth. In my defence, when I saw him pack the knife away (after he made it clear none of us should be running around with it in case we tripped and stabbed ourselves, sounding like some old grandmother warning children not to run with scissors), I ignored him and swiped it when he left the room.

Okay, that's not much of a defence.

'Give me back the knife. You lead them ahead,' Logan commands, presenting his open palm in expectation.

'No, it's my fault we're out here. I'll stay in the back, and *you* lead them ahead,' I argue, hands on my hips, the knife out of his reach.

'Oh my God! Guys! This is *not* the time to argue. There's frigging wolves out there closing in on us,' Alex implores, his brown eyes wide.

'Fine, you can have the knife. But I'm protecting the back with you. Charlie can lead,' I concede with a hint of defiance, reluctantly handing the knife back to Logan.

'Thank you.' Logan's dry tone belies his words. 'Charlie, Dawn, and Alex, stay in front. We won't be far behind you.' He brandishes the knife and tucks the sheath into the waistband of his jeans.

Charlie shakes his head in disbelief at us as he leads Dawn and Alex back the way we came. Their pace is quick yet cautious. Logan grabs my sleeve and tugs me along with him. We're several feet behind the rest, keeping watch in case of attack.

'I'm quite capable of walking without an aid, you know. You don't have to hold onto me,' I snip, yanking my arm out of Logan's grasp.

His pale eyes snap to me, the muscles in his jaw working. 'Then keep pace,' he grinds out, clearly still annoyed about the stolen knife.

Ignoring the bitterness in his tone, I make sure to move faster than him out of pettiness alone as we stalk back through the trees.

Minutes crawl by without another chorus of the chilling wolf song. It's more unsettling now that they've slipped into silence. There's only the faint sounds of crunching twigs and dried leaves under our hurried feet. I'm hoping the wolves have already passed by. We may be able to carry on with the escape plan if they've moved on. A lick of hope brightens my eyes at the prospect, momentarily easing the tension in my limbs.

Then, out of nowhere, the growls begin.

Logan and I freeze in our tracks and spin around when a low snarl sounds out from behind us. There's nothing to see. The snarling perpetrator is concealed somewhere behind the thick greenery. I can tell, from the absence of soft crunching, that the others have paused as well. Glaring their way, I motion them on with harsh flicks of my wrist. Charlie hesitates, not wanting to leave us behind.

'Keep going!' *It doesn't matter if you're loud now since they've already found us*, I reason, ignoring Logan's exasperated sigh. 'We'll be right behind you,' I assure them in a softer tone.

Concern is etched on Charlie's impish face, but he continues to push on with a panicked Dawn and Alex in tow.

On high alert, Logan and I slowly and carefully creep backwards. He still has the knife unsheathed and pointed in front of us. His arm spreads across, shielding me. I wish I'd kept the knife for myself now so I could be the one protecting us. Granted, I'm pretty sure that if a wolf *were* to attack us, he'd be foolish enough to put himself in front of me, whether he had the knife or not. Maybe it's for the best that he *does* have it.

Another menacing growl rumbles from somewhere in the forest ahead. A glimpse of a silver shadow slinks through the gap between two trees. My heart jerks in my chest, skipping over beats. I doubt they'll simply pass us by. They're on the hunt.

Hunting *us*.

Now I'm the one yanking on Logan's arm to keep him moving back with me as quickly as possible. We can't let the others roam too far ahead of us, in case the wolves go around our meagre blockade and close in on them from the sides. I glance back to check on them. They're still in sight. Although we're lagging behind. We'll lose track of them soon if we don't hurry.

'Come on, we have to catch up with the others. They're disappearing,' I breathe to Logan. And, when I peer over my shoulder again, panic strikes me as I watch their shapes evaporate into the trees.

They're gone.

Logan's free hand grazes my hip as though he's checking I'm still behind him. 'If we turn our backs now, they will attack.'

A surge of fear liquidates my limbs. My heart falters as I struggle to process his warning. Ever since that Alsatian attacked me and my mum when I was a kid, I've had recurring nightmares about dogs chasing me. This is ten times worse than those nightmares because there's no doubt that a wolf bites much harder than any dog.

'Then we'll just have to run and hope they don't catch us,' I suggest, attempting to thrust my fear aside. 'We're losing the light. We can't continue with this impasse for much longer. Those wolves will have more of an advantage in the dark.'

'Fine. Go! Run as fast as you can,' Logan orders, caving in.

Immediately, I take off in a sprint, my pulse already ahead of me. Logan is only seconds behind. I run as fast as my legs will allow. They're shaking dangerously as my feet repeatedly thump against the uneven ground.

A moment later, Charlie, Dawn, and Alex are visible again. Their heads turn when the noise of us crashing through the foliage reaches them.

'Run!' I shout, vigorously waving them on.

They heed my command, darting faster through the trees. And as I continue pushing myself on, I throw anxious glances over my shoulder to check we're not being pursued by hungry beasts. Logan is still right behind me. Relief sets in when I can't spot anything on our tail—there are no wolf-shaped shadows looming.

Without warning, a mighty, silver force of fur leaps out from the trees to our right. It knocks Logan off his feet. Faster than I can scream, the grey and white wolf pins him to the ground, its jaw locking onto his forearm. It shakes Logan with a low growl and his grasp on the knife loosens.

'No!' I scream, stumbling at the sight. My face hits the dirt a second later. It punches me into a daze. My vision swirling, I raise my head enough to see Logan wrestling with the wolf.

'Ruby, get out of here!' Logan shouts, seeing me crawling towards him as I struggle to shake away the swaying stars in my eyes.

Pushing myself upright, I ignore him and charge at the wolf while shouting at it to release him. Clocking me, the wolf releases Logan to strike a defensive pose; its hackles up, teeth bared, a low yet vicious growl erupting from its throat.

I grab at Logan's good arm and drag him up. His other arm is badly wounded. There are puncture wounds visible through his torn shirt—blood gushing out and dripping down to stain the leafy carpet crimson. The knife has disappeared, lost to the forest floor. At this point, I don't care. It's hard to focus on anything other than the terrifying beast blocking our path, ready to pounce.

My desperate mind is frantically sifting through solutions to our predicament. If we continue to run, turning our backs on it, then it will certainly attack. And I imagine it will catch us without much trouble. Despite that, we can't simply stare it down all night. We need a distraction before its buddies show up and we're completely outnumbered.

Food—that's what it wants. It may like the thrill of a hunt, but I'm sure most predators are also opportunists. If we offer it food, it might not try to make *us* the meal.

'Logan, give me the pack,' I whisper, and he instantly shrugs the backpack off his shoulder without further information.

His tiny movements make the wolf lurch forward and snap. We take a startled step back and so does the wolf. Its posture is still tense and poised for battle.

Slowly, I unzip the backpack and grab the first tin of food I find—it's the hot dogs. *That was a lucky pick*, I tell myself, my stomach unclenching a little. I don't suppose wolves would be as tempted by French onion soup.

I pull the tin ring and peel back the top. The wolf continues to snarl at my movements, though it doesn't lurch forward again.

Capitalising on the animal's hesitation, I pluck out a hot dog and wave it around, the juices flinging off. The wolf's growls quieten when the scent of the meat overwhelms its senses. Its nose twitches in interest.

Taking the risk, I chuck the hot dog over to it in hopes it will be enough to wrench its focus from us.

For a moment, the wolf is distracted by the offering and lunges for it—which gives Logan and me a chance to gain some distance from it. But, as soon as the wolf hears us moving backwards, it instantly resumes its stance against us, closing the gap we made.

Logan touches my shoulder and leans close to murmur, 'Throw the whole tin.' His hand glides down my spine to rest on the small of my back, and I can't help the shiver that ripples through me.

If he felt you do that, he'll assume it was from fear, I reassure myself, trying to focus back on this life-or-death situation.

'Pass me the backpack so you can throw it further.' Logan carefully takes the backpack from me, his cool fingers brushing my arm as he slowly slides the strap down, causing goosebumps to rise.

Is he doing this on purpose to distract me? And if so, why is it working?

Unburdened, but completely weighted to the spot by a curling heat in my abdomen, I reel my arm back and cast the tin away with some force. Three hot dogs spill out along the way, which grabs the wolf's attention. The animal instinctively follows its nose, turning to inspect the flying food. However, it suddenly changes its mind, rounding back to us before we can escape.

My heart sinks. It didn't work. The distracting heat inside me fades as quickly as it spread, leaving me shivering with chilling fear once again.

New grunts and growls linger on the whipping breeze, lashing us with the threat of their proximity. The other wolves have caught up. In a minute or so, we'll have a whole pack to contend with. One is frightening enough.

Dread is a sickness, stirring up more panic in my stomach. This can't be happening. I'm going to be eaten by wolves—my worst fear realised.

'Logan,' I squeak, my tears as threatening as those approaching snarls. Sensing my hopeless terror, Logan hastily fishes for another tin of food from the backpack. But instead of opening it, he throws the tin directly at the wolf in our sight. It hits it squarely on the nose, startling it. It jumps back with a whimper.

Not wasting a second, Logan clasps his good hand around my arm and yanks me back. We race away through a crowd of thick trees together, hoping to camouflage ourselves from the stunned wolf and its approaching army.

Our feet spring off the ground, harder and faster. The painful vibrations ripple through my calves as we sprint for our lives. I don't dare look back. There's no need as I'm already acutely aware that we're being hunted.

The whispers of its soft pads glide over fallen leaves. Its raspy, panted breaths sound closer and closer with each effortless stride as it surpasses our heavy, clumsy ones with ease. Even if we had a hefty head start, it wouldn't have been enough. Its sleek design makes it perfect for pursuit. It's meant to catch its prey.

It will all be over soon.

A terrifying growl and a snap of teeth come from near my ankle. It must have narrowly missed clamping onto my foot. My heart nearly stops at the realisation.

I'm about to be ripped apart. I only hope Logan will race ahead and help the others to safety when it catches me. At least it'll buy them some time to get away.

Another growl rumbles in the throat of the wolf on my tail. This is it. *Its jaws will claim you this time*, I tell myself, resigned to the inevitable. The death part doesn't scare me. It's the inescapable pain that will precede it, which is distilling pure, quaking terror into every cell of my body.

Something knocks me off course. At first, I think it's the wolf. But I don't feel any teeth sink into my flesh. It felt more like a wind-tipped hand, blowing me away.

As the force veers me to the right, I catch sight of the wolf rising up and grabbing hold of Logan instead. He must have shoved me out of the way of the attack, taking the vengeful animal on himself.

The weight of the wolf forces Logan to the ground again. I attempt to stop the momentum of my legs and succeed after a metre or so. Swiftly, I pivot back, managing to keep my balance. Logan's face is pressed down in the dirt, the wolf ripping into his back. For some reason, he doesn't cry out. He only groans as he strains to push himself up. That's when I realise the wolf isn't ripping into flesh; it's biting into the backpack.

In desperation, I shriek, 'Take off the pack!'

Logan scrambles to slip his arms out of the harness while the wolf shakes him around like a rag doll. I clamber over, not caring if the wolf decides to pounce on me instead. Reaching down, I struggle to pull Logan out from under the wolf, who's thankfully still preoccupied with tearing the backpack up.

After a few tense beats of my overworked heart, Logan wriggles free. And, since the wolf is sufficiently distracted, we both seize the opportunity to escape. We stumble through the forest as quickly as we can. Adrenaline courses through my bloodstream. Burning gasps rip at my throat as I continue running for my life. This time, I can't hear the horrifying sounds of a wolf in pursuit. I don't think we're being chased anymore.

'Are you okay?' I manage to ask Logan after a minute, my voice a husky huff.

'Yeah, keep going. They could still catch up,' he rasps back, lightly encouraging me forward with his good arm.

Blood is dripping out of his wound. He holds his injured arm close to his chest. Scarlet droplets flick out as he moves, leaving a trail. The metallic scent in the air has my stomach churning. As a result, my head starts to swim. It's also hard to control my legs as they wobble.

Luckily, I manage to run for another ten seconds before my whole body turns to jelly. My heart is bursting out of my chest. I can't keep this up for much longer. Hundreds of tiny black dots obscure my vision.

Despite this sudden near-blindness, up ahead I can just make out Charlie waiting up a tree. His long legs are dangling over a branch. Further up the tree are Dawn and Alex, holding onto each other for dear life.

When Charlie spots us, his face lights up. He immediately jumps down from his branch and gallops towards us.

'Ah, thank goodness!' he calls out in relief as he approaches. Dawn and Alex also descend from their hiding place, just as happy to see us.

As soon as Charlie is near enough, he reaches out to embrace me. I stumble into his arms, my legs finally failing. My body revolts in protest—seizing up when I come to a stop. Charlie lowers me to the ground with him.

Then I fall into the mass of black dots.

I'm in central London. It's a bright afternoon.

Big Ben is peeking out behind some buildings in the distance. I'm sitting comfortably on my sleeping bag on a busy street. Usually, I prefer to avoid central London because these large crowds are too intimidating. Today, though, people pass me by, completely ignoring my presence. A typical day for me. It's equal parts insulting and yearned for.

Disorientated, I stare up at them, trying to remember how I got here. That's when I notice there's something wrong with their faces.

Every face that passes me is a blur. I can't make out their features. It must be my eyes. Am I going blind?

No, I can't be losing my vision because I see everything else clearly enough: the bricks of the old buildings across the road, the light glinting off the black cabs as they speed by, and the specks of green glass from a smashed beer bottle on the side of the road. All of that detail is well-defined. It's only the sea of faces that's murky.

This must be a dream. Or possibly another memory.

At least I have my old pack with me this time. Rifling through it, I find my cracked compact mirror at the bottom and open it up to check my face. It's not blurred like the rest. Although I do appear younger: maybe twenty-seven. My hair is a lot shorter.

My tummy rumbles aggressively. The gnawing hunger pains attacking my stomach are indication enough that I'm slowly starving, as per usual. I search my pack and conclude there's nothing I can eat inside, except some flavoured Lypsyl. I can tell I haven't eaten for a day or two.

Staring blankly at my black beanie hat on the pavement beside me, I think over my options. There's a pound at most in it. It might be enough to buy a bottle of water for tonight. It won't do much for the hunger, though.

This must have been before I resorted to stealing from shops, I assume. Most of my measly benefit money went on hostel beds, back then. Unfortunately, there wasn't much to spare on food. Most days, I had to choose between a bed or a meal.

I wonder why I'm myself this time and not watching the memory from the outside. In this one, I'm reliving it, not a spectator standing by, helpless. I hope nothing bad happens to me.

A pair of legs pause in front of me. I peer up to see a hooded man, his face blurred like the others. He bends down to my level and takes a wad of notes out of his pocket. He drops them into my hat. He says something I can't quite make out—the sound is muffled here, too.

The kind stranger has given me four twenty-pound notes—eighty quid! This must be a mistake on his part. You can't accept that much from him, *I tell myself, guilt and shame whirling to the surface.*

Before the hooded man can leave, I pick up three of the notes and hand them back to him. He rejects my offer, enclosing my hand with his, so the notes are trapped inside my palm. He utters something else I don't catch and then walks away, a fresh wave of faceless people sweeping past to swallow him whole.

A slight recognition of this generous stranger sparks within my mind. I'm sure I've lived this moment before. This surprise and gratitude are too familiar. Why can't I remember his face? Why am I recalling this lost memory now?

The sun drops from the sky in a rush, my surroundings dipping into ink. It's not a natural sunset. It all happens within a few blinks. Buildings and cars melt into the ground.

The street is now an opaque haze.

My world has fallen into another black hole.

I wake in a dimly lit room with a dark wood ceiling. My vision is still misty, so I shut my eyes again. Murmured voices hiss over the crackle of the fireplace. I listen to them, pretending to be asleep.

'It's a good thing we came back out to find you. I don't think you could have carried them both here without our help before the wolves caught up with the smell of blood,' a deep voice mutters somewhere in the room.

'Absolutely. We would have been easy prey,' someone replies. I recognise that voice—it's Charlie.

'We were easy prey anyway, man.' I can make out the tenor of Alex's voice, too.

With my head gradually clearing away the heavy cloud of unconsciousness, I take a deeper breath. My vision improves the second time I open my eyes. *This isn't London, Ruby. You're back in the fucking cabin again, still kidnapped.* I groan internally at the reminder. Someone must have carried me back here while I was unconscious.

'I think Ruby's waking up,' a soft, feminine voice says next to me.

'About time,' Charlie responds, rushing to my side. His face slides into my eyeline. He's smiling, though there's worry behind its tightness. 'How are you feeling?'

Everything comes flooding back to me: the wolf attack, Logan being bitten, blood squirting everywhere. My head swims again at the memory, so I push it to the back of my mind.

'Logan? Is Logan okay?' I mumble, struggling to sit up. I'm weak, my body numb and tingly. Charlie stops me with a soft touch to my shoulder.

'He's stable. We managed to stop the bleeding, although he will need stitches. They're coming to collect him soon,' Charlie relays to me, but I can't grasp his words.

Tilting away from Charlie, I push myself up to sit despite my lingering weakness and spinning head. I take a moment to process, my eyes exploring the room. I'm on the sofa in the cabin living room. Sasha and Eli, along with Alex and Dawn, are all studying me as intently as Charlie.

Sasha is in the chair beside me. She smiles down at me sympathetically. A sudden rush of relief hits me, realising they're okay—they also made it back.

'You're here! You're not dead,' I manage to say without my voice cracking.

Sasha snickers. 'We're fine. I'm glad you're okay, too.' Her voice is warm. She leans over to squeeze my arm reassuringly.

'Where are Ben and Freya?' Panic sets in again when I can't find their faces.

'They're with Logan, upstairs. So is Zoe. They're keeping an eye on him until *they* come to take him,' Sasha says, her tone ominous.

Confused, I stare at her, my forehead crinkling. Charlie said something similar. My stomach lurches as the information begins to sink in.

'Until *they* take him?' I repeat, still unsure. 'Who?'

'The Haven Initiative. That's what they call themselves. They rang us earlier when you were unconscious. They told us they're coming to collect Logan—to give him the medical treatment he needs,' Alex informs me, a wary look on his face.

'They're not happy with us. They said we gave them no choice but to release the wolves—to retrieve our backpacks. I don't think they were meant to bite Logan, though. The man on the phone said that, if we stop them taking him, or attempt another escape, they'll shut off our water so we'll have no supplies left,' Dawn adds, shaking her head.

All this new information is too much for me to comprehend. Especially since I've only recently awoken from fainting. My mind is still muddled.

All I can gather is that our kidnappers are coming to take Logan away, and there's nothing we can do about it.

Chapter 16

AWAITING DARKNESS

Once my addled mind has fully grasped the ominous news, I insist on going upstairs to check on Logan. I want to make sure he's all right before the so-called 'Haven Initiative' comes to whisk him away.

I wish I'd been awake for their phone call. The fact that there's even a phone to call was news to me. Apparently, it's in one of the bedrooms upstairs. Freya spoke to our captors, and Charlie mentioned how calm and polite she was throughout the short exchange. If *I* had answered the phone, it would have been a different story.

In the ten minutes I've been awake, Sasha and Eli filled me in on their group's failed escape. They didn't receive an eerie vocal warning like my group did. They simply crossed paths with the wolves shortly after entering the forest. Then, after a tense standoff, one of the wolves attacked Sasha, ripping the assigned backpack to shreds.

The wolves didn't bite her like one did Logan. They only snatched the backpack, then left to hunt my group down.

After making it safely back to the cabin, Ben, Sasha, and Eli decided to venture back out to look for us. It's lucky they did because both Logan and I were unconscious when they found us. It took all of them to carry us back to the cabin. Eli told me that he bandaged up Logan's wound, but thinks he'll need stitches and antibiotics to fully recover.

'Are you sure you don't want a cup of sugary tea first? Your body is still recovering from that fainting spell. You should be sitting down, relaxing,' Sasha suggests as she helps me up off the sofa.

'I can sit and relax upstairs,' I maintain, trying to regain my balance. My legs are still wobbly from running so hard earlier. 'What time do you think it is?'

'It's after nine. We plugged the microwave in. It has the time displayed on it, which is handy,' Dawn answers.

With Sasha and Charlie on either side of me, in case I stumble over my unstable legs, I make my way slowly towards the staircase. 'When are they coming to collect Logan? And do we know *how* yet?'

'They said an hour, about an hour ago, soooo... not long. No idea how they're gonna take him, though. Maybe they'll knock on the door? Stroll right in and stay for a cuppa? Who knows?' Alex replies, sliding the curtain to one side to peek out the window. Outside, dusk has settled to blacken the glade. There's no way we could leave now, anyway—we'd be stumbling about in the dark.

Charlie scoffs. 'How delightful.' His tone is dry. 'Perhaps they'll clear a few other things up for us if they *do* decide to pop in.'

We make it to the staircase as a door squeaks open on the first floor. A moment later, Ben appears at the top of the stairs. He beams a smile at me, and I think it's the first time I've really seen his teeth in a grin. He flies down the stairs to bear-hug me, picking me up off my feet.

'Ah, I'm proper chuffed you didn't get ripped apart by wolves, like,' Ben says, more humour than I expect in his voice.

I'm still lightheaded, so him literally sweeping me off my feet is only making matters worse, but I don't particularly care because it's so good to see him safe.

'I'm glad you didn't get taken and tortured in some dungeon somewhere,' I reply with a faint giggle.

Ben finally sets my feet back down on the solid wood floor. I keep ahold of his arm to steady myself. Noticing my struggle, he places an anchoring hand on my shoulder. 'I'm guessing you wanna see Logue before those bastards come to take him away, eh?' There's clear contempt written on every inch of his face and laced in his voice. He must be as angry as I am about the situation.

'Yeah. If they come in here, you know things will kick off. We have to confront them. I don't give a shit about the consequences.'

Ben snorts with dark amusement. 'I'm with you, trust me. But I don't think they're daft enough to just waltz in here.'

'Yeah. They know we're frustrated and angry with them. We're too unpredictable to deal with face-to-face. Plus, I doubt they'd want a barrage of endless questions about why they're doing this to us and who they are.'

'Is Logan conscious now?' Sasha queries, not joining our frustrated rant.

'Nah, I think his body's still in shock, like,' Ben reports, his brow heavier.

'He hasn't woken up yet? I assumed when you said he was all right... I—I thought you meant he was up and talking. What if he's lost too much blood and is in a coma or something?' The words rush out in a sudden fluster. My tummy tumbles with acidic queasiness, thinking Logan could be hurt worse than I anticipated.

'He's fine, Ruby. Eli says it's only a flesh wound, and he didn't lose too much blood. He's just sleeping, like you were, whilst his body recovers from the shock. Go up and see for yourself,' Alex reassures me, taking a seat next to Dawn on the sofa. How can he be so blasé about this? As if I'm overreacting?

A frenzy ignites within me as adrenaline kicks in. I manoeuvre past Ben and scramble up the stairs. Someone follows me up, but I'm too focused on finding Logan to bother checking who it is. I need to see him for myself. I need to see how he is before he's snatched away from me.

The door to our allocated bedroom is ajar. Reaching the threshold, I swing it open.

Zoe is hovering over a peaceful yet unconscious Logan, tenderly whispering something in his ear. Seeing me burst in, a smirk curls her lips and she leans back on the bed across from his, looking smug.

Freya, perched at the end of Logan's bed, turns at my chaotic entrance. 'Ruby, you're awake!' She immediately springs up to give me a brief hug. 'How are you feeling? You look white as a sheet,' she mentions, her dainty features pinching in concern.

'She scrambled up the stairs like one of those disturbingly scary children you'd see in a horror film. I have to stay close for when she realises her legs aren't working properly yet,' Charlie remarks behind me, breathless.

Charlie slides an arm around my waist for safekeeping, and I'm glad for it because the sudden burst of energy I expelled, racing up those stairs, has left me on a downward spiral towards total depletion. He was right to follow me. My legs *are* brittle sticks, merely propping me up at this point.

'I'm fine... but sitting down couldn't hurt,' I admit, accepting Charlie's assistance.

'I'm glad you're okay, Ruby. I'll go down to make us some tea. These bedrooms are too tiny for more than three or four of us,' Freya announces lightly, prancing out of the room.

Charlie shuffles me towards the bed next to Logan's, which I guess is technically *my* bed. Despite going years without a bed to call my own, I don't particularly want to claim this one. Sleeping in this bed tonight will only seal my defeat.

Zoe hops across to sit on Logan's bed. She shoots me a look of distaste at the prospect of sitting within touching distance of me. Why is she even in here? She hasn't cared about anyone or anything up until now. I've sensed her interest in Logan, though. There's been hints of desire in her sideways glances at him. He *is* an incredibly attractive guy. Plus, he seems to be a decent human on top of that. Am I surprised that Zoe fancies him? No. What surprises me is the sudden, strange need to claim him for myself.

Logan will never be yours because you have nothing to give him in return. And even if you did, you wouldn't let yourself.

Wincing, I carefully lower myself onto the mattress. The bed is springy and temptingly comfy. The soft pillows are calling for my tired head to rest. I resist the urge to lie down. Instead, I focus my full attention on Logan. His ashen face is serene, despite the slight sheen of sweat coating his forehead. His bowed lips are parted as he breathes, with only a mild whisper when the exhaled air escapes. I glance down at his wound, which has been dressed with a tight bandage. Alex did mention that they found a basic medical kit in the bathroom cupboard.

There's a dark red stain soaking through the layers of material holding Logan's ripped skin together. He really does need stitches, and also something to stop an infection from creeping in. I doubt that bandage will continue to staunch the bleeding for much longer.

Surprisingly, I'm relieved Logan will receive the medical attention he needs, even if they must take him away for it. Eli has done his best in cleaning and dressing the wound. Still, it's not enough: Logan needs an actual doctor. I couldn't live with myself if he bled to death, just because of some risky escape plan I concocted. And it was all due to me being too stubborn to stay here and do what I was told.

It's *my* fault he was injured.

As if she can read my mind, Zoe interrupts my thoughts. 'I told you there was no point wasting your time. It's *your* fault he was injured, you stubborn cow.'

Her words hit me right in the heart. I swore to myself that I'd never again let anyone be hurt because of me, and I've broken that promise. I'm lucky no one else was bitten, or worse. I convinced everyone to go. I practically strong-armed them into it. People were content to stay and put up with this ridiculous situation for two weeks before I meddled and decided to play leader.

Defending me, Charlie pipes up. 'Zoe, why do you have to act like that? There's no need to be malicious. It's not––'

I cut him off. 'No, Charlie, she's right. I knew they wouldn't let us walk out of here. I was being stubborn and reckless.' I bow my head in shame.

It's hard to see Logan lying there—lifeless and ghostly white. Before I came along and caused this mess, he was so strong and capable, his presence so commanding. He's a better leader than I am. Now, he's weak, unconscious, and bleeding. And I find myself hoping the kidnapping, tree-cutting, wolf-wielding bastards hurry up and tend to him already.

'Zoe, we should allow Ruby some time alone. This is *her* room, after all,' Charlie says, soft yet authoritative.

He must have noticed my demeanour. I'm definitely not in the mood for company right now, especially a soul-crushing presence like Zoe. I'm glad I didn't have to ask them to leave. I thought it impossible to like Charlie more than I already did, yet I'm warmed by a new wave of affection for him and his little Peter Pan face.

Zoe tuts, then huffs out of the room as if it's a big ask. Before Charlie can follow her out, I grab his hand. 'Thanks, Pan,' I convey, offering him an equally warm smile. *Pan*. That nickname suits him. It feels natural to show my affection for him in that way—cementing our friendship.

Bending, Charlie kisses the top of my head before wordlessly exiting the room. He doesn't shut the door. I assume he kept it open in case I call for assistance.

The last time someone kissed the top of my head was the night I said goodbye to my brother, when he left my dad and me to move out and on towards a better life. The memory of that goodbye stings me to this day. Though being reminded of it now only hollows me—my heart emptying in preparation. The sharp ache in my chest isn't there like it used to be. It's as if those painful memories are finally fading. Or I'm somehow finding the strength to bear them. What once filled me with sorrow and loss has been replaced with Charlie's warmth and friendship. The last time someone kissed the top of my head is now the night I was feeling sorry for myself, so my best friend did exactly what I needed and comforted me without words.

The night I felt like I had a brother again.

Now that I'm alone with Logan, I don't know what to do with myself. There's no point in attempting to talk to him as I doubt he can hear me. If I do start talking to him, there's a chance he could wake up, and I'm not sure that's a good idea. If I tell him our captors plan to take him, would he attempt to fight them? Would it lead him to be hurt even worse? There's no way to predict how he'll react to the news. I don't know him well enough to guess.

Tentatively, I shuffle up my mattress so I'm close enough to reach out and touch Logan's uninjured hand: the one that's resting on his stomach. His skin is smooth yet cold, which immediately has my panic flaring. Trying to be gentle, I bring his hand closer to inspect it. His skin has a mottled blue tint to it. I'm not sure I've heard the whisper of his breath since the others left the room, either. What if he died while I was too busy with my own thoughts to notice?

As my heart drops to my stomach, I propel myself from my bed to hover over Logan's face. I place a hand on his chest to feel for movement. If he is breathing, they must be very shallow breaths because his chest hardly moves.

Fearing the worst, I speak his name with whispered urgency. 'Logan? Logan!' He doesn't respond, though I didn't expect him to. A lump forms in my throat, one I can't swallow down.

I move my hand up to his nose and hold it there. After a few anxiety-ridden seconds, a slight push of air warms my palm. Lowering my hand, I release the breath I was holding, my heart relaxing a little.

Good, he's not dead, just very weak. Please hurry up, you government scum!

Guilt is the chasm beneath it all. I'm the cause of this. Well, I can't take all the blame. The Haven Initiative are the arseholes who released their wolves to terrorise us. How did they think that was a good idea? Did they not foresee us being hurt in the process? They're huge, fuck-off *wolves*, for God's sake, not golden retrievers.

Nevertheless, I was the troublemaker who defied them and had these punishments imposed upon us. If they could use the threat of falling trees to drive us towards the cabin, of course they'd send wolves out to scare us back there. I wouldn't like to guess what else they have up their sleeves.

Wolves. Fucking *wolves*! I still can't believe this has happened. This organisation has trained wolves?! *Seriously*? Maybe they're actually a Russian government agency trying to recruit us as spies. It makes me wonder why we're so certain we're still in the UK. I'm pretty sure there are no wolves wandering around the Scottish Highlands. Not wild ones, anyway.

Pushing my thoughts aside, I stare down at a still-unconscious Logan. He's so motionless and frail that the sudden urge to cry is burning. I can't remember the last time I let myself cry. I rarely allow those emotions to slip past my mental defences. Being vulnerable is unthinkable to me because that's giving up power—that's losing control. Self-pity is only acceptable if it emerges from a place of bitterness, not sadness.

Focusing on my anger is the only thing which keeps me strong enough to survive.

Holding back the persistent tears is only tiring me further. I need to lie down before I strain myself too much and faint again. I've already used all of my energy racing up the stairs. I also nearly had that mini heart attack when I thought Logan was dead. All I can do now is spend the next few minutes by his side, until they come to steal him from me.

Raising Logan's good arm, I crawl into the crook of his shoulder, then rest my head on his chest. I lift my jelly legs off the floor and lay them beside his, taking comfort in the faint humming of his heart in my ear. I can monitor him like this. Also, being so close to him brings a sense of solace. It's easier when he's unconscious. We can't argue with each other and there are no power struggles or miscommunications.

We're lying side-by-side, our bodies relaxed... no more confusion... no more tension. Only the low strumming of his heart is filling my head. It's comforting.

It's louder now. The sound spills out into the room—it's booming. The vibrations reverberate through me... I'm a hummingbird.

My eyelids are too heavy to open. My mind is drifting into less cognitive thoughts. Sleep is a siren song—a sweet, unavoidable lure. Sleep weighs down on me like a thick slab of ice. Though there's no pain, only a frozen numbness. A cold chill descends upon me, from my head to my toes. I fall under its icy spell.

Instead of crushing me, it suddenly lifts me up. I'm floating—projecting out of my body. Any second now, I'll fly away.

I let go and soar into the awaiting darkness.

'Ruby? Ruby! Wake up!'

'Do you think they injected her with summat?'

'I dunno, but she won't wake up.'

'She could have fainted again.'

'It's too convenient that she just happened to faint when they came to take him.'

'They must have sedated her somehow, then.'

Distant voices echo through my mind before being swallowed by the darkness. I'm unable to grasp them, but I can hear them—faintly, like a whisper. Nothing seems real. I'm not in a dream, yet I'm not quite here. Or *anywhere.*

I'm lost.

Perhaps I should follow the voices so I can reorient myself. Currently, all I'm aware of is darkness—opaque space.

Nothingness.

I'm floating in it.

'I swear, I did not *shut the door when I left. I have no idea why it wouldn't open. The ruddy thing doesn't even have a lock on it, does it?'*

'But they must have locked it somehow. Maybe it's magnetic or something?'

The voices are growing louder. I want to reach them, but something deep down is telling me I shouldn't. I must find my own way out of here.

'Wake up, sweetie. Come on, open your eyes.'

My body is numb—detached. I'm not sure I even have a body to feel *with* right now. I'm someplace else. This must all be in my head because I can still *think*—I'm still *me*.

Something is very, *very* wrong, though.

I'm not asleep or awake.

I'm trapped. And I need to find a way out.

'Something's wrong. She's not breathing.'

'Somebody do something!'

I'm fighting as hard as I can against this strange, invisible force. I can't identify it, but I know it's holding me here—holding me back from where I'm supposed to be.

'Help her!'

'Ruby, come on—breathe. Stay with us.'

But I can't stay here. This isn't the right place for me. I need to escape—to get back to where I belong.

'Ruby, stay with us!'

Struggling, I aim to pull away from this tangible black haze. It has invaded my brain and enclosed me like a cold, steel trap.

It has made me a prisoner in my own fucking mind.

Suddenly, a light appears, blinking into existence. A tiny pinprick of hope in the unmeasurable distance. It's like the first star born in an empty universe. It becomes my target—my beacon.

'Come on, Rubes. Don't leave us.'

As I battle against the shackling shadows of my mind, the light expands into a small circle, seeming bigger—closer—as if it senses my need to reach it.

'Is she dying?!'

'Ruby, please! Breathe!'

'Come back to us!'

I'm in reaching distance now. I don't possess a body to reach out *with*, so I'm only using the power of my mind to push against this pull.

I'm so close. Just one more heave and I'll be free.

'No, Ruby. Stop! Don't--'

The familiar voices instantly cut off when I slip through the circle of light.

Everything is white. It's too bright to process. Gravity is pressing me down, like I've woken up from a deep sleep. I'm too stiff and heavy to move a muscle. My eyes aren't even open yet, I realise; bright light is seeping in through the thin skin of my eyelids.

I have to concentrate on my body. I have to will my eyes open, in spite of the harsh glow. *Come on, you weakling. Open your eyes*! I command myself, growing more frustrated with each passing second of immobility.

When my right eye finally cracks open, the bright light pours in, stinging enough for both of my eyes to water. At least it's a start.

Next, I will my left eye to open with every fibre of my being. And I manage to roll both eyes around their sockets before my left eyelid eventually frees itself, cracking the same as my right.

I regain enough bodily control to open them further, hoping my pupils adjust to the bright light without watering again. My face is tilted to the side despite lying on my back. It must have been instinctive for me to turn away from the harshness of that light. But my neck is too weak to lift my head.

The mist of tears evaporates, clearing my vision. There's a large, body-length, rectangular lamp hovering above me. Eight bulbs-like orbs shine down, warming my face and body. Next to the lamp is something else—some sort of grey monitoring machine. Lights and numbers are flickering on it, like glowing buttons on a switchboard. My name is there on the screen, in the left-hand corner of it.

A buzzing sound startles me. Not like a bee. It's more like a small alarm clock going off.

The numbness in my limbs ebbs, pins and needles prickling. I tap a slick surface with my index finger. It's made of some kind of metal. I must be lying down on a metal surface with medical machines around me. Though *why* eludes me. It's not *un*comfortable. In fact, I think it's shaped to fit my body. And it's surprisingly warm.

I'm not thinking clearly. None of this makes any sense. I can't move the rest of my body yet, either. Something still has me in its cold grip.

Ruby, sit the fuck up, I urge myself, but my body doesn't listen.

'She's found her way back.'

'Do something—quickly. She's not ready.'

I'm hearing voices again. Although these seem more tangible—more real. They're not in my head anymore.

'Perhaps we should terminate. There's too much going wrong with this one.'

'It just needs more time. You find the rebel and I'll work on the subs.'

The lamp above me brightens sharply, forcing my eyes to snap shut again. *No!* I just got those fuckers open.

More tears form, flooding my eyelids. Then a cold sensation over-whelms me, like an icy wind has caught me in an updraft. It originates in my head, then descends down to my toes. If I could move, I'd be shivering.

'Stop fighting. It's not the right time. You have to go back.'

It's then I notice something besides the overpowering chill—a soft touch travelling in a circular motion on my hand—a second before the veil of blackness envelops me again, and I lose myself to it.

I fall back into the empty in-between.

'She's gone. I can't believe she's gone.'

'Wait. I feel a pulse. She has a pulse!'

I'm floating again, but this time I'm drifting backwards, away from the tiny star of light. I'm delving deeper into nothingness.

Faster and faster, I soar. I can't fight it any longer.

I've lost control.

'Ruby—come on. Come back.'

A desperate breath burns my throat, my lungs expanding to their full capacity.

'She's alive!'

'Ruby? Can you hear me?'

Opening my eyes, Sasha's face comes into focus. My chest hurts as if it's been crushed.

'Can you hear me? Can you understand me?' Sasha continues to quiz me, worry furrowing her forehead.

'What happened?' I croak. Speaking also hurts.

Sasha draws in a deep, steadying breath. 'You want to know what happened? Ruby... You *died*.'

Chapter 17

Time To Think

'I was *dead*?' I squeak in shock.

'Sasha brought you back. She didn't stop giving you chest compressions even when we all thought you were gone,' Dawn informs me, wiping away tears.

I guess that's why my chest hurts so much.

I sit up gradually. My weakened body is a trembling mess, so I prop myself up on my elbow. My strained eyes scan the room. It's not only Dawn's face that's tear-stained. Ben's eyes are also glistening as he stands hunched by the wardrobe.

My gaze finds Charlie, whose face is red and puffy from crying. He's slumped at the end of my bed, unable to look at me. He's trying to calm himself down by collecting deeper breaths. My heart swells with warmth for him. Also, guilt; the threat of my death has clearly wrecked him. Even though it's not *my* fault that I died. He finally makes eye contact with me, and more tears spill down his flushed cheeks.

'I thought I'd lost you,' Charlie chokes out, his face contorting with grief.

'You haven't. I'm still here.' My voice is also thick.

Charlie kneels next to my bed and buries his face into my neck. His arms come around me. I stroke his floppy bronze hair to comfort him as his hold on me tightens. It's amazing how strongly we've bonded in this short space of time. We really do care about each other. We're more than friends—we're like family. I'm sure I'd be equally as upset if our roles were reversed.

Squeezing him back, I murmur, 'I'm okay, Pan.'

Charlie sighs deeply in relief. He breaks away to sit opposite me on Logan's bed, which I finally realise is empty.

'Where's Logan?' I question, shooting into an upright position. The jerky movement hurts my chest, though that's the least of my worries right now.

'They took him by helicopter. We heard it hovering behind here, so we legged it upstairs. They locked this door so we couldn't get in, like. They must have come in through the window, because when the door finally unlocked itself, we burst in and found you unconscious with the window open. Logan was already gone,' Ben relays to me.

'I heard something before I fell asleep—humming. I thought it was Logan's heartbeat. I—I was lying down next to him at the time. But the humming was growing louder and louder. I felt the vibrations,' I recall, somewhat reluctantly. I hate to admit I was basically snuggling up to Logan when he was unconscious. It makes me sound like a creep.

'Do you remember how they sedated you? Did you feel the pinch of a needle?' Eli quizzes me. He's in the corner of the room with his arms crossed and his body stiff.

Needles terrify me, so I'd emphatically remember if I were pricked by one. 'No, all I remember was that I suddenly felt drowsy, so I laid down. It was as if I was high or something—like I was floating out of my body,' I recount, straining to make my brain work.

Something strange occurred when I fell asleep; that's all I know. It's right there—niggling at me, yet I'm unable to fully grasp the memory. It's like a dream I'm desperate to hold on to; but it's slowly slipping away as my conscious mind takes control and pushes it to the back, just out of reach.

Everyone is crammed into the room around me, excluding Zoe, who's watching us from the hallway. Compared to the others, she appears calm and unfazed. We make eye contact for a beat before she spins on her heel to leave down the stairs. I imagine she wouldn't have cared if I had stayed dead. She might have even preferred it.

'Do you remember anything else?' Sasha asks me.

'Any pearly gates?' Alex adds.

'I'm not sure. Something strange happened to me but I can't quite remember what.'

'It doesn't really matter now. What matters is that you're all right,' Sasha says, her smile kind.

'Do you think they'll bring Logan back when he's sorted?' I ask her, hoping she says what I want to hear. The thought of never seeing Logan again makes my throat constrict. Just imagining that he's gone for good hurts more than my crushed chest.

'I assume so. There must be a good reason for putting us into pairs, so I doubt they'll stop the programme or try to replace him now. He'll come back,' she replies with conviction, like she believes that enough for the both of us.

'Let's hope he can tell us summat about 'em, when he does,' Ben remarks before a yawn.

'It's been a long day. I think it's time for bed. We should let Ruby get some rest and recover from this ordeal,' Freya announces, moving to open the door for the others.

'I'll sleep in here. You shouldn't be left alone,' Charlie declares, taking my hand in his.

'You can't! The rules state that only the allocated pairs are allowed to sleep in their assigned rooms, so you and Zoe must stay in your room together. They'll shut off our water if you sleep in here. We'd have to travel to the stream every day and boil everything again because there's no way I'd drink that disgusting lake water,' Freya warns him in a rush, not stopping for breath.

'For heaven's sake! Ruby nearly died!' Charlie snaps back. It's the first time he's raised his voice with any of us. From the look on her face, Freya is just as surprised as I am, although she quickly masks it.

'I know that but... Ruby, do you really need someone in here with you?' Freya changes her approach. She must have gathered that I'm the type of person to say I'm fine even when I'm nowhere near.

'I'll be fine on my own. Don't worry, Pan,' I answer dishonestly, plastering on a fake smile while giving his hand a tentative yet reassuring squeeze. Charlie shakes his head and sighs, but doesn't push it further.

The truth is: I'm terrified to stay here on my own. Any other time or place, I would relish this solitude. However, sleeping here tonight—in this log prison—in this unfamiliar room—in this death bed...

I couldn't be more afraid of being alone.

I've spent the past hour lying in bed, trying to collect and piece together the tiny fragments of what happened to me when I died. Everyone else has returned to their own rooms. Charlie only agreed to go to bed if he could keep both our doors open, making it easier for him to hear me call if I needed anything. This prompted Ben to suggest we hold all the doors open with chairs, lest the Haven Initiative decides to lock them again with what we suspect is the magnetic locking system.

Thus far, all I can recall from my near-death experience is floating into nothingness, lost and confused. Except I have this unexplainable inkling that, somewhere deep down, I know what happened—that it's vital information.

Figuring out how to force my memory to cooperate with me is taking my mind off the fact I just died, and now I'm all alone in the dark. All the while, someone I care about is probably fighting for his life in the hands of those inhuman bastards who kidnapped us. Anyway, there's one thing I'm certain of: I'm not sleeping any time soon.

Being so mentally and physically exhausted lured me into thinking I'd be out like a light. Especially as I've recently lived through the trauma of dying. You'd think that was enough to warrant a good night's sleep—not forgetting that I've been forced into unconsciousness more times in the last two days than I have in my entire life. Before this, I don't think I've ever had a panic attack, fainted, or even been sedated for an operation. I'm like a bloody narcoleptic mess all of a sudden.

In all seriousness, I'm surprised by how well I'm coping with everything recently. I'm still somehow managing to stay rational and sane... I think. Am I trapped in a delusional state? Perhaps none of this is real and it's all a product of my imagination. I could in reality be in my alleyway in London on some sort of acid trip. Not that I would knowingly take acid, or any drug for that matter. Still, it seems like a more reasonable explanation than what's happened to me here. Or I could have been murdered and this is purgatory. Which may sound completely implausible, yet it's starting to feel a lot more logical than this place is turning out to be—if I even know what logic is anymore.

Years of dealing with unfortunate situations and bad luck have clearly left me able to handle stress when things go awry. If I've stayed sane surviving on the streets alone all these years, then why can't I survive this? Why am I doubting myself and my ability to adapt to what I'm facing now? Yeah, it's an unbelievable and overwhelming situation, but I'm capable, I'm resourceful, and I'm mentally equipped to deal with this life-or-death level of pressure.

You can keep it together. You can get through this.

Thinking about it, it hasn't really been me keeping it together, all on my own. I may be feeling lonely at this moment. However, the rest of the time I've been here (bar the first few hours in the valleys), I've been supported by other people—sharing the load with them. That's the real reason I've made it through this ordeal. I would have given up on that hill if it weren't for Logan. He was that glimmer of hope. It was enough for me to get the fuck up and push myself through more pain and turmoil. I've shared the weight of the decisions with them, the stress, the trials, and tribulations. I've invested more compassion and trust into them than I have with anyone in years, within only hours of meeting them all.

We've learnt that we're all in this together and we've leaned on each other to make this situation bearable. I realise now: it's not them that need me. I thought I was the one taking care of them, when, in actuality, I'm the one who needs *them* to care for *me*. They're the reason I'm still sane. They're the reason I haven't given up yet.

They saved me.

Moving forwards, I have to rely on them, at least a little.

It's hard to admit that to myself because it's relinquishing an element of control. It's usually too dangerous for me to open myself up to others—to be vulnerable in that way. Except, in this situation, it could be the only way to survive this: being part of a team.

This programme is working too well on me. It's so frustratingly efficient. Despite that, it also feels good to be a part of something—to finally have something to care about again.

Maybe I should suck it up and see where two weeks here gets me. I'm leaning towards the possibility that our kidnappers don't actually want to kill us because they were quick to come and assist Logan. And, deep down, I don't wholeheartedly believe they intended for me to react badly to sedation. My body was obviously too weak to cope with it and shut down. I only wish they would have gone about everything differently—given us a choice in the matter. Though, to be fair, if some tossers in suits approached me on the street and said they wanted me for some government training programme, I would have laughed in their face and run away as fast as I could. With that in mind, I guess there's no easy way to recruit someone like me—an outcast; a despondent loner who's disconnected from society and humanity in general.

Admittedly, kidnapping would probably be the easiest option.

Having this time to think things through has made me do a one-eighty on myself. I'm supposed to be trying to remember what strange thing occurred within my mind. Instead, my recent tangent of thought has led me into betraying my own character, by even entertaining the notion of letting our kidnappers win—of staying here as they intended. Unfortunately, there doesn't seem to be a viable counter-option.

Anyway, I have to stop being so stubborn as it's only made things worse. And, for once in my life, I can in truth see an opportunity. If I stay here, then I can continue to build these relationships with the people I've begun to care for. I can finally make some friends and stop feeling so alone in the world.

Why am I so eager to return to being just another unfortunate homeless person? Isolated from the rest of society? Constantly struggling to survive?

By comparison, this cabin, with these rations and comfy beds, could end up being the easier life. Especially since I have company here; I have support. There's even a chance this programme could pave the way into a government position, despite this being the most implausible thought I've had tonight. I don't see myself running around in a black suit being a secret spy agent. It makes me want to laugh out loud. Nonetheless, a job is a job when some nights you're living off leftover pizza from a bin. I must have been picked for a reason. It's not that improbable to believe what they're telling us has some truth to it.

Well, I guess I'm a sell-out and Logan was right: it's not giving up, it's accepting the best option and putting pride to one side. It seems that my best option is to stop fighting against this, stay here for two weeks, then see what happens. That's painfully hard to admit; it's going against my instincts and thinking with my head for once. I can't let go of my stubbornness entirely, though. I refuse to tell Logan he was right. He'll flash me that cocky, dimpled smirk of his. The one that annoys and flusters me simultaneously.

Thinking about him brings a smile to my lips. But then my chest tightens uncomfortably at the same time.

I miss him already.

It took hours for my whirling mind to settle enough for sleep to find me. Though it was restless. And now my body is aching from all the stress it's been under since I've been here: the running, the dehydration, lack of food, panic attacks, unconsciousness. Not forgetting coming back from the brink of death and all.

Sasha really went to town on my ribcage. Every breath brings a fresh, invisible stab wound. All my muscles seem to be made of stone, like a layer of airtight cement has encased them. Each time I move a millimetre, my sensitive nerves rub against the rough, gravelly texture—eroding them.

Luckily, I didn't dream last night. Not that I remember, anyway. I'm not in the mood to decode my thoughts today. I'll happily have a day off to recover. I've already decided to stop fighting, so there's no better time to start than the present. I'm going to be a good candidate and contribute to surviving here, as the task demands. I'm the reason our food and supplies were taken away, therefore I'll have to make up for that by fishing on the lake or gathering berries.

Today, my aim is to provide a meal for everyone in my little team. Hopefully, then they'll give Logan back, and it might also make me feel less guilty about the whole incident yesterday.

The first glimmer of morning light peeks in through the bedroom curtains. I've already been awake for half an hour, struggling to move or even breathe deeply without crying in pain. I resort to massaging my own legs as I curl into the foetal position in bed.

Hurried footsteps scuffle down the landing. I can already guess who it is.

'You haven't kicked the bucket, have you?' Charlie asks sleepily.

'Not yet. My legs aren't working.'

'Technically, it's morning now so I can come in,' he says, shuffling into the room. He drops onto Logan's bed, his eyes shut.

'You're not allowed to sleep in his bed, though. Respect the rules, Pan, you rebel. You'll get our water shut off and then I'll have to stop being your friend,' I tease, sounding a bit like Freya. With a dozy laugh, he sits up. 'I'm joking, you don't have to get up.'

Charlie stands anyway. 'No, I wouldn't want to break the rules. I'll have to slide into *your* bed. Aren't you lucky?' he replies cheekily, waiting by my bedside with an expectant look.

A beat passes before I sigh. 'No cuddling,' I state, relenting. I lift my covers up for him to slip in. A noise of discomfort grinds out of my mouth as my aching muscles rebel against my movements.

'I'm also rather achy. Although I can't imagine how horrid you're feeling right now. I'm sure the after-effects of dying trumps a bit of running,' he mentions, crawling under the covers beside me.

'Yep, I'm determined to have a chilled-out day. No drama. I'm planning to relax, and then I'm going fishing. You want to come with? I think one of the rules was that we're not allowed onto the lake alone. There's also the problem of my having no fishing experience to speak of.'

'You've never been fishing? I used to go quite frequently. Which doesn't mean I'm an expert fisherman, by any stretch of the imagination. To be honest with you, I've never actually caught anything,' he admits, scoffing at himself.

'Well then, it seems like we'll have a better chance jumping into the lake and scaring all the fish out.'

'You simply hold a stick out with bait attached to the end of it. There's no real skill involved. We'll be fine,' Charlie concludes, turning onto his side to drape his arm over my stomach.

'Pan, I said no cuddling,' I remind him, feigning a stern tone.

'You said it yourself, I'm a rebel,' he responds, smirking proudly. I shake my head, fighting a smile.

It's surprising how normal it feels to have Charlie here like this. I'm not threatened by his presence or worried he might do something untoward.

I'm sure he'd never push me too far or hurt me in any way. Snuggling with him only makes me feel safe and comforted.

It's a complete contrast to Logan. When he's been close enough to touch me previously, I've felt that crackle of tension in those separating centimetres, and I've been acutely aware of any skin-to-skin contact, like my skin was kindling, and his the spark. Our relationship isn't as innocent. It's more dangerous. It's not intentional on Logan's part. I know he's not going to attack me or anything like that. Still, it's more the idea of where things could lead with us which concerns me.

On the other hand, being close to Charlie is much simpler. There's no threat of things developing into something which could end up hurting me.

'Seriously, if you wish to be alone, I won't take offence,' Charlie mumbles, half-asleep now.

'Nah, you're all right. It's warmer like this anyway. Good for the muscles,' I justify, snuggling up to him. Thankfully, Charlie's body warmth is truly persuading my muscles to ease up. It's no lie.

Cuddling isn't that *bad*, I concede, moments before I fall blissfully back to sleep.

Chapter 18

Underwater

'Morning. Aww, aren't you two cute?' Dawn's sweet voice rouses me from my slumber. I open my eyes to see her beaming at me from the doorway. 'Everyone's downstairs. Thought I'd see if you wanted some tea?'

'What time is it?' I ask groggily, freeing my arm from under Charlie's to rub my eyes, which causes him to stir, too.

'It's nineish,' she answers.

'Okay, we'll be down soon.'

Dawn nods once before exiting down the staircase.

Stretching out, Charlie rolls onto his back. 'That was cosy, wasn't it? You were sleeping like a baby,' he mumbles, yawning widely.

'I do feel more rested now,' I admit, sitting up stiffly.

My muscle ache hasn't improved much. Regardless, I need to force myself up to do something productive today. Lying in bed—useless—may be appealing, but it's not an option. So, gritting my teeth, I bear it.

'Are you ready to be immeasurably bored watching a stick all day? You do realise it will take hours on that boat to get even a whiff of a fish? I'll be surprised if we manage to catch a cold between the two of us,' Charlie says.

I shrug. 'I was the one who messed up yesterday. There's no food because of me. I have to at least try,' I reply dismally, hoisting myself up from the bed by grabbing onto the wardrobe door. All I can do is stand for a minute, hoping I grow accustomed to the intense ache all over my body.

'Come to think of it, Ben mentioned he was rather good at fishing. I would hate to miss out on the opportunity to mock you all day—you hunched over like a little old lady—but perhaps you'll have more luck with him in the boat with you,' Charlie suggests, rising from the bed. He then supports my elbow to help me walk.

As much as I like Ben, I haven't been alone with him enough to have a one-to-one conversation. I'm almost certain that if Charlie and I were fishing all day together we'd have fun. Charlie is great at holding conversations. I'm not sure Ben has the same ability. Hopefully, it's not awkward with him. Although I doubt either of us is the type to bother attempting small talk.

Something tells me this afternoon will be a quiet one.

After finishing my morning tea at the dining table, speculating about Logan's return with the others, Ben and I grab the fishing equipment and row out to the middle of the lake.

He takes over rowing less than a minute in because my arms are still too weak and stiff. I've been struggling to mask my pain, not fooling anyone with my awful attempts to smile through it. Some of the others have been babying me since I woke up. Dawn helped me dress in comfortable leggings and a loose jumper, Charlie has been fussing over me, and Freya even asked if I needed help brushing my teeth.

At least this kind of fishing is a sit-down activity. It's barely a sport, in my opinion. Thankfully, there's not been much action involved for me thus far.

The relatively balmy breeze dries the droplets of lake water which have already found their way onto the exposed skin of my forearms.

Since we set up the fishing gear, it's been silent between Ben and me. We're on opposite sides of the boat, watching the calm water ripple around us as it rocks with our tiny movements. Charlie and Freya are talking together on the decking. Occasionally, they send a smile our way.

'So, Rubes, how are you really feeling now? I know you told us not to worry—that you're sound as a pound and all that bollocks, but I can tell summat's up,' Ben comes out with, catching me off-guard.

'Erm, I don't know. Are you talking physically?'

'I think anyone can see you're in a right state physically. You're not fooling anyone there, love,' he mocks, and we both chuckle lightly. 'I'm talking about what you think we should do now, in this shite situation we're stuck in.'

'Well, I'm done leading the rebellion, that's for sure... Honestly, Ben, I don't see any other option than to see these two weeks through. At least we're all together. And maybe, if we cooperate, they'll give us more food or something,' I mumble before sighing in defeat. Already, I'm not looking forward to his reply. I wince in preparation.

'You've changed your tune quickly, haven't you? Do you hear yourself? You're handing over all your power to 'em,' he bites back, his head shaking in disappointment.

'I'm sorry, but I'm just too fucking tired. We can't win against them. They have bloody wolves on tap for Christ's sake.' In exasperation, I throw my hands up, and then immediately come to regret that action. I wince again in pain.

Bowing my head, I let out another sigh. Ben's disappointment in me has my heart curling into a tight ball in my chest. But regardless, I've made my choice and I'm not going back on it now. This doesn't need to turn into an argument. I can't be bothered to have these sorts of heavy discussions today. I'd rather relax and not be made to feel guilty for trying to do the right thing.

Clearly sensing this, Ben rubs his face and sighs, too. 'I know. I don't blame you, love. But... I just thought you were the one person here who would fight to the death with me. I dunno what to do now, like. I'm lost,' he discloses in a dejected tone.

I'm surprised he's being so open. I thought he was disappointed in me, when in fact, loneliness is the problem; he thinks no one can understand how this situation is affecting him.

'I did fight to the death... literally,' I remind him, trying to lighten the mood. This forces a weary laugh from him.

'Aye, and you're never gonna let us forget that now, are you? Mate, remember when I died? Yeah? So, go on, make me a brew and gimme the last Custard Cream while you're at it,' he teases.

'Of course. I'd die for tea and biscuits. Who wouldn't? And few people can say they kicked it then came back to life. You're the only friends I have. I've got no one else to tell it to, so get used to it. The last biscuit *will* be mine, Benjamin. Maybe I'll even use it to get out of the washing up. It's like a get-out-of-jail-free-card,' I banter, mocking myself, but my words hit me after.

When I *do* finally leave this place, I have no one to explain this situation to—no one to be there for me—no support. Also, I won't need an excuse to get out of washing up because I have no sink, and any cutlery I use is disposable. I can't believe I now view washing up as a luxury. Pathetic.

'I doubt anyone will believe us, anyway. Imagine if a friend told you they were abducted by the government for some secret training programme in the forest,' he scoffs, securing a new colourful bait on the end of his fishing line.

'Don't forget the wolves they've trained to keep us from escaping. People will lap that shit up,' I add with a snort of amusement.

'We'd be sectioned so fast our heads would spin.'

Worrying about spending time with Ben out here was a wasted effort. He's not as serious as he makes out. He's actually quite easy to talk to.

The next hour rushes by. We discuss how strange our predicament is and speculate as to why we've been chosen. We also talk about what foods we wish were on our dinner plates tonight, plus other topics which delve a bit deeper, such as politics and religion. We seem to have similar views. To be fair, we're mostly discussing our mutual disdain for the right-wing parties and our lack of belief in the whole concept of religion in general.

We also bond over our Jewish roots. Ben tells me his maternal grandmother relocated from Jamaica on the Windrush and married a Mancunian man, whereas his father was a Turkish Jew who immigrated in the late eighties. I would tell him my ancestry, if I knew more about it, but my mum never mentioned her family much because they disowned her for marrying my dad.

It's been unexpectedly fun fishing with Ben. I even squeal in frightened delight when I come close to nabbing a fish. It wriggles free before

I can reel it in, though. Ben has more luck—effortlessly catching a few small ones.

'So, Ben, when did you learn how to fish?'

'Hmm, well... when I was younger, me dad used to take me once in a while, like. You know, it's how we bonded,' Ben answers, keeping his walnut-brown eyes fixed on the water.

Adjusting my position on the rough wood seat, I ask, 'When was the last time you went?'

'I haven't been fishing with him since I was around ten. He didn't come to visit me much in me foster homes,' Ben casually reveals, shrugging a shoulder.

Sneaking a peek at him, I try to make out his expression but he's facing away. 'Sorry. I didn't mean to pry,' I mumble, afraid that I've hit a nerve.

Ben shakes his head. 'Nah mate, I'm not embarrassed by it. I was a foster kid; it is what it is.'

'Of course, there's nothing to be ashamed of. It's not your fault,' I mutter, treading carefully.

Being mindful of someone else's boundaries is important in personal conversations like this. I don't want to say anything triggering as I know how it feels when people start questioning me about my past. Trauma is no one else's business and something people shouldn't have to explain unless they're comfortable enough to do so. Of course, it would be nice if Ben *did* feel comfortable enough to open up to me because I'm genuinely intrigued. On the other hand, I'm not sure I'm ready to tell anyone about my situation in the real world yet. It's rude to allow someone to share their story with you without reciprocating. I felt bad enough when Charlie confided in me about his life and I left him hanging.

'I've always had to fend for me'self. It's made me a more resilient bloke, I guess.' He shrugs again, as though talking about this sensitive topic doesn't particularly bother him.

Ben seems to relax into the conversation. He's turning towards me as if he wants to engage—unload. I'm still not sure if it's polite to ask more questions about it or not. I take his recent body language into account and go for it.

'If you don't mind me asking... what happened to your mum?' My tentative question hangs in the air for a moment, long enough for me to wonder if I've overstepped.

'Long and short of it... she was addicted to drugs and alcohol. I was taken by social services when she overdosed the first time. She tried to get clean, like, but she couldn't do it for more than a week or two. She was a goner by the third overdose. She snuffed it a week before my sixteenth birthday,' he answers candidly. There's no emotion in his response. It's all a matter of fact.

'I'm sorry.' I can't think of anything else to say after that.

'Cheers, love, but I don't really dwell on that stuff anymore. It messed me up when I was a teen. I got hooked on booze and gambled a lot. In the end, though, I sorted me'self out. I realised I didn't wanna end up like her. I have slip-ups now and again. The night we were kidnapped, for example... I was hammered and nodded off at a train station,' he confides, laughing to himself. 'At least I didn't wake up here, hanging out me arse.'

I chuckle at that. 'Well, I think you're one of the most resourceful and level-headed blokes I've ever met, Ben. I wish I could control my temper as well as you can.'

Ben smiles. 'Nah, you don't give yourself enough credit, love. You've got a good head on your shoulders there. I'm not the only one who respects you and trusts your judgement.'

'Thanks, I trust yours, too,' I convey, my smile widening.

That's no lie. I do trust Ben in that way. Yet, for some reason, I can't bring myself to tell him about my life in return. He may not be embarrassed about being a foster kid, but I still haven't managed to sort myself out. I'm at the lowest point of my life and being homeless brings with it tremendous shame. Ben believes some of the others respect me. But I'm sure that, as soon as they find out what I am, that will change.

As the next hour passes by, we make some progress with fishing. 'We' meaning Ben. I haven't caught a single thing all fucking morning. Whereas he's managed to catch another small fish—that we don't know the name of—and a medium-sized Perch.

Sasha and Eli decide to journey into the forest in search of a berry bush they think they saw when we attempted our escape. We're only allowed to explore the forest in pairs now, according to the new rules Freya said our captors implemented on the phone after the incident with the wolves. Which means the others are waiting around, bored, and useless.

Dawn, Alex, Charlie, and Freya leave the decking area, heading back inside the cabin. They're obviously tired of watching me fail miserably at fishing.

Apparently, Zoe has been hiding in her bedroom all morning, not interacting with anyone else. That's probably best for keeping the mood lighter. Although I'm starting to feel sorry for her. She's intent on isolating herself and I can relate to that way of thinking. She has her barriers firmly up and will fight anyone who tries to take them down. That was my default before this place—these people—burrowed through my defences.

'What's going on with you and posh boy, then?' Ben enquires out of the blue, a cheeky smirk tilting his mouth.

I was worried people would start questioning my friendship with Charlie after our little cuddle in bed this morning. I'm only surprised it's Ben asking because I wouldn't have guessed he'd be interested in such things.

My face flushes. 'Nothing. We're just friends. I know it might look like more but I'm sure, given the chance, you'd be snuggling with him at night, too,' I joke, masking my embarrassment.

'Maybe. If I can tape over his gob, I'd consider it.'

I laugh. 'You love him really.'

'He's like the annoying little brother I never wanted. He's a good'un, though. Bloody irritating but I guess he can be a laugh... occasionally. Don't tell him I said that,' Ben says, trying not to smile.

'So... you and Freya? Is it like me and Charlie or Dawn and Alex?' I imply with narrow eyes, getting my own back.

Swiftly, Ben drops his gaze, but I catch the shy grin. Coughing with discomfort, he fiddles with the fishing rod. 'Erm, we better start concentrating on fishing. We'll need a break soon, anyway.' His awkward attempt to change the subject makes me chortle.

'That's what I thought,' I reply knowingly.

Ben snatches up one of the small fish he nabbed earlier and pretends he's about to chuck it at me. We both laugh harder.

'All right, all right. Keep laughing and I'll throw you in the lake. You'll probably catch a fish better in there, anyway,' he playfully threatens, winking.

'Now, that's really hit a nerve. I can't believe you'd mock my fishing capabilities.' I pretend to look offended. 'You've gone too far, Benjamin.' As I wag my finger at him, he shakes his head in faux shame.

'Ah, I'm proper sorry, like. Obviously, you're just warming up by catching thin air,' he quips, a smug expression replacing his contrite one.

'Ooh, you'll see. By the end of the day, I'll have at least *seen* a fish in the vicinity of my rod.' To illustrate my point, I swirl the line around in the water, trying to temp one up.

'That's the spirit, love. Always aim high,' he replies sarcastically, punching me lightly on the arm.

I've enjoyed this opportunity to build a rapport with Ben. I'm proud of myself for keeping up with his banter. Unlike Charlie, whose jovial humour is used to mask his insecurities, Ben's is more straightforward. I can completely rinse him and know he'd give as good as he gets, with no hard feelings. With Logan, our conversations tend to be more serious, like each sentence has another meaning behind it. It's not like either type of conversation is better than the other: it's just refreshing to interact with people in different ways. I've never been able to do that with friends before. Thinking about it, I guess I've never had any *real* friends. Developing these relationships with Logan, Charlie, and Ben has made me more confident in pursuing closer bonds with the others, especially the women.

Growing up in a male-dominated household after my mum died, I pushed aside my femininity in favour of the more typically 'boyish' things my brother was into. I even tried getting on the boys' football team but they wouldn't let me. I wasn't interested in much else so I ended up not fitting in anywhere at school. Honestly, I never felt like I could relate to the girls in my year and the boys didn't accept me, either. Therefore, I wound up floating around somewhere in the middle, not making any real connections. Hopefully, in the next two weeks, I can overcome that fear of rejection and find my place.

Suddenly, tiny vibrations travel up the rod in my grasp and excitement springs up inside me. I quickly tighten my grip.

'Hey, Ben, I think something's nibbling.' I sit up straighter, preparing myself.

'Be patient. Don't do nowt yet,' he instructs, swivelling to face me.

My rod vibrates again, enough to see it shake this time. I peer over the side of the boat, unable to spot anything in the water. It's too murky. The rod continues to vibrate, growing stronger by the second.

'Hold on tight, it looks like it might go for it,' Ben says, adjusting his own rod.

Shifting my hands further apart, I cover more of the rod to stabilise it. As I do this, there's a swift pull, which nearly forces me to lose my grip completely.

'Wow, it's strong,' I mention, bracing my feet against the boat for the next pull.

'You're doing fine, Rubes. Lift it a bit higher now.'

I do as Ben instructs, wrenching the rod up with both hands. However, as soon as I do, it tugs back down sharply. The force of it jolts the boat and it sways from side to side.

'I'll need help keeping this rod if it continues doing that, Ben,' I admit, starting to panic. I can't lose a rod after getting all our supplies stripped from us yesterday.

The rod is vibrating so intensely now that my hands are going numb. Before Ben can make his way over to me, a formidable force drags the rod down. Somehow, I manage to keep hold of it. Still, the boat steadily dips to the side, tempting water in.

'Wait, hang on,' Ben urges before he manoeuvres across the boat to me.

The rod suddenly slackens, causing the boat to jump upwards again. Ben nearly falls overboard, though he quickly regains his balance. When he reaches me, he grabs onto the rod, lending me extra support. It lurches down again, tipping the boat to the water's surface. A lick of water rolls into the boat, wetting my boots.

'Must be a big ol' bastard,' he guesses, struggling to yank the rod back up. 'Can you start reeling it in, love?'

Before I can rotate the lever, another sharp jolt rocks the boat harshly, and more water spills inside. Beads of sweat trickle down Ben's forehead as he maintains his position and gains ground. Between reeling, I help him haul it in, using our combined strength. We both have our feet braced against the side of the boat, leaning back heavily so it doesn't capsize on us.

Despite our strenuous efforts, the rod veers fiercely down again. Both Ben and I are striving to keep it up with all our might. The strain is killing my muscles, which are already in bad shape.

'We have to cut it loose. It's gonna tip the boat over,' Ben predicts, his voice tight. 'There's a small knife in the tackle box. Bring it here, will you?'

'Okay, wait a second,' I mutter, releasing the rod to reach over to the box.

Fumbling through it, I find the knife sitting at the bottom. Ben is groaning with the effort of managing the rod on his own. The boat is practically tipping below the surface of the lake now, the water inside rising fast, sinking it gradually. If I don't cut this cord, we could lose the boat as well.

'Come on—quick. I can't hold on for much longer,' Ben calls out impatiently.

'I've got it,' I tell him, steadying myself so I can stand up and cut the cord.

Just before I manage to rise, the rod slackens again and the boat jerks back, hitting the water hard. Ben, who had been bracing himself against the pull, is suddenly swung back, the force knocking his head against the other side of the boat. He drops the rod and falls unconscious into the small pool of water which has accumulated in our boat.

'Ben! Ben, are you okay?!' I rush to turn him over so his face isn't underwater. His eyes are closed, his jaw slack. He doesn't respond.

My heart is racing. Who knew that fishing could be so dangerous? I heave Ben up and rest his head on the seat, then turn my attention to the rod. It's stopped vibrating. It's sinister in its stillness, resting innocently on the lip of the boat.

Hesitantly, I pick it up. Nothing happens. *Quickly reel it in and row back to land, Ruby. Don't be a wuss*, I say to myself, ignoring the tremor in my hands. Hopefully, Ben won't be knocked out for long. The others are inside with the door closed so won't hear me calling, anyway.

I cautiously peek over the side of the boat to see if the fish is still attached. All I make out in the murky water is a dark shadow lurking below our boat. It seems to be growing, like it's rising fast.

Before I catch on to what's happening, something snags my wrist, and in a blink, I'm tugged over the edge of the boat. I hit the water so fast I forget to gulp down air, sweeping beneath it with hollow lungs. My body revolts in panic while I attempt to fight off whatever has ensnared me. It releases my wrist but latches onto my foot as I start to rise back up.

Plummeting deeper and deeper into the darkening water, my lungs burn from lack of oxygen and my mind begins to scream out for air. I need to return to the surface or I'll soon drown.

In a desperate frenzy, I fight as hard as I can against the weight of the water as it bears down on me—the pressure squeezing and closing in from all sides. The empty expanse of my mind calls for me to drift—to sink into its calmer depths. I must be losing consciousness. *No.* I refuse to let my mind shut off.

Fight harder. Get yourself free. Fight or die, Ruby. Make it a choice.

My eyes sting when I force them open, staring down at my feet. It's hard to see anything in this dirty blur but I can just make out my black boots. My heart freezes when I see what's holding onto my ankle. It's not the mouth of a fish pulling me to my death but a large, pale hand. It's not *something* that has me—it's *someone*.

Agonising seconds tick by slowly as I flail and kick. I can't fight for much longer. Any second now, it will all be over.

My eyes droop as I drift in and out of the dark corners of my subconscious. My body is now limp; I have no energy left. Life is leaving me.

The pressure around my ankle eases and I start drifting up again. Although it doesn't make much of a difference: I'm too far gone. I've sunk too deep. I won't be able to reach the surface in time. Still, I attempt but it's no use—my legs are made of lead. They're weighing me down.

It's game over.

Just as I resign myself to death, something else hooks onto me. Its firm yet tender touch is under my arms, lifting me up. With its help, I rise more rapidly from the depths of the lake. I can't hold my breath a second longer, though; I can't fight the burning urge to breathe.

My mind fades into the blackness for a moment and I accidentally inhale. Pain fills my lungs with the clogging intake of water and I choke.

Returning to the surface, the water lightens, and the pressure around my chest, and inside my head, recedes. The sensation of drowning is terrifying and painful. This is a horrible way to die. But it's happening, and I can't control the natural impulses of my dying body. Floundering, I gasp, sucking in more water.

A beat later, I breach the surface—the cold air hitting my face. I try to breathe but it's impossible with all the space in my lungs already full.

'I've got you. You'll be all right, Ruby. Hang on—we're nearly there,' a familiar voice tells me as I'm dragged backwards through the water. 'Grab her. Get her in the boat,' the voice demands from another.

A second pair of hands grip my sodden jumper to haul me up over the side of the boat. There's a blurry film over my eyes, preventing me from seeing anything.

'Rubes, did you swallow any water?' a deeper voice asks in a Northern accent. A fuzzy face appears in front of mine but I'm too out of it to connect the dots.

Unable to answer, I gurgle, slipping in and out of consciousness. Just because I'm out of the water doesn't mean I'm out of danger.

I'm still drowning.

'She has water in her lungs. Move over,' the first voice orders. The fuzzy face disappears from view a second before my vision blackens. I float into the blank spaces of my mind again. The nothingness is welcoming. I'm drawn in.

A tiny star appears. I've seen that before somewhere, I'm sure of it.

I'm vaguely aware of several pushes on my chest in quick succession, only due to the pain it causes, and then a mouth on mine. My lips tingle as a rush of air forces its way into my lungs. It happens a couple more times before the water trapped inside begins to bubble up.

'Come on, Ruby. Let it out—breathe. Please,' the voice begs, cracking with desperation.

The intermittent pressure on my chest increases, surging the water up. It rises to my throat and I'm forced to choke again—salty lake water spurting out of my mouth in waves. I finally inhale, gasping and spluttering. The burning breaths fill my beaten lungs with the oxygen it needs to wake my body up. The star fades into the blackness beyond.

'Hey! What's going on? Is Ruby hurt?' That's Charlie's voice, calling from further away.

'She needs help!' the first voice shouts. 'Ben, are you strong enough to row back?' The voice is too familiar. I know who it is. Yet I don't trust my instincts or the way my heart leaps in hope.

I force my eyes open to see a very wet, smiling face staring down at me. It's Logan.

Chapter 19

SABOTAGE

'Do you have some sort of death wish?!' Charlie exclaims when Ben informs the others of my near-drowning.

After gallantly carrying me into the cabin, Logan carefully lowers my exhausted body onto the sofa. My throat is burning so much that each breath stings with a fiery intensity. My stomach is also churning up the dirty lake water I inadvertently swallowed.

I wish I had the strength to rush upstairs to the bathroom because I can't think of anything worse than vomiting in front of everyone. I'm already embarrassed enough that I've nearly died twice in less than twenty-four hours.

'What the fuck happened? One minute we were reeling in the fish, like, and the next I'm waking up with a bleeding headache and Logan's pulling you up from the lake half-drowned,' Ben questions me, drying his hands on one of the towels Freya fetched for us. On his forehead, a deep frown is carved, along with a trickle of blood escaping the thin yet angry-looking gash where he hit his head on the boat.

A hoarse cough inhibits my response. It rips at my already-raw throat, the pain so sharp I wonder if I've somehow swallowed glass.

'I think we should save our questions for later. Ruby needs to dry off, warm up, and recover a little first,' Logan instructs them, wrapping a towel around my shoulders. 'Sash, can you help her get changed upstairs?' He's clearly just as exhausted as I am, his chest heaving not only from pulling me from the lake but also carrying me inside. He grabs a towel for himself with trembling hands.

Sasha nods before rushing over to assist me.

I hate how weak and disorientated I am—still shaking from the shock. I can't concentrate on how the others are reacting to this new drama. I'm soaked, cold, and shivering in violent bursts. I need time to process what I've experienced before I'm around everyone, having to answer their difficult questions.

'Come here, love. You're breaking me heart,' Ben says, effortlessly scooping me up. He carries me across the room with Sasha following closely behind. He shouldn't be carrying me anywhere after his spell of unconsciousness but I'm too weak to argue.

The others can't hide their concern for me, either. It's obvious that Charlie is itching to come with us, although I'm sure he knows there's not much he can do. Sasha is a more appropriate choice to help me change into dry clothes.

'By the way, it's good to have you back, Logue. Don't answer any questions 'til I come back down,' Ben specifies, climbing the stairs with me in his muscular arms.

Before we enter my bedroom, Freya calls up, 'Before all that, we'll need to sort your head wound out, Benjamin.'

After Ben places me onto my bed, he practically runs back down to hear Logan's story. Sasha proceeds to dry me with more warm towels, then helps me change into fresh clothes. She's been kind enough not to badger me with questions. Instead, she remains silent, occasionally offering me sympathetic glances when I wince and groan from discomfort, caused by the numerous sources of pain across my broken-down body.

'You scrub up well for someone who's been raised from the dead several times, I have to say,' she jokes, stepping back to admire the simple outfit she's dressed me in—blue faded jeans, a soft, cream woollen shirt, and a navy jumper. I'm not as comfortable as I would like, but at least I'm warm.

'I'm sure I don't have to tell you that Logan will be *insufferable* from now on. He'll be buzzing around you like a hornet waiting to strike. I wouldn't be surprised if he's already on the other side of the door on guard duty,' she continues to jest, knowing I can't retort. What happened to the companionable silence I was enjoying?

Suppressing a smile, my eyes roll at the ridiculous notion of needing a bodyguard. Especially if it's Logan. What makes her think he cares for me that much? Yeah, he dove into the lake for me, but wouldn't anyone do that if someone were drowning? From what I've seen, Sasha and Logan have barely spoken one-to-one. This must be an assumption rather than an observation.

Sasha plonks down on Logan's bed. 'Are you feeling better now? Just nod if you are.'

Sighing painfully, I nod. The entirety of my sore body is an unwelcome distraction—the heated stab that accompanies each movement snatches my attention every time—which means I'm still hopelessly confused about what occurred in the lake. But, as I calm down, my mind gradually clears away the panicked clutter. It also helps that I'm no longer cold and wet.

I'm not looking forward to explaining the truth of my experience to the others. Was I imagining what I saw in the depths of the lake? Maybe my brain, through lack of oxygen, conjured the existence of the unknown lake-dweller. No one will believe the hand was real; it sounds beyond any realm of reason. I should probably dismiss that spooky detail and assume it was some rare, hand-shaped fish that dragged me under the water.

'At least you won't go fishing again. You were pretty bad at it,' Sasha mentions, a teasing smirk on her face. I'm strong enough to hold up my middle finger, which makes her snort a laugh.

I lie back on my bed, resting my aching head on the pillow. As soon as my eyes shut, I drift off.

'You shouldn't sleep for a few hours at least. You might be at risk of secondary drowning; I read it somewhere. I don't really know what it means, but it doesn't sound too good, and we don't need you dying again. It's not a party trick, you know.' Sasha dives onto my bed to shock me awake. Her teasing smile fades. 'Seriously, Rubes, I'm worried. Stay awake for me. Please?'

Rubbing energy back into my face, I nod then sit up again.

I undeniably misjudged Sasha upon introduction. Like me, she has shields up most of the time, but occasionally, I glimpse the softness of her heart. I imagine she's a fiercely loyal friend to those she allows past her defences. I want to be one of those people.

What I *am* looking forward to is spending more time with her. If I manage to survive the rest of the day, that is.

Half an hour of Sasha gushing about her nephew and his cuteness is making me want to fall asleep again. I'm not a baby person, mainly because I've never been around them. Luckily, before I rudely dose off, there's a knock at my bedroom door.

'She's decent,' Sasha says.

Logan and Charlie enter the room and Charlie immediately springs over to my side.

'Ruby, when I said you had to watch the stick all day, I didn't mean you had to guard it with your life,' Charlie mocks, draping an arm around my shoulders. 'It was fishing, not babysitting.'

Sick of the jokes already, I shrug him off and huff.

'My sincere apologies. Too soon? Should I wait until the next near-death experience?' he carries on, pouting. 'And don't worry, even as a zombie, you're ravishing. Not rav*enous*, I hope,' he adds, deadpan, and I punch his shoulder weakly. He snickers at my reaction, his arm snaking back around me.

'I've been keeping the others busy downstairs with the story of what happened to me in our kidnappers' care. They also filled me in on what happened to you after I was extracted. I won't make any jokes, though, I promise,' Logan assures me, stepping closer with a forced smile in place. He stays standing, his icy eyes catching on Charlie's arm. His lips press into a hard line, his smile tightening even more.

I suppress the sudden urge to fling myself into Logan's arms. Perhaps because last night I was so worried about his well-being. And now, he's here, and he's just saved me from drowning. Plus, I haven't had the chance to greet him properly yet. I'm desperate to hear all the details of his brief stint with our kidnappers. But I'm sure our friends downstairs—already familiar with his story—are more eager to know what happened to me in the lake. The quicker I get through this, the sooner I can have a one-to-one conversation with Logan.

'Let's go downstairs. I only want to have to tell this story once,' I croak, fighting a wince.

Ten minutes later, we're all in the kitchen, sitting around the dining table. Everyone is listening intently as I recount my harrowing tale, though it's mostly because I'm having to whisper, due to my uncooperative throat. I detail the lead-up to my unexpected plunge into the lake easily enough. The next part is harder to express in words. Under the table, my clammy palms slide against each other.

'The rod had gone completely still so I looked over the edge of the boat and then...' I hesitate—deciding whether or not to tell them about the hand I saw.

'Then what? You decided to dive in and flail around like a worm to entice it back? Or did you *fall in* to garner more sympathy from everyone?' Zoe derides me.

'Zoe, let her finish please,' Logan asserts after an exasperated sigh.

Zoe chucks Logan a dirty look. She hasn't been interested in what I've had to say from the get-go. She's slumped in her chair, staring up at the ceiling. *She'll pick at whatever you say, so you may as well tell the truth*, I convince myself, sucking in a brave breath.

'I didn't fall in; I was *pulled* in. Not by a fish, but by a *person*,' I state as clearly as I can, making sure my words have emphasis.

'What?!' Ben and a few others exclaim in shock.

'Someone pulled you into the water? How do you know it was a person?' Freya questions, her light eyebrows knotting together.

'I looked down at what held my ankle and I saw a hand,' I clarify, fidgeting nervously in my seat.

'I don't get how that's even possible. No one else was about before I knocked me head,' Ben claims, visibly perplexed. 'A human can only hold their breath for a few minutes, you know.'

'Are you sure you weren't just deprived of oxygen and you imagined the hand?' Alex asks gently.

'That did cross my mind, but I know what I saw. I wasn't hallucinating,' I protest, a little defensively. I knew it would sound too far-fetched. Now they're going to pick me apart. I shouldn't have told them.

'If she saw a hand, she saw a hand,' Sasha says simply, and I gape at her, surprised she believes me.

Eli speaks up, to everyone's surprise. 'It's possible. Someone could've been waiting under the water the whole time you were out there if they had some sort of breathing apparatus. I've been diving before and those oxygen tanks last about an hour each. Were there any bubbles in the water?' His eyes dart between Ben and me.

'There could've been, but I—I must have thought it were a fish or summat,' Ben replies, scratching his jaw.

'Even so, it's still a wild theory. Why would someone attempt to drown Ruby? That's a lot of effort to go to—hiding under the water all that time. Ruby was in her room on her own last night; why not try to kill her then? You know, after she died the first time?' Freya queries, raising her eyebrows.

'I don't think The Haven Initiative is behind this attack. I reckon it's someone else; an individual trying to mess with their programme,' Logan speculates, resting his elbows on the table as he sits forward. He's picking at the bandage on his arm, distracting himself.

We all pause for a moment to contemplate it. That would make more sense. I was struggling to see how it would benefit The Haven Initiative to herd us back to the cabin, when their wolves could have easily ripped us apart, then save Logan to gain our trust, only to mess it all up by elaborately staging an attempt on my life when they could have simply plucked me out last night. They only sedated me and left with Logan.

'So... someone else could be trying to sabotage this? Someone hoping to stay under the radar—from us and The Initiative,' Sasha sums up, her eyes narrow.

'I do remember hearing something—when I was at the hospital—and now it makes more sense,' Logan offers, nodding his head, deep in thought.

'What did you hear?' Eli enquires, leaning forward with interest.

'I heard two people talking outside my room about a rebel wanting to ruin them. At the time, I thought they were referring to Ruby and our escape plan, but maybe not,' Logan answers.

So Logan was taken to a hospital. I can't wait to find out more—to see if he interacted with anyone or found out more about the people who kidnapped us. However, right now, what's unfolding here, in this conversation, takes precedence.

'If there is someone out there, hoping to sabotage this programme, and obviously knowing they were unsuccessful, might they attempt to do it again?' Charlie glances at me, worry making his usually bright eyes weary.

'They could hurt any of us next,' Dawn squeaks, then gulps. Alex wraps an arm around her while she bites her nails anxiously, her wide doe-eyes dashing to the window as if she expects someone to break through it at any moment.

'We need to stick together from now on—look out for one another. One rebel can't take on ten of us,' Alex says, trying to sound optimistic.

'I'm not gonna stay around you lot all day for two weeks. I'd rather die,' Zoe interjects, a disgusted look on her face.

'This cabin is secure enough; it's an enclosed space with few hiding places. It's riskier outside in the forest. I think, if we have to go out, it should be in groups of four instead of pairs. One rebel would have trouble taking on four of us at once. I'm sure our kidnappers would allow us to revert to our original rules if it's to keep us safe and we don't attempt another escape,' Logan suggests, relaxing back in his chair. The others nod in agreement.

I'm still shocked that most of them believe me, seeing as I even doubted myself. I'm glad we've been able to piece together what could be happening, with the aid of Logan's hospital eavesdropping. Otherwise, we wouldn't have known about another possible threat to our safety here—a rebel. The funny thing is, we may in fact be forced to rely on our kidnappers to keep us from harm. This situation can't get any more unbelievably complicated, surely.

'Urgh, I'm so tired of all this. And, quite frankly, I've had it with all of you. I can't do two weeks here. I want out!' Zoe shouts to the cabin ceiling, as if she's addressing our captors, not us.

'My God, will you shut the fuck up?! None of this is ideal for any of us. So suck it up, work with us, and stop being such a brat,' Sasha snaps at her.

'Why don't you come and make me, bitch,' Zoe goads, shooting up from her chair.

Sasha springs up too, although Logan is quick to intervene by standing between the two women. 'I think there's been enough drama for one day. Sash, please. Ignore her,' he pronounces in a steady, calming tone.

With firmly pursed lips, Sasha backs down, slowly blowing out a resentful sigh through her nose.

Zoe sneers at Sasha before sliding back into her own chair.

'Team Sasha. That was brilliant,' Charlie whispers in my ear.

Zoe catches my answering snicker and glowers my way.

'What do we do now? We're stuck here with nothing to do, and worst of all, we're all grumpy and hungry. Tonight's not gonna be fun at all,' Alex complains, trying to change the subject.

'Maybe we can all get to know each other better?' Dawn throws in, perking up, and Zoe scoffs, as though the idea is unthinkable.

Unfortunately, I share Zoe's opinion on this one. I'm not overly keen on the idea of a glorified sharing circle. Don't get me wrong: I'd be happy to learn more about these people and have a calmer evening tonight. But with that comes the expectation to open up in return, and the thought still terrifies me. I prefer one-to-ones where I can squirm my way out of giving specific details by deflecting and being a good listener. More mouths equals more questions, and there's more pressure to answer—more eyes and ears trained on you.

Out of nowhere, a loud crash from outside makes us jump. We all race to the window to locate the source of the commotion.

Outside, about fifty meters from the cabin, sits a huge wooden crate with a red parachute attached to it. I assume it fell to the ground from an aircraft of some kind. We must have been speaking too loudly to hear the plane.

We make our way outside to inspect the crate. On one side, in bold, black lettering, is the word 'Haven'. And on the other is a graphic design that must be their logo. It looks to be a tree with two diverging branches inside a circle. The roots of that tree growing from open palms.

Logan opens the latch on the crate and lifts the lid. 'I don't think we have to worry about tonight being boring,' he says, a grin making his dimples pop.

Stepping up, I peer inside the crate. There's a variety of supplies stacked on top of each other: food items, a fair few bottles of wine, and a couple of board games.

'Finally. I was contemplating cannibalism for a minute there, honestly,' Charlie jokes, rubbing his hands together in anticipation. 'Ooh, there's premium beef!'

He's like a kid in a sweet shop. Smiling, I scan the others for their reactions. They all have that same excitement lighting their faces. Thinking about it, the prospect of a fancy meal washed down with wine is incredibly soul-soothing, considering what we've been through these past few days. All this dying business has been rather taxing; I'm definitely in need of a break.

I'm not even doubting it anymore. I don't suspect it's been poisoned or is suspicious in any way. The Haven Initiative has rewarded us, and I'm profoundly grateful for it.

I guess that means I've swapped my pride for food and comfort. Though at present, dinner is the thing which will keep me going—fuel my internal fire for another day.

I have to swallow my pride.

For now.

Chapter 20

GOODNIGHT

In the kitchen, I'm helping Dawn set the table while Logan, Charlie, Freya, and Eli are busy cooking. I'm glad they took over that task because I can't think of anything worse than attempting to cook a decent meal. Beans on toast is a stretch for me. The best I usually do for myself is to open a tin and eat whatever's inside—cold with an old plastic spoon. Hot food in general is a luxury for me as I don't have a portable kitchen just lying around the streets of London for my culinary needs.

Ben, Alex, and Sasha decided to fish on the bank of the lake, not risking using the boat again since the incident this morning. We already have beef for dinner. Regardless, waiting around while the others cooked made them feel a little redundant. They chose to chance it so we could add some protein to tomorrow's meal.

Lightning rarely strikes the same place twice, right?

Zoe, on the other hand, hasn't wanted to contribute in the slightest. She's alone in the living room, resting those malicious eyes of hers. Every time I've had to walk past her, she's used them at full force, searing holes into me. I don't understand her. I've tried to. What I can't figure out is *why* she hates me in particular. I could relate to her isolating herself if it were due to mistrust or if she were shy. But to actually have this level of disgust for us—all this venom aimed at *me* especially—simply isn't warranted or justifiable. There must be an underlying reason.

'What are you thinking about?' Dawn probes, her head tilting as she observes me.

Snapping out of my tangent of thought, I realise I've been wiping down the same plate for five minutes; it's the cleanest plate in the world.

'Erm... just wondering why Zoe hates me so much,' I answer honestly. I assume the others sense the same venom from Zoe so I'm not afraid to voice it.

'Usually, if someone gives you looks that dirty, it's because they're jealous of you,' Dawn imparts, setting the cutlery beside each plate I've placed on the dining table.

'I doubt that very much,' I scoff, unable to think of a reason anyone would be jealous of me.

'You're pretty, smart, funny, respected by everyone here. I could carry on. Even I'm a wee bit jealous,' she admits with a light chuckle.

This throws me off, heat rising to my cheeks. I'm not comfortable receiving compliments, especially so many in quick succession. Also, I'm still perplexed as to why people keep saying stuff like this to me: that I'm respected and trustworthy. They're the comments which stand out the most for me because everything else you'd just say to make someone feel better about themselves, regardless of the truth. 'Respected' seems like a more genuine and plausible comment. It's something I'm more willing to accept. It's something I've always been desperate for.

Taking a seat at the table, I say sheepishly, 'Thanks, Dawn. You're sweet, but I really don't think that's the case. Maybe I remind her of someone she doesn't like.'

Dawn sits down opposite me. 'Could be. But I've been around girls like her before. I used to work in a boutique in Dublin. The girls there would bitch about me all the time. Sometimes purposely loud enough that I'd hear. One day, I asked one of them outright why they had a problem with me, and she said they thought I drove a car that was too fancy for my class. That was it. It's funny when you think about it.' She shrugs, resigned.

'That's awful. Just because you worked hard to buy something nice for yourself?' How could anyone be that mean to someone so sweet and genuine?

'That's the kicker; I would never buy a fancy car even if I had the money saved. I inherited that car from my mam who had just passed away from cancer. She got the car from my da when he died, which was before I was even born. So they were jealous of something I would have given up in a heartbeat for something they had—a parent.' Her eyes shine for a moment, but then she blinks and forces a smile.

'Your dad died before you were born?' I ask timidly, tiptoeing around my desire to ask a hundred questions.

'Hmm, he was a fireman. He died trying to save one of his crew who'd gotten trapped in a burning building. They didn't make it out. My mam received a medal from the Lord Mayor, in honour of da and his last act of bravery. That's the one thing I miss while being stuck in this situation. I used to carry the medal around with me in my purse, but obviously we didn't have any personal items with us when we woke up here. It doesn't just make me think of my da: it reminds me of my mam, too. She used to hold the medal to her lips when she was worried about something. She said it made her feel brave. She did that a lot when she was going through chemo. I usually have it on me, in case I ever need it. I'm a right wimp so I kissed it often enough,' she confides, laughing at herself, though the roughness of pain is hiding beneath it all.

'You're not a wimp. You're kind—you try to take care of everyone. And it takes a tremendous amount of courage to be so open and genuine with people. I'm afraid to do that. That's something I'm envious of,' I share with her, offering an encouraging smile. She tilts her head again, smiling back. 'I'm sorry about your parents.' My voice is a thick whisper now, my mouth seeming full of hot honey. I want to tell her I understand her loss; how devastated I was when my mum died. Yet I can't bring myself to say it. Instead, I focus on the plates again, feeling the words disintegrate—ruining our moment.

Charlie interrupts whatever Dawn is about to say next, and I'm glad when he swans over with two bottles of wine in hand. '*Bonjour Mademoiselles. Blanc* or... what's the word for red again?' he queries in a terrible French accent.

'Rouge, but I'll have white please,' Dawn replies, beaming a brighter smile his way.

Charlie places the red wine down on the table then lifts the other bottle—filled with white wine—up to Dawn's glass to pour some in.

I pick up the red wine and smell the open top; the aroma is bitterly sweet, like unripe blackcurrant on a warm summer's day. Much like the situation we're in. Even with the comparison fresh in mind, the smell makes my mouth water. I haven't tasted wine in such a long time. When I worked as a waitress, I used to drink once in a while, if I could afford it; mainly to cope with the abrupt change in my life and to try and socialise with colleagues I otherwise struggled to connect with. The bar staff used to let us have a few sneaky glasses here and there, when there was an open bottle. I haven't really drunk since I lost that job.

In the mood for one, I pour myself a glass. One will do me fine for the evening. I doubt I'd be able to handle any more than that. I've always been a lightweight.

'Can someone tell the others that dinner's nearly ready, please?' Freya asks the room, obviously meaning Dawn or myself, because we're the only people who aren't busy and who also aren't a particular sullen blonde with a short temper and vicious tongue who wouldn't lift a finger even if begged.

Dawn quickly springs up, knowing movement is still a painful task for me. As she passes me by, she places a hand on my shoulder and squeezes lightly before she leaves the room. It makes me smile. It's funny how a small gesture like that can be such a good indication of an important feeling—of a moment of understanding and gratitude. It's possible she read the thoughts on my face before I closed myself off again.

Dawn reminds me a bit of my mum—kind, thoughtful, always looking to help out and spread positivity. My mum loved to express her gratitude through silent gestures, too—a touch of my hand, a sweep of my hair, or an extra chocolate bar in my school lunch box.

I remember one time, when I was six or seven, a boy I used to play with on my street was crying because his bike broke. Without thinking twice, I gave him mine to keep. Later, my mum asked me why, and I told her I knew it would make him feel happy again, and that I was already happy so I didn't need it like he did. She tilted her head and gifted me the warmest smile, which made me happier than that bike ever could.

Dinner suddenly becomes a feast. Once all the food is arranged on the table, we realise our cooks have gone above and beyond. We have a creamy mushroom soup that Eli conjured up for our starter, with warm, crisp rolls, which are perfect to dunk into it. I would usually be satisfied with that for my meal. But after we finish it, we move on to the main course.

There are succulent beef medallions and roast potatoes. There's also a variety of steamed vegetables, Yorkshire puddings, and sage and onion stuffing balls. It's similar to Christmases when I was a child: stuffing my face as quickly as possible because I was so excited to sample everything. Even with ten people, eating like pigs, we still have leftovers. We quickly find out that our eyes are bigger than our stomachs. Especially as they've shrunk from the lack of food over the past few days.

Zoe moans about how she hates cold leftovers, but I sure as hell don't mind eating more of this tomorrow. It's the best meal I ever remember having. Forget sandwiches or spaghetti bolognese; roast dinners are my favourite.

In addition, the wine flows more easily than I anticipated. I finish off my glass of red, head to the bathroom, and, when I return to the table, I find my glass full again. After my second glass, Sasha tops it up for another. Which I protest, at first, yet end up drinking anyway. With my system unused to the influx of alcohol, I slip into tipsiness by the third glass, which results in my muscles relaxing; I'm not in as much pain as I move around. I'm also significantly more joyous.

The feast continues with a serving of dessert. Freya has made some sort of honey sponge cake, which we pair with thick, creamy custard. I don't know how we fit it all in. By the end, we're all stuffed and hardly able to move. Everyone, including Zoe, is noticeably more blissful with a full belly.

Conversation around the dinner table changes throughout the meal. The more relaxed we become, the more we laugh—mostly due to the wine. Our chat started off polite and reserved. Now, since we've finished pudding, we're full-on mocking each other, swapping inappropriate stories, and getting to know one another on a more personal level.

We find out that, after a few glasses of wine, Eli certainly becomes chattier. He tells us stories from when he was in the army; the stuff he used to get up to with his squadron at his base in West London—practical jokes, drinking games, and bad wingman experiences which seem way out of character for him. I'm not shocked that he was in the military, though. He says he left as soon as he could for his mental health but doesn't go into detail, and we don't push.

Ben is the only one of us not drinking alcohol, due to his past experiences with substance abuse. He's opted for water throughout the evening. Despite this, he's still getting into the spirit of things. He's just as merry as the rest of us.

Naturally, Zoe is the opposite. It seems the more wine she consumes, the more cutting her comments become. Thankfully, we manage to ignore her, and she stops after a while, when she realises she can't get a rise out of us.

I also learn more about what everyone does for a living when the topic of work is broached. Logan vaguely states he's an engineer but doesn't go into much detail. He claims it's boring, and that he only chose that career path because it's what his father wanted for him. Ben is a youth worker, which doesn't surprise me, given his past. Freya is a chef. Again, pretty fitting. Tonight is a fine example of her cooking. As for Eli, he's obviously ex-army, but doesn't offer much else regarding his current employment. Sasha simply says she works in HR. Dawn tells us she works in sales and is between jobs at the moment. Alex is a working session musician who plays guitar and piano, which impresses me. I'm excited to hear him play sometime, although it's unlikely a piano could fit into the next crate of supplies. After Alex, Charlie unashamedly discloses that he's never needed a job because he was left a large inheritance. Though apparently, he does charity work instead, which I admire. When I'm asked, I just mumble something about being a waitress, then divert the conversation away from me by asking Charlie more about his charity work.

After we're finished with dinner, we shuffle into the living room. It's clear we're all ready to roll over and fall asleep. Except we did promise Freya and Dawn we would play some games before bed.

Attempting to play charades while tipsy is probably the funniest thing to watch. By the end, Charlie is struggling to describe *Blade Runner* and accidentally smashes into the wall, thoroughly disorientated. Then, instead of seeing if he's okay, we spend five minutes raucously laughing at him until we're all nearly sick.

After some card games, we collectively agree it's getting late. My heavy eyelids keep closing of their own volition. All day, Sasha hasn't even let me blink for more than a second because she was worried I still had water in my lungs.

Tonight has been the most fun I've had in years. If every night here was like this then I'd be content to stay in this cabin, in spite of what the last two days have put me through.

As we all drag ourselves to bed, we say our goodnights to each other. Charlie pulls me into a hug before he trudges into his and Zoe's room, a pouty look on his face. He told me earlier that sleeping in the same room as Zoe is a stressful experience, as he's afraid she'll end up suffocating him in his sleep one of these nights.

The idea of sleeping in the same room as Logan tonight has been whipping my anxiety into a frenzy all evening. The alcohol has hardly helped.

Logan follows me into our assigned bedroom and shuts the door behind us. We stand there awkwardly, unsure of how to act now the others aren't around to chaperone. This is the first time we've been alone since he returned. My tummy is fumbling, trying to process my meal as well as these foreign emotions.

'It's been a good evening, hasn't it? I think it's made up for the last few days,' Logan says, easing the tension.

'Yeah, I think that was the H.I.'s attempt at an apology for the whole *we nearly killed you both* thing.'

He breathes a laugh. 'The H.I.? You've nicknamed them?'

'The Haven Initiative is a bit of a mouthful. It's not a term of endearment. My Stockholm Syndrome isn't advancing that quickly,' I retort, throwing in an eye roll.

Needing comfort, I perch on my bed, still tense from muscle ache, and I suspect nerves as well. Silence creeps back into the room again. I know I should be asking all the questions I was waiting to bombard Logan with earlier, but the wine has fogged up my brain. How can I hold a coherent conversation with him when my mind is chucking a million different things my way, unable to grasp onto anything specific? Especially now I'm so close to him—my pulse quickening.

I'm acutely aware that I'll be alone in a bedroom, all night long, with an incredibly attractive guy, who is not only kind and attentive, but also seems just as drawn to me as I am to him. I'm eternally grateful for the twin beds. If we had to share a double, I think I'd combust. There's no way I trust myself to think clearly tonight.

'So... are you sleeping in your clothes? Because that shirt doesn't look very comfortable,' Logan murmurs, more shy than seductive.

I blush on top of my drink-induced flush. 'Erm, well, I usually sleep in my clothes.' A second after the words fall out of my mouth, I remember he doesn't know I'm homeless. 'You know... like jogging bottoms and a loose T-shirt. I—I don't like pyjamas,' I add hastily, to draw less attention to that slip-up.

'Yeah, I usually sleep in the same,' he replies, unbuttoning his light blue shirt. Immediately, I avert my gaze to the floor, flustered. It's not enough. I whirl around so my back is to him.

'Do you want me to leave the room for a bit?' I ask, slightly breathless.

'Nah, no need. You turned around so quickly then, I'm surprised you don't have whiplash,' he jokes, a smile in his voice.

'What's the alternative? I stare at you while you get undressed, like some creep?' I respond, laughing nervously. I hear the wardrobe open and close.

'Don't pretend you haven't been undressing me with your eyes. I'm not a piece of meat, you know,' Logan continues to jest, but his tone is smokier now. My insides liquify.

'The wolves would disagree on that one,' I throw back, and a laugh puffs out of him.

'You can look now,' Logan says, still chuckling. I spin back around to see he's changed into a white T-shirt and grey joggers—sexy. The short sleeves highlight the bandage wrapped around his forearm—not as sexy.

'I forgot to ask... your arm,' I mumble, pointing to the bandage.

'Six stitches and antibiotics to prevent infections. I shouldn't really have drunk anything tonight. But oh well. It's fine. Might leave a scar, but scars make cool stories, right?' Logan drops onto his bed opposite me and his knee touches mine. My attention snaps to that point of contact, my body flooding with heat. 'What I haven't had the chance to say is thank you. You saved me from that wolf,' he conveys earnestly, his eyes softly searching my face.

Panicking internally, I avoid his gaze, struggling to focus on controlling my jagged breaths.

Fiddling with the hem of my shirt, I clear my throat. 'I didn't save you. You've saved me three times now—coming back for Zoe and me, with the falling tree. You also pushed me out of the way of that wolf attack before I helped you. And then what happened at the lake today. I'm the one who needs to thank you.'

Logan frowns in apparent confusion. 'I don't remember pushing you. I must have just knocked into you when we were running. And with the tree... you only went back to rescue Zoe. So really, *we* saved her, not you. Basically, we're even. You saved me, I saved you, we all saved Zoe. Hopefully, we stick to that, and no more incidents need occur.'

This fills me with some relief. I was worried I owed him too much. But if he really wants to call it even then I won't argue.

Logan continues, 'I'm surprised you haven't asked me a million questions by now. I thought once I shut our door, I'd be grilled like a steak.'

'I've had too much wine; my brain's not catching up with my mouth. I'm sure you can guess what I want to know, anyway,' I respond, bravely knocking my knee against his.

Something flares in Logan's light eyes, darkening them. Or maybe I imagined it. 'Okay, I'll spare you the boring details. Brief version: I woke up in a hospital bed, all fixed up, and no matter how many questions I asked, or how agitated I was, nobody answered me. The nurses wouldn't speak to me. Obviously, from what I said earlier, I overheard a few things, but that's it. I didn't see anything out of the ordinary. And I have no idea where the hospital was even located,' he says hurriedly.

'Oh, that's disappointing. You really need to work on your story-telling,' I tease. Although I *am* obviously dissatisfied with his answer. I was hoping he'd find the missing piece of this frustrating puzzle. Or at least a clue. 'So, all you found out was that they may have a rebel trying to bring them down?'

'Mm-hmm. It was a wasted opportunity, I guess. They had me locked in a room so I couldn't go snooping around, unfortunately.' Sighing, he hunches his shoulders, his lips pursing.

'Oh well, at least you're better. I was worried you'd stopped breathing at one point. I had to hold my hand up to your nose to check,' I disclose sheepishly, omitting the fact that I slid into his bed and snuggled with him while he was unconscious.

'Yeah, I'm fine now. How are you feeling? You must be exhausted after everything you've been through. I was gone for less than a day and you managed to get yourself into that much trouble? I'll have to watch you like a hawk, just in case one swoops in and tries to fly you back to its nest or something,' he remarks, amused.

'Um, I'm feeling a little better. Knackered, but hopefully by morning, I'll be more myself,' I answer, shifting my weight on the edge of the mattress.

Logan flashes his eyebrows. 'Yeah, you'll be you, with a mild hang-over.'

Both chuckling, our eyes meet, and the sound of our mirth tapers off. There's electricity behind his stare. My head was already swimming thanks to the wine, but now, my giddiness soars to new heights. My cheeks relish the heat of this moment, and my heart becomes an untamed beast—wildly bucking inside my chest. Swallowing hard, I snap up to my feet, separating myself from his thrilling gaze and our entwined legs.

'I need to dress for bed,' I mumble, opening the wardrobe.

Without another word, Logan twists towards the wall so I can dress with a modicum of privacy. I pick out a black T-shirt and grey joggers from my side of the wardrobe. Swiftly and awkwardly, I change into them, wincing as my stiff, tender muscles strive to work effectively.

'A massage might help your muscle ache,' Logan mentions, almost too quietly to hear. When I don't answer straight away, he adds, 'You could ask Sasha or Freya tomorrow. I'm sure they wouldn't mind helping you out.'

I'm still too stunned to speak. My mouth is open but uncooperative. At first, I thought he was offering to massage me right this second. The idea alone sets my body on fire. The image in my mind is so clear—Logan, straddling my hips as I lie face-down on the bed, kneading my bare back; his firm hands sliding up my spine and down again.

Something hard of his pressing against my arse...

Fuck. What is happening to me?

Before I can melt into a puddle, I shake off the intrusive thought and ignore the excitable butterflies dipping into the heat of my core.

The room is silent again when I slip under the covers, hoping my face isn't as red as it feels. He does the same. We're lying in separate beds, but our proximity still feels weirdly intimate.

'I have got one question,' I breathe suddenly. Logan turns onto his side so we're facing each other. 'How did you manage to reach me just in time today? I didn't hear a helicopter before I fell into the water.' As soon as the question is out, hanging in the air, I realise it sounds more like an accusation.

'They didn't drop me off near the cabin. I assume they couldn't be bothered to start trapping all of you in here, or sedating people again, after what happened to you. As I was walking back, I heard a splash, so I ran. I was only a few minutes' walk away. When I reached the glade, I saw Ben unconscious in the boat and bubbles in the water. I dove in not knowing it was you who had fallen in until I pulled you up.' He frowns. 'Why did you ask me that?' There's a shadow of hurt in his eyes.

Guilt churns in my belly. 'I only thought it was lucky, that's all,' I cover. I don't want Logan to think I don't trust him and his motivations, because I do. Not one hundred per cent, but I don't even trust myself one hundred per cent, especially around him.

This explanation seems to undo the damage because he offers me a soft smile before murmuring, 'All right. Well... you should get some sleep. Hopefully, tomorrow will be a better day for you.'

'Yeah, you too.' I return the smile, my butterflies finally dozing.

Logan switches off the light then flips over onto his back. I raise the duvet to my chin, squirming to get more comfortable.

'Goodnight,' Logan whispers warmly.

'Until morning light,' I whisper back with equal verve. My eyelids are so heavy that they succumb to the weight almost instantly. Taking a deep breath, I wish for the kind of peace only sleep can bring.

Drifting in and out of consciousness, I lazily ponder.

I've come a long way since I was dropped into this place. Initially, I was so eager to fight and escape. In contrast, all I want to do now is spend more time with the others—swapping stories, sharing meals, laughing together, and generally learning more about them as people—friends.

I guess I'm learning a lot about myself, too.

Chapter 21

Week Two

'Ruby!'

As I jolt awake and sit bolt upright, my face smashes into something spongy and cold.

There's an eruption of laughter from all corners of my bedroom. I jerk my head back from a frosted cake held up by Charlie, who's silently laughing to the point of tears because my face is literally *caked* with white buttercream.

'Happy 31st birthday!' Charlie squeaks out between giggles.

After wiping the frosting from my eyes, I learn that everyone (minus Zoe) is in on the prank. They start singing *Happy Birthday* to me but stop as soon as I throw my first handful of cake their way.

'You absolute bastards! You all better run,' I growl in good humour before I chase them down the stairs, armed with handfuls of cakey buttercream. I can't help laughing along when I catch Charlie and smear some into his precious hair. Annoyingly, I fail to grab Logan or Sasha before they dash out the front door of the cabin. I won't nab anyone now they've all escaped outside. But it's still fun to try.

For a reason I don't fully understand, I let slip to Dawn a few days ago, when we were making lunch together, that today is my birthday. Instantly regretting it, I swore her to secrecy. But I knew from her sweet little placating smile that everyone would know within the hour.

I don't celebrate arbitrary milestones in my life. There's no point. You can't really have a party for one, and it's pretty pathetic to buy yourself a present because no one else will. At least at Christmas, there were charities that received donated gifts for the homeless. The rare times I'd ever engage with people were when I'd slink into a CCTV-monitored day centre to have a small roast dinner with a load of other homeless wanderers, who also couldn't stand being alone and hungry on Christmas Day. We'd each receive a small gift, like hygiene essentials, or second-hand clothes, and we'd sit there making small talk, simply appreciating the respite from the cold, dreading when the day centre closed its doors, because then we'd have to face our pitifully lonely reality once again.

After Dawn let the cat out of the birthday bag, they all swore to me they wouldn't make a huge deal of it. Obviously, they're all fucking liars. I *will* plot my revenge. I'll sneak salt in their tea or pour ice on someone in the shower; one way or another, they'll get what's coming to them.

Until then, I'll lick the rest of the frosting and cake crumbs off my fingers because it tastes fucking amazing.

Today marks the end of our first week in the cabin. Only seven days to go before it's all over and we find out why we've been stolen from our lives so mysteriously, as promised by the H.I.

The last few days have been near-death-experience free, thank fuck. It's been uneventful in terms of drama. Even Zoe has calmed down with her tirade of verbal abuse against us.

Another crate full of supplies dropped from the sky the other day, when we were running low on food. It even had a DVD player in it, with some old films from the fifties, which we've been watching as a group every night, snuggled up together on the living room floor, cocooned in our duvets. There were also several books crammed in the crate. Yesterday, I read *The Handmaid's Tale* by Margaret Atwood. Unsurprisingly, I've had limited access to books in recent years. Though as a teen, reading provided an escape—a hiding place, tucked between the pages of a book. The main characters were interesting enough to love and root for. Unlike me.

Ben braved the boat again; he's managed to catch a fish or two for us each night. Since my near-drowning, I've stayed far away from the edge of the lake. That being said, when Ben does go fishing, with Logan or one of the others, I help to keep watch by the cabin, just in case the rebel reappears. Instead of making use of myself where I'm use*less*, I've ventured out with Logan, Sasha, and Eli into the forest, foraging for berries from the bushes Sasha found. Freya bakes delicious muffins with them.

The days here are surprisingly relaxing for a lesson on survival. We hang out, we prepare meals together, and Logan is even teaching me how to cook. Then, in the evenings, we play games and watch a film. It's the nights which haven't been so pleasant; I keep having nightmares. Actually, it's more of those disturbing lost memories resurfacing again, I suspect.

One night, I woke the whole cabin up when I started screaming in my sleep. That one wasn't exactly a lost memory, only a purposefully repressed one.

I'm eleven, ringing my front doorbell after walking home from school because I forgot my key. No one answers, so I climb in through the open back window, assuming Mum must be out food shopping. But her car is on the driveway, *I think, perplexed. The house is cold—empty of its usual warmth. I call for her but she doesn't answer.* Asleep, maybe?

Feeling a little mischievous, I decide to scare her awake by jumping onto her bed, loudly announcing my return. After slipping my shoes off, I creep up the stairs, grinning to myself. But, before I reach halfway, I stop dead. Mum's bare feet are peeking out from behind the bannister at the top of the stairs. As I force myself to climb a couple more steps, legs trembling, the rest of her body soon comes into view. She's resting face-down on the landing, unmoving.

The urgency of the situation dawning on me, I scramble up the rest of the stairs to her. But it's already too late; her skin is stone-cold, lips blue, eyes unseeing. Her body is an empty shell. And all I do is keep screaming and screaming for her to wake up.

She never does.

I haven't relived that memory for many years. I thought I'd pushed it down deep enough to forget. When Logan woke me, and the others ran in to see what all the fuss was about, I had to make up a lie about wolves chasing me because I still haven't told them much about my life before the cabin. I especially didn't want to describe to them the day I found my mum dead. I don't plan on speaking about it—*her*—to anyone. Ever.

The other nightmares have been recurring. The one where the shadow man saved me from the attack by my alleyway resurfaced again. There's also a new one: the time I witnessed a man dying outside a club one night. He had overdosed on some drug, and I desperately tried to keep him alive, but I failed. He died in my arms before paramedics could arrive. A hooded man with a blurred face appeared, hoping to aid me in resuscitation. But once I knew there was no saving the dead man, I ran, tears in my eyes and no air in my lungs. I can see why I buried that memory—I woke up crying with a mixture of grief and guilt.

Logan wanted to comfort me—calm me down. He tried enveloping me in his arms, but I pushed him away, insisting it was only a bad dream I didn't want to discuss. He didn't press me on it, so I quickly rolled over and pretended to go back to sleep. I could feel his eyes on me for a long time afterwards. I reckon he also feigned sleep as he looked as worn-out as I did that morning. As far as I'm aware, he didn't mention it to anyone, which I very much appreciate.

Now, I'm afraid to sleep. Luckily, last night was dreamless and memory free.

This week, I've bonded more with the women in our group. Sasha is easy to hang out with because we have similar personalities. Whereas I've had to make more of an effort with Freya and Dawn. They're so much friendlier than I am. They also like to ask a lot more questions. Which, at first, I was struggling to dodge, but now, I simply give them a yes or no answer with little detail. They've come to realise it's better not to ask me too many personal questions and to talk more about themselves. In turn, I've learnt that I'm a patient listener.

Since I was already closer to Logan, Charlie, and Ben, I strove to get to know Alex and Eli on a more personal level this week, too. Alex is similar to Dawn; he's very talkative, and a genuinely nice guy. He carries our conversations. Eli, on the other hand, is shy and tentative. Still, after some awkward starts, trying to spend time with him—forcing it even—he's beginning to seek me out for company to sit quietly together and read. Sometimes, Sasha and I will encourage him to read aloud to us on the decking of the cabin, when no one else is around. He doesn't seem to mind that.

The only time Eli really comes out of his shell is when he gulps down a few glasses of wine. We were supplied with five bottles in the last crate, although I avoided drinking any more of it. Going to bed each night with Logan, I have to remain in control of myself. A clear head is essential when I'm lying in a bed adjacent to him, hearing him talk of the things he's passionate about. Most nights, the urge to crawl into his bed again is almost irresistible. To rest my head on his chest with my body pressed against his... fuck. It's tempting. However, with him conscious, it seems a lot scarier to consider actually doing. If I throw alcohol into the mix, I'm afraid I wouldn't be afraid anymore.

On the flip side, hugging Charlie is as easy as breathing now. It's a part of our morning and nightly routine. Though I try not to indulge him too often because people have begun commenting on how cute we are together. Charlie laughs it off while I scowl and give them the finger. Ben only says it to tease me; whereas Logan ends up leaving the room whenever Charlie and I act chummier with each other. It makes me feel a little guilty. So now, when Logan is present, I don't pander to Charlie's friendly affection as much.

After ridding myself of cake frosting in the shower, I wrap a cream, fluffy towel around my freshly clean body. I scrunch excess water out of my curls over the sink before I leave the bathroom.

Mortified at the idea of being caught in only a towel, I make sure no one else is on the landing, then dart towards my bedroom.

I've successfully avoided anyone seeing me after a shower, thus far. Others haven't been as lucky. Yesterday, I was so flustered when I ran into

Ben—his massive muscles gleaming with water—that I nearly walked into my door. He just laughed at me.

Rushing into my bedroom, I don't notice it's occupied at first. I shut the door and startle when I turn to see Logan hanging up clean clothes in the wardrobe. I almost bumped right into him. Jumping back, I grab the tucked corner of my towel as it slips down a little, revealing more of my chest.

Logan stiffens, dropping the jumper he was about to hang. 'Fuck,' he breathes, his eyes going wide as they track down my body. His Adam's apple dunks. That's the first time I've heard him swear. It does strange things to my body. All surprisingly pleasurable.

We stare at each other for a blinking beat, searching our rattled minds for an appropriate response. I watch his eyes darken as if a less-than-innocent thought crossed his mind.

Clearing his throat, Logan closes the wardrobe door then fists a hand in his hair. 'I—I didn't know... I'm sorry. I wasn't waiting here for you to come in... you know... like that,' he claims, his gaze dropping to my cleavage for a split second before he looks away, searching for anything else to focus on. His cheeks redden and he rubs his neck, his overall demeanour awkward.

'Erm, no worries,' I mutter, my body heating despite the cool air chilling my damp skin. Feeling exposed, I hunch my shoulders, the situation finally sinking in. I'm standing in front of Logan in only a small towel, enclosed in this tiny bedroom, with him looking at me as if I'm temptation incarnate. 'I'll go back to the bathroom to dress. I just need to grab some clothes.' My voice comes out raspy and unsure.

'No. No. I'll go. I—I just need to squeeze past you.' He points to the door I'm blocking.

'Oh, sorry. Yeah,' I mumble, flattening against the wardrobe to let him by.

Logan steps towards the door but his foot catches on the jumper he dropped. Tripping, he knocks into me, my hands automatically reaching out to steady him, leaving my towel unattended. Its corner dislodges from its position. Before it can fall out of place, Logan grasps hold of it to keep me covered, his fingers grazing my cleavage, only an inch away from my nipple, which has suddenly become taut.

His touch is a lightning bolt through my veins. I gasp, unable to move a muscle.

'Sorry,' he whispers, his chest heaving as rapidly as mine. 'That was accidental, I swear.'

'I know,' I squeak, hyper-aware of the fact that, each time I drag in a husky breath, his fingers brush against my flushed skin, again and again. I make no effort to slow them.

'You need to take this from me.' His rougher voice is almost pleading, his gaze lowering to my lips, then further down to where his hand is placed, keeping the towel from revealing me. He clenches his jaw, his throat working harder.

Coming to my senses, I take the corner of the towel from him and tuck it back in tightly. 'Thanks. That would have been embarrassing.'

'Hmm,' Logan hums absent-mindedly as his eyes linger on the corner of my towel. He stays close. Close enough that I feel his warm, exhaled breath skate across the red-tinged skin of my chest, leaving goosebumps in its wake.

My tummy coils tightly, something hot and dark inside of me yearning for attention—seeking to be released.

'I should go,' Logan murmurs, yet he doesn't make a move. Only his gaze lifts slightly, not to my eyes—to my lips, which impulsively I take between my teeth.

Unable to form words, I produce a small noise of agreement. Do I want him to go? There's a repressed part of me that wishes he hadn't caught my towel in time.

When Logan's almost-black eyes finally find mine again, there's an ember of what I hope is lust smouldering in them. He steals another moment to study my expression, his lips parting for the flick of his tongue as it wets his lips. His probing look causes me to automatically flinch away.

Whatever Logan finds on my face in that unfortunate, reflexive moment immediately extinguishes our flicker of flame. He lurches back, and without another word, hastily exits the bedroom, shutting the door on his way out.

Expelling pent-up air, I deflate back against the wardrobe, struggling to process what's just occurred between us.

For a moment, I thought he was going to kiss me. Maybe even rip my towel away.

Fuck. Why is that idea making me sweat? I fan myself with my hand, my pulse still charged with electricity.

Don't think too deeply about it, Ruby. Most men would have had that reaction to any woman in the same situation. It doesn't mean he likes you. It doesn't even mean he's attracted to you, I tell myself, the cold creeping back in, making me shudder.

Calm enough to move again, I brush off what I hoped that meant and accept the more logical rationale.

That was simply an awkward run-in between friends. Nothing more.

Successfully burying that indecent incident with Logan, I finish getting ready for the day and then head downstairs for breakfast. Luckily, Logan hasn't mentioned what happened to anyone and we manage to continue as if he never saw me in a towel. Hopefully, him practically touching my boobs will be a long-forgotten memory by the end of the day.

After breakfast, Ben, Charlie, Logan and I prepare for our journey into the forest. Ben suggested setting up snares in the hopes of catching rabbits or squirrels. He likes his meat for dinner, and he didn't have much luck with fishing yesterday. We also don't know when the next crate is coming. If there is a next one.

Alex, Sasha, and Freya are planning to fish this afternoon. None of them are keen on the idea of catching and killing fluffy little animals. I'm not particularly, either. Saying that, as long as it's quick and clean then I'm all for hunting for supper. It's not like there's a supermarket around the corner.

When I was younger, I was a vegetarian for years, after I learnt where pork actually came from, and I had a deep love for the film *Babe*. But living on the street, I couldn't be too picky. If I had the choice between a half-eaten bacon sandwich left on a park bench, or going hungry for another day, I'd stuff that porky little critter into my guilty yet ravenous mouth.

At first, we search around the edges of the forest, to see if there are any signs of animal habitation. We wander around for about an hour, not finding much, so we decide to journey further.

Anxiety takes root in my chest as we delve deeper into the forest. The berry bushes are usually only a fifteen-minute walk from the glade. When we've come out here before, I felt as though I could run back to safety within minutes if anything happened. This is the first time, since the failed escape attempt, that we've ventured nearly two miles away from the safety of the cabin. My heart rate increases and I start to sweat despite our slow and steady pace.

'This looks to be an alright spot to set some traps. The ground's even, and there are a few bushes and stuff to cover 'em, like,' Ben suggests, crouching down and rustling the bushes, clearly hoping something will spring out.

'Have you done this before?' Charlie asks him.

'Nah, mate. Seen it on survival shows, though. Bear Grylls is God,' Ben answers, organising his materials.

Logan kneels beside Ben to assist. Charlie and I are on lookout duty, as we're the useless ones.

'I really should have used the bathroom before we left, but Zoe was taking so long in the shower,' Charlie whispers to me, squirming with discomfort.

I point to a place down a grassy slope. 'There's a big group of trees and bushes over there.'

Charlie smirks as he passes me. 'Brilliant. I'll be back in a minute. No need to pine after me while I'm gone.'

'Oh, Pan, I don't know how I'll cope a whole two minutes without you,' I respond sarcastically, my eyes rolling skyward.

Charlie strides down the slight decline and then stumbles on a root. He recovers quickly, but I'm already laughing at him. 'I meant to do that. Anything to make you laugh, Hazy,' he claims with an exaggerated grin.

Hazy is Charlie's new nickname for me. He started calling me *Miss Hayes* when he addressed me because I said he was posh once. Now, he's moved on to *Hazy*, as apparently, that's how I looked after I came to from my various unconscious moments. I'm just glad it's not something like *Zombie*, or worse.

269

Scoffing, I shake my head at his false arrogance. And when he disappears behind the trees, I glance behind me; Logan and Ben are furiously working on the snares.

After two minutes tick by without Charlie's return, worry creeps in, so I call his name. Ben swiftly chides me for scaring off our potential dinner. So instead, I shuffle down the slope towards the cluster of trees to find my lost boy.

'Pan?' I whisper harshly. 'Are you decent?'

I merge into the denser forest. Then, all of a sudden, a hand reaches around a thick tree trunk to yank me behind it.

'Shh, be quiet,' Charlie whispers, clasping his other hand over my mouth before I can call out to the others. He lets me go as soon as I stop struggling.

'Why? What is it?' I question, impatient.

'You need to see something. I don't think the others should know. Promise me that you won't tell anyone else what you see,' he implores. His usually jovial face has turned serious.

'Okay, I promise. Just tell me before Logan realises we're gone and comes to find us,' I push. My heart beats tenfold, either due to excitement or fear. Probably a bit of both.

Charlie leads me through the trees and stops in front of an old, ragged oak with long winding branches that brush the forest floor.

I don't notice it straight away; it's the glint of the sharp steel surface which catches my eye. At the top of the trunk, stuck in deep, is a knife. The same sort of knife we lost in the wolf attack last week. Under the knife are lines of writing, cut into the bark. A chill ripples down my spine as I read it.

Trust no one. Not your friends. Not real. All lies. Death is only escape.

I stare blankly at the words for a minute, struggling to comprehend the message. Charlie snaps me out of my trance, whipping me around to face him.

'Ruby, I heard Logan calling for you. We must rush back before anyone else spots this. We shouldn't speak of it until we're alone later, right?'

Slowly, I nod in agreement.

I'm too stunned and confused to attempt to decipher it now, anyway. Also, we've already been missing for an extended period, and Logan is on his way. Comprehension can wait.

Charlie and I jog back through the trees, hand-in-hand. As we emerge into the clearing, we nearly collide with Logan.

'Where did you two go?' Logan demands, suspicion rife in his voice.

'We thought we saw a rabbit!' Charlie says in a rush. 'We got over-excited and chased after it. It wasn't long before we realised it was just a fat bird.' He shrugs. 'It flew away. Shocking, I know.' He forces a smile.

Logan frowns rather sceptically, but then his expression relaxes, and he too shrugs. 'Unlucky. Maybe next time you see a *rabbit*, you call us for help.' He shoots me a penetrating look, and I notice him linger on the word 'rabbit' like he doesn't believe the story. He probably thinks we snuck away for a moment alone together. The thought makes me blush, which I'm sure only adds to his idea. Hastily, I rip my hand away from Charlie's, hoping I haven't fuelled the fire.

We all walk back to Ben; he's finishing up on the second snare. 'Oi, what'd you think? Logue and I managed to make Bear Grylls look like a bleeding novice while yous two love-birds were busy sneaking off like naughty teenagers,' Ben teases, elbowing me lightly.

I shoot Ben the deadliest stare I can muster before I push him away playfully. Although secretly, my intention is to knock him over. I catch a glimpse of Logan; with a prominent scowl, he quickly strides away from us, fists clenching at his sides.

'Come on—we need to set more traps,' Logan commands, stamping through a bush. Why do I get the impression he's imagining that bush is Charlie's face?

Seething, I throw Ben a scathing look. He grits his teeth awkwardly, knowing he's caused some trouble. Then he follows Logan's manmade path. Charlie and I share a worried glance before we trudge after them.

Anyway, even if our little bird story wasn't that believable, and they now think they have more apparent 'evidence' of my speculated 'secret relationship' with Charlie, I'd rather they suspect that than the truth. *Do* you *even know what the truth is anymore*? I ask myself, my chest tight. What the message suggests is that the comfort I've been enjoying here is not to be trusted. That these people—whom I now regard as friends—are not to be trusted.

What a shitty birthday this is turning out to be. Not that I'm surprised. I'm used to shitty birthdays. But this is definitely not the best start to week two.

Chapter 22

Spiralling

We set up a series of snares on the way back to the cabin. We plan to return first thing tomorrow to collect any animals unfortunate enough to be caught. I, however, don't intend to journey into the forest again after what Charlie and I found. The rebel likely left the message. The rebel who tried to *kill* me.

As we travel back through the trees, the sensation of being watched—*hunted*—causes the little hairs on the back of my neck to prickle. I'm projecting the appearance of calm so Logan and Ben won't suspect anything, but it feels as though I'm trapped out here—caged by my own fear.

Inside, I'm rattling the bars—trembling and on the verge of breaking.

Logan is too perceptive about me. He keeps glancing my way, his worried eyes searching for any crack in my fortified defence. I instinctively react by dropping my gaze to the forest floor, my arms wrapping around myself to subdue any nervous twitches. Thankfully, he hasn't said anything... yet. I'll have to avoid him for the rest of the day. Although sharing the same small bedroom makes that more difficult. *Never mind. Jump over that hurdle when you come to it.*

Another reason I'd rather not check the snares tomorrow is that, since reading the message, I've started empathising with whatever animal becomes tangled in those traps—the poor thing being so terrified and alone. I know how it feels to have the looming presence of death shadow my steps. The thought of witnessing a death, however swift and clean, turns my stomach more than before. I can't deny that I'll still eat a nice rabbit stew, though; killing and eating the spoils are two separate things for me. Like I said before: survival trumps guilt in my world. I have to push any empathy back into that pit of useless things my mind throws back at me sometimes.

It turns out that London and Arkinwood Forest aren't as dissimilar as I first thought. Each is a wilderness in its own right. I've learnt to adapt and survive in both. I've overcome the obstacles which have held me back—things like emotions. All of them are regularly stuffed back in the useless pit. Anger and resentment are regular escapees, though.

Ben, on the other hand, seems to have an even stronger survival instinct than I do. He's not squeamish; he'd kill a fluffy little bunny for food without a second thought. Not because he's lacking empathy: he's a sensitive guy under his tough exterior. It's because we need him to be that person for us: the kind of person who puts his friends first and gets the necessary done. He's been in his element out here. I'm lucky to have people like him in this situation who are willing to do the dirty work for me.

I say that I'm lucky to have them, like they're on my team. But, if I were to believe the message I read on the old oak, then they're not really my friends.

If they're not your friends, then... what are they?

I'm still stuck on this question when we reach the outer edge of the glade. The others are milling around the decking, laughing together. These people I've come to care about—they could all be liars. The bonds I have with them may not be genuine.

That thought makes my heart hide, shivering in the pit of my stomach. Of course, I don't want to accept the message is true.

Can I really believe that Ben, Logan, or Sasha would lie to me after I've grown so close to them? Can I imagine someone as kind and innocent as Dawn being anything other than herself? Someone as outspoken and honest as Freya being complicit? A man as deep and sturdy as Eli being fickle and fraudulent? That none of them really care about me after everything we've been through this week?

Zoe is the only one who has ever been unkind to me. That could mean she's the only truthful person here. I'm so confused. I need to discuss this with Charlie as soon as possible—privately.

It's strange that I automatically trust Charlie. Maybe it's because he automatically trusted me in spite of the message warning him not to trust anyone. He showed it to me, regardless.

This would have been easy to accept a week ago. Now, looking at Ben and Logan, I'm struggling to imagine that they could be faking our friendships, or even be my enemies. It's unbearable to think true—an impossible notion.

But apparently, it's not. So, to keep myself sane, my guard will have to snap back into place—my emotions will need to be forced back into that pit deep inside of me.

That's the only way I'm going to survive this.

'Hey, did you catch anything?' Dawn asks as we approach them on the decking. Her tight-lipped smile indicates that she wants the answer to be no.

'Nah, they probably heard us, so we'll go back first thing tomorrow,' Ben informs her, passing Freya the bag of berries we collected today.

Dawn struggles to suppress a smile. She doesn't even like the idea of killing fish, let alone cute little bunnies. How can I believe someone so empathetic could have negative intentions towards me? Surely I'm more important to her than a fish? Or I'm completely wrong and she's actually a ruthless hunter—the sweet vegetarian thing is all an act.

'We wrangled a few fish for dinner. Who wants to help me cook them tonight?' Freya asks, her baby blue eyes settling on me. 'Ruby? I can take over the cooking lessons from Logan?' An encouraging smile brightens her doll-like face.

Why me? I wonder, my suspicion overloading. She could have waited for someone to offer, but instead, she asked me. Does she want to gain my trust? Teach me how to cook to keep up this bonding charade?

Shit. I can't do this. I can't be around them. I'm analysing every word they say. I can't even look at them without questioning every expression.

Panic incites a riot inside me. And, before I know it, I'm barging past Freya into the cabin. I dart up the stairs and race towards the only room with a lock: the bathroom. I hurry to shut the door, imprisoning myself. Then, I slide onto the cold, hard tiles of the floor. To clear my head, I inhale deeply, numerous times.

It's impossible to hide how the message has affected me. It's spooked me—brought my fears and insecurities rushing back to the surface. I can't pretend I'm all right. The doubts are infesting my brain. And now, they all know something is wrong—that maybe I know too much.

My head aching, I release my curls from their messy bun and run my fingers through the roots, which calms me a little. I can't stay in this bathroom forever. Sooner rather than later, I'll have to face them and make up some excuse for my strange behaviour.

A soft knock at the door makes me jump. 'It's Logan. Can I come in?'

'No! Erm... I'm just about to hop in the shower,' I lie unconvincingly. *He knows you already had a shower this morning, you twit.*

'Come on, Ruby. I know something's up. Charlie said you told him you were feeling sick, but that's not true, is it? Something's worrying you.' Logan's grounding voice is muffled slightly by the wood separating us.

I knew he was going to do this—check on me—try to coax me back out of my protective shell. I can't hide from him.

'The others believe what Charlie said, and I promise I won't tell them any differently. You can trust me,' Logan implores, pleadingly.

'*Can I, though?*' I reply in my mind.

Usually, I always go with what my gut tells me. My gut—or instincts—tell me that Logan *does* honestly care about my well-being. I've looked into those magnetic blue eyes and I've *felt* a connection. That can't be faked. Can it? My stomach churns. Now I really *do* feel sick.

Sighing, I push to my feet and tentatively open the door, still not sure if I should let him in. With a crinkled brow, Logan stands there for a moment, measuring me. I search his eyes to work out if he's genuine—if our connection is real. He appears nothing more than concerned. He must sense I'm conflicted because he doesn't rush in. He lingers in the doorway, waiting for an invite.

If I close the door on Logan now, then I'm deciding to throw away what we might have. And I'm afraid he'll think he means nothing to me if I don't confide in him. On the other hand, I promised Charlie I wouldn't tell anyone what we saw until we discussed it. Charlie trusts me to keep my word and I don't want him to think that he's wrong about me. So, I can either shut the door, lie to Logan about being ill, which he can see through—hurting him. Or, I can break my promise to Charlie, which might make him doubt our friendship. Maybe I can find a compromise—let Logan know I do trust him without explaining my fear.

Standing aside, I allow room for Logan to pass. With relief evident in his expression, he steps in, and I shut the door after him, locking it for good measure.

'Ruby, you're scaring me. What's—'

Before Logan can finish his sentence, I spin around and launch myself at him, my arms winding around his waist, my head hitting his chest. Shocked and unprepared, he stumbles back a step. But then, after a short beat, his arms wrap around me, too.

I bury my face into his jumper and sigh, taking in his pleasantly smoky scent. He must have been the one to light the fireplace before breakfast today. I had wondered who came down early and I remember that yesterday, I had complained about being cold in the mornings. He warmed the place up for me. The realisation has my heart unfurling in my chest. How could I have doubted him? How could I have thought for one second that our friendship wasn't real?

Neither of us speaks. We simply stand in the middle of the bathroom in our locked embrace. He tenderly strokes my hair before he kisses the top of my head. Closing my eyes, I accept defeat. I needed this. I needed him to comfort me—to be my friend.

Warmth spreads through my entire body, my expanding heart beating faster as butterflies stir in my belly. It's hard to think of Logan as purely a friend when my body reacts this way to him. Nevertheless, I can't allow myself to indulge in the fantasy of us. Especially now, when I'm so confused about everything else.

I'm unable to say how long we stand in each other's arms, but it's long enough that my feet start to ache.

Reluctantly, I break away from Logan and we smile shyly at each other. I'm surprised I'm not more embarrassed about my bold show of affection. And even more astonishingly, I'm not worrying that I've revealed some vulnerable part of myself to him. I simply enjoyed our moment together.

'I'm guessing you don't want to talk about it yet. That's all right. I only wanted to be here for you,' he says softly, his eyes still sparkling with concern. Despite that, he's resigned to let me keep my worries to myself, for now.

'I'll be okay. Thank you. I'm glad you were here.' I sweep the weight of my hair off my shoulders and rub the back of my warm, damp neck. 'I wonder why hugs comfort people so much. It's strange, huh?' I ask rhetorically, not expecting an actual answer.

Logan reaches out to push a rogue curl away from my face. 'Well, I guess sometimes, you need something real to hold onto when you feel like you may be spiralling.'

'Yeah,' I whisper, offering him a coy smile.

Logan really hit the nail on the head with that one: *something real*. I'm choosing to trust the safe, comforting feeling of being in his arms. I'm as certain as I can be that he wouldn't purposely hurt me. During our embrace, the sound of his rapid heart fluttering filled my head and my heart with hope. Also, come to think of it, his breath was just as uneven as my own. He must have some genuine affection for me. There's no actor *that* good.

As we lock eyes, my tummy does a backflip. I swallow thickly and again choose to ignore our obvious attraction. *Not now, Ruby. Not when you're this vulnerable.*

Logan's regular dimpled smirk reappears. 'So, how violently sick are we saying you were?' His tone is lighter.

'We can't make it sound too bad. I still want dinner,' I answer, and we laugh.

Fighting to forget the rebel's message, I follow Logan downstairs. It's almost impossible to force all my doubts to the back of my mind. Suspicion lingers when the others seem overly worried about my fake sickness. I say I'm feeling better and pretend to laugh with them at my unlucky streak of health issues since being here.

Charlie is also subdued; he's not his natural jolly self. Even *he* can't act like nothing is wrong.

Later, Ben mentions that Charlie is not being as annoying as usual, and Charlie worms his way out of it by saying he might have caught my fake sickness. I try not to let my eyes wander to Charlie as often as I want, just in case anyone notices our pained looks at each other. Plus, every time I glimpse his uncharacteristically sombre face, I'm reminded of what the message said, and my charade falters.

The rest of the afternoon is a blur. I'm unable to focus on any conversations. It's deliberate. Not paying attention means that I don't have to overthink anything they say. I mostly read on the decking with Eli. I manage to immerse myself in another world, far away from here.

Today, I picked up *The Hobbit* by J.R.R. Tolkien. But, when I reach the middle of the story, I start to envy Bilbo and the friendships he develops with his companions as they journey through the woods of Middle Earth. That's when I quickly shut the book and decide that maybe reading isn't such a good idea after all.

Heart dragging low, I trudge back inside the cabin and place the half-read book on the near-empty shelves. Continuing, I take a seat at the dining table to watch Sasha, Freya, and Alex cook dinner. Then, when dinner is served, I convince everyone I'm well enough to eat with them. Despite being hungry, I only end up playing with my food, moving it around my plate while I listen to the others talk and laugh.

Logan made sure that he sat next to me. He went as far as to move Dawn's plate down a setting. He even dragged my chair closer to his—while I was *sitting* in it—which did funny things to my lower abdomen. Now, I keep catching him in my peripheral vision, assessing me, his brow furrowed. My reluctance to confide in him is clearly eating away at his own peace of mind. I'd be feeling the same way if I didn't know what was torturing Charlie, if he *had* kept that message to himself.

'Ruby, did you hear me?' Freya asks from across the table.

I snap out of my dissociated state to look up at her in bewilderment. 'Sorry?'

'I know you didn't want your birthday mentioned again, but last night we all made you a card when you went upstairs for a nap,' she reveals, an excited smile stretching the freckles on her cheeks.

'Not all of us,' Zoe interjects, rolling her eyes.

'Those of us who matter did,' Sasha adds, sneering at Zoe.

Freya passes me a decorated white card that's folded in two. For a moment, I wonder where they got the resources to make this, then I remember that the last crate had some art supplies in it.

Surprise has me hesitating for a heartbeat before I slowly reach out to accept it. When the card is in my hands, I examine the front of it. Someone has drawn an elaborate picture of the cabin, with smoke billowing out of the chimney, and people reading on the decking. It appears to be an artist's depiction of Sasha, Eli, and myself; I recognise my curly hair. There are also people fishing by the lake: Freya, with her fiery locks, and perhaps the others are Ben and Logan. I spot Dawn, Alex, and Charlie in the corner, lounging under a tree, having a picnic. We're all drawn in the scene. Even Zoe is visible in the window of the cabin, watching us with a moody look on her face. A burst of laughter nearly escapes me at that.

'Eli's an amazing artist, isn't he?' Sasha asks proudly.

In awe, I look to Eli, who stiffens at the compliment. He touches his face, his gaze lowered. His dark skin conceals the blush I know is heating his cheeks.

'This is beautiful,' I convey to him. And he mumbles his thanks while he stares down at his twiddling thumbs.

'Wait until you see the inside,' Dawn says, smiling widely.

I open the card. Inside, there's various messages from each of them. I read them from the top:

Happy, happy birthday, Ruby!!! I hope we can make the day special for you. I'm so pleased I met you (despite the circumstances) and that I can call you my friend through all of this. Lots of love, Dawn xxxxxxx

Hey, Ruby! Enjoy your birthday. I know it will be a hard task because you're too cool for birthdays, but you should at least try to accept that it's happening, whether you like it or not. Much love, Alex :)

I hope your 31st year in this world brings you nothing but happiness and luck. It hasn't had the best start, being trapped in this place. But seeing how you've handled yourself so far, I have faith that you'll be okay, and tackle whatever is thrown your way in future. Eli.

Happy birthday, sweetie. I'm sure you'll hate me saying that, but just deal with it. I will celebrate your birthday even if you refuse to. Seriously, though, I really admire everything I've seen you do in the short time I've known you. Whatever happens to us, I know I can count on you. You're a star. Love Freya xxx

Rubes, I'm sorry that we've done this to you. It wasn't my idea. I hate birthdays, too. Although I'm glad I have this chance to tell you how much you've inspired me. I think you can relate to finding mushy things like this easier to write down than to say out loud. You've been so brave, and I aspire to be as capable as you are in tough situations. I feel as though I've finally found someone I can moan to without judgement. I hope that whatever's waiting for us (after this shitty cabin) doesn't ruin the little family we've created here, and we remain good friends. Sasha x

Alright, love, I know it's your birthday and all that, but please, don't get over-excited. We don't want you to keel over again. You know I enjoy torturing you, and today's gonna be no different. You might even suffer more abuse. So, prepare yourself for a rinsing and ready that awkward embarrassed face you do. The one I'm sure you're doing right now, reading this. Love Ben. P.S. Charlie's next, and I'm sure your heart's about to flutter. P.P.S. It took me ages to write this—Dyslexia is a fucking pain in the arse.

Hazy, aka the respectable Miss Hayes. Of course, you've been anxiously awaiting my incredibly wise words to come up on this card. I bet you expect me to write something hilarious, and I certainly will. But first, I want to say that, even though we've only known each other a week, you've been a really good friend to me—the bestest friend I've ever had. Good grief, I sound like a nine-year-old girl. In a way, I'm thankful to have been thrown into this place, simply because I got to meet you. Soppy, I know. I told Freya to have a box of tissues handy as I'm sure you're tearing up right now—realising how amazing I am. Anyway, happy birthday. I'm almost certain that you'll be dying for a birthday cuddle from me after this. 'Dying' isn't a word I should really use with you, is it? ;) Lots of love and hugs, the one and only, Peter Pan xxx

Dear Ruby, I hope you have a great birthday. I remember when I first saw you on that hill, back in the valleys: it was then I realised I wasn't alone anymore. I'd found someone who made me stronger than I'd ever felt before. Someone I could rely on. Someone to trust. I was lucky to have you with me. Then, the more time I got to spend with you, the more I saw how special you are. As long as you're around, I know I don't have to be afraid. I'll never forget that moment of hope when I first laid eyes on your face. Thank you for that, and every moment after. Logan x

The card ends with that, and it's lucky because tears are burning in my eyes, threatening to overflow. I swallow numerous times, my throat thick. I've been fighting against these tears since I started reading to myself. The messages from Charlie and Logan nearly tipped me over the edge. Struggling to contain myself, I bite my bottom lip until I taste blood and close my eyes tight. Some droplets manage to escape out of the corners. They trickle down my warm cheeks for all eyes to see. I hastily wipe them away with my sleeve.

My face hot, I lower the card to the table, laying it down next to my plate of now mixed-up and mashed-together food. I keep my gaze secured on it, acutely aware that everyone is staring at me, waiting for a verbal response. My reaction should be answer enough—the sparkling wet lines marking my face are a big clue.

'Aww, sweetie. I'm so glad you liked it,' Freya says, a hint of triumph in her voice.

She must get some satisfaction in finally forcing emotion out of me. That's clearly what most of them intended the sentimental card to do.

But sentiment is not the only reason I'm upset. It's also the worry that everything I've just read is a work of fiction. It's hard to swallow because it could be laced with deceit. All those messages from my friends—those kind words that tug at my heartstrings—might all be lies. I ache for them to be real. I wish I hadn't seen the rebel's message before I had the chance to read theirs. Because, no matter how I receive them, they're all tainted. Ridding myself of the doubt implanted in my mind seems unachievable.

I want to run away. I want to escape this table and hide from all of those kind, targeting eyes. The only face I can rely on to understand what I'm going through is Charlie's. I finally lift my head to find him sitting solemnly at the end of the table. He's already staring at me, mirroring my tortured expression.

I could pretend that I'm feeling sick again—lock myself away in the bathroom for the rest of the night. But that won't help matters, and it won't help me feel any better. It will only allow me to wallow in it—to let the poison seep in. I'll be encouraging my own downward spiral, and like Logan said before: what you need sometimes is to hold onto something real. I don't know what I can find this time to help me through this moment—to steady myself.

As if he can read my mind, Logan finds my hand under the table, squeezing it lightly in his. The warmth of his skin seeps into my own, and my heart skips a beat. I don't turn to him. I don't need to. Because I know he's here for me. I understand his words to me now: as long as he's around, I don't have to be afraid. Gripping his hand, I find what I need to hold on to.

My feelings. They're not lies. That's what I can put my trust in. Even if the rebel's poisonous message is true, it can't detract from the positive change I've discovered within myself this past week. The bonds I've developed here have made me feel human again.

Straightening my spine, I face the rest of the table to convey my thanks to them. I hug each of them, trying to concentrate on the affection I have for each individual, instead of what they might really think of me.

I must embrace this pain. That's how I know that these people mean a lot to me. That's why I'm sure that it's all real *for me*.

I guess that little pit of useless things, where I usually bury my emotions, is about to erupt. Nevertheless, I'm determined not to let them bring me down.

Instead, I will use them to hold on.

Chapter 23

A Thimble

Keeping everything bottled up won't help me anymore; I realise that now. Still, I have to act like nothing is amiss and force on my cheery, birthday girl persona like it's a too-tight stinger suit until Charlie and I decipher the rebel's message together.

I need to trust the bonds I share with Charlie and Logan, at least for now. They're the two people who I know, deep in my bones, genuinely care for me. I can work the others out later. Although any hopes I had, regarding the H.I.'s promises, are non-existent at present.

Logan seems pleased by my apparent change of mood. I thought I was over-acting: smiling at everyone and laughing too loudly at our group film in the living room. But they all seem to have bought it. Even Charlie glances my way at times, riddled with confusion. I can't be fooling him, though, surely? He must know it's all for show.

As our film, *The Day the Earth Stood Still*, finishes, my performance has left me so exhausted that I say goodnight and head straight to bed before the games start, my temples throbbing with stress. I'm hoping this offers Charlie the chance to talk to me alone. We haven't found an opportunity to speak privately yet, and I'm dying to share my concerns with him—with *anyone*.

He doesn't come up.

I'm upstairs for a good half an hour on my own before the others drift up to bed. The opportunity for a secret meeting tonight with Charlie has been and gone. As I lie stiffly in bed, I seethe over his lack of urgency.

Logan creeps in and soundlessly closes the door, leaving it a fraction ajar. When he realises I'm still awake, he smiles at me before he starts undressing. Of course, I cover my eyes as our routine demands. We discuss the film as he dresses, and I have to remind myself that I'm pretending to be happy again. So I make an effort to keep the chat light, telling him I really enjoyed the rest of our evening, while inwardly hoping he doesn't realise my sudden mood change was only a performance.

When Logan swallows my lies, control slowly slips back into my hands. This is a lot easier than I expected. That means that other people can probably mislead just as well as I can: a thought I have to keep in mind. Although I shouldn't really dwell on it right now. Not when I'm alone with Logan.

Not when he looks at me like this.

After I uncover my eyes, I find him sitting on his bed, his body leaning forwards, his elbows on his knees, as if he needs to be as close to me as possible without breaking the invisible boundary I've wordlessly set.

Logan peers down at me, his lips quirking as his eyes soften. 'Are you warm enough under there? You're all rolled up in your duvet like a...'

'A pig in a blanket?' I finish for him.

He shakes his head. 'Something far cuter than a pig.'

'A pig*let*? They're cute.'

Logan laughs. 'They are, but I wasn't about to compare you to a farmyard animal, just so you know.' His fingers find the corner of my duvet and he fiddles with it as I watch him, wondering why he hasn't slid into his bed yet as he usually does. He swallows, his eyes focused on his tiny ministrations. Is he imagining touching my skin that same way? Am I imagining it? 'If you're cold… maybe I could—'

Logan stops mid-sentence when the stairs creak outside our door; a small group are climbing the stairs, chatting amongst themselves. It's Ben, Freya, and Charlie. They're the last to come up. My attention snaps to the door, waiting for Charlie to pop his head through the thin slither Logan left ajar. Maybe Charlie will pull me aside before bed, since everyone is shut in their rooms. Instead, he strides with purpose right past without so much as a goodnight. He always gives me a hug before bed. Is he avoiding me? Why?

My stomach tightens and I worry my lips. I quickly run through our evening in my head; nothing to warrant a cold shoulder springs to mind. My brief moment of feeling in control of things slips away as confusion rushes back in.

Perhaps my acting earlier was *too* good. Charlie could be under the impression that I'm not at all concerned about the rebel's warning. I hope he doesn't have any doubts about our friendship or believe I've been lying to him all along. It would break my heart if he harboured the same suspicions I do, but towards me.

'Are you okay?' Logan asks, noticing my mood has shifted back to pensive. He's withdrawn from my bed since the last time he held my attention. Wasn't he about to ask me something?

'Er… yeah, just thinking about what I can do tomorrow,' I lie, forcing a smile.

Logan slips under the duvet of his own bed, and for some reason I'm disappointed. 'I have an idea. If you want, we could spend the day together? Just you and me? We can have a picnic in the meadow, around the back of the cabin, and maybe do some painting? Play a board game?

Relax?' He says this as casually as he can, though I detect a tremor of nerves.

As well as the disarming shyness, I'm a little taken aback by his offer. It sounds like he's asking me out on a date. But how do I respond when I'm not sure of his intention? I can't just ask him outright. What if I'm way off the mark? That would be too embarrassing.

Sitting upright in bed, Logan patiently waits for my answer, his expressive eyes shielded by his thick, ebony lashes as he fiddles with his own duvet.

'Erm... I—I don't know. Maybe? We can see what the weather's like,' I mumble awkwardly, scratching my newly-flushed neck.

'If you don't feel like it, that's fine. I only thought you might want to get away from the others for a while, after whatever happened this afternoon,' he clarifies, settling more comfortably in his bed.

There doesn't seem to be disappointment in his expression, though he's more guarded than he's been with me recently. I must have been too presumptuous in assuming he meant it as a date. It would be nice not to have the stress of acting as much tomorrow.

'Actually, I think that's a great idea. I'm a terrible artist, though. I'm no Eli,' I say hurriedly before the offer stales.

Smiling, Logan shrugs. 'You can't be good at everything. It would be unfair on everyone else if you were *too* perfect.' To complement his compliment, he throws a wink my way, the blatant flirtation shocking the sense out of me.

My gaping mouth dries up along with any reply that isn't *huh*?

Was I right about it being a date?

Unable to handle the sudden rush of my blood to every possible inch of skin, I roll onto my side, facing the wall so Logan can't see how his words have affected me.

His breathy chuckle is so low, it's hard to hear, but I catch it and store it in my brain for later; for a time when I know I'm alone and free to imagine it tickle the skin of my inner thigh before he licks across to... *fuck. Stop, Ruby! Save these thoughts for when you're not kidnapped and forced to sleep in the same room as him.*

The whisper of Logan's duvet is loud in this knowing silence as he settles down beneath it.

Tomorrow, I'll be spending the day alone with Logan on some kind of date. The mere idea of it makes my insides swoop and dip. At least my mind will be off the rebel's message.

'Goodnight.' My voice is higher than I intend.

After a brief, pressurised pause, Logan murmurs, 'Until morning light.' Then he switches off our shared lamp, the darkness strangely sensitising.

As expected, my birthday has been another awful reminder of everything I hate about myself and my circumstances in life. Yet somehow, Logan has managed to sugar-coat the shit I've been presented with today.

That's Logan's gift to me—a birthday wish I wouldn't have had the courage to ask for myself.

The chance for us to become *more*.

'Hey,' a voice breathes in my ear, rousing me awake.

My heavy, crusted eyelids open, but the darkness hasn't receded. It must still be night-time. Charlie comes into focus, his face completely shadowed. He raises a finger to his lips to shush me.

'Come with me,' he whispers, barely audible.

I lift my covers and crawl out of bed as quietly as I can. Charlie feels for my hand in the darkness. Once he has it in his clutches, he hurries us out of my bedroom and down the hall to the bathroom. He shuts and locks the door behind us.

'Why are we in the bathroom?' I question, still a little disorientated from sleep.

'Shh, wait a moment,' he instructs, turning both taps on.

I fold my arms across my chest and frown. 'What are you doing?'

Charlie finally swivels to face me. 'Assuming this place is bugged. I saw it done in a film once,' he explains, shrugging. 'It can't hurt.'

The look I give him is all scepticism. If this place is bugged, I doubt a trickle of running water will drown us out.

'Why didn't you come up before bed? We had a half-hour window to speak privately.' Frustration seeps into my tone; it took me a while to find sleep tonight, and now it's disrupted again.

'To avoid suspicion, I thought we should wait until they're all asleep. Also, I feel more like a spy on a secret mission now,' Charlie jokes, waggling an eyebrow at me.

Biting on a smile, I roll my eyes. 'Anyway, so this message... obviously it's from the rebel,' I start.

'Yes, I assume so, too. A bit of a shock, wasn't it? You reacted terribly by the way. Did you tell Logan?' His question holds no accusation. Still, I imagine he's eager to find out if I went against my word.

'No, of course not. He knows something's up, though. He saw right through the fake sickness.'

'I thought as much. I'm guessing the whole '*hardy har har, you're all wonderful*' thing was merely an act earlier?' He raises his eyebrows at me, his lips curling up at one corner. I didn't fool him after all.

I sigh, then admit, 'Yeah. At first, I wanted to hide away and never speak to any of them again, but that's not the easiest to do while we're stuck in this cabin together.'

'Hmm, I understand all too well how you feel. I *cannot* get that message out of my head. It's driving me up the wall,' Charlie responds, his voice terse. He's rubbing his temple like he has a headache.

'Do you believe it? Do you think the others could be lying to us?' I quiz, hoping the answers are '*no*' and '*of course not.*'

'I have no idea. I hope not, obviously. This whole situation we've been dropped into is incredibly sinister, whichever way you look at it. There's no way to know what's really going on. It would be senseless to rule it out entirely, though. Our best bet is to try to think objectively,' Charlie answers, more level-headed about this than I am.

'I doubt either of us can be objective here. The fact that we care about these people will cloud our judgement, any which way.' Perching down on the toilet seat lid, I drop my face in my hands to rub the weariness away.

'I know. I know.' Charlie's forehead scrunches with concentration. 'If the message is genuine, why do you reckon they'd set us up like this? Befriend us? What would their mission be? I can't detect any logical reasoning for it.' He fires the questions out as though he can't hold them in any longer.

'Control? If some of them are lying to us, then they must be working with the H.I. as insiders. They could have been implanted into our group to keep the peace—to keep us on the right track or something,' I speculate, my heart aching at the possibility.

'That could mean they were involved with our kidnapping and so they know significantly more about the H.I. than we do. In that case, it's impossible to determine who we can trust with this information.'

'Oh yeah, I wanted to ask... why did you trust me when the message said not to trust anyone?' I'm fishing for a compliment, I know. But I want to hear him voice my own feelings about our connection back to me.

Charlie shrugs a shoulder. 'I'm not sure. I just did. It was automatic—instantaneous—you and I. We're on the same team. I doubt I could have handled the information on my own, anyway. I needed you with me on this.' He offers me a shy smile.

'I'm glad you did. Well, not *glad*. It's not a nice feeling to wonder if all your friends are fakes. But, as long as we can count on each other...' I say softly, returning the gesture.

Charlie drags out an exhale. 'I've been thinking over the alternative, too. Supposing the message is a falsehood, it's clearly meant to divide us. The rebel *does* want to take down the H.I. after all. Therefore, it's quite likely that he, or she, is attempting to drive us apart. To the point where we isolate ourselves—becoming more vulnerable,' he reasons. It's a good argument against the validity of the message.

'I hadn't really thought of that—that the message could be a deception tactic in and of itself. I've only been focusing on what it could mean if it were true,' I mutter, guilt nibbling at my gut for assuming the worst.

'That's because you're a pessimist, Hazy.' He levels me with a look that's more affectionate than derisive. 'Think about it. The rebel attempted to kill you. They're not on your side. Do you remember what the end of the message said?' Charlie prompts, pushing me to think for myself.

'Death is only escape,' I recall, a shiver flitting down my spine. The rebel must have been in a rush when they were carving it into the bark.

'A bit ominous, isn't it? I imagine the rebel is suggesting we kill ourselves.'

Pursing my lips, I frown in thought. 'I forgot about that part. So really, if we were thinking logically, then we'd conclude that this message is most likely a device to cause trouble?' I put forward, trying to be objective for once, while hopeful at the same time.

'Perhaps you're not a pessimist after all,' Charlie comments, his smile as warm as his tone. 'Whatever happens at the end of this week, good or bad, at least I know I have you by my side. I meant what I said in your card.' His trusting, hazel eyes lock with mine. 'You're my best friend.'

Overcome, I lurch forward to embrace him tightly and whisper, 'You're mine too, Pan.' My eyes mist unexpectedly, and I swiftly blink away the unguarded emotion.

'I missed our goodnight hug. It felt odd walking past your room without it,' Charlie confesses, squeezing me back.

Relief settles my swirling anxiety and affection blunts the annoyance I felt for being woken up in the middle of the night. Our little chat has made me feel a lot better. Charlie has pushed me to see the other side of this; the less gullible, less pessimistic side. I'm always so eager to accept and even *expect* the worst from humankind. Even so, I can't forget that this could still be a legitimate warning.

We break apart, both heaving sighs. I think together we sense the weight lift off our shoulders slightly, as if we bear the brunt better between us.

Charlie turns off the taps and then unlocks the door. 'We should creep back to bed before anyone notices. If the circumstances were different, this would feel sort of cool—sneaking around, having secret rendezvous.' He cracks the door an inch to check the landing. 'The coast is clear, Miss Hayes,' he says, opening the door for me.

I make my exit, and Charlie is hot on my heels like he's afraid the bathroom door will snap shut on him. I begin to tiptoe back to my room when he stops me with a tap on my shoulder. I turn back to face him.

'I forgot to give you this earlier.' Charlie digs into his dressing gown pocket. 'You said that you didn't want any birthday presents, but I wanted you to have this,' he utters, placing a small, silver object in my hand.

I give him a bewildered look in return. 'What is it?'

'It's a thimble, like in Peter Pan,' Charlie explains, a coy smile playing on his lips.

The thimble is weightless in my open palm. 'I don't get it,' I mutter, still confused. He must have taken it from the sewing kit we received in the last crate.

Without warning, Charlie leans in to press his mouth to mine. I don't realise what's happening until he takes my face in his hands. He's *kissing* me. A real kiss! On the *mouth*! I'm too shocked to pull away. His tongue flicks lightly against the seam of my lips but I don't part them for him. I don't think I could even if I wanted to. I'm too unprepared.

The kiss only lasts a few more seconds before Charlie steps back with a puzzled expression. I'm sure my face is just as perturbed as his.

'That's not quite how I imagined it,' Charlie says, his disappointment evident.

My mouth is sealed shut. I'm still too stunned to speak. Wait, does that mean he thinks I'm a terrible kisser? Insecurity burns its way up to my face.

Our eyes wide, we stare at each other for a long beat. Then, all at once, our smiles crack completely, and we both struggle to stifle our giggles behind our hands. Any awkwardness or embarrassment crumbles as soon as we finish laughing.

'What was that, Pan?' I playfully shove him away, no force behind it.

Charlie grimaces. 'It looked more romantic when Wendy did it in the film.'

'It would have been romantic if––'

'If it weren't so strange. I know. It was like I was kissing my sister. Not that I would know. I don't have a sister. Nonetheless, that's what I would guess it would feel like,' he rambles, pinpointing my exact thoughts.

'Yeah, incest isn't sexy,' I joke, making light of it already.

I'm glad we can laugh about this and I don't have to have an awkward conversation with him where I try to let him down gently. We both seem to be on the same page now.

'I'm sorry. I just had to see,' Charlie says simply, his expression a little forlorn. I can't be sure if it's the kiss he's regretting, or the expectation of an emotion neither of us felt during it.

'Okay. Well... we should get to bed.'

'Yes. Goodnight. Keep the thimble. I'm sure you don't want to *ever* forget this moment,' Charlie jests, a dry laugh in his voice. As he creeps back to his room, he shakes his head at himself, as though in disbelief at his own actions.

When he disappears from view, I pivot on my heel to return to my room. Luckily, Logan is still asleep, so I silently slink back into bed, hiding the thimble under my pillow before I rest my head down on it.

Charlie is right: I don't want to forget this memory. And, despite the kiss not really working out for us, I do feel closer to him, more so than ever before. He's my best friend. A brother figure, even. And we're sure of that now. Plus, I'd forgotten what kissing someone was actually like, and it's suddenly sparked my interest.

The last man I locked lips with was a co-worker from the restaurant that made me redundant. It was on a drunken night out in my mid-twenties. I know the kiss with Charlie wasn't what it should be like.

Nevertheless, I'm eager to be reminded of what a proper romantic kiss feels like.

You should expel that silly notion out of your head before you do something really senseless, Ruby. Especially considering you have that date-thing with Logan tomorrow. You don't need these urges *burning the other thoughts from your mind right now. You'll only tense up and act awkwardly.*

Images of Logan leaning close, just as Charlie did, his tongue swiping at the seam of my lips, begging for entry, flicker in my mind's eye. *Stop thinking about it and go to sleep*! I command myself, the heat of that thought searing a hole in my lower belly.

I roll over and shut my eyes tight, forcefully dragging my thoughts back to Charlie. I do admire his bravery tonight. Few things people do shock me, yet I definitely didn't see *that* coming. Have I been giving him mixed signals with my willingness to cuddle him? Maybe it was more curiosity to see if we could lead anywhere else. For me, though, the thought hasn't really crossed my mind—I've never regarded him as anything more than a friend. Still, I understand why he wanted to try; we do have a strong connection.

Whether or not our kiss was bad, it's completely distracted me from our conversation in the bathroom. Thank fuck. I owe Charlie for that one. I can actually relax now. Maybe even get a good night's sleep.

That's only if I can somehow stop my imagination from running wild about my date tomorrow.

Chapter 24

TRY ME

I wake up feeling more refreshed than I expected. My talk last night with Charlie must have done wonders, because I doubt my improved mood has anything to do with our silly little kiss.

There could also be another reason...

Excitement fizzes in my stomach.

Rolling over, I find Logan's bed empty. The heady image of him rising early to prepare for our picnic sends a little thrill shooting through me. The fizzing intensifies.

On my way to the bathroom, I prance past Charlie's room. He's still fast asleep. Zoe isn't in her bed, though; she must be downstairs with Logan. The others have their doors shut.

In the first week, we kept our bedroom doors propped open with chairs. However, over the last couple of nights, I've noticed that many of the pairs have been craving more privacy at bedtime.

The other night, I tiptoed to the bathroom when I thought everyone was asleep and heard what sounded like kissing noises drifting from Dawn and Alex's room. That wasn't exactly a surprise, as I've seen them kissing before. But on my way back to bed, the same sloppy noises were coming from Ben and Freya's room, which made me pause a step.

I haven't poked Ben about it yet. He totally deserves it, as he's always teasing me about Charlie. With that said, I've chosen to take the higher road. I won't try to get back at him by bringing up the noises in conversation. Mostly because we both know that, when he jokes about Charlie and me being romantic, there's no truth to it. Well, there might have been for a few seconds last night, during our kiss, but no one will ever find out about that so it doesn't matter.

After a speedy shower, I hurry to dress in my room. Catching my reflection in the mirror, I remember that I'm supposed to be going on a date, not lounging around the cabin like I usually do. Currently, I'm wearing blue ripped jeans and an oversized grey hoodie, my damp hair hanging in listless curls past my breasts. *Ruby, come on. You have to make more effort than this.* Groaning, I open the wardrobe again in search of something a tad fancier.

On my second try, I pick out a cream blouse with a Peter Pan collar, a tie waist, and pearl buttons. This will hopefully make me look more feminine. To complement it, I choose a pair of black ankle boots, then braid the front of my hair, blow-drying the rest into my natural dark curls. No messy bun today.

Over the past week, I've been applying subtle makeup in the mornings. Each room has a makeup bag, plus perfumes for the women and aftershave for the men. I have no idea why they're counted as essentials here. The H.I. probably think we'd feel more comfortable in this place with the usual everyday things, despite me not being a usual everyday type of person. To me, everything is a luxury.

Before I ended up on the streets, I used to enjoy putting on makeup; it was a mask to hide behind. For the last couple of years, I haven't been able to afford any products so it's been nice to have some here—a small comfort.

I apply some light foundation, mascara, blusher too, and stain my lips a darker shade of rose. When I'm finished, I stand back to check my reflection. It's strange seeing myself like this—almost pretty. Well, pretty compared to my usual self. I hope it doesn't look as though I've made too much effort. I'm still not sure if it's meant to be a date or not.

When I'm as satisfied as I can be with my appearance, I head downstairs. There's some rustling coming from the other bedrooms. The others must be awake now, too.

With a spring in my step, I stroll into the empty living room. This is the point where I'd usually feel the warmth from the fire Logan lights for me. Today, however, the fireplace is still ashy and cold. I wish I'd worn something warmer now, but I'm not bothering to change again.

I carry on through to the kitchen and swing the door open, expecting to see Logan preparing our picnic. Instead, he's hunched at the table with Zoe in the seat beside him. They must have been talking about something intense because they're leaning into one another. Zoe has her hand on his as it rests on the dining table. They stop talking immediately when they see me enter.

Logan casually moves his hand out from under Zoe's, using it to pick up his mug of coffee to take a sip. All the while, he refuses to look at me. Zoe, on the other hand, is holding my gaze, even offering a sly smirk.

'Good morning. Did you have a good sleep?' she asks in a strangely pleasant tone. Too pleasant, almost mocking. 'You look different. Yeah, you could almost pass for female today.' Her smirk widens into a malicious grin.

My heart deflates like an overblown balloon. I was right: her tone was unequivocally mocking.

I look to Logan to tell her off but he doesn't. He always defends me when she throws an insult. Not today, apparently. He remains silent, his focus still on his coffee. Maybe he was too lost in his thoughts to hear her.

With his jaw clenching, Logan rises to wash his mug in the sink.

'Logan, shall I throw together that picnic for the two of us? It looks like it will be a lovely day in the meadow; the sun's out,' I mention, making sure Zoe knows about our plans for the day.

'No, don't bother. I don't really feel like going to the meadow today. I'll check the snares in the forest with Ben instead,' he replies in an even tone, his back to me.

'I'm going too, remember?' Zoe interjects, her eyes bright. 'Good idea about a picnic, though, Ruby. I can prepare one for us, Logan. We could even pick some berries to put in our brie rolls. It always makes them extra sweet,' she says directly to me, sneering triumphantly. She's making it glaringly obvious that she intends to steal my date.

'Sure,' Logan responds absentmindedly, sorting clean cutlery into the correct compartments in the drawer.

I'm still standing awkwardly in the kitchen doorway. One minute, I was excited to spend the day with Logan on our sort-of-date, and now I'm a third wheel. I don't understand why he's suddenly changed his mind. Why is he withdrawing—giving me the cold shoulder? Maybe I'm reading too much into it. It might not have been a date at all. He probably feels obliged to assist Ben with the snares after yesterday. *Give him the benefit of the doubt and stop being so pessimistic.*

'You need a fourth person in the forest with you in case the rebel shows up. I'll come,' I offer, not caring if I have to spend the afternoon with Zoe while she flirts with Logan right in front of me.

'I think Eli would be a better fourth. We may have to kill and skin an animal. I'm not sure you have the guts to do it,' Logan returns in an overly frosty tone.

Ouch. I'm zero for two. He's undoubtedly annoyed with me about something. This kitchen may as well be made of ice.

With my stomach digesting my sunken heart, I step into the room, unsure of whether I should ask what's wrong.

Before I can open my mouth, Zoe says, 'Yeah, and anyway, wouldn't you rather stay here with your little midnight kissing buddy?' Her smile is so wide I'm surprised her cheeks don't split.

All of my insides drop to the floor. They know about my kiss with Charlie last night. That's why Logan is acting this way; he's hurt. In his eyes, I agreed to spend quality time with him, just the two of us, and then kissed another man a few hours later. How did they find out? Charlie is still asleep, so he couldn't have told anyone, and of course *I* didn't. In my mind, I filter through other possibilities. *Maybe you said something while you were asleep? Confessed to it, and Logan heard?* I can't stand this. I have to ask.

'How do you know about that?' I cross my arms over my chest, needing the protective barrier.

'Late last night, I woke to find you weren't in bed. Hearing hushed voices, I got up. And when I looked out into the hall, you were kissing Charlie. So, I went back to sleep and left you to it,' Logan answers dryly, turning to face me. 'You two make a great couple.' His words are thick with resentment. Eyes narrow, he strides forwards. 'Excuse me.'

Realising I'm blocking his exit, I hurry to side-step. He walks straight past without meeting my wide, guilt-ridden gaze.

Zoe snorts in amusement as she bounces up to follow Logan out of the kitchen. But instead of an 'excuse me', she barges past with a shove.

A churning wave of sickness hits me, like I've done something un-forgivable. I can tell that, even if I try to explain what really happened, Logan and I will never be the same. There are no more date-type things in our future. There might not even be a friend-type thing between us anymore.

The thought leaves me as cold and lifeless as the grate where a fire once burned for us.

The day dragging at a snail's pace, I struggle to keep myself busy. It's an arduous task, since I'm also trying to avoid everyone due to the doubts I still have about trusting them. My only option, therefore, is sneaking off to devour a book.

The sun is high in the sky as I settle myself down on the shorter grass patch in the meadow with my copy of *Brave New World* by Aldous Huxley. Dawn and Freya find me a short while later to ask if I want to participate in arts and crafts with them. I swiftly decline. Arts and crafts require patience, which I lack at the best of times.

Ten minutes later, Charlie appears to ask if I want to fish with him, Sasha, and Alex. He already knows it's a pointless question as I've said often enough this week that I have no desire to go anywhere near that lake again. I suspect he just needed an excuse to check up on me.

Ben, Logan, Zoe, and Eli have been absent all afternoon, yet I can't stop thinking about what happened in the kitchen this morning. When I tell Charlie that Logan caught us on the landing, he just laughs it off.

It doesn't really mean much to him—that Logan was hurt seeing us kiss—because they're not the closest here. There's always been this tension between them. It's become apparent that it was due to an unspoken rivalry for my attention. Not that it makes a difference now. Charlie realised that we're only meant to be friends, and Logan is gallivanting in the forest somewhere with Zoe, writing me off.

After Charlie leaves, I desperately try to concentrate on reading again. All I end up doing is scanning over the same page three times before I give up and slam the book shut.

Expelling a frustrated breath, I lie back on the spongy grass to soak up the warmth of the sun when it manages to escape the clutches of the clouds. It disappears again and my body reacts to its chilling absence. The idea of retreating to the cabin isn't a tempting one. With the rebel's warning still creeping in the shadows of my mind, I'm not ready to force myself to integrate again. Even with the likelihood of it being a ploy for division, it's worked well on me; I'm struggling to forget it.

Stress exhausting my every cell and neuron, I doze.

Sasha's voice rouses me. 'The guys are back from the forest.' She's already kneeling on the grass beside me. I didn't hear her approach.

Removing a numb arm from behind my head, I search the sky above. It must be an hour or so later because the sun has shifted its position. I don't sit up, I just laze, allowing my eyes to fall shut again. Hopefully, she'll take the hint and leave me in peace.

When her shadow still shades the entirety of my left arm, a minute later, I ask half-heartedly, 'Did they catch anything?'

'A couple of rabbits,' Sasha answers, lying down and making herself comfortable. I guess she won't be leaving any time soon, then. 'You shouldn't really have been out here on your own all afternoon. Not with the rebel still at large.'

'I needed some time alone. Being around everyone all the time can be a bit overwhelming. I'm used to being on my own,' I hint again, hoping she catches my drift.

'I get what you mean. I don't have a lot of close friends back home, either. The only family I have is my sister and nephew. When I'm not with them, I'm usually alone. Saroyce is busy being a mum to Darwin. And if I'm around them too much, I'm afraid I'll only be in the way of that,' she divulges, her tone sombre.

Despite not wanting to delve into a heavy conversation with anyone right now, I hum a response as if I can empathise. Maybe I do in some way. I've always felt as though I didn't fit in anywhere: as if I'm always in the way of other people's lives, watching from the outskirts.

'You should wear your hair down more often. Your curls are actually well-defined. When we get out of here, I'll give you my spare silk sleeping cap to help stop the morning frizz,' Sasha offers, twirling one of her own curls.

'It's the Jewish genes in me,' I say, almost smiling. 'I got it from my m—'

When my mum's face surfaces in my mind, I nearly choke.

There's a long silence before Sasha finally moves on to another subject. Although this one is just as dreadful as the last. 'I heard about your kiss with Charlie.'

I roll onto my front and prop my head up on my elbows. 'Did Charlie tell you?' I ask after a sigh. I should have known it would get out eventually. This is fast, though.

Sasha pulls up the zipper of her hoodie, the sun disappearing behind another cloud. 'Yeah, he explained what happened when we were out on the boat, and that Logan saw. Charlie feels a bit guilty about it now.'

I scoff. 'He laughed earlier when I told him what Logan said.'

Sasha flashes her eyebrows at me. 'He told me that, too. But I think he sees how much it's affected you today. He said he'll explain it all to Logan later—tell him you're just friends.'

'Urgh. Tell him not to bother. This is so juvenile. It's like we're back at school,' I moan, cringing.

Sasha chuckles. 'Logan already knows there's nothing between you and Charlie. I reckon it's just a case of wounded pride and insecurity. He'll be over it by tomorrow.'

'Not if Zoe's got her hooks into him already,' I mutter, flopping back down on the grass.

Sasha shakes her head. 'No chance. I don't think you know just how much Logan cares about you. It's blatantly obvious to all of us. We all see the way he looks at you.' She props herself up on one elbow to get a better look at me. 'You really don't know?'

'Know what?'

'That he's fallen for you,' she says, a knowing smile curving her lips.

My stomach twists at that, a pleasurable sort of discomfort. 'I don't think so. He barely knows me,' I respond, my tone defensive as I set a scowl in place. I'm confused about why I suddenly feel attacked by that notion. It's probably because I don't believe it—*can't* believe it. It's another lie.

'You're not that mysterious, Ruby. You might not be comfortable talking about yourself, but that doesn't mean you haven't shown us exactly who you really are. You've been your true self here. We all love you,' she claims, her smile warming. 'Stop forcing me to say nice shit to cheer you up and just believe me.'

I don't know how to respond to that. I should be happy hearing it, yet the only thing welling up is suspicion. How can anyone love me when they don't really know me? It's impossible.

Forcing a smile, I mumble, 'We should go in and help cook dinner. I haven't done anything productive today.' I jump to my feet and rush off, not waiting for her to catch up.

Dinner is predictably awkward.

Logan hasn't said a word to Charlie or me all evening, and Zoe has been rubbing salt into my wounds every chance she gets. At present, she's talking about her and Logan's berry picking adventure. It's the most animated and talkative she's been since arriving here. I didn't think she could get any more annoying—since she's acted moody the whole time—but I was wrong. She's worse now that she's happier. Mainly because it's at my expense.

As soon as we finish dinner, Logan says to no one in particular that he's tired. And while everyone else gets themselves cosy in the living room, in preparation for tonight's film, he slinks off upstairs.

As for me, I scurry back to the kitchen and grab a soapy cloth to wipe the counters, needing my own excuse to separate myself. Sasha finds me again not long after.

'Are you coming to watch the film, or are you going to talk to Logan? You know that's why he went upstairs, right? He wants you to follow him,' she states as if it's a fact.

'He went upstairs to be as far from me as possible,' I refute, my voice low.

'Trust me, I know Logan. Well, I've known guys *like* Logan. He wants you to make the first move. Your emotions are harder to read than his.

He's not sure if you care as much as he does. So, if you *do* care, *show* him,' Sasha concludes, striding out of the kitchen before I can respond.

The problem with Sasha's point is that I don't know how to show Logan I care. The thought of opening up to him about my feelings has bile rising to my throat. I admit, I *am* hard to read. It's purposeful. I consciously try to conceal my emotions at all times. It's my defence mechanism; it keeps me safe. On the other hand, I need to break this pattern of behaviour if I'm ever going to make things right with him. I don't want our last days here to be uncomfortable and tense. And the truth is... I *do* care about him, in a different way to how I care for Charlie, or anyone else for that matter. I've tried not to. I've been denying it to myself for a while now.

The disappointment I felt this morning in the kitchen was horrible, yes, but it was also oddly clarifying. I want Logan to keep looking at me. The kind of looks that make me feel special—that make me feel like I'm real and I matter. I want him to *see* me, like no one has before.

My mind made up, I tiptoe through the living room. Luckily, the film is already on so the group's attention is focused on the television as I creep up the stairs to the landing.

I peek into mine and Logan's bedroom; it's empty. The bathroom is free, so I check all the bedrooms and still come up short.

Where the fuck is he?

Panic rising, I rush back to our room for a second look. Still nothing. But, before I close the door, the rustle of the curtain alerts me to the open window. Stepping in, I spot the back of Logan's grey jumper through the glass. He's sitting on the slanted roof of the kitchen outside our window. He's staring out to the forest; under the moonlight, its spooky glow seems unearthly.

Logan must hear me approach because he mutters, 'Why are you up here, Ruby? Shouldn't you be snuggling with Charlie, watching the film?' His poisonous tone nearly makes me spin on my heel and run.

I resist the urge to revert back to my old ways.

'Can I join you?' I ask, ignoring his childish remarks.

'If you must.'

I climb up over the bedside table to the window then swing my leg through it. The roof isn't high, but I'm also not the most graceful of people, so I'm hesitant in my movements. Logan senses my struggle and offers me his hand without hesitation. I take it and manage to place myself beside him on the roof without much trouble.

The frosty night air raises goosebumps on my arms. Fighting off the chill, I pull my sleeves down and rub my forearms. Nerves are also a factor in this action. It's a comforting motion which keeps my shaky hands busy.

I steal glances at Logan, tentative in approaching a meaningful conversation. He has his knees up, arms firmly around them as he stares off, avoiding eye contact. 'So... why are you out here?'

'I thought it would be a good place to clear my head,' Logan answers, monotone.

'I tried to do that today in the meadow. I wanted to be alone to think.'

'Did it work?' he asks, his eyes still fixed on the shadowed landscape. At least he's willing to talk to me and isn't being as dismissive as he was earlier.

'Not really. It didn't help me clear my thoughts at all. It only muddled them up worse—produced more questions. I've realised that you need to talk things through to find answers.' Sharing my worries last night with Charlie has proved that to me.

Logan's scowl deepens. 'Talk things through? That's interesting. You haven't practised that on me yet. You don't *talk* to me about anything

310

important. You never *talk* about your life before the forest. You only hugged me yesterday to get out of *talking*,' he points out, no humour in his exaggeration because it's too on the nose.

When I don't answer, he finally turns his head to cut me with a sharp look, driving his point home. His eyebrows raise, goading me.

We stare each other down for a painful beat before I buckle. 'Okay—I get it. I'm sorry, Logan, but I'm just not used to talking about... myself. I'm not used to talking, full stop.'

'Why not? What's stopping you?'

'I'm... afraid to,' I mumble, shrinking in on myself.

Logan turns, leaning closer, not allowing me to hide from him. 'Afraid of what?'

I huff. 'Of people seeing me for what I am,' I mutter, louder now.

'And what's that? What are you?' He continues to push—continues to invade my space with his overstimulating presence.

My body flushes with sudden, blistering anger. 'I'm nothing, okay?! I'm nothing special. I'm worthless. I'm fucking worthless!' I shout, rounding on him.

Logan is frowning. I'm frowning. We're both breathing heavily, the night air revealing our breaths in thick, foggy wisps.

My inescapable truth hangs in the space between us like a malignant spirit. Blinking in shock, I retreat, snapping my mouth shut again. Though I seem more surprised by my outburst than Logan is.

He shakes his head in exasperation, his hand inching closer to mine as it rests on the roof. 'You're so wrong, Ruby. So incredibly wrong. You're not seeing yourself the way we do. Your reality is warped if that's what you believe.'

I cool down just as rapidly as I heated up. A chill ripples through me again. I move my hand out of reach of his. 'You don't know what my reality is, Logan. You have no idea,' I dismiss, wrapping my arms around my knees as I glare into the darkness ahead of us.

'I might if you gave me the chance,' Logan murmurs, trying to find my eyes. I can see him in my peripheral vision, tempting me with that look which makes me believe he really cares to know me. That he cares *about* me.

Trembling, I allow him to see my face, wondering if he can already read the truth written there. 'I know, as soon as I tell you, you'll never look at me like that again.' My words taper off into a whisper. I breathe a weighted sigh, my throat tight and raw.

'Try me,' Logan urges, his eyes wide and sparkling. 'Please, Ruby. *Try me*.'

Trust me is what he's really saying—imploring. More desperately genuine than I've ever known anyone to be.

I stare into the depths of Logan's encouraging eyes, dimly lit by our bedroom light, and fall into them so deeply that I forget my fears.

Chapter 25

THE TRUTH

'I lied when I said I was taken from my flat. The truth is... I've been living on and off the streets for over four years. I've struggled to find a job. I don't have any friends or family. I have nothing,' I admit, my checks burning with shame. In contrast, the rest of my body is numb with cold. A full-body shiver has my teeth chattering.

Logan stares at me for what feels like an eternity, deep in thought. I brace myself for judgement. 'Having nothing and being nothing are completely separate things; they're not synonymous. You believe your struggles in life have made you worthless? I would say it's the exact opposite,' he says softly.

His response throws me off-kilter; I was expecting shock and disgust. I'd imagined he'd cringe when he learnt of my circumstances. I thought he'd jerk away from me as quickly as possible, believing homelessness to be a contagious disease. I bet he's only being nice because he feels sorry for me. After this conversation, I'll become invisible to him, if not worse.

'Why are you so afraid to talk about that? I don't think anyone here would see you any differently,' Logan continues after a minute of silence.

'Yeah, you say that, but have you ever been friends with a homeless person before? Have you even had a real conversation with one?' I don't wait for his answer. 'The reality is: I can sit in a shop doorway all day and not draw a single look. Not one smile. Not one word. I'm the reality nobody wants to face, so they try not to see me at all. And if they do, I'm reduced to an object in the background—not human. I'm only the dirt that has to be swept away because I make them feel uncomfortable—make them feel too guilty. So, they just keep on walking past as if I don't exist,' I mutter despondently, clutching my knees in a vice-like grip. 'It's a lot easier to ignore problems than solve them, especially if you think they won't affect you. And it's even easier to lie to yourself than to face the truth that one day it will.'

Nodding, Logan sighs. 'Hmm. Humans are so selfish sometimes, blissful in their ignorance until it affects them,' he agrees, turning to face the darkness with me once again. 'But this whole experience should only prove to you that it doesn't matter where you come from; circumstances do *not* define who you are. Here, everyone's different. We're all individuals with distinct personalities and backgrounds. We all have our own trauma and issues, too. That's a given—that's living in a sometimes-harsh reality. Yet together, we've built a sense of community, not based on socially constructed, superficial things which separate us like money, race, gender, age, or beauty. We've surpassed those binary limitations because we share a purpose. We're bonded by what truly matters: our hearts and minds. Those two things are ever-changing—growing—evolving. Our past may shape us, but how we live in the present and how we plan for our futures are what define those lines and fill in what's left with colour.' He looks back to me, but I limit my gaze to the landscape, absorbing his words. 'We haven't needed to know anything about your life before this forest to know what kind of person you are, Ruby. You just need to start seeing yourself the way we do.'

'Well, I've known myself for a lot longer than you have,' I reply in a dismal tone. 'In the end, you'll wish you never saw me. I always disappoint.' Logan shakes his head but doesn't bother arguing.

Another long pause stretches. I don't think either of us knows how to proceed after my confession of self-hatred.

Logan blows out a loud breath. 'The funny thing is, I spent a long time wishing I was invisible. For years, people looked at me with this pitying guilt in their eyes. Not really guilt: more sympathy. Which is sometimes worse. They used to remind me of the worst moment of my life nearly every day.' He catches my perplexed expression. 'You see... my mother was murdered by my best friend a few years ago. Actually, I guess it's nearly seven years ago now,' he reveals, his voice raw. I stare at him in disbelief, too shocked to respond.

Logan pushes on. 'Random people would approach me to ask about it: the *hows* and the *whys*. They wanted to know every gory detail without bothering to get to know me first. Then I'd have family and friends asking different questions, like '*How did you not know your best friend was a murderer?*', or '*Why didn't you do more to stop it?*'.'

Empathy squeezing my heart, I peek over at him. His focus is on his fingers as they fiddle with a fraying spot on his jeans. 'That's awful. What kind of person would ask those things?'

Logan huffs a laugh full of dark amusement. 'You'd be surprised. That last question was from my father.'

My tummy twists painfully at that. I know exactly how it feels to have a critical and unsympathetic father. 'I'm sorry,' is all I can think to say in return.

'It's okay. My father and I have rebuilt some bridges since then. Rickety though they may be.'

'What was your mum like?' I enquire, needing to know if he at least had the kind of love I was lucky enough to enjoy, if only for a time.

Logan lifts his gaze to me then, his face twitching in surprise. 'You know, every time I've told someone about my mother, that question has never come up. They would rather hear about the circumstances of the death, not the life of the person.' His smile is only small but it's contagious.

'That's depressing. It seems as though humanity is becoming more and more inhuman,' I comment, and he laughs darkly, seeming to agree.

'Anyway, you asked what she was like... she was amazing. I'm sure a lot of people think their mum's the best, but mine really was. She was resilient, assertive, she knew what she wanted and achieved it. She could do almost anything and was invincible in my eyes growing up. She managed to accomplish so much, yet she still had enough time for me—to give me all the love I could ever want. I feel like I still need her around to help me make decisions and push me to be a better person. I try my best without her, but I make so many mistakes,' Logan says gruffly, his emotions taking hold.

'What was her name?' I request, my chest tightening in solidarity.

'Ha—Hayley,' he stammers out. Then he frowns.

I offer Logan an empathetic smile, and his lips twitch up despite the tears glistening in his eyes. 'She sounds like someone I would have wanted to know,' I say, my voice gentler than I've ever known it.

'You're very much like her. Only personality-wise, though. It would be weird if I fancied someone who looked like my mum,' Logan mentions casually, scanning my face for a reaction.

Holy shit. Did I hear him right?

With wide eyes and a galloping heart, I gulp down the urge to return an admission of attraction. Instead, I sweep my startled gaze away, concealing the blush that's burning a path downwards from my cheeks to my neck and chest.

'You must have known. I haven't been able to hide it very well. Although I tried to tone it down, because every time I inched that little bit closer to you—close enough to touch—close enough to tell you how I felt—I got the distinct impression that you wanted to run away,' he tells me, his tone still serious. It's as if he doesn't want me to brush this off or try to turn it into a joke.

My pulse skitters at that truth, my fight or flight response rearing; my body tenses up, limiting my intake of air.

'You're doing it right now; it looks as if you're about ready to jump off this roof to escape me,' Logan jokes, snickering, though his eyes betray him; there's some hurt there. My silence is obviously making him insecure.

'You just make me nervous. I'm not used to this kind of attention,' I mumble, hiding my face in my hands. Feeling like a complete coward, I peek through my fingers to check he's still staring—witnessing this weakness. He is.

'I think it runs deeper than that. It's not nerves: it's fear. You're afraid to let me in—to let me get too close.' Logan's forehead furrows again. His gaze roams over me, searching for a crack in my metaphorical armour. It's clear that he's desperate for me to open up to him—to tell him the real reason why I'm so scared to let someone touch my heart.

'It's not only you. I'm afraid to let anyone get too close to me. I've changed a little for the better since being here—I've trusted people more than I would have anywhere else.' I drop my hands to my lap again, my jeans a comfort to pick at.

'Like Charlie. You seem really comfortable around him,' Logan remarks with a hint of sadness.

The jaws of guilt gnaw at my stomach. 'Yeah. Charlie's a strange one. We share this connection even though we're worlds apart. He's like my comfort blanket. I know he won't hurt me,' I try to explain, sensing that this answer will have implications.

'How could you think I would want to hurt you?' Logan questions, his face contorting as if I've caused him injury.

'I'm sure you wouldn't *intentionally* hurt me. But even people who cared about me the most ended up doing so, one way or another.'

'So... someone who was supposed to love you let you down somehow, and now you won't trust anyone?' he guesses correctly.

I want to say, '*Yes, that's the best way to be. It keeps you safe. Just lock yourself up and throw away the key.*' However, I realise now that this way of protecting myself has only made me cold, bitter, and lonely over the years. I can't keep avoiding real relationships for the rest of my life because I'm scared of getting hurt again. I have to tear down these walls and stop confining myself to the prison I've built in my own mind.

Society may have conditioned me to think I deserve this—this poor, lonely, barely there existence—but I'm the one reinforcing these punishments each time I decide to choose the easiest option: running—hiding. I say I've never given up, but isn't that exactly what I've been doing all these years? Letting society win by internalising these limitations?

Resigned to at least try, I close my eyes and dive off this self-imposed barrier, trusting Logan to hold me if I spiral. 'I was eleven when I came home to find my mum dead—a brain aneurysm. The doctors told me it was instantaneous—no pain... as if that would make me feel better about it. My brother, Jack, was the strongest of us after that. He was only two years older, yet he was the one who protected me; he was my shield when my dad used to break down and hit us, as if it was our fault she was gone. For years, I counted on Jack, and he was there for me... until the day he wasn't.' I pause, my heart aching so much I think it might crack. I place a palm to my chest, trying to soothe its pain.

'He left home at eighteen—left me alone to deal with my dad's violent meltdowns. I understood why, though; I wanted to escape just as badly. What helped me through that time was the thought of seeing Jack again. So, when I finally had the courage to leave home myself, I tracked him down. He was living in this little house in Yorkshire with a woman; his girlfriend, I presumed. I knocked on his door, so excited to see him because we were both finally free, you know?' Tears prickle in the corners of my eyes, my throat closing up to restrain the truth from pouring out of me, unfettered. I push on past those limits, needing to expose this festering wound to the air at last.

'He opened the door and looked right through me, like I was a ghost. He said that I shouldn't have come... that all I did was remind him of the life he wanted to leave behind. He knew I had nowhere to go but he shut the door on me anyway. I never saw him again,' I choke out through tears that have been waiting to fall for years. 'A few years later... erm... his girlfriend left him... and he killed himself. In his suicide note, he said he'd lost the only person he loved and he couldn't stand to be alone.' I turn to Logan, enraged with sadness. 'He didn't have to be alone, though; he could have had *me*. He could have been my big brother again, but he chose death instead.' With that, I break. A sob claws its way out of me like it's been trapped inside for years. It has. I bite the sleeve of my shirt to try to hold it back, but it's no use.

Logan gives me his body to cling to. He draws me in, my head against his chest, so his jumper can absorb my tears. His arms tighten around me as I use him to stabilise myself. 'Ruby, despite all of that, you've come here and protected us—cared for us. You've done what your brother was too afraid to do. You're not like him. You've tried to be all these years but you're not. Your heart is too big to lock away,' he states, hoping to comfort me. 'Like you said to Zoe: you've wanted to give up before, yet you didn't. You *can't*. Because that's not you. You're a survivor.' His face

319

is hovering above mine, angled down, his breath warming the shell of my ear. His closeness makes my heart stutter now that I'm not entirely consumed by my postponed grief. 'You deserve so much more than you've been dealt in life. You deserve to be cared for. And you are.' He sweeps my fringe away from my forehead to brush a kiss there.

Ignoring the stirrings of more pleasant feelings, I heave a tired sigh. 'It's just so hard to believe—that this is all real. That people here really do care about me. This place seems too good to be true. *You're* too good to be true,' I profess in a strangled whisper, my throat still clogged by my volcanic emotions.

Logan's fingers come under my chin to tilt my face up to his. He gently wipes away the wet trails on my cheeks with his thumbs, and I exhale audibly, allowing myself to melt into his touch. His intense, shadowed eyes lock on to mine, sending chills racing up and down my spine. I shudder with a mixture of relief and desire—simultaneously unburdened by my secrets, yet weighted again by his magnetism. I'm captured—ensnared by his tenderness and understanding.

'I want to kiss you so fucking badly, Ruby,' Logan whispers, his nose nudging mine. 'I've been desperate to for a while now.' His jaw clenches as if he's trying to restrain himself from doing just that.

'Why don't you?' My voice is all breath, his admission inciting a riot in my body.

Logan shuts his eyes tightly, continuing to fight the compulsion. 'Because I didn't want to do it when... It wouldn't be right to kiss you when you're upset—vulnerable. It would be taking advantage,' he reasons, shaking his head. Despite his honourable hesitation, he hasn't let me go, hasn't withdrawn from me. If anything, he's closer, his lips only inches away, wordlessly calling for me to make the decision for him—for us.

Throwing caution to the wind, I answer that call, closing the inconsequential distance separating us. When our lips fuse, they burn white-hot.

The butterflies in my stomach beat their wings harder and faster—furiously ecstatic.

The kiss is soft at first, but our spark soon ignites, fiery passion building. His tongue is a warm tickle as it briefly swipes the seam of my lips, and I open up to him for the second time tonight. He quickly seizes the opportunity with teasing flicks.

Stunned by the heady taste of him, I hold my breath. Dizziness overtakes me before I recall how to use my lungs. Not that it matters because I'm in Logan's arms now and there's no way he'd let me fall. So I embrace the sensation. I give myself up to it—to him.

Logan's breathing becomes a chorus of laboured gasps as he clutches my hair with one hand, his fingers combing and stroking, while his other hand lowers to my hip to forcibly drag me nearer, caging me against his body possessively. I'm surprised by how positively my body responds to the dominating action. I shiver, feeling his need mounting alongside my own.

My heart is humming its own lavish song in my chest, singing its tantalising melody to every part of me. His mouth claims mine like it's his life force, as if the air in my lungs is all he ever wants to breathe. *You need to take in more air, Ruby, or you'll faint again*, I remind myself, my lungs burning as intensely as the rest of my body.

Panting, I break away, completely shell-shocked. Logan sits back, catching his breath too. Despite the frozen night air, my entire body is an uncontrollable flame. *That's what a real kiss feels like*, I say to myself, still breathless and shaken to the core. It's so much better than I remember.

'Oi, what are yous two doing on the roof, eh?' Ben calls out from behind us.

Both Logan and I whip our heads around to find our Northern friend standing in the open doorway, smirking.

'We were having a chat,' Logan rasps, his chest still heaving.

Ben arches an eyebrow. 'Aye, if that's what they call *making out* nowadays, like,' he teases laughingly, shutting our door for us.

Logan and I glance coyly at each other, tittering nervously.

'See, sometimes it's good to be invisible,' he jokes, placing his hand on top of mine.

With Logan, I know that I will never feel invisible again.

We catch the last half of the film, although my attention is elsewhere. I'm more focused on Logan's hand as it holds mine: the heat of his palm, the smoothness of the back, his fingers interlocking with my own. His thumb occasionally brushes my skin with absent-minded strokes, which tickles in the most pleasant of ways.

Imagining being alone with Logan again in our bedroom is provoking palpitations.

The credits roll and we all say our goodnights. But, before anyone else has a chance to move, Logan grabs my wrist; not too tight, yet tight enough to make my blood sing. He hastily leads me upstairs to our bedroom. There's a bit of force behind it, as though he can't wait another minute. The thought of him so desperate to get me alone again makes my mouth run dry and my tummy clench.

We usually keep our door ajar. However, tonight, as soon as we step into our room, Logan sweeps the chair away from the door, letting it fall completely shut. We have some privacy now. I'm starting to like this assertive side of Logan. In these circumstances, it's fucking sexy.

'I don't know about you, but I couldn't wait for that film to finish.' Logan aims a boyish grin my way before stepping closer. His eyes darken under his lashes as they track down my face to my lips. He licks his own then inhales sharply. 'Can I touch you?' he whispers, and I nod a little too enthusiastically, my body tensing ever so slightly in anticipation. No one has ever asked for consent before touching me.

Logan leans in slowly, placing his right hand at my waist and the other at the top of my arm. When he presses me to his body, my heart skips a few beats. His lips skim over my cheekbone and my eyes instinctively flutter closed. My stomach backflips when his rapid exhalations tingle hot on my skin. Needing to draw in a gasped breath, my mouth parts. His left hand sweeps the curls off my shoulder, exposing my neck. And I'm frozen, so still as he touches me, unable to concentrate on anything other than these thrilling sensations.

The thrumming vibration of my heart resonates through my entire body, like a herd of stampeding butterflies.

Logan kisses the corner of my mouth then tilts back to check my expression. I look up at him, disappointed by the break. His eyes find mine and my body has a heavy heat to it under his dark, smouldering gaze. My breath snags somewhere between a gasp and a yelp.

'You still look petrified. Am I moving things too fast?' he asks, a worried expression creeping onto his handsome features.

God, he's so hot. *How the hell have you resisted him for this long?* I question myself, amazed at my restraint. Now that I've tasted him, I can't imagine denying myself this craving a moment longer.

'No... not fast enough,' I exhale, grabbing Logan's collar with one hand to yank him back to me. I crush my lips to his, my other hand sliding up into his hair, keeping him close.

This is undeniably intoxicating; something extremely addictive.

Logan's scent is smoky like our fire yet as fresh as our meadow. His lips are soft and as eager as mine. We fall back onto his bed, gripping each other tightly—desperately. His weight forces me down, the spongy mattress moulding to the curves of my writhing body. And, as soon as I hook a leg over his hip, he strokes up my thigh. In response, I sweep a hand under his jumper, my fingers exploring the small of his back while he presses hot, wet kisses into my neck. A soft moan escapes my lips, and he groans in response—the animalistic noise vibrating in his chest. My own body vibrates in tandem, little shivers dancing over my sizzling skin.

I had no idea how hungry I was for him—for this kind of contact. The feelings I've been avoiding for years have resurfaced all at once, and they're electrifying every cell of my body. Blood is pounding through my veins with a feverish delight.

I want him. I want him *inside* me.

My body starts to throb with desire—pulsing with my newfound arousal. Pleasure twinges deep inside the lost recesses of my belly.

Then Logan's hand glides over my breast, and my nipples stiffen automatically.

He squeezes.

Oh, God.

There's instant dampness in the space between my legs, and I bite my bottom lip to stifle another moan.

'Do you like me touching you, Ruby?' Logan asks, his voice all smoke and gravel.

'Yes,' I hiss, more turned on than I've ever been. I never want him to stop touching me.

'God, my imagination has *not* done you justice. I didn't know someone could feel this good—taste this good.' Logan's demanding lips move to mine again with a renewed frenzy. His greedy hand roams down to my hip, sliding around to grope my backside. 'And it will only feel more intense after this. I can't fucking wait,' he breathes against my lips.

As he stokes the flames in my body, I tingle with need. In turn, my hands drop to my shirt and start undoing the tiny pearl buttons in a hurry. I want him to truly feel me, skin-to-skin. I want him to taste a hungrier part of me.

Logan finally notices what I'm doing enough to stop kissing me. He lifts his head, peering down at what I'm starting to reveal to him. At first, there's a haze of lust clouding his dilated eyes. He licks his lips as he stares at my cleavage, wicked intent clear. But then, a strange look crosses his face. His eyebrows pinch. I can't tell exactly what emotion it is, but it causes his hands to swiftly retract from pawing at me, as if he's remembered something important. He swiftly rolls off me to sit at the end of the bed, breathing heavily, his face flushed.

My stomach plummets. What did I do wrong?

As my cheeks burn, I quickly redo my buttons. Then, without looking up, I ask, 'What's the matter?'

We're both still gasping for air. Logan rubs his face, sighing. 'We *are* going too fast. I don't think we should take things any further whilst we're here. The H.I. could be watching,' he answers in a rush, his eyes searching for the cameras we never found.

'I forgot about them. You're right. Sorry. I don't know what I was thinking,' I mumble, mortified.

'The same thing that I was.' Logan pushes out a shaky laugh, although his expression tightens with guilt. He shifts back over to kiss me lightly on the lips again, then he playfully ruffles my hair. 'I'm sure you can control yourself for a few more days,' he jests, his smirk all male arrogance.

'You were the one with your hands all over me. I think *I'll* manage just fine, thanks,' I retort snarkily, rolling my eyes. I give him a little shove before dropping down on my own bed.

Logan chuckles at my response then rigidly stands up. Only after a full minute, I notice. A flicker of self-confidence sparks within me, knowing I had that effect on him. He tries to nonchalantly adjust himself, stealing embarrassed glances at me over his shoulder.

After Logan has finished *rearranging*, he clears his throat and opens the wardrobe. He pulls up his jumper, and I quickly shut my eyes like I normally do.

Logan laughs again. 'You don't have to look away if you don't want to.'

'I'm avoiding temptation,' I tell him, my face prickling with warmth again.

'I'm not sure I can do the same when it's your turn,' he murmurs flirtatiously. And I swallow thickly at that.

It's not long before it *is* my turn to change clothes. I pick out my usual combination of T-shirt and joggers, then lay them flat on my bed. Logan is propped up in his own bed, pretending to hide his bright eyes behind his hands. He's leaving exaggerated gaps between his fingers on purpose.

Starting off slowly, I untie the braid at the front of my hair, struggling to make the task look at all sexy. After that, I fumble with the first button of my blouse, suddenly nervous as he watches me expose myself, even though it's only underwear. It's not like I'll be naked in front of him. All the steam powering me for that earlier, during the kissing, has evaporated. Now, I'm turning shy.

'I'm joking, I won't peek,' Logan assures me, bringing the duvet up to cover his head.

I laugh, relief easing the stiffness in my stance. I change in less than a minute.

More comfortable, I hop over to my bed, ready to peel back the covers. Logan says my name to draw my attention. He has his own duvet pulled back now: to show he's made space for me in his bed.

'I'm sure cuddling won't be putting on that much of a show for the H.I.,' he says, his tempting lips turning up into a devilish grin.

My pulse charges again, making me hesitate. For some reason, the idea of cuddling Logan all night seems much more intimate than what we nearly did five minutes ago. Despite that thought, I relent, climbing into Logan's bed with a shy smile. He wraps his arms around me as I lay my head on his chest, like I did when he was unconscious that night after the wolf attack. He was so cold and lifeless last time that tonight is a complete contrast; his whole body is warm and inviting.

I don't have an ounce of worry left in me.

We're both safe here in our little snug.

'Goodnight,' I utter, delighting in his heat and feeling more content than I have in years.

Logan kisses the top of my head, and my eyelids immediately feel weighted with the promise of a restful sleep.

'Until morning light,' I hear him whisper into my hair, before I drift off into blissful oblivion.

Chapter 26

Halo

The next few days fly by. Once I start trying to embrace this experience—to cherish every moment—time begins to slip away. Not that I'd ever admit it out loud, but I'm almost thankful the H.I. kidnapped me.

What I will admit is: this unfamiliar state of well-being is mostly due to Logan and our leap into a romantic relationship. We haven't defined what we have together yet, but we're inseparable in the cabin, much to everyone's amusement. Ben offers us an endless supply of banter. And thankfully, Charlie doesn't seem to mind Logan and me being an unofficial couple.

I'm glad the romantic shift with Logan hasn't detracted from what I have with Charlie. Charlie is still his cheeky, tactile self, and we're as close as ever. Plus, now, when Charlie pulls me in for a hug, Logan doesn't react jealously, as he knows Charlie is no longer a threat.

Since our rooftop confessions, I've thrown myself into the deep end with Logan, baring my heart and soul to him. My old wounds are now open to the air, needing that healing touch only trust can bring. Each night, we crawl under the covers of his bed, my head on his chest, his arms around me, and I unload my past pain onto him, and he bears it for me. Every ounce of truth I spill, like blood out of stone, is rewarded with a soothing touch—a kiss—a story of his own to show me I'm not alone in my suffering.

Zoe is the only person who reacts badly to the news. I sensed she had her beady little eyes on Logan from the get-go. But now that she knows she wasted her time, she seems to have given up on this experience altogether. She spends her days alone in her room or out in the meadow reading. If anyone tries to join her, she screams at them to go away. We've all made the effort to include her in the group to no avail. A small part of me feels guilty. It must be hard to see Logan and me together. I would have been equally as upset if roles were reversed and Logan chose her instead of me.

Despite everyone figuring out that our relationship is no longer platonic, Logan and I don't often indulge in public displays of affection. Romance is uncharted territory for me so I'm taking baby steps. Logan sometimes forgets that and tries to kiss me when others are in the room but stops when I tense up with embarrassment. He doesn't mind waiting until we're alone to quench his thirst for affection. But at night in our bedroom, we struggle to stop ourselves from taking the physical contact to the next level; it's too easy to lose control and be swept up in the heat of the moment.

During the day, I occasionally indulge Logan, allowing an arm around my shoulders or waist, even if the others are around to witness. I've been trying to push myself beyond my comfort zone, for his sake. He's a lot more affectionate than I am and I don't want to keep rejecting him. On the other hand, my boundaries also allow me to be comfortable enough to take those next steps. Luckily, Logan has been mindful of that, not pushing me too far. I've returned the same respect in regard to the *nothing-more-than-kissing-and-the-cheeky-occasional-grope* rule he's set for us until we leave the cabin. It's extremely frustrating for both of us. But the risk of unknowingly becoming exhibitionists is too high a price. Even though we've checked for cameras many times, there's still a chance they're there in some microscopic form.

We're also not the only relationship to progress. Yesterday, Ben and Freya finally outed themselves as a couple. Like me, Ben is more guarded with his emotions. Freya is trying to be as understanding as Logan, but the sting of rejection is more evident on her dainty features.

Dawn and Alex are the only pair who aren't afraid to publicly flaunt their affection. It gets to a point where I have to leave the room if they start making out. It can go from cute to cringey in a matter of seconds.

I'm surprised Sasha and Eli haven't jumped on the romance bandwagon with us. They seem really in tune with each other. Sasha can even interpret Eli's silences for me. Also, Eli often seems transfixed by Sasha when she talks, like he's hanging on her every word.

We've been engaging in lots of group activities this week. I think we're all worried that our days together are numbered. The next four could be our last as a group. The H.I. could split us up or send some of us back to our old lives, once this stage of the programme is over. I'm tempted to continue with whatever's next, so long as I'm still with them—the people I would now call friends. If they separate us then I'm out. I don't care what job they offer me. I'll be my usual stubborn self.

Remarkably, I've managed to push the rebel's message to the back of my mind since the night Logan and I first kissed. It doesn't seem important now. Perhaps I've just accepted that it's a divisive tactic. Or I'm drunk on the bliss of wilful ignorance.

The last few days have been easier to enjoy, more than I thought possible. I've re-read my birthday card, consciously choosing to believe those messages of love and support. I'm believing in the people who seem to really care for me—people who have saved my life, even—over the message of an anonymous rebel who tried to kill me.

We received another crate yesterday, full of food, alcohol, and leisure activities. Last night, we played a game of Twister after we'd drained several bottles of wine. I can't remember laughing so hard.

Today, I'm going berry picking with Sasha, Eli, and Logan. Logan wants the two of us to bake a berry pie tonight. My cooking skills have improved significantly with Logan and Freya's help, although I'm still terrible at baking.

Ben and Logan found more berry bushes to the east, near where we set up the snares the last time I went out with them. And I made sure to volunteer for this particular trip as I plan on sneaking off to check if the rebel's warning is still engraved on that old oak tree. The overwhelming urge to see it again has been simmering under the surface of my skin, despite my attempts to forget it.

We start out at an even pace, talking as we walk. Eli leads from the front. That way, he doesn't have to join in our conversations. The introvert in me recognises his avoidance tactics. Not that any of us take it personally. We know by now that Eli is just the strong, silent type. There's nothing wrong with that. It doesn't mean he's not interested in what we have to say. Like me, he's a good listener.

After nearly an hour of travelling, we locate the bushes. Some are blooming with orangey-red berries, others almost black. None of us know their names but we've tested them in smaller quantities and they seem safe to eat.

On the last leg of our journey here, when Sasha and Logan were busy arguing about nature versus nurture, I started planning my escape. I'm going to pretend that I need to find a 'bush bathroom', as we like to call it, then 'get lost'. I won't have much time before someone (Logan) comes to find me, so I have to run to the old oak and back. I think I remember where it is.

'Shall we collect them all today or leave some for later?' Sasha asks, opening a plastic storage container.

'Let's take all of them. We need to make two pies if we're going to have a decent piece each,' Logan replies, stripping a branch of its berry clusters.

'You'll probably need some backup pies too, if Ruby's helping,' Sasha teases, sliding me a cheeky look.

'Har har. I'll purposely burn your piece now,' I retort dryly.

Eli joins in with my roast. 'We can scrape off the burnt bits, can't we?'

'If we did that then we'd only be left with a few berries,' Sasha concludes, aiming an exaggerated grin my way.

Recently, I've taken some flak for my baking skills. Mostly because, the last time I attempted to make a cake with Freya, I was in charge of the oven, and I nearly set the cabin on fire. I haven't lived it down since.

'There are still some tinned pears in the cupboard; you could add those to the pie,' Eli mentions.

'No, I hate pears,' Logan replies with a grimace. 'So does Ruby.'

How does Logan remember so many inconsequential details about me when I can't even recall what I ate for breakfast this morning? Did Logan make me scrambled eggs? Or was that yesterday morning?

Anyway, now that they're busy berry-picking, it's a good time to excuse myself. 'I'm going to find a bush bathroom,' I announce, casually strolling off.

'Don't go too far,' Logan calls to me, his head turning briefly to check my direction.

As soon as all eyes are off me, I quicken my pace. Then, once I'm far enough from their line of sight, I bolt. I race through the trees until I come across the patch of grass where we set up the snares the other day.

Just down the hill, in that dense cluster of trees, is the old oak with the rebel's warning.

Now I'm here—reliving this secret Charlie and I chose to keep—nerves get the better of me; a pit is forming in my stomach, so deep it's a chasm of doom. *Why did you think this was a good idea, Ruby?* I ask myself, knowing I'm just looking for trouble.

My head is telling me to turn back yet my body moves forward, down the slope to the trees. I've slowed considerably, although that's only because my legs are trembling with a sense of foreboding.

As the stealthy breeze dries my perspiration, I drift through the towering natural archway. And, when their leafy shadows engulf me, a chill clings to my skin. The old oak is concealed here somewhere, its message a scab I'm wilfully picking at, knowing it will bleed.

It's not long before I see it: the winding branches, the thick flaking trunk. What I don't see is the message. It's vanished—like it was never there. I expected it to have been cut out or scratched off, but I don't see any manmade marks at all. There's no evidence that anything was ever cut into it. The chasm in my stomach fills with dread as I see the old oak as good as new, casting doubt on my sanity. I couldn't have imagined the message—Charlie was a witness to it, too. How could the rebel have rebuilt the trunk to cover it up? I wrack my brain, but confusion is a wall I can't seem to scale. What's going on? Have I got the wrong tree? I swear I'm in the right place, though. It looks exactly the same, minus the absent warning and missing knife.

'Ruby!' Logan's voice echoes in the near distance, bouncing off the trees like searching sonar; he's on his way to find me.

You need to hurry back so it's plausible that you got lost and didn't travel this far on purpose, I tell myself, my heart caught between a jump and a fall.

A shiver of awareness rakes over my skin before I see him: the man cloaked in black. He's there when I spin around, between two trees, camouflaged in the same shadows that welcomed me in.

I only realise he's there when he steps towards me, the glint of his knife catching my eye. For some reason, my first thought is to wonder if it's the same knife that was embedded in the old oak, above the vanished warning.

For a moment, I'm a statue, shock holding me in place. However, as soon as he takes another step forwards, I pelt it in the other direction, my feet finally catching up with my racing mind. It's no use, though; he's already too close.

The cloaked man pursues me with efficiency as if he'd planned for this moment. It's only a matter of seconds before I'm falling hard to the ground, tripped up by a calculated sweep of his leg. Rolling onto my back, I catch sight of the knife hurtling towards my head. Relying on reflex, I shift my body to the right, and the blade slices into my left shoulder. The knife deflects into the ground afterwards, its momentum already decided. It lodges there.

Ignoring the pain, I kick out at the cloaked man, and one flail connects with his stomach. It doesn't deter him for long as he's quick to recover and jump on top of me before I can scramble away.

The knife, rigid in the dirt, knocks into my injured shoulder. I try to reach for it while attempting to fend off my attacker. After a laborious struggle, my fingers find the hilt and I yank it free. However, the cloaked man manages to pin my wrist, the knife in my hand still useless. His other arm is a barring force across my chest, holding me down, so he can't easily snatch the knife from me. I have to somehow free my hand so I can swipe at him with the blade. *Headbutt him. He'll instinctively move his hands to his face if you do that*, I reason, my fighting instincts kicking in.

He figures out my next move before I can carry it out. He sweeps the knife out of my grasp while his other hand jumps to my throat. I can't move my head. The knife is now out of reach but he doesn't need it to hurt me. His superior size and strength are his crucial advantage. His grip on my throat tightens. Both hands now—wrapped around my neck—squeeze all the air out.

My heart is a pounding roar in my ears as my lungs scream for their next breath. I'm focused on the cloaked man, though his face is too shadowed to distinguish his features. As he strangles me, I'm unsure of whether it's the light-shielding canopy, or the black spots in my vision, which obscure his identity.

This reminds me of my near-drowning, although it's a much sharper feeling; my lungs are drier as they begin shrivelling like a deflated balloon. My head feels like it could explode, the pressure so intense that I have to close my eyes, scared they might pop out of their sockets.

That's when I see the star.

That little flickering beacon in the black space of my dying mind. The light I saw the night Logan was taken by the H.I.—when their mysterious sedative worked too well and nearly killed me. I also remember seeing it for a split second in the lake.

I'm floating again—drifting away from this place. From pain. From fear. It morphs into intention; the urge to escape it all rising in my phantom chest.

I've been here before. I can't remember what was beyond that star, but I must find out.

I push my conscious mind to the light then force my way through it.

The light overpowers the dark, burning through whatever tether had me bound.

My eyes fling open.

There's no cloaked man above me. His hands are no longer around my neck, choking the life out of me. All that's within my line of sight is a white-tiled ceiling. There's no rustle of leaves over the desperate splutters which pushed their way out of me, a mere moment ago: only a soft beeping sound. Yet I still can't seem to move my body. I'm so stiff, as if I've been asleep for a long time.

Chemicals rob the air of their natural musk. It's a clean smell—very clinical. I must be at a hospital. Someone must have saved me.

My vision sharpens enough to focus on a large lamp to my right, its warming light bathing me. I look to my left and realise I'm practically enclosed in some type of machine pod. Luckily, there isn't a lid trapping me inside. My hands glide over a slick, warm surface beneath me, solid yet moulded to the shape of my body.

I'm still too stiff to sit up, and my limbs tingle with numbness. I try to lift an arm to test its strength, and it takes a full minute before it shakily complies; I tentatively stroke my neck, finding no pain where I touch. The H.I. doctors have done a good job with my painkillers. That, or I've been unconscious for days, long enough for the bruises to fade.

Next, I touch my face, my unsure fingers skimming over something unexpected on my forehead. Fear gripping my heart again, I quickly paw at it. It's some kind of metal contraption. It's secured around the top of my head, like a headband—a halo. A halo that's fused to my fucking temples!

Not strong enough yet to remove it, I give up wasting my limited energy. Instead, I use my remaining strength to sit up to look beyond this unusual hospital bed.

I place both elbows on the moulded metal surface beneath me, pushing up as hard as I can. My body follows. And, after some strenuous effort, I'm upright.

That's when I notice the drip embedded and taped to my left hand, which is connected by a long tube to bags of various coloured fluids. I pull the tube away from the cannula but leave the needle in place for now. I shudder; I hate needles. I don't think I could stomach removing it myself. It's likely I'd faint. Even seeing it stuck in my skin makes me more lightheaded than I already am.

My mind is slowly clearing away the fog of induced sleep. I rub my eyes before I dare to look around the room. I need them to focus so I can find an exit. Logan told us he was initially bound to his hospital bed when he woke up here. Thankfully, our captors didn't think to do the same to me.

Still blinking away the misty film of sleep, I search beyond my little hospital pod. But what I find doesn't register for an extended beat.

I see *them*—the others. They're here too: Logan, Ben, Freya, Charlie, Zoe, Sasha, Eli, Dawn, and Alex. Everyone is here—asleep. Stunned, I scowl, then scrub at my eyes again. This can't be right.

We're arranged in a circle around some sort of mainframe. We're each in our own personal pods, yet it looks as though we're linked by very thin silvery cables that attach to our individual halos.

I would have thought they were all dead if it weren't for the beeping of the machines monitoring their vitals. My beeping has increased above theirs; my heart is a constant flutter in my chest, disbelief and confusion powering it. We're all dressed in long, white hospital gowns. And, with our silver halos catching the light, we look like angels.

Speech is something my laden tongue can't seem to manage. I want to wake them up but my words grate against my throat, like my morning voice does—raspy and dry—because I haven't spoken in a long while.

There's something I'm missing. Some piece of the puzzle I'm not quite sharp enough to pinpoint. My eyes dart around the spacious, white room. The walls are tiled to match the ceiling. The only sources of light seem to be artificial. I check behind me. There's a closed grey door with no visible handle, beside a small glass window, looking into an adjoining room full of high-tech computers. I assume the H.I. doctors monitor us from there, safe from our wrath behind glass.

Since I was attacked by the cloaked man, whom I presume is the rebel, the H.I. must have knocked us all out and finished the programme prematurely because it was too dangerous to continue. I guess I woke up earlier than they anticipated as I can't see anyone in that windowed room. Maybe they're on a break?

You need to wake the others up, Ruby. You can't wander around this hospital on your own; *you need backup*, I tell myself, fear making my useless muscles twitch. Adrenaline courses through my veins, my heart monitor showing that my elevated levels are creeping higher and higher, until the beeping is almost a constant hum.

Taking a calming breath, my attention centres again on my present circumstances. I need to claw this fucking halo thing off my head before I can drag myself out of this strange monitoring station/lidless sensory pod/hospital bed. My limbs are still weak, tremors jarring even my tiniest movements. I don't have the time to wait around for them to strengthen; a doctor or nurse is bound to check on us soon.

When I bring my hands up to my head to prise the contraption off, a cold sensation tickles my temples and spreads, like cool water trickling over my skin, then sinking beneath it to dilute my blood, thinning it to the point where I feel weightless—as faint as a whisper of breath.

What the fuck is happening to me? I'm losing myself again. This disorientating chill is shutting off my senses and making me drowsy—dazed. I struggle to fight it off but shaking my head only makes matters worse. Desperate to escape my pod-bed, I clumsily reach for the side and slump over the edge.

That's when a mature, silky voice murmurs, 'Don't fight it, Miss Hayes. It's a wasted effort. It's not yet time to wake up.' The voice—male—is exasperated and impatient. He's not physically in the room with me; his voice crackles out from a speaker. 'Lie back down before you hurt yourself.'

I'm trying my best to stay upright but my entire body is sluggish—too heavy and numb to control. Logan is in the pod beside mine. *Wake him up so at least he has a chance at escape*, I order myself, losing hope fast.

Reaching out as far as I can, my fingertips barely brush Logan's hand. I'm only able to tap him a few times. Although it's not much use: he maintains his slumber.

You can't give up now. Try harder!

Glancing over my shoulder, I spot the man. He's perhaps in his mid-fifties, yet his hair is jet-black with only a few grey streaks at his temples. He's watching me from the windowed monitor room, his expression impassive, almost bored. Turning away from him, I figure that my best option is to escape this pod and disconnect my halo from the mainframe. That's probably how he's controlling me.

With one last heave, I thrust my body over the lip of my pod and fall to the floor with a hard thunk. Luckily, my body is numb enough to ignore the pain, yet I still sense the impact of it. Winded, I wince, then gasp in more air to recover.

I hear the light whoosh of a door opening. Then soft clicks and a slight drag of shoe soles on the tiled floor as the man makes his way over to me.

Despite knowing it's futile, I crawl away, dragging my limp lower half behind me. Any moment now, I'll fall under—this nefarious cold will submerge me into its icy depths.

'Insufferably stubborn. Foolishly so. I have no idea why he wants you so much,' the man comments, exasperated.

I roll onto my back to see him looming over me, the familiar sneer of disgust shaping his mouth. That look of judgement is something I've grown accustomed to over the years. He's glaring at me with sharp, pale blue eyes, similar to a frosted lake. He looks familiar but I'm too out of it to make the connection. My eyes... I think they're green; green like the moss growing on the stones surrounding the lake. They're overpowered by the weight of sleep—forced shut again against my wavering will.

'Goodnight, Miss Hayes. Morning light will have to wait,' I hear him say in a faintly mocking tone, before all sound falls away with me into a black hole of nothingness.

A tangible darkness is the only safety net that catches me.

In its cold clutch, I hurtle away from my beacon of hope. The light retracts, smaller and smaller until it's only a pinprick.

I remember this place. This has happened to me before. But last time, when I woke up, I forgot. *You can't forget this time, Ruby.*

My mind suddenly stills.

'Ruby?' Logan's voice echoes in my ears.

Before I can register anything else, intense pain shoots through me—my neck, my arm.

'Please, open your eyes,' Logan begs, desperation making his voice shake.

Heeding his command, my eyes flutter. His face is close to mine, his forehead slick with sweat, his eyes shining with unshed tears. The forest is behind him, swaying with the wind. No, not the wind. He's moving—*we're* moving. I'm in his arms; he's carrying me.

'Ruby, what happened? I found you lying on the ground, barely breathing. Your shoulder is sliced open and your neck is bright red,' Logan says in a breathless rush.

'Rebel,' I whimper. Speaking is pure pain; worse than after my near-drowning.

'He attacked you again?! Have you been stabbed anywhere else?' Logan is bordering on frantic now; his eyes are bulging.

'Str—ang...' I strive to finish the word, but the pain is too sharp.

'He strangled you?' Logan guesses, his face scrunching in rage.

'Ruby? Logan? Where are you?' Sasha calls out from further away.

Logan returns her call. 'Sash! Help! Ruby's been attacked!'

A moment later, the scuffle of rushed footsteps can be heard over Logan's strained gasps.

'Oh, fuck! What happened to her?!' Sasha demands, horror-stricken.

Logan lowers me to the ground, then Sasha is there, hovering over me, Eli right behind her. Logan yanks at the slashed, blood-soaked sleeve of my jumper to rip it clean off, so they can better tend to my wound.

'The rebel throttled her. She must have put up a good fight because there was a knife right beside her, but she only seems to have that cut on her shoulder,' Logan relays to them, filling in the gaps.

'Did you see the rebel? Where is he now?' Eli quizzes him.

'No. I don't know. I heard the sounds of a struggle and followed them to find her unconscious on the ground, her blood everywhere,' Logan replies, catching his breath. His pale, bloodshot eyes glisten again. 'At first, I thought she was dead.'

'You must have scared him off before he had the chance to kill her,' Eli assumes, his arched eyebrows drawing together.

'What do we do? It's an hour's walk back to the cabin. She could bleed out before we get there,' Logan stresses, his voice breaking. 'She can't die! I can't lose her now, Sash.'

'Logan, calm down. You know I won't let that happen,' Sasha placates him in a soothing tone while she applies pressure to my shoulder wound. It fucking hurts but I'm too weak from blood loss to make a sound of protest. All I can muster is a faint whimper.

'We can't hold it shut like that when we're moving around. It needs to be plugged or stitched!' Logan shouts, his frustration growing.

'Logan, you're not helping,' Eli interjects calmly. 'I can assist. I've done some field medic training in the past.'

Logan waves him off. 'That's not the issue here. Just give me a second to think.' He grips his hair at the temples, jaw tight.

'Just find me some moss. Both of you—go!' Sasha commands them sternly.

Eli is quick to comply, whereas Logan takes a few seconds longer, apparently too overwhelmed to fully function.

Moss—wasn't I just thinking about green moss?

I'm left alone with Sasha. She presses down more firmly with both hands, stemming the flow of blood so it's only a dribble.

'You need to stop scaring us like this, Rubes. When Ben finds out you nearly died again, he'll never relent on those jokes. He'll have a field day,' she jests, trying her best to calm me, but my mind blanks as my body hollows. My teeth chatter loudly. 'Did you see the rebel's face?'

I shake my head, and she sighs. 'When you fell unconscious, did you... do you remember anything else? From before or after?' she mumbles, struggling to keep my wound closed.

I shake my head again as Sasha finds the right amount of pressure to apply. She visibly relaxes.

'That's a shame,' she mutters, distracted.

Logan and Eli appear with handfuls of spongy moss. They pass it to Sasha, who hastily stuffs some into my knife wound, plugging it up.

'You really think that will be enough to stop the bleeding?' Logan asks, sceptical.

'For your information, moss saved a lot of lives in World War Two,' Sasha teaches, but Logan, still not satisfied, pulls off his jumper and T-shirt in one swift move, throwing the latter to her before he pulls his jumper back on. She ties his T-shirt around my shoulder tightly, making me cry out.

Eli brushes the dirt off his hands. 'We need to get her back to the cabin as fast as we can. The emergency medical kit they sent us in the last crate had stitches, bandages, and antiseptic. I think it even had a local anaesthetic.'

'If we do a good enough job, she may not need the hospital,' Logan adds, rubbing a hand over his face, leaving a smudge of dirt on his forehead.

Hospital—that word registers somewhere in my brain. Why is it standing out?

Eli frowns. 'She'll need to go to the hospital, Logan. Just in case.'

'We may never see her again if she does,' Logan counters, panic flaring in his eyes.

'Didn't you say she was strangled? That must have caused some damage to her throat,' Eli argues, gesturing to the marks that must be visible around my neck.

Sasha groans. 'We can argue about this later. Anyway, it should be for Ruby to decide, not us.'

'I'll carry her for a while,' Eli offers.

'No, I want to,' Logan insists, kneeling down at my side.

Sasha stops him from trying to pick me up. 'You're shaking. You'll end up dropping her.'

Eli takes Logan's place. 'You can carry her when you've recovered.'

'No... I... wal—k,' I somehow get out in a painful rasp. I don't want to burden them with my weight the whole way back to the cabin; I'm not the lightest person. My insecurity makes me cringe. That's probably not what I should be worrying about right now, when my life is on the line.

'Stop being so stubborn,' Logan growls, letting Eli scoops me up in his strong arms.

Stubborn.

That word triggers the memory; a flash of an older man with jet-black hair and frosted-blue eyes. The cold numbness I'm feeling now is also familiar. The hospital—I woke up there: the white room, the chemical smell, warm moulded metal, monitors beeping... It's all coming back to me in a haze—a jumbled mess of memory—fragmented; the pieces not quite fitting together.

I must not have been at a hospital, though, because I'm still injured. I haven't been anywhere since the rebel attacked me. The programme isn't over, and I'm still in the forest with everyone, just as I was before.

Then I remember that we were all angels.

Chapter 27

SEE THE LIGHT

We make it back to the cabin in less than an hour. The moss has proven useful in reducing blood loss. I'm still alive and, thankfully, conscious this time.

This is the third occasion that I've had to be carried into this cabin. The others must think I'm either extremely unlucky, or a dramatic attention seeker.

As soon as Freya, Dawn, Alex, Charlie, and Ben spot Logan emerging from the forest with me cradled in his arms, they rush to my aid. None of them seem surprised that I'm the one injured.

Sasha fills them in on what happened while Logan lowers me onto a dining chair in the kitchen. Eli grabs the medical kit and Freya fills a container full of warm water to wash my wound clean of the bloody moss.

My head still swims with shock from the attack. The loss of blood, mixed with the images which continue to reform in my memory of what I saw through the star—the hospital, the monitoring pod, the halo, the man with the frosted-blue eyes, and the others asleep in a circle—they swirl around my mind in a loop. All I know for certain was that I *wasn't* taken to a hospital. It must have happened inside my head. I had the same doubts about the hand I saw wrapped around my ankle in the lake. Most of them believed me when I divulged that information, though I don't expect they'll be as understanding this time. Explaining everything I witnessed to them—when I was unconscious from strangulation—seems pointless. Even *I* know that it was most likely my imagination running wild between life and death. Still, it's hard to shake off because it all felt so real.

'Why did you leave her alone to be attacked?' Ben demands, rounding on Logan.

Logan shrugs, guilt tightening his features. 'She wandered off.'

'My... fault,' I state hoarsely. 'I went... to check... snares. They... didn't know.' My voice is a fraction better, although it's still painful to talk. The 'I got lost' excuse won't work because I was found too far away for it to be believable. I catch Charlie's eye and gather he knows the truth; he knows I went back to check the old oak.

'Mate, I know you're hurt and all that, but I have to say it: you're a muppet,' Ben chastises me, shaking his head, yet his tone conveys fondness.

I allow Freya and Sasha to wash my wound, and only let a sound of discomfort escape when they pour the cleaning solution on to kill the bacteria. The sharp sting takes a while to subside. Eli prepares the medical needle and stitches, ready to sew me up. That's the part I'm dreading most. Now I *wish* I were still unconscious.

'Have you done this before?' Charlie asks Eli. I had the same question but I'm glad Charlie got there first; I don't want Eli to think I doubt his skills.

'A couple times—in Afghanistan. I was never the official medic, but when you're in the field, with people falling injured all around you, even squaddies pick up a few things,' he assures us, picking up another needle attached to a syringe.

'What's...?' I ask, my voice too raw and shaky to say more, so I simply point to the syringe with an equally shaky finger.

Noticing my reluctance, Eli says, 'It would be near impossible to bear the pain of stitches without a local anaesthetic.'

Trying to be brave, I nod despite my whole body revolting at the thought of a needle piercing my skin. Sweat drips down my back under my mud-covered jumper. I know it's silly, since I've literally been sliced open with a knife and didn't bat an eye. But there's just something about needles that makes me nauseous. It's probably because I was full of adrenaline during the attack and wasn't expecting it. Now, I'm watching Eli prep the tools he'll be using to close my extremely sore wound.

Logan is by my side in the blink of an eye, taking my hand in his. 'Squeeze as tight as you want,' he says softly, though he doesn't meet my gaze. Is he annoyed at me?

I plan to soldier through it. However, as soon as Eli unsheathes the needle, my wooziness intensifies, and then everything dissolves to darkness.

In what feels like a few seconds, I come to, finding myself lying against Logan's chest at the dining table, my arse in his lap. Eli is busy bandaging my shoulder while everyone else is milling about the kitchen, shooting me concerned looks.

'Did I pass out?' I ask, my throat dry and sore, though the ache is bearable.

Eli nods. 'Lucky for you. I gave you the anaesthetic anyway, just in case.'

Still dizzy, my head lolls back to rest on Logan's shoulder. I'm too weak to let my mortification take hold, but I'm sure I'll look back on this later and cringe. I can't believe I fainted at the sight of a needle. How pathetic.

AMBER BAYLEY

Even though I'm sitting in Logan's lap, our bodies touching, the emotional distance between us is noticeable. Peeking up, I see that he's lost in thought, still looking worried, or pissed off, or a mixture of the two. He has one arm around my waist, and the other is holding my injured arm still for Eli. I lift my good arm so I can place a hand over his at my waist. He removes it as soon as he feels the tentative brush of my thumb, pushing me to sit up a little so he can readjust in the seat, creating more space between our bodies.

Shit. He's not just annoyed at me; he's angry.

'There—all done. It wasn't as deep as I thought, so as long as you keep it clean, I doubt it will cause you much trouble,' Eli concludes, tucking the end of the bandage in to keep it secure.

'Thanks, Eli,' I convey, wiping sweat and dirt away from my forehead with the back of my hand. 'Logan—look—we're bandage buddies,' I joke, smiling at him over my shoulder, but Logan doesn't look impressed. He simply grunts in response, and I swallow down my hurt.

'Here, sweetie—drink some water.' Freya hands me a cup of room-temperature water and two painkillers. I gulp them down, ignoring the sharp stab in the back of my tight throat.

'This is the second time the rebel's gone for you, Rubes. Why you? Why not someone else?' Ben questions, leaning against the kitchen counter, his thick arms crossed over his chest.

'A coincidence? Wrong place at the wrong time? It only happened because she went off on her own.' Alex shoots a glance at me then hastily adds, 'Not that it's your fault or anything.'

Without warning, Logan stands up with me in his arms. My shoulder hurts too much to move my arm, so it just hangs limply as he carries me through to the living area. Before anyone can follow, Logan cuts them a sharp look that says, *'Don't'.*

My body, broken and bruised as it is, is still aware enough to react to Logan's proximity, his dominant display making me a little giddy. 'Where are you taking me?'

'You're caked in blood and dirt. I can't look at you when you're like this,' Logan grinds out, climbing the stairs with me still cradled.

'Yeah, I'm sure I don't look my best right now,' I mutter, my face heating at his clear disgust. 'Not that I'm any better looking cleaned up.'

Logan finally meets my eyes when we reach the landing. 'It's nothing to do with attractiveness, Ruby. What I mean is... it upsets me to see you hurt—in pain. I just keep picturing you lying on the ground... the knife... the blood.' He pauses, shutting his eyes tightly as if to stave off the tormenting mental image. 'I wasn't there when you needed me. It's my fault you—'

I cut him off before he can spiral. 'It wasn't your fault. You found me in time. I'm okay.' Pushing through the pain, I lift my hand to cup his clenched jaw as he walks us into the bathroom.

'Why would you stroll off on your own like that?' Logan enquires, his eyebrows knitting together. He sets me down on the closed toilet seat.

'I'm sorry, I wasn't thinking. I just wanted to be useful,' I lie, unable to speak the truth. If Charlie and I hadn't sworn each other to secrecy, I'd probably tell Logan the real reason I ran off. I know in my heart that I can trust him. If he didn't care about me, he wouldn't be so affected by my ordeal or blame himself for my pain.

This seems to ease his anger. He leans down to kiss me lightly on the lips, his hand snaking around to gently cup the back of my neck for support. 'You terrify me sometimes.' He stares down at the marks the rebel left on my throat, with the fear he speaks of flashing in his eyes.

'I'm sorry, I don't mean to.' I'm not lying now; I *do* feel sincerely guilty for making everyone, especially him, worry so much.

Still bending over, Logan presses his forehead to mine. The intimacy of the action has my heart melting. Sighing again, his eyes close, as if he's relishing the relief he feels at having me here, safe.

Logan straightens to run a flannel under the tap. 'Can you stand? Or are you still too light-headed?'

'I think I'm steady enough now.'

Logan helps me to my feet. He shows me what's in his other hand: a small pair of hair-cutting scissors. 'Can I?' With his eyes, he gestures down to my soiled jumper, now with one sleeve missing.

My pulse jumping, I nod.

'If I were a better person, I'd let one of the girls help you get cleaned up,' he murmurs, taking the bottom of my jumper in hand to cut up the seam.

When Logan's fingers graze my skin, my teeth sink into my bottom lip, and what remains of my blood pumps to very intimate places.

'Are you wearing underwear?' Logan whispers, and I'm not sure what he'd prefer my answer to be. His dilated pupils aren't indication enough.

'Yes,' I manage to say, though it's breathy.

'Good,' is all he replies. Again, I'm unsure if he's disappointed or thankful.

A second later, what remains of my ruined jumper falls to the bathroom floor. I'm standing in front of him wearing only my equally dirty leggings and a sports bra that unfortunately doesn't showcase my breasts. Regardless, the amount of my skin on show makes me feel bare. Especially considering my stomach isn't flat by any means and it's looked down on in our society to be anything other than thin. If Logan were anyone else, I'd feel vulnerable like this. But with him, I feel safe—accepted as I am.

Logan makes a point of not looking at my body. He keeps his eyes locked with mine. He places the scissors down on the sink cabinet then passes me the warm, wet cloth and soap. 'No shower, I'm afraid. You shouldn't get your shoulder wet. I'll fetch you a change of clothes. And when I come back, I'll help you wash your hair in the sink.' He turns me around to face the sink, his hands lingering on my naked waist. In the mirror in front of us, I catch the dunk of his Adam's apple. 'I can pull these down, if that also helps?' He pinches at the elastic waist of my leggings, his index finger running along the cusp. The tickle of it has my nipples pebbling and my body aching for those fingers of his to dip lower. 'Save you bending over and using your arms too much.'

Desire pounds through my veins, hearing the rough edge now present in his voice, and the mental image of me bent over with him so close behind me... lined up perfectly.

'Okay.'

'I won't look, even though I really, *really* want to,' he promises, and despite the sharp ache in my throat, I laugh.

In the mirror, I watch Logan shut his eyes. Then slowly, he teases the material down my thighs until it pools at my feet. He dips down, knees bending, to collect my leggings, which I step out of for him. His head is inches away from my arse. But when I look over my shoulder to check, his eyes are still closed.

Before Logan stands, his smooth palm strokes up my calf, and the contact has me shivering with delight. I'm so glad I shaved my legs in the shower this morning.

When his face appears in the mirror again, I notice that his cheeks are redder than they were. He's blushing as brightly as I am. That's comforting, and cute. Really cute.

'On second thought, I'm not sure I'm strong enough to help you get changed,' he admits, his hands now back on my waist. 'I think I've used up all of my self-control for today.'

Smiling shyly, I say, 'Don't worry, I'm sure I can wash and dress myself without assistance. The painkillers are kicking in now, anyway.'

Logan nods. 'I'll bring you clothes to sleep in. Then, when you're ready, I'll wash your hair for you. I can do that without combusting,' he jokes, his thumbs stroking the curve of my hips, right above the elastic of my plain black cotton knickers. It only encourages the throbbing between my legs.

I offer him a small smile, unable to think of anything witty to respond. All I can focus on is where he's touching me, and that I'm standing right in front of him in just my underwear. Even though he's trying his best not to sneak a peek. Unfortunately for me, he's too gallant.

I kind of wish he wasn't. Even though I'm in no fit state to do much more than stand on my own two feet. Let alone make out or... *God, Ruby, you definitely shouldn't be thinking about sex right now.*

'Stamp your feet if you need me. I'll listen out.' With my tattered clothes in hand, Logan leaves the bathroom so I can wash.

As I clean myself up, my mind wanders back to the dilemma I face: should I inform the others about the dream/out-of-body experience I had? The same thing has happened twice now. Well, three times if I count the brief moment in the lake. The whole 'light at the end of the tunnel' thing—with the star in the darkness—is what makes me think it's all nonsense my mind conjured to deal with its deactivation process.

What other possibility is there? That it was real? That I was transported somewhere else? I can't find any logic in those ridiculous theories. No sensible person would entertain such otherworldly notions. I won't allow myself to descend into irrationality. I must stay within the realms of reality.

It's the next morning. There are only three days to go before the big secret of our kidnapping is revealed. And the closer this programme is to ending, the more nervous I become. It's not only the fear of the unknown; it's that I might be tackling it without my friends. I may never see any of them again after this.

My sleep last night was plagued by traumatic flashbacks from the attack, and the mystery of what occurred afterwards. The man from the monitoring room kept staring at me. The more I think about him, the more recognisable he becomes. Have I met him before? If he's a figment of my imagination, have I based his appearance on someone from my past?

When Logan returned to the bathroom the second time, after I'd washed and changed, he shampooed my hair for me. The experience was surprisingly intimate, especially when he took the time to massage my temples.

On occasion, being a woman can have its advantages: the evidence of my arousal isn't noticeable, for one. Unfortunately for Logan, after I let an embarrassing moan tumble from my lips—too caught up in the tingling scalp massage he was delivering—the evidence of *his* arousal was plain to see, his joggers not doing much to hide it. We didn't address it, and I tried to avoid the temptation of looking—of *touching*—providing him with the same courtesy he gave me when I was stripped down to my underwear. But it was a hard thing to ignore. Quite literally.

As soon as Logan had finished rinsing me off, he wrapped my hair in a towel and made a quick exit. He called for Sasha to come up to help me set and dry my curls before bed. And when I was finally ready for sleep, Logan was there, though he didn't make room for me in his bed, saying that he didn't want to hurt me and that sleeping separately was best. I'm sure a large part of that decision was based on reducing temptation. Especially after the sexual tension we both felt mounting in the bathroom.

My neck and arm are both incredibly swollen today. The throbbing pain is what I'd imagine being stung by a hive of bees would feel like. Charlie and Eli tried to persuade me to ask the H.I. for an examination in their hospital, to make sure there was no lasting damage. But I decided against that idea. Logan's words stuck with me: if I were extracted for medical care now, I might never return to my friends. I can't risk it. Anyway, I don't actually feel that terrible, considering I've been dragged through hell and back numerous times these past two weeks.

Bedrest has been strongly advised in its place, but I don't want to miss out on anything. Wasting one of my last days here by sleeping doesn't appeal to me. So I join the others in the meadow for a game of football. Obviously, I'm not able to participate, because of my injuries, so I play referee for them instead. That makes even teams as Zoe is unlikely to play either.

The two teams consist of Logan, Sasha, Alex, and Freya, against Ben, Charlie, Dawn, and Eli. As the referee, I'm sitting on the sidelines in the middle of the meadow pitch, between two jumper goalposts, watching the others have fun without me. I received a brief lesson from Ben on the rules of the game as it's been about fifteen years since I played. It can't be that hard, though. I'll just wait until someone moans about something the other team did and then agree one way or the other.

Zoe, to everyone's surprise, has left her room and made an appearance. She's standing nearer the cabin, watching from a distance, nowhere near me.

The game begins.

Most of them, I already assume, are going to be competitive. Logan and Ben tackle each other for the ball, and Sasha is shadowing Eli to make sure he doesn't receive a pass. The more she blocks him, the wider his grin. Then, when she intercepts the ball and manoeuvres past him to score the first goal, his laugh is full of pride. It's the first time I've seen him really laugh out loud like that—so uninhibited.

When Eli gives Sasha a congratulatory hug, I spot the sparkle in both their eyes. There's definitely potential there for more than friendship. I don't think I'm just wishful thinking.

Ten minutes later, I'm pulled into a dispute about a handball. Apparently, the ball accidentally grazed Charlie's forearm when he attempted to block Logan's kick to goal. I know I'm referee but I don't want to choose between the two. Luckily, Charlie doesn't care as much about the game as everyone else so he lets Logan have a penalty, much to Ben's dismay. Ben goes to goal and manages to block Logan's attempt, which cheers him up significantly.

I'm so engrossed in the game that I don't notice Zoe is beside me until she speaks. 'You've been resurrected more times than Jesus now.'

I snort a laugh. 'Yeah, except I feel more like a walking corpse than the supposed Messiah.'

'You certainly look like one, too,' Zoe quips, sneering. I knew that was coming so shrugging it off isn't a problem.

After a long minute, she continues, 'Did you see the light?'

Fast as a whip, my head snaps in Zoe's direction, and I instantly regret it; a scalding knife slices at my neck. Only figuratively, of course. I groan, slowly moving my head back to the centre. She finds my suffering highly amusing.

'Nope, no light at the end of the tunnel. No pearly gates. No angels either, sorry,' I mutter, keeping my eyes on the game.

'Hmm. Not exactly Heaven, was it? That dull white room is more like Hell,' she mentions casually. A chill scurries its way down my spine as my eyes widen. She knows about the room in my death dream. 'Wait a minute before you follow me.' She stands, then slinks off into the forest, not looking back.

The others are too distracted by the game to notice Zoe's absence. Not to be big-headed, but they're more likely to notice my absence. Nevertheless, I'll have to risk it to find out what she knows.

I wait sixty seconds, preparing to casually walk into the forest after Zoe while the others run towards the opposite end of the meadow. My chance arises when Alex intercepts a pass and travels up the pitch towards goal, the ball in his control.

Unnecessarily panicked, I scramble up and scurry backwards until the forest conceals me from view. *So much for being casual, Ruby.*

Searching for Zoe, I slow my pace. She only had a minute's head start yet she's nowhere to be found. I continue walking, cautiously scanning the trees for any movement. I'm contemplating turning back when she springs out from behind a tree, making me jump, hurting my neck again in the process.

'It's a shame I'm not the rebel, eh?' Zoe says darkly.

'Just tell me about the white room,' I demand, my glare impatient. I'm not interested in playing her cruel games anymore.

'So, you *did* see the light?' Her laugh is mocking. 'I'm surprised you've kept it to yourself. Don't you trust them? You're all so chummy all the time. It's sickening.'

'I thought it was all in my head,' I reply in a low voice.

'It is. It's *all* in your head,' she delivers with a sly grimace, placing her hands on her hips.

Face dropping into a scowl, I cross my arms under my bust. 'What are you on about, Zoe?'

'Listen,' she commands, her dark sea-green eyes roaming around.

'Listen to what?' I automatically do the same, my paranoia triggered.

'The forest.'

Rolling my eyes, I do as Zoe instructs. We spend half a minute in silence.

'Can you hear anything?' she asks.

'No, am I supposed to?'

'Yeah, you're supposed to. It's a forest, you dimwit. Don't you think it would have more distinctive sounds in it? Not just stock background noises?' Zoe retorts, matching my aggravated tone.

In reply to my confused expression, she continues, 'Since being here, have you ever seen a bird, a deer, or even a beetle? Anything that wasn't consciously planned? Things that served no purpose, unlike the wolves?'

I think on it, struggling to remember even one instance which has stood out to me. There haven't been any weird bird calls, or bees buzzing around my face, or anything you'd expect travelling through different parts of a forest. Still, I don't understand what she's getting at.

'Nothing stands out, does it? That's because none of that stuff is at the forefront of our minds. We only have what we need in here. The fish that appear at the end of a rod, the rabbits ready for us in the snares, even the berry bushes. No use for anything else so we just don't think about it. It doesn't manifest,' Zoe explains, still frustratingly vague.

The pit of doom reforms in my stomach when I come to comprehend her words; this place is set up. It must be a fake forest. 'Is this forest manmade? Like a film set or something?'

Zoe huffs. 'I'm basically giving you the fucking answer and you still don't get it?' She lets out a groan of frustration while massaging her temples. 'Have you ever wondered why you're so in tune with everyone—with their thoughts and feelings all the time? How you've all grown so close so quickly?' She pronounces it slowly, as if talking to an infant.

'Yeah, like sometimes they can read my mind,' I reply, ignoring her patronising tone.

'Maybe they are. Maybe we're all *connected*,' Zoe emphasises, and I swallow hard, dread creeping down my spine.

Painful goosebumps rise up on my forearms when it registers. 'The halos—they were connecting us together,' I whisper, my mouth running dry. 'Are you saying that what I saw in the white room was real?'

'That's for you to decide. They're all about choice here, apparently,' she says bitterly, sauntering off towards the meadow.

I spend a full minute processing what Zoe is implying. The idea that this forest isn't what it seems, and that we only have what we need in here... it sounds far-fetched, to say the least. But isn't being kidnapped for a supposed government survival training programme, meant for recruitment, just as unbelievable? What did she mean about the other stuff not being at the forefront of our minds? Just that we don't notice that stuff, like birds and insects? Or that we haven't noticed they don't exist here at all?

Zoe was heavily hinting that the white room was real. However, when I asked her at the beginning of the conversation if that experience was all in my head, she said it was. She must be messing with me, trying to make me doubt myself—to make me feel like I'm losing my grip on reality. On the other hand, if it wasn't real, then how did she know about the white room? I haven't told anyone, so the only way she could know is if she'd been there, too. And, as far as I'm aware, she hasn't had any near-death experiences.

Ugh, this is so frustrating! Why couldn't Zoe simply tell me outright what she meant? Why did she have to be so vague? She's so fucking annoying. Why can't I connect the dots?

Head spinning, I jog back the way I came. Hopefully, nobody noticed my short absence. It's only been a few minutes, and I haven't heard anyone calling my name.

Reaching the meadow, I recall the image of all of us as angels, lying in those capsule-like hospital pods, with metal bands and wires connecting us together.

The others are still focused on playing football while Zoe strolls back to the cabin. I swiftly reclaim my referee spot on the ground, pretending I haven't moved a muscle.

I feel in my gut that the white room was real. And because I'm almost positive that I haven't acquired any psychic abilities, I reckon it *happened* (past tense), and not *will* happen; it's not some kind of premonition about future events or time travel. Which means I must have been transported somewhere else.

It's still beyond the realms of physics, though, right? If I can't allow myself to believe in time travel then I certainly can't believe in transportation of mind or matter. Anyway, it doesn't explain why the others were there with me.

If Zoe's intention was to derail my rational thinking process, then it's working. Between the rebel's warning, and Zoe's word games, I'm spiralling—my mind unravelling before me.

I'm brought back to reality when I hear Logan's team cheering. They must have won the match because it was the first team to three goals.

After their celebration, we all head back inside to prepare dinner. Logan must notice my pensive mood as he urges me to take a nap, saying he'll wake me when dinner is ready.

I trudge upstairs, lost in thought. Climbing the last step, I lift my head to see Zoe on the landing, waiting for me. I'm about to ask her for more information but she raises a finger to her lips to stop me; she must suspect the cabin is bugged or that someone will overhear. Nonetheless,

I'm so desperate to quiz her about the white room that I don't care who's listening.

Sensing my eagerness to ignore her shushing, Zoe speaks before I can. 'You're planning on taking a nap before dinner, are you? Well, just make sure you *wake up* on time. Okay?' With that, she hurries into her room and shuts the door behind her.

'*Wake up*' were the words she emphasised. They ring a bell. Somewhere inside my brain, something is tugging on those words—pulling memories from the corners of my mind until they collide together in the middle, presenting themselves in a neat little bow.

The words that were said to me in the white room, by the man over the speaker: '*Don't fight it, Miss Hayes. It's a wasted effort. It's not yet time to wake up.*'

I had woken up in the monitoring pod but the others hadn't; they were all still asleep. The man had to put me back under with the help of the halo, used to control me. That's when I woke up in the forest.

The realisation nearly floors me.

We're all asleep—this forest isn't real.

It's all in our heads.

Chapter 28

BULLET TO THE HEAD

All of the air in my lungs exits as the room begins to spin. I have to lean against the wall for support. My legs are suddenly jelly. Yet despite this physical reaction, my mind isn't foggy. On the contrary, I'm finally seeing things clearly.

None of this is real: we're dreaming, our bodies trapped in some kind of suspended animation. How is that even possible?

And Zoe is somehow aware of it. She could be the only one. But the rebel's message said not to trust anyone, and perhaps this was why—because more of them know. How could Zoe have this information without being in on the secret? She must work for the H.I.

It's then that I recall part of the rebel's message, the part I've overlooked until now: *Not real. All lies.* I thought it implied that my friends weren't real. Yet, all along, the rebel has been warning me about the dream I'm in. It all makes sense now.

It also means that the end of his message—'*death is only escape*'—is another clue, not a threat. The occasions I woke from this forest dream were the moments death's shadow was cast upon me. Apart from when

I was drowning: Logan managed to pump the water out of my lungs before I fell unconscious. The two times the rebel tried to kill me may not have been malicious; he could only have been attempting to wake me up.

The rebel might be the shadow man from my dream memories—the man who saved me from the attack by my alleyway. How am I dreaming within a dream, though? How do I sleep each night when it's already the constant state I've been forced into?

Enough! You don't have time to dwell on these complicated questions. You need to escape.

My best bet is to keep this revelation to myself. I can't be sure what the H.I. will do to me if they discover I'm *aware*. I need to prove this theory on my own. I can't trust anyone to help me, not even Logan or Charlie.

With the shock wearing off, an idea takes shape: I need to hear what the rebel has to say. Maybe he's waiting for me by the old oak, hoping I figure things out in time.

The first part of my plan is clear...

I have to sneak out.

Knowing there's no way I could sneak out the front door, I end up climbing out of my bedroom window onto the sloping roof of the kitchen instead.

Flat on my stomach, I peer down through the downstairs window. Logan, Freya, and Alex are busy cooking dinner. Dread demolishes my confidence when I realise I'll have to roll off the roof instead of dangling because they'd easily see me hanging there.

Psyching myself up, I position my body along the edge of the roof. Luckily, because of the slight decline, it's not much higher than one storey, and the bushes below will likely soften my fall. I cross my arms over my chest, locking my neck and tucking in my chin, then let myself roll off, front first.

Fortunately, my neck and wounded shoulder don't absorb the brunt of the fall, but they still suffer the shockwaves from it; tremors of pain have me gasping and writhing—the wind is completely knocked out of me. I'm forced to recuperate on a prickly bed of bushes for a full five minutes before the consequences subside enough for me to function.

Eventually, I'm able to shakily push myself to stand, then stagger off into the forest as quickly as my body will allow. Hopefully, nobody has seen me leave.

My heart is a hummingbird, hovering in my throat. I'm a dizzy mess, yet I force myself on. The truth is all I care about now; all my thoughts swirl around it—this void shrouded in secrecy, dark and gravitational.

The rebel may be my only ally here. I *need* to find him.

One of my stitches must have pulled in the fall because a growing red patch of blood is seeping through my grey sweatshirt. That can't be good.

The forest gradually deepens around me, shadows dancing, as the sun creeps lower in the delicate pink sky. The wind picks up, whistling through the trees and whipping my curls into a frenzy. I wish I'd thought to secure my hair in a bun before I left. Remembering to wear a jacket would also have been useful. I blame the painkillers for robbing me of sense. Maybe that's why I decided to practically jump off a roof and venture into a cold, eerie forest just before nightfall to pursue someone who's tried to kill me twice.

Anyways, what's done is done and I'm out here already. If I don't move faster, it will be too dark for the return journey. Or perhaps I won't want to return to the cabin after I learn the truth. I haven't planned that far ahead yet.

After an hour or so of walking, I finally stumble across our snare patch. I hurry down the slope, eager to locate the old oak and hopefully the rebel.

Reaching the oak, I search the vicinity, though there's no sign of the cloaked man who strangled me yesterday. What I do find is the knife, lying on the ground under some fallen autumn leaves. I pick it up and grip the hilt loosely in hand. As I inspect it, I deduce that it *is* the same army knife we were provided with on the first day. It's not sheathed so I can't slide it into my pocket or waistband. Walking around with the knife in hand, I hope the rebel doesn't think I'm here to enact my revenge. I'll have to state my intentions clearly.

'Hello! Is anyone here? I understand your message now. I know you're not here to hurt me. You're here to wake me up, right? Come out. I need to know the truth!' I shout out into the impending night.

In the inactive pause, I savour rest—my perspiration drying—yet my heartrate refuses to slow. There's no response from the rebel, only the answering murmur of brittle leaves in the ghostly wind. It's reasonable to assume he hasn't lingered, wary of retaliation from the H.I. after attacking me. *You should keep searching*, I tell myself, not ready to accept defeat just yet.

I parade around the empty forest for half an hour, repeating the same words over and over, attempting to coax the rebel out. But there's still no sign of him.

Dusk departs in a blink of an eye. I nearly stumble over a fallen branch which I fail to notice as I stamp around clumsily. My ripped stitch is starting to gnaw at the relief my painkillers provided. My whole body is practically one big bruise and I'm so very tired. It's probably wisest to return to the cabin, then try again in the morning. But what if the others have already noticed my absence and I have no excuse for why I left? I guess I could say that the rebel kidnapped me and I somehow escaped. I can't tell them the truth without any evidence. They'll likely call for my extraction, assuming the attack scrambled my brain.

Knowing my limits, I decide to head back. *For fuck's sake.* It will be a stressful night from here on out. Not that it isn't already. But I'll be worrying about everyone's intentions again. Yet what other choice do I have? I can't stumble around the forest in the dark all night, freezing to death.

That's when the intrusive thought hits me and a chill tries to prick at my cold, numb skin.

Perhaps that's not such a bad idea. *Death.* That could be the proof I need.

Death is only escape.

If I kill myself, I should wake up in the white room. I don't need the rebel. I can just stab myself with this knife. *But what if you're wrong?* The rational part of my brain nags at me, full of doubt. If I stab myself, I can't come back from that. If I'm mistaken, then I'm really dead. For good this time.

I have to take that risk. I'm sure I'm right about this, and it's the only other option I have at my disposal.

Disregarding the very real risk of death, I hold the knife in front of me, the sharp tip pointed towards my chest. I stare at the cool, silver blade as it battles against the darkness to find the tiny sliver of light. My breath quickens at the thought of going all *Romeo and Juliet* and plunging it into my chest. Can I really do it? Kill myself to prove a point? Fear trickles into each vein of my body, turning them into ice. Goosebumps cover every inch of my skin. I'm shivering now. My teeth ache as they clash from violent chattering.

Is this how my brother felt before he took his own life?

That question only summons another plague of doubt along with a sharp stab of guilt.

This is not *the same as that; if anything, it's the opposite—you're not giving up, you're fighting back. This is you struggling to survive by any means necessary.*

Adding to the sombre mood, rain starts to fall. The tiny droplets splash onto my trembling, blotchy-white hands while they grip the knife handle tightly. I'm already losing my resolve when I spot Logan rushing into a clearing in the distance, about two hundred metres away. He clocks me and gapes in confusion, his body going rigid. Then all the blood drains from his face when he realises I have a knife pointed at my chest.

'Ruby, what are you doing?!' Logan demands, shouting across the distance. 'Put that knife down!' He takes a few steps towards me, abject horror written all over his pallid face.

'Stop! Don't come any closer, Logan,' I warn him, my voice shaking as fiercely as my hands.

Logan abruptly halts, his hands raising, palms out. 'Why are you pointing a knife at yourself? Ruby, you're really scaring me.'

'I need to do this. I need to find out... something,' I reply, too vaguely to prove that my sanity isn't as frayed as it must seem.

'Hey! What's going on? Have you found her?' I hear Charlie enquire, appearing out of the forest behind Logan. Ben and Sasha join them a moment later. They all freeze when they catch sight of me.

'Ruby?' From this far away, I have to read Charlie's lips to understand what he's saying. The fear shining in his eyes breaks my heart.

'Rubes! What the hell's going on?!' Ben gesticulates wildly, his face scrunched. 'Are you off your head?! Put that bleeding knife away!' he yells, the distance no match for his booming voice.

'Can we just talk about this for a minute? Can you please explain *why* you want to stab yourself?' Sasha asks me, attempting to calm the situation.

I should come clean. To them, I'm sure this looks like some sort of mental breakdown. Perhaps it is. But if I can somehow explain my train of thought to them, then surely they'll understand, right? They're the closest friends I have here. The closest friends I have *anywhere*. If I were to trust anyone with this information, it would be the four of them.

'I've realised something. I—I know it sounds ridiculous and unbelievable, but I think this place isn't real life. I believe that this forest is a dream or... or some kind of digital simulation—that we're all asleep and death is the only escape. It's... it's the only way we can wake up,' I explain in earnest, trying to sound as coherent as possible, although my voice cracks with urgency. I spot recognition of the rebel's warning on Charlie's face; he's contemplating my rationale. The others exchange worried glances, apparently believing my mind is already lost.

'Wh—why would you think that? Where has this all come from?' Logan questions, anxiety making him tremble.

'Each of the times I've died here, I've woken up in another place: a white room with strange machines and monitors. We were all asleep in a circle with metal bands on our heads, linking us together. There was an older man with black hair and blue eyes, who forced me back to sleep. Seconds later, I woke up here again. It's happened twice now,' I inform them, the words coming out in a dizzying rush. Their confused expressions don't disappear.

'Ruby, you're basing this theory on the moments your brain was in a state of shutting down. What if they were only dreams? From what I've witnessed, you seem to have *very* vivid ones,' Logan reasons.

'Hazy, I know what the rebel's message said, but please don't take it so literally. Don't do this. You could very well be wrong,' Charlie pleads, his voice thick.

'What message?' Ben turns to Charlie. 'You never mentioned a message.'

Charlie pushes his damp bronze hair away from his face. 'Ruby and I saw it a few days ago, carved on a tree. It said not to trust anyone—that you're not really our friends and that death was the only escape.'

'Charlie, it also said '*Not real. All lies*'. It was warning us that the *forest* isn't real—everything here is a lie,' I stress. He considers that for a moment before shaking his head.

'You're assuming too much. You're trying too hard to figure it out, and you're filling in gaps which may not even be there,' Charlie argues. 'Are you really willing to gamble with your life? Because I'm not.' His voice catches at the end, tears misting his hazel eyes.

'Rubes, please! We all care about you. We don't wanna see you hurt, like. *Please*. Put that knife down and we can all work it out together,' Ben begs. He gestures for me to come to them, his arms opening as though he's ready to embrace me.

What do I do? I was so sure of this course of action five minutes ago. But if Charlie thinks I'm jumping too quickly to conclusions then maybe I should think more before I do something I can't take back. With this situation as dangerous as it is, I shouldn't let my impulses win over reason. Plus, the stricken looks in everyone's eyes are hard to stomach. Watching me stab myself could traumatise them.

'I'm begging you, don't do this. I can't lose you, Ruby. I love you too much,' Logan declares, fighting back tears. 'I wish I could have told you under different circumstances, but that's the truth. It's been the truth since the moment I saw you. Please, Ruby. I love you.'

With those soul-changing words burrowing deep into my marrow, the knife drops from my grasp as a sob breaks loose.

I give in.

How can I kill myself now? I can't risk it. Not when I've finally found someone who loves me.

The force of Logan's love has me falling to my knees. They all start running towards me.

There's renewed fear in their eyes.

'Ruby! *Run!*' Logan shouts, dismayed.

Out of nowhere, there's a bone-cracking blow to the left side of my face.

The punch knocks me to the ground, mud claiming me. And it's like the whole left side of my face has suddenly burst into flames, the pain radiating through my skull. I look up to find the cloaked man standing over me, a gun in hand.

'No!' Logan screams from too far away.

The rebel raises the gun, but it's not pointed at me; he aims the barrel at the others, who are racing towards us. They scatter when the rebel starts shooting at them, jumping behind trees and bushes to avoid the spray of bullets.

'Stop! Just kill me,' I beseech, pure terror invading every cell of my body at the prospect of the others being hurt in my place. 'I know I'll wake up. I—I know that you're on my side—that you're not here to hurt me.' My plea is a quake of garbled words shuddering out of my mouth.

The rebel turns his attention back to me, and his spine-tingling laugh has my stomach squirming. He must be wearing a mask under his hood because the sound is muffled.

AMBER BAYLEY

'I'm not on your side, silly girl. And I *do* want to hurt you. It will bring me great pleasure,' the rebel pronounces, pointing the gun at my good arm.

The rebel pulls the trigger, and a searing force impacts my shoulder in an instant, the flash momentarily illuminating the forest around us. The pain is excruciating. I cry out, sobs racking my body, and he chuckles, enjoying watching me suffer. The smell of my own flesh burning has me close to vomiting.

The rebel brings the gun up again. This time, it's aimed at my head. I stare down the barrel, fear paralysing me. Knowing there's no point in carrying on, my heart stops pre-emptively, and my last breath stutters out.

I was wrong about everything, and now, I'm going to pay the price. Now, I'm going to die.

Denying my killer the satisfaction of seeing the light leave them, I shut my eyes.

I prepare myself for death, but a shy, sturdy soldier appears instead: Eli. He barrels into the rebel, knocking him to the ground with one swift blow. They wrestle in the mud, and I seize the opportunity to crawl away, towards the others.

Dawn and Alex come up from behind. With their hands under my arms, they drag me towards some trees we can use for cover.

'Eli!' Sasha screams as he fights to disarm the rebel. It seems she can't simply stand by and watch. She hurtles towards them, and Logan, Charlie, and Ben, who are now joined by Freya, are close on her heels.

A single shot rings out a moment before the gun drops to the ground. The rebel throws Eli off him, and Eli's lifeless body slams into the wet earth. To our horror, we see that Eli has taken a bullet to the head.

He's dead.

The second that fact registers with Sasha, a bloodcurdling scream rips from her throat. She continues to sprint towards his body. The rebel scrambles to retrieve the gun and shoots towards them until he's out of bullets.

Logan is the first to collide with the newly unarmed rebel, and they scrabble for purchase in the thickening mud. Ben tries to join in, but the rebel is too fast; he punches Ben to the ground with the butt of his gun. Ben appears to be rendered unconscious before he even had the chance to fight.

Sasha is kneeling beside Eli's body, kissing his face and apologising over and over. When Freya reaches me, she scrambles to cover my gunshot wound with her hands. She presses hard to stem the bleeding. I'm too numb to feel anything. Her lips are moving but my brain refuses to process a single word. I'm just sitting by, watching the horrifying scene unfold before me.

Useless.

Hopeless.

This is really happening. Clearly, the rebel only wanted to watch us suffer and die. And the person who pushed me into believing his message isn't even here.

Zoe.

Maybe she's been working with the rebel this entire time—encouraging the doubts he planted in my mind to bloom into irrational actions.

I was ready to *kill* myself.

And now Eli is dead because of my foolish gullibility.

With rage taking sorrow's place, Sasha rises to attack the rebel, who's now managed to knock down Logan, too. She jumps onto the rebel's back, raining blows down on his head with her closed fist. For a minute, she seems to be winning, until the rebel smashes her back into a tree trunk. She yelps, dropping to the ground in a daze.

The rebel retrieves the knife I dropped. Logan is up again with Alex by his side. They move in to tackle the rebel from behind. Together, they manage to wrestle him to the ground, but he kicks out, his boot connecting with Alex's face, who stumbles back, holding a bloody nose.

It's just Logan and the rebel in it now, and the rebel has the knife.

The rebel springs up, swiping at Logan with the blade, but Logan dodges the skilled attacks with surprising ease. An impressive kick of Logan's lands in the rebel's stomach, winding him for a brief moment before he lurches forward again. He slices at Logan's arm and blood spills out. Logan groans out a breath before successfully spinning away, out of danger. His jumper was already soaked from the rain, but his sleeve is now running red. My stomach turns, knowing he's at an even greater disadvantage with an injury like that.

Despite the odds, Logan recovers and surges on, grabbing the rebel's wrist before he has a chance to sink the knife into his chest. Logan twists the rebel's arm at an angle, and the rebel groans but doesn't drop the knife. Instead, quick on the offensive, the rebel elbows Logan in the face.

The rebel then flips Logan onto his back, the knife hurtling towards him again. Logan blocks the attack with his forearm. But, as the rebel pushes down with his body's full weight, the knife inches closer and closer to Logan's right eye.

This is all my fault. Eli is dead because of me. I must do something. I can't let Logan die, too. I love him.

I love him.

A surge of something indescribable has me pushing to my feet, forgetting my weakness, my pain, my fear. I swipe a large, rounded rock from the ground on my way up. Once I'm upright, my legs threaten to buckle again but I straighten my spine anyway, determined. Freya and Dawn struggle to hold me back. They're begging me to stay put, but I don't listen. Somehow, I find the strength to push them away.

Time slows as I charge at full speed towards the rebel, the rock heavy and rough in my palm. My body is powered by my will alone.

With a strenuous effort, Logan leads the knife away from his face. Although now, it lingers over his heart. The tip of the blade presses into his chest and he growls out in pain as it slowly slides in. Any second now, it will reach his heart and he'll be gone. I'll never see him again.

What happens next is a blur. Reaching the rebel, I strike like an angry viper; I smash the rock into his skull over and over—I can't stop. Warm blood sprays my face. A metallic tang invades my mouth. Still, I keep hitting. It's only when Logan grabs me—prying the newly slick rock from my aching hand—that I realise there's nothing left to hit.

'Ruby, stop. It's okay. We're safe now,' Logan whispers to me, stroking my face and wiping the rebel's blood from my eyes.

Soaked through, more with blood than rain, I tremble violently in Logan's arms, stunned by the brutality of my actions. My chest is heaving, the air hard to catch. Logan allows me a minute to process and recover. All the while, his words are soothing, and his kisses are soft; my wet, blood-smeared forehead is peppered with them.

As the adrenaline dissipates, my senses return. Looking up, I stare wide-eyed at Logan.

He's still here. I saved him.

The others also appear to be gradually absorbing the outcome of the fight. Sasha has dragged herself over to Eli's body and is crying on his chest. Freya is cradling a still-unconscious Ben in her lap, and Dawn and Alex are holding onto each other for dear life. That's when I notice who's missing: Charlie.

I push off Logan's chest and step back, my eyes darting around the night-cloaked forest. 'Charlie?!' I call, my panic spiking again. 'Pan, where are you?!'

There's still enough light in the moonlit sky to distinguish his long legs from broken tree branches. About twenty meters away, behind some bushes, they're sprawled unmoving on the wet ground. My stomach drops while my heart does the opposite, sticking in my throat.

This scene is all too familiar.

I sprint over as fast as my shaky legs allow.

As I close in, I notice the blood-woven stream flowing down the slight decline. And when I reach my lost boy, it's as if I'm punched in the gut.

Charlie is lying face-up in the mud with a gunshot wound to his stomach. He's still awake and even smiles when he sees me.

'Hazy, you're safe,' Charlie manages to puff out between strained gasps. Blood dribbles from his mouth.

Crumbling, I fold to my knees beside him. 'No, this can't be happening,' I cry, applying pressure on the gunshot wound. Logan appears, kneeling down, on the other side of him.

'Logan, wh—what do we do? I don't know what to do. Help him!' I splutter, my throat closing up.

Logan assesses Charlie's injury. 'I don't think there's anything we can do. I'm sorry, Ruby,' he says solemnly, rocking back to sit on his heels.

Blood seeps between my fingers, my hands slipping. 'No, no. We have to do something. The Haven Initiative can take him to the hospital. He will be okay. He *has* to be okay!'

For a long beat, Logan only stares at me, unreadable emotions flitting across his mud-splattered face. Then his eyes shutter as he rises to his feet, and just like that, he walks away.

'Logan? Logan, don't leave! *Please*, help me!' I shout after him, but he doesn't return.

I focus back on Charlie. 'Hold on, Pan. You'll be fine. We'll get you to a hospital.' I want to keep calm for him but I can't stop the tears from giving me away.

'It's all right, Hazy. I'm just glad I met you. Now I know what a true friend is. With you here, I found joy. I found happiness. Thank you,' he voices weakly. His blue-tinged lips hook up into a small smile before he starts coughing, which brings up more blood. The gleam of life his eyes always seem to showcase slowly dims.

'Please don't go. You're my family,' I beg, a sob tearing through.

Charlie holds my gaze for one more precious moment before his eyes droop to a close, and his final breath leaves him behind.

Dazed with grief, I slump back. I just watched my best friend die. He's really dead. My actions have killed him, too.

In disbelief, I stroke Charlie's rain-soaked, lifeless hair with my bloodied hands, and kiss his forehead. 'Goodbye, Pan. I'm so sorry,' I whimper, praying he can still somehow hear me.

For one more agonising heartbeat, I take in his little lost boy face, committing it to memory. Then I drag myself away, back to the others.

The pain of losing Charlie is overwhelming; it's as if my chest is caving in on itself. It's unbearable.

Just like Sasha, my rage is quick to fight its way to the forefront. Logan walked away and left me alone to deal with my best friend dying in my arms. He got up and walked away—he *abandoned* me. Just like my brother did all those years ago.

The people you love the most always hurt you the worst in the end. Whether in life or death.

Logan is in the middle of a huddle, whispering with Alex, Sasha, and Freya, while Dawn is trying to wake Ben up on the sidelines.

'You just walked away! How could you leave us there like that?' I shriek, tears streaming down my already wet, puffy face. Logan turns to me but can't meet my eyes.

'I'm sorry, Ruby. I'm sorry for everything,' Logan mutters in a desolate voice. He doesn't come to comfort me; he simply stands there with his head lowered. He's only a few feet away but it feels like a mile.

'No, it's *my* fault. Charlie died because of *me*. Eli died because of *me*.' My voice is a strangled gasp—choked by raw emotion. I need Logan to hold me and make everything stop hurting—to make everything all right again.

'Just tell her, Logan. It will be over in a minute anyway. Put the poor, pathetic thing out of her misery,' Zoe says, stepping out from behind the trees to our left.

Logan's face hardens, his jaw clenching. 'It was you, wasn't it? You planted the seed,' he growls, his tone now deadly.

'The seed was already planted. I only helped it grow. She saw the rebel's message first. And anyway, I'm not the one who couldn't keep her alive,' Zoe snaps back, unfazed.

'What are you talking about? Logan?' I glare at him, a million questions in my eyes.

Logan quickly shifts his gaze away, his head shaking. He heaves a heavy sigh, defeat slumping his shoulders. His mouth opens but no words come out.

'You lot are so cruel, torturing her like this. And there was me thinking *I* was the villain,' Zoe remarks to the group before she strides away, disappearing into the forest again.

Straightening my spine, I fight against a shiver as the cold, indifferent wind berates me. 'What does she mean? Tell me!'

'Ruby, please don't hate us. Just know that we really *do* care about all of you,' Sasha chokes out, fresh tears brimming in her big, hazel eyes. She, Logan, Freya, and Alex all bow their heads in shame.

I gape at them as what's left of my blood freezes in my veins. 'I was right, wasn't I?' I say calmly, the truth both painful and relieving. The group which stands before me are all in on it; they're the liars the rebel warned me about. They're not my friends. They never were. It was all an elaborate ruse.

Sasha, who was one of my closest friends here—even Logan, who I've grown to *love*— have betrayed me—all of them have. The relationships we formed here are built on a foundation of lies and manipulation. They're all fraudulent. I thought I'd finally found a new family that I could rely on, but they've turned out to be just like my old one. Maybe worse.

Ben is awake now, too, and he appears just as confused as Dawn. They must not have been a part of it. They must be what I am—a fool.

Words are an impossible task for my gaping mouth, so all I do is stare at Logan in disbelief, shocked that, of all people, he's done this to me. I *trusted* him. I swallowed his lies so easily, starved of companionship for so long that I gobbled up all of his bullshit without question.

I'm a fucking mug. A lonely, desperate, gullible, pathetic loser.

I deserve this.

Logan finally looks up as if he can read my thoughts, and his pale, frosted eyes find mine. They're full of sorrow and guilt, but mine are only full of hate. Cautiously, he approaches me.

When Logan is close enough, I flail my weak, wounded arms, trying to land a hit as I curse him with every expletive that comes to mind. The fire of my fury burns a hole in my chest where my wounded heart ceases to beat for him. He catches my wrists, bringing me to my knees. And I can't stop myself from crying; it's guttural, like the broken yowls of a dying animal. This endless, all-consuming pain—the sorrow, confusion, betrayal, and anger—it's impossible to keep it all contained; it erupts out of me like scorching waves of lava, obliterating what's left of us in his desperate embrace. I scream into his chest, his arms tight around me, controlling my uncontrolled outburst.

'I never wanted to hurt you, Ruby. I thought this was the only way. I'm so sorry. I'll make it quick,' Logan whispers into my hair before the knife slides in.

Immediately, my wail becomes a gasp as the cold, smooth steel effortlessly penetrates through my ribcage to my heart.

Numb with shock, I glance up at Logan's grief-twisted face, his intense eyes overflowing with tears. They appear to have lost all their colour now. They're no longer electric. They're only the grey eyes of my killer.

The pain slips away. All of it.

Logan lowers me to the ground with him until I'm resting in his lap—*dying* in his lap. Sobbing, he kisses my forehead and murmurs, 'Until morning light.'

My last thought is of my mother's face. She has a scarlet rose in her hair. It begins to wilt, and then it crumbles away to dust. Her skin follows suit, and soon, her kind face scatters into the wind, replaced with emptiness—with hollow hopes and very real fears.

Swallowing my last shallow breath, the forest fades to black.

Chapter 29

DEBRIEF

LOGAN

I default to fidgeting as I anxiously wait in the extremely clean, minimal white office, the diffused smell of citrus permeating the filtered air. Over the past two weeks, I've grown accustomed to wearing casual clothing, so this trouser/shirt combination is something I'll have to reacquaint myself with.

The sturdy metal chair provides just as little comfort. That said, not much could comfort me at present. I haven't been the same since that devastating final night in the forest. It's been two days, but that was mostly recovery time—coaxing the neglected muscles in my body to cooperate with my conscious mind again.

Now, it's time to face him. If he hurries the fuck up. He's half an hour late. I want to get this over with. I have more important things to deal with today.

The distinctive sound of his footsteps echoes down the corridor. I can always tell it's him from the clip then slide of his feet, his artificial leg slightly dragging on the glossed floor. I've never understood why he prefers the mechanical leg. He's always been old-fashioned, I guess.

The door slides open, revealing him. His jet-black hair is slicked back to look more presentable at work, with the thin streaks of grey barely visible at his temples. He's wearing his white technician coat; he must have come directly from the lab. His icy blue eyes drift to me, and I sit up straighter in my chair. It's an automatic response to the familiar critical look, which seems to be *his* default when dealing with me. He doesn't greet me. Instead, he shuts the door and then silently glides over to his frosted glass desk to claim the seat opposite me.

'It seems we have a lot to discuss in this meeting, Logan,' Noah starts, his expression stony. Again, familiar. 'Is your body more in sync now? How's your coordination?' His tone conveys only medical professionalism, with no hint of fondness or genuine concern.

'Yes, Noah. It's back to normal. I've fully recovered,' I assure him, not that it matters much to him.

'Good. Now, are you ready to evaluate your sim experience? As you know, the board would like to review your account of what factors contributed to the early termination of the Arkinwood sim,' he clarifies, skipping any more pleasantries. He taps lightly on the small metallic circle imprinted on his skin by his right ear to record our conversation.

'There was only one major factor which caused issues, and that was the rebel's interventions. His sabotage attempts generated mistrust and panic. The rebel was the reason the Arkinwood Forest simulation failed,' I state for the record.

'Yes, that was a major contributing factor. However, there were also other problems you encountered, outside of the rebel's corruption,' Noah pushes, his eyes narrowing.

I clear my throat. It's suddenly tighter. 'There may have been a few instances of rebellion from some of the subjects. Nevertheless, that was to be expected. This programme is only in its fifth year of development. There are a few... kinks that we need to straighten out. The methods with which we maintain the safety of both subjects and guardians may need to be revised, as well as the guidelines on interactions and the ethics surrounding the use of uninformed consent. The programme generally remains in its experimental phase,' I admit, my body temperature rising quickly.

Noah nods, his lips pouting. 'Can you elaborate for the board, please? Perhaps you can provide us with examples of what you witnessed in the simulation, which accounted for its early termination,' he suggests politely, wanting to appear patient to the board.

'It started according to plan: all five guardians recovered their matches from the valley initiation, leading them to the forest with very little pushback. In the forest, all five subjects began the bonding process with their respective guards to sufficient standards. Some showed more progress than others in that early stage,' I recount evenly.

'In your opinion, do you believe Guardian Zoelle Morgannig did a sufficient job bonding with her match, Charles Winshaw?' Noah questions, leaning back and folding his arms across his chest, challenging me already.

'Zoelle was not pleased with her matched subject prior to the sim. She was a late candidate for the guardiancy course, and therefore did not have adequate time to learn about her match before the sim began. I confronted her about it, the morning of the second day of the sim. She told me of her indifference towards her match, and that she wished to quit the programme. I assured her that she would bond as soon as she was open to trying.'

I'm sure Noah is aware of the real reason Zoe was indifferent to Charlie, though the board wouldn't be. Zoe was in love with me—*unrequited* love. She did *not* like my involvement in the programme. When I started my official training for this sim, she was there as another volunteer. I gathered that she only put herself forward to keep her eye on me. She only wanted to ruin my chances of success with Ruby.

Noah steeples his fingers. 'Were you aware that subjects Hayes and Winshaw had witnessed you both returning from that meeting and expressed their suspicion?'

'Yes. I could tell that my match in particular was suspicious, especially of Zoelle. Even so, my match bonded better than anticipated to everyone else,' I reply in haste, sweat beading on my forehead.

What Zoe did—hinting to Ruby about the simulation—was pure malice; it was the driving force that led to the unfortunate events at the end. Despite that, I don't wish to be spiteful. Even though Zoe deserves it, I won't drop her in trouble in any official capacity. When Zoe volunteered, she entered into a contract, and she broke that contract on many occasions. As did I, in a different way. If the board found out about her sabotage, she'd be fired from the facility and perhaps prosecuted. Even Sasha, who can't stand Zoe, agreed to lay the blame solely on the rebel.

'Hmm. We also saw a particularly strong bond form between subjects Hayes and Winshaw. Subject Winshaw even had romantic contact with your match before you did. How did that develop?' Noah probes, a frown forming. Is he trying to rile me?

With my insides twisting, I chew out a breath. 'They had a connection which ended up being purely platonic. The romantic element was tested and quickly dismissed by both parties. This was partially due to Subject Winshaw's lack of connection to Zoelle and partially due to my eagerness to connect with my match. This sometimes resulted in her withdrawing from me. Nonetheless, after their romantic contact failed, it wasn't long before I fulfilled my objective; my match opened up to me about her past, and romantic contact between us was established.' It's difficult to sum it up in these terms but I have to. To stop myself from saying more on the tender subject, I literally bite my tongue.

'That wasn't the only instance Subject Hayes went off course though, was it? There were numerous occasions, excluding the rebel's interventions, that demonstrated she was difficult to control. The flashback anomalies, for example. Can you explain those?' He watches me squirm in my seat with no visible remorse.

'Some of the dreams my match experienced were not unusual: the memories of her mother, for instance. There were only a couple of rare occurrences when other memories—those we thought we had terminated—resurfaced somehow. These never had a significant enough impact on the mission to cause concern,' I answer confidently, attempting to hide the nervous twitch of my mouth with my hand.

Noah glares at me. 'Subject Hayes nearly unmasked you in those flashbacks. We would have had to terminate the simulation then and there, if she had. How was that not a cause for concern? It also calls into question our methods of slating.' His lips press into a hard line, his patient facade slipping.

Ignoring the ticking of my jittery heart, I swallow hard and set my jaw. 'The process of slating has worked on all previous subs over the entire five years of operations. Subject Hayes is the only participant to exhibit these anomalies. No other sub has ever had a targeted memory resurface after we deleted it,' I fire back swiftly.

'That's not the only anomaly we encountered with Subject Hayes. She found her way out of the void twice of her own accord. I, alone, had to deal with her on the second occasion. It was lucky I returned to the monitoring room when I did; she was about to escape her medipod.'

To stop myself from shifting in discomfort again, I grip the armrests of my chair. 'I was just as curious witnessing it myself, the first time, when I returned to discuss the rebel. Subject Hayes was placed inside the void to subdue her whilst I was pulled from the sim. Somehow, she became aware of her change in state and her mind also pulled away from its digital tether. She found her portal and escaped. Unfortunately, the other subjects were present when she left her simulated body. Therefore, they assumed that she was deceased. Luckily, Director West and I managed to subdue and reinsert her before too much time had passed. Guardian Sashire Reedenoh successfully convinced the other subjects that Subject Hayes had been resuscitated. However, unbeknownst to the team here, the rebel discovered that Ruby—I mean, Subject Hayes—had that ability and used it to his advantage. The same situation was avoided the next day, when Subject Hayes was nearly drowned. I quickly reinserted myself into the sim to retrieve her from the lake before it had a chance to reoccur.

'The rebel used a remotely-controlled insert machine to code his digitally-generated arm into the sim to pull Subject Hayes under the water's surface. He managed to bypass the firewall to tamper with our code. He grew bolder by the end, causing distractions—like setting that fire in recovery room two—to secure the uninterrupted time with which to hack into the sim mainframe and insert himself fully.' *You don't need to delve into logistics right now, Logan. Just stick to the script*, I chastise myself, losing focus.

I rub a hand over my face, my mind still frazzled from lack of sleep. 'Anyway, erm... Subject Hayes saw the rebel's hand around her ankle, but a plausible theory was put forth as to how he was hiding under the water. Nevertheless, the rebel was a known danger to the subjects after that. Using the trees as a weapon was our first indicator of subterfuge from a member of staff. However, the *subs* assumed it was a tool used by The Haven Initiative to draw them to the cabin, like the wolves were. The guardians were the only participants aware of the rebel at that early stage, after an unplanned fallen branch hit Freyessa Clarkail—sending her into the void. It was then we realised there had been a breach. Thankfully, the blow to the head didn't significantly damage Freyessa's brain functions, and she managed to reinsert herself after some time. The group wasn't supposed to begin the integration procedures until the second morning. However, this incident forced Subject Mendel to seek assistance. The method of slow integration between the subjects was still successful despite this—no subject fractured away. They adapted quickly, and, as in previous sims, the situation encouraged teamwork,' I report clearly, hoping I've supplied enough information to satisfy Noah and the board. And extra pieces to distract them from the complications with Ruby.

Noah nods, content to accept my spiel. 'The last incident, when the rebel strangled your match: after I reinserted her, did she seem unsettled to you? Was there any indication that she knew the truth of her situation?'

'Not at first. She was extremely confused and weak. It wasn't until the next day that she pieced it all together.'

'And what do you believe brought on this sudden realisation?' Noah observes me carefully. He must suspect that Zoe was involved.

'I assume it was a combination of the rebel's earlier message which she and Subject Winshaw discovered, the flashback anomalies, and her successful void escape attempts. Subject Hayes is very intelligent and intuitive. She was even bold enough to attempt suicide to prove her theory.' I can't help my pride at Ruby's wits on this. No other subject has ever come close to figuring out the simulation.

A humourless smile pulls up the edges of Noah's mouth. 'Dangerous and stubborn are the words that come to *my* mind. Even if she *had* managed to navigate the void before, any death inside the simulation is a huge risk to the subject's state of mind and is *not* an acceptable method of termination, unless used as a last resort.'

My stomach churns with guilt-riddled apprehension, anticipating his next question: the one I've been dreading the most.

'With that said, explain why it was necessary to terminate Subject Hayes yourself, after your betrayal was revealed.' His voice is stern and unforgiving.

I clear my throat again, my mouth drying out. 'Subject Hayes was inconsolable from witnessing subjects Conteh and Winshaw die at the hands of the rebel. She realised that her suspicions were correct and was in extreme pain, both emotionally and physically. She was unpredictable, unstable, and potentially dangerous to others in the sim, including herself. Let's not forget that she was near death anyway, from blood loss. The situation needed to be dealt with swiftly to minimise the risk of trauma. It was the easiest and safest option I had available to me at the time,' I answer, almost honestly. I chew on my lips, my nervousness hard to hide.

'Very well, then. Logan, I think you have adequately answered the board's questions. At least for now. I will inform you of their findings from the review at a later date,' Noah states before he double taps behind his ear again to end the recording.

My fraying muscles relax slightly. 'Has the rebel's true identity been uncovered?' I enquire, my stomach settling.

The question has been burning away at me since Noah entered the room. I've been kept out of the loop since my return. All I know is that the rebel turned out to be Oren Colerig—one of the facility's engineers. That's why it was so easy for him to gain access to the sim control rooms without suspicion. Luckily, the main room (where we were all asleep in the medipods) was under heavy guard. That meant he couldn't slip in to harm our vulnerable bodies whilst our minds were connected to the sim.

'His real name was Stratton Drohgue. He was a spy for the rebel group Ascendant,' Noah informs me with a wave of his hand, as though this information is of little importance.

'Kyder Fain's cult?' I spit, recoiling as the name of my mother's murderer leaves my lips. Kyder Fain—previously my best friend, a brother in all but blood, and now the leader of one of the biggest rebel groups that stands against us and everything we're working towards here at the facility.

'Yes. That's why Stratton was targeting Subject Hayes specifically: to hurt you,' Noah comments matter-of-factly, his expression unreadable.

'Where's Stratton now?' I demand, anger charging through my veins.

'The morgue. Subject Hayes caused him severe brain damage. He died within hours of being pulled from the sim. We couldn't extract any information from him as he never regained consciousness,' Noah delivers in an indifferent tone.

My anger dissipates. Stratton got what he deserved. 'The board won't hear this, Noah. You can call her Ruby,' I say flatly.

Noah's mouth tightens, but he doesn't respond.

'Has Elijah regained consciousness?' I ask, my forehead aching from frowning so much.

'No. Unfortunately, his mind is still lost in the void, the last I heard. His body continues to lie in his medipod. We're keeping him connected to the sim, for now. Hopefully, his brain isn't as damaged as Stratton's was,' he reports regretfully, the slightest hint of sympathy softening his expression for once.

My heart drags itself down to the pit of my empty stomach. Dying in the simulation is dangerous. Sometimes a mind isn't strong enough to find its way back to the subject's body. It becomes trapped in a digital in-between place we call a void. Especially if the subject experiences brain trauma in the sim itself. Eli took a bullet to the head; he may never wake up. I imagine Sasha is devastated.

'Now that the debrief is finished, will you be visiting the cells?' Noah's question is more a demand.

A heavy weight presses me down into my seat, my shoulders slumping under the invisible pressure. 'Yes, it's about time I go,' I respond with a sigh.

'What are you planning to tell her?'

'The truth,' I answer simply.

'Are you sure that's the wisest decision? With her anomalies, inform-ing her of who we really are could be a danger to us if her mind rejects the slating process again,' Noah warns, the creases in his brow illustrating his concern.

'Why are you so sure she'll need to be slated? She could accept it. Just because the sim terminated early, doesn't mean the experiment wasn't a success. The connection was made, and it was one of the strongest in all of the candidates for the programmes thus far, in the five years we've been doing this. You saw her levels on the chart,' I argue, the knot in my stomach tightening.

'I also saw the look she gave you when she realised your deceit.'

Shit, Noah must have filtered through some of the sim's digital signa-tures already and converted the code to playback. What else has he seen?

'You knew the risks with her before the sim began. I told you she was too strong-willed—too damaged,' Noah maintains.

Chilling dread trickles down my spine at the very real possibility that Noah is right. 'Is she still not communicating?' I ask, changing the sub-ject.

'She hasn't spoken a word since she woke from the sim. She recovered quicker than the others, though she isn't responsive, according to the psychiatric team. They suggest we slate her immediately and send her back. If we leave it any longer, she may never recover mentally,' Noah informs me, his scowl conveying his judgement.

Panicking, I swallow down a hard lump in my throat. 'I need a chance to explain the situation to her myself. You know I have to try. I can't lose her without a fight. I *love* her, Noah!'

Noah's expression softens again. Twice in one interaction: that's rare. Sighing, he shakes his head. 'I understand that, Logan. I do. I just don't want you to get your hopes up.'

'We've seen subs in the past who we thought were lost causes accept the programme and even excel in it,' I remind him, my resolve fierce. 'I have to believe that's still possible.'

Noah exhales a more resigned sigh. 'Fine. You are excused. Sashire, Freyessa, and Alexel are waiting for you in reflector room two,' he says, dismissing me with a wave of his hand. He brings up a holographic screen using the small metallic symbol on his left wrist. He's busy scrolling through documents when I leave my seat and walk to the door.

'And, Logan...' Noah begins.

Ready for another cutting remark, I twist my head to face him. 'Yes?'

'I should warn you that I've decided to terminate Zoelle Morannig's contract. Today will be her last day at The West Haven Facility,' he informs me impassively, not lifting his eyes from his work.

'Thank you for letting me know.' I can't say I'm surprised by that.

'Logan, you may be my son. But that does not mean you can withhold important information from me without consequences. I am still the director of this facility. The board, on the other hand... what they don't know won't hurt them.' He throws me a pointed look before his attention falls back to his wrist.

Suppressing a smile, I exit his office, leaving my father to finish damage control.

A short while later, I enter reflector room two; it's been the main reflector room for seven years now, after the first was sealed off.

My heart pangs and I instantly cut off my trail of thought.

Just three people occupy the room: Sasha, Freya, and Alex. They aren't looking my way and my presence goes unnoticed. They're focused on the memory projection Freya is currently supplying. A metal band—an infilter—rests on her crown. The machine she's hooked up to is called a reflector: it collects memories we wish to save in case our minds are ever slated.

Every guardian (from the previous sim experiments we've run so far) has stored their first-person account in the reflector. Anything a guardian deems an important moment in the mission is saved onto our system for the record. Each time, we learn valuable information on what works and what doesn't so the next sim experiment can improve its procedures.

We also use it to train volunteers for the upcoming annual sim. It's basically a template for how guardians should handle themselves once their mind is transported into the digital world. They're hooked up to the machine so they can relive our memories and experiences as if they are their own.

As Freya relives her moments from inside the sim, the projected memories—through her eyes—flash up for the rest of us to see onscreen. But only to see, not experience. We'd need an infilter for that.

Hidden in shadow, I lurk by the door, watching carefully as moments from our nights in the cabin replay. They've turned the sound off so it's only images of us: our meals around the dining table, our games, and all of us cosied up in the living area, preparing to watch a film. It must be embarrassing for Freya to show the moments of her and Ben alone in their room: their private conversations recorded, their kisses and embraces shared with select members of staff. Granted, every guardian has to do it. That's why we have strict rules on how we engage with our matches. Rules a few of us were close to breaking.

As guardians, our main objective is to get the subjects we've been matched with to fall in love with us. This cannot be forced in any way; we have to allow them choices at every stage of development. We simply guide them to that choice, with as little manipulation as possible, hoping the strength of the connection is enough to fill in the gaps of what we must withhold of ourselves. The subject has to be the first to initiate romantic contact even if interest is expressed. A guardian can only embrace or kiss their match with consent, either verbal or strongly implied. Even then, the guardians have strict limits on what romantic contact occurs. We're only allowed to progress as far as kissing on the mouth. Any further physical contact is prohibited. Alex and I found that rule the hardest to stick to.

I watch intently as Freya projects the memories of that fateful last day. My heart jerks to a halt when I see Ruby and I together—my arms around her, engaging in a kiss as Freya walks in, interrupting us. Melancholy creeping back in, I swallow hard. If it's difficult to watch—projected from Freya's memory—then I have no clue how I'll cope in the reflector chair myself, reliving my relationship with Ruby and its downfall... again.

Then the conclusion of our sim proceeds: finding out that Ruby was missing, Charlie suggesting we check the part of the forest where we'd laid the snares. Understanding how he knew where she was. Witnessing Ruby being shot by the rebel. That makes my stomach lurch, bile rising to my throat. Continuing, I study the haunting echo of Ruby's face when Eli was murdered in front of her. Freya must have been trying to care for Ruby at that point, whilst I was busy battling Stratton.

It shows the moment Ruby intervenes in my fight with Stratton—her bashing his skull in. Ben unconscious. Freya stroking his face. She must have feared he'd die and be lost to the void after a head wound like that.

Suddenly, Ruby is there, staring at simulation me in absolute pain and confusion. Zoe appearing, and Ruby's expression changing: the look of betrayal, of repulsion, then hate tainting her tortured face. I have to shut my eyes because I know what's coming: the last look she gave me when I had to end it. I couldn't stand her looking at me like that, and I couldn't bear to see her in that much pain. I broke the rules when I ended it the way I did—sliding that knife into her heart. It wasn't real, yet it sure as hell felt like it. I threw up three times before my father finally pulled the rest of us out, once he realised the fire Stratton caused was a distraction.

As soon as Alex, Sasha, Freya, Zoe, and I were back in our own bodies, we were separated from our matches. Apparently, Ruby had already woken up and was sedated again because she started fighting against her medical team. I had to stay for the mandatory health tests but left for my apartment as soon as I was strong enough to walk unaided. The coward I've become, I ran and hid, weakened by the idea that Ruby might never forgive me—that I might never forgive myself. At the time, I couldn't handle it—couldn't cope. Not much has changed in the days since, though I woke up this morning knowing I couldn't put it off any longer, for her sake as well as mine.

I need to face Ruby and explain everything before a decision is made.

The projection ends and Freya removes the infilter band. She rises from the reflector chair, a solemn expression on her face. She wipes her watery eyes, a sigh blowing past her trembling lips. Sasha peers around the chair, spotting me. She must guess that I've been watching for a while because she offers me an empathetic smile. Coughing once, I make the others aware of my presence.

Alex rushes over to pull me into an embrace. 'Logs! Oh man, it's so good to see you. Where have you been?' he asks, his voice breathy with relief. 'You haven't been answering my calls.'

'Sorry. I've been recovering in the north wing. I needed some time on my own,' I reply, half-heartedly shrugging one shoulder.

'How did the debrief go?' Sasha enquires, her eyes red-rimmed and puffy.

'Better than expected. My father will handle things with the board. I'm sure it will all be fine. I don't think we'll be reprimanded,' I assure them.

'Guess what?' Freya asks, now smiling. 'Eli just woke up. He's been transferred to a recovery room.' She places an arm around Sasha, jostling her in excitement.

Sasha allows herself to smile along with Freya, although I assume she's probably still incredibly anxious. Maybe that's why she's keeping herself busy here instead of pacing the medical block, waiting to be cleared to see her match.

'That's amazing, *amazing* news. He'll recover quickly, I'm sure of it,' I convey to Sasha, offering her a warm smile. I hesitate before continuing. 'How are the others doing?'

'Dawn's good, man. She's accepted; she's decided to stay for the trial period.' Alex beams, his happiness shining through.

I squeeze Alex's shoulder. 'Congratulations. I'm happy for you. I really hope it works out,' I say to him, forcing my smile this time. We've always been close. My family unofficially adopted both him and Kyder when I was a toddler. He's the closest thing to a brother I have. Still, the stab of jealousy in my gut is unavoidable.

'Ben's doing all right. He's letting me talk to him now, at least. He's onto the history stage and is understandably sceptical. But hopefully, by the next stage, he'll be more accepting,' Freya tells me, slightly dejected. 'If only we had those final two days to ease them into the truth, like we were supposed to...'

'And Charlie?' I query, ignoring Freya's wistfulness; there's no point dwelling on what was supposed to happen.

'He's been informed of the basics but Zoe hasn't been in to see him. I don't know if she plans to, either.' Sasha frowns. 'I can't believe she's just left him to sit in his cell, confused and scared, for *this* long,' she voices, her judgement clear. Then her eyes widen as she realises I've done the same to Ruby.

Everyone stands rigid with awkwardness for a long beat, their eyes on anything that isn't me.

'I'm heading to the cells now,' I mutter in a small voice, my face hot with shame.

'I tried visiting Ruby this morning but she didn't even want to look at me, let alone speak to me,' Freya mentions, saddened again.

'Anyway, we should carry on with reflection. I just want to get this over with,' Sasha mumbles, sinking into the reflector chair. 'Good luck with Ruby, Logan. I really hope she believes you.'

'Best of luck, brother. If it doesn't work out, you still have me,' Alex jokes, patting my back.

'Alex!' Freya reprimands him for his insensitivity.

'Thanks, mophead. That makes me feel *so* much better about it,' I retort sardonically, but we smile at each other, anyway. 'See you later.'

They call out their goodbyes as I swiftly make my exit.

The cells are where we hold the subs after they've recovered. Physically, I should say. It's only for a short period whilst they adjust to the facility and absorb the information provided to them. It may be called the cell block, but they're not prison-like in the slightest. It's a safe space where the subs can't inflict harm upon themselves or members of staff. It's more like a luxury hotel they can't escape.

They're only supposed to be in there for a day or two. During which time, their guardian visits to ease them back to reality. They're seen by a team of medical specialists and are guided through the various stages post-recovery: the history lessons, the joint counselling session with their guardian, and the guided tours before they're interviewed by my father and the security team to acquire a limited security pass which permits them to explore the rest of the facility and integrate.

In the interview, they're offered a choice to either stay and participate in a trial run of habitation, which lasts six months, or return to their regular lives. Either party can terminate the trial run at any time, if they're unhappy or dissatisfied with their relationship. After the trial run, there's a review by the board, where a final decision is made on whether they can stay as a permanent resident or not. I'm hoping to guide Ruby to that point at least. Although that will be a tough feat, according to the negative levels on her most recent chart.

I knew, when I chose Ruby as my match, that she wasn't a desirable candidate. Her trust levels were extremely low, almost non-existent. She has a very strong will, and is deeply stubborn, belligerent, and fiercely set in her ways. She also has undiagnosed ADHD, which I'm not sure she's aware of. Despite all of that, I could tell this wasn't really her; it was only the person she was forced to become because of the unfortunate circumstances life threw at her from a young age. I thought I could help her find herself again, and I think she did. That could all be for nothing now, though. The Ruby she discovered and let shine may be lost to trauma again. All because I was too cowardly to face up to the reality that I've left her to endure alone. The pain my betrayal caused her has been hard to face, quite literally.

With all that in mind, there's still hope in my heart when I finally reach Ruby's cell.

Studying the monitor screen outside her door, I see that she's sitting on the floor in the corner of the room. She has a variety of comfy chairs in her cell. Plus, there are films, games, and books with which she could easily occupy her time. Yet she chooses to simply stare into thin air, with her arms wrapped around her knees, leaning her back against the wall—a shell of the person she was in the forest.

It's now or never; I have to walk in there and tell her the truth. I have to be brave, as brave as she was in the forest. Nauseated, I struggle to digest my fear. This won't be easy to explain. As part of pre-sim preparations, all guardians are trained on how to handle this sensitive situation. However, actually *doing* it—saying what I need to and exposing my secrets—is a terrifying task to navigate.

In the back of my mind, another worry sinks my gut: will Ruby be afraid of me after I ki—... ended her suffering in the sim? That's another hurdle we might need to overcome before I start dropping more shocking bombshells.

It will rip my heart into pieces if I walk in there and she blanches in fear of me. Especially considering the abuse she suffered in the past. I'd rather she hate me with a passion than associate me with the same dread her father instilled in her.

Logan, stop searching for reasons to delay this further and get in there!

Inhaling courage, I place my sweaty palm on the door. It slides open and I take that first heart-stalling step.

Chapter 30

SECRET

LOGAN

I clear the door of Ruby's cell. It shuts silently behind me, locking automatically. It will only open again at my touch.

Ruby's living space is decorated in muted tones, and the fabrics of the furnishings are soft and inviting, yet unused. The place is still pristine, as though she's refused to move from that spot in the corner. The door to her bathroom is ajar, and her chestnut curls are a little damp, which tells me she's at least content enough to use the shower. In the sim, she told me she doesn't take hot water for granted, and that being clean was always a priority for her, living on the streets. I guess it's something she still cares about even when she's numb to everything else.

Hot with anxiety, my clammy hands shake as I approach Ruby. My muscles twitch out of sync with my movements; I can't seem to harness control.

Ruby is unmoving. I'm in her peripheral vision yet she continues to stare into space, as though I no longer exist to her.

At least she's not recoiling in terror.

With my tail between my legs, I shuffle closer and lower myself down onto a cushioned seat opposite her. She's now only a metre or two away but has yet to bat an eye at my presence. *Unresponsive*, the psychiatric team concluded. She never answered any of their questions and hasn't spoken a word since she woke up.

The team informed Ruby of the basics: that the forest was a simulation, and that Sasha, Alex, Freya, Zoe, and I were guardians for each of our chosen candidates. Ruby already figured that part out for herself, anyway. The team then went on to explain that Charlie and Eli didn't actually die, though they neglected to mention how serious Eli's condition was. It doesn't particularly matter now that he's finally woken up.

Prior to my visit today, Ruby was also informed that the purpose of the experiment was to build romantic relationships between the matched pairs. However, she's not yet been told of the precise reasons behind it. It's my job as her guardian to deliver that information personally, accepting that mistrust and disbelief will be tough obstacles to overcome. It always is in the first conversation after a sim ends, no matter how much love and trust was previously built between a couple.

Lastly, Ruby understands that, when she's recovered enough, she can make the decision to stay here for the trial run or to wipe clear her memories of this whole experience and return home, as if none of this ever happened.

Unable to think of an adequate starting point, I keep it simple and mumble, 'Hello, Ruby. It's good to see you.'

No response.

Wringing my hands, I continue, my mouth painfully dry. 'I need to explain some things to you... things you need to be made aware of before you decide which option to take. Obviously, you may not wish to converse with me. I would completely understand your reluctance. And if you'd prefer to remain silent, that's fine. I'm not expecting anything from you. I only hope that you listen to what I have to say.'

Silence.

Okay, it's awkward but it's a start, at least. Relax. I blow out a breath.

I continue, 'I'm sure this won't mean much to you, coming from me, but I want to tell you the truth. I want to explain why it had to happen this way.'

I'm met with more empty stillness, the low hum of the air purifier not loud enough to fill the space. Before I carry on, I rub my temples. The pressure has been building there all day. I need to think of something that will elicit a response from her.

'Do you want to see Charlie later?' I blurt out.

Ruby's eyes flicker to me as soon as that name tumbles off my tongue. She studies me with her beautiful, narrowed green gaze. I'm not supposed to let her leave this room to integrate yet, not until she's been cleared by the psychiatric team. But that didn't stop the words flying out of my mouth and now I can't take them back. I *am* the junior director of this facility and it's not as if this is the first time I've bent the rules for her. At least I have her attention now. And that attention, even saturated with scornful scrutiny, heats my blood like no other.

'If you listen to what I have to say, and if you promise you won't become violent or anything, then I can break you out of here to visit Charlie,' I swear to her, hand on my heart.

Ruby slowly nods; it's a cautious movement. She must understand what I'm saying, though. Clearly, she was only pretending to be unresponsive to the team. She continues to fascinate me.

Savouring the small victory, I clap my hands down on my thighs. 'Okay. I'll get on with what I have to say, then. Feel free to interrupt to ask questions at any time,' I tell her, fidgeting in my seat.

Unsure how to proceed, I delay by inhaling a lung-filling breath, then smooth my hair down, self-conscious under her hollow gaze. Despite having two days to prepare, I still haven't decided how to broach this topic. There's no easy way to explain myself or the situation in general. I just have to jump in somewhere and work my way through.

'What I'm about to tell you might sound unbelievable, and I know I have no right to ask you to trust me, but neverthe—'

'Yes, it will be unbelievable, and no, you fucking don't,' Ruby interjects, emotionless. Her voice is soft but not gentle; it's as cold as steel.

My heart twists, trying to avoid that shard of ice. It's unsuccessful. The sharp pain has me rubbing at my chest. 'Well, I'll try anyway. I want you to know all the facts before you decide anything,' I mutter, wiping my sweaty palms on my trousers. To stop them shaking, I clasp my hands in my lap, then dive in again before I completely lose my nerve.

'Ruby, I'm sorry I withheld information and—'

'You mean you lied,' she corrects me, cutting in again.

I don't let this throw me off. 'I did lie about some things in the forest, yes. But you have to know that everything I felt for you was genuine.' She rolls her eyes, but I carry on regardless. 'I chose you as my match. I had strong feelings for you before you even knew I existed. Every guardian monitors their match for nearly a year prior to the extraction from... their lives, so they can gauge who their potential love interest is—who they are as a person and how they handle themselves. Most guardians develop attachments to their match at this stage, before they meet them in person.'

'So, you stalk us. How romantic,' Ruby says dryly.

'I guess that's one word for it. Guardians are only allowed to monitor from afar; they analyse online data and social media, they watch footage from CCTV, and sometimes from hidden cameras. That wasn't enough for me, though. I needed to be closer to you. I broke the rules and started to shadow you. Mostly at night. I was scared for your safety; you were so vulnerable on the street alone. It crushed me with worry. One night, my worst fear manifested: a man began to pursue you. Then, when you saw him and ran, he chased you down and attacked you. That's when I intervened. You saw it unfold in your first flashback,' I reveal, biting my thumbnail.

'You were the shadow man. I should have guessed,' Ruby says flatly, shaking her head.

'Yes. I was also there outside that club, when the man died of an overdose. Other people just walked past him as he lay lifeless on that street, but you didn't; you tried your best to revive him even though his heart had already failed. You were so distraught. You ran from me when I tried to help. After that, I implemented a different method of approach; I'd walk past you on the street sometimes. And when I suspected that you hadn't eaten for a while, I handed you some money or left you food where I knew you'd find it. Too often, I tried to start a conversation, though you'd only say a few polite words to me each time. It never felt like enough.'

'Hmm. Then you go and erase a whole year of stalking. All that effort you went to—*wasted*.' Ruby's sarcasm is thick yet she doesn't outwardly display her anger. She looks tired, like feeling anything is too bothersome for her.

'No, it wasn't a year. That's how long guardians usually have prior to their sim. I had actually been monitoring you for almost five years. You see, I was supposed to be a guardian the first year West Haven ran this programme. My father is the director of this facility and, as his son, I was to lead the first sim. We searched for potential candidates; people without any close family or friends were the obvious choices. Because if *they* went missing for two weeks, or potentially longer, it wouldn't arouse much suspicion. The moment I saw you, I knew... I knew you were the one. But my father didn't agree. I was told that you weren't viable—that you were too suspicious, too affected by your past experiences. And I was strongly encouraged to pick someone else—someone more trusting, less stubborn, and not as strong-willed... but I couldn't. Those were the things that I liked about you, and I couldn't seem to let you go. I withdrew myself from the first sim experiment, to my father's dismay. It was the same for the next three. This year, my father relented, and you were finally approved. Your vague memories of me were wiped from your mind and then we really met for the first time, when I was able to finally introduce myself. I was so eager for you to like me that I broke some rules along the way. But I just... I had cared about you for so long and I was worried that you would never feel the same way about me. I didn't think I could love you any more than I already did, but you kept surprising me every day. I had the pleasure of watching you blossom in that forest. And I really hope, more than anything, that this isn't the end for us,' I express earnestly, blistering tears brimming. I dab them away with my cuff then roll both sleeves up to my elbows.

You need to pour your heart out if Ruby is ever going to believe a single word of this. You owe it to her and to yourself, even if she destroys your heart the way you did hers that night.

Ruby's forehead crinkles before she looks away, showing the first sign of an emotional response. 'Is that it?' she finally asks, her expression blank again.

'No... I still haven't told you my secret,' I whisper. The shaking has spread to my legs now. It's my body's feeble attempt to cope with the dread rising inside me as I come closer and closer to telling her. She's interested again, focusing back on me.

'What secret?' Ruby demands in a low voice, her eyes narrowing to slits.

Once I tell her the truth about me, she'll have to understand. I'm hoping beyond reason that it will make all the difference, and she'll finally see why we had to do it this way—why I did what I did to her.

I fill my lungs to the brim again, my pulse thrumming under my damp, itchy skin. 'I'm... different. I'm not like you. None of us... *here* are. I—I... It's hard to explain,' I stammer, dancing around my point, too afraid to just say it.

'Whatever you tell me won't make a difference, Logan. You know that. That's why you're putting it off. You know it doesn't matter anymore, so you're prolonging it. Save us some time and get to the fucking point before I fall asleep,' Ruby says coldly, resting her head on the wall and closing her eyes.

Also needing the safe space only the darkness behind my eyelids can bring, I shut them tight. 'We're not in the United Kingdom, Ruby. We're not even on your planet; this isn't Earth,' I say through an exhalation.

As soon as the truth is out, a weight lifts off my shoulders. My curiosity gets the better of me; I open my eyes to study her reaction.

Ruby's eyes fling open a second after mine. They widen as she comprehends my words. The silence is roaring in my ears as I wait patiently for her to respond. A variety of emotions shoot across her face: shock, confusion, realisation, and doubt. Then she simply stares at me, mouth agape. Fear dilates her pupils.

'If we're not on Earth, then that means... you're not human.' Ruby's words push out, a little choked.

'No, technically not,' I admit, scratching my neck.

'*Technically* not? What the fuck are you, then?' she presses, anger settling on her pale face, returning the colour to her cheeks.

'Well, to put it simply... I'm your ancestor. That sounds weird. Erm, let me rephrase... my kind came across your planet over a hundred thousand years ago, through a rip in space: a portal that we call a link. Humans might liken it to a black hole in appearance. Although it's more of a wormhole, really. Anyways, erm... it was an accident, the first time. One was created in an explosion, and someone fell into it—a female—Aiddah, we think her name was. We call her The First Scientist. It was written that she was sucked into a void of nothingness, like the in-between place you discovered when you died in the simulation. And like you, Aiddah managed to find her way out. However, it wasn't back to where she had come from. The First Scientist clawed her way into *your* world.'

I pause briefly, allowing time for Ruby to respond, but all she does is stare, mouth parted, the whites of her eyes still visible. So I continue.

'After many years of studying Earth's environment, and some further experiments, my kind decided to inhabit Earth. There was already a native species of a similar anatomical makeup—Neanderthals—who were widespread at the time. There's a real possibility that an unrecorded, prehistoric link was their reason for existing, too. Though it can never be proven. But that's a theory we can discuss another time... Where was I? Erm... oh yeah... My kind proceeded regardless, sending a select number of people through the link to start exploring and setting up base camps. A hundred or so in total, we believe. And of course, at some point, it all went wrong. Apparently, there were too many people for the link to handle and it closed up without warning. The rip just disappeared, as did our people—lost on Earth without our supplies, without our medicines or technology. Although, back then, we weren't as advanced as we are now, obviously. They're considered primitive compared to our current c apabilities.'

Ruby is still listening intently, though her expression tightens a little, like she's finding it difficult to follow this thread.

Stop flooding her with unimportant information and reduce the flow before her head explodes, I chastise myself, wiping the sweat from my brow.

'So... erm... the settlers on Earth had to start from scratch. It was a new world and they had to find ways to adapt and survive. Our kind forgot about them and forgot about Earth. Until just over a hundred years ago, when another rip was formed in this very facility, by my great-grandfather, Perrin West. What he discovered changed my world. My kind saw that what we left behind had flourished to become the dominant species. A new world was at our fingertips. The descendants of those settlers—*humans*—over thousands of years, had evolved slightly differently from us, due to the new environment, or some cross-species breeding with the natives—we're not entirely sure. Despite that, we were still the same in many ways. There were hardly any differences in our genetic makeup—the way we looked, the way in which we respond to physical and emotional stimuli. Not much had changed on the surface. But there was something that stood out. And with that difference came our salvation,' I explain as straightforwardly as possible.

'Salvation?' Ruby echoes, more confused.

'We had found a new gene pool.' I let the words hang in the air, allowing Ruby time to process—allowing time for her to connect the dots of what I've left unsaid.

'You want to *breed* with us?' she asks in a hushed tone, her bewilderment morphing into disgust.

My insides scrunch up, hit by that change in her expression and tone. 'You have no idea what we go through here. In my world, most of us don't live past the age of five. Over the last few thousand years, my kind has developed problems with our genes—they're corrupted. We don't know how or why, but we know the effects all too well. Our offspring have high mortality rates because a lot of them are born sick; it's a disease called Infadroniah. There's no cure as each case is different. It mutates slightly, like your common cold. That means antibodies can't fight it and it's why our scientists can't identify the corrupted gene until it manifests after a child is born. They die a slow and painful death. It might take a couple of years to kill them, but as soon as that baby is here, those parents know that their son or daughter will never see adolescence. They have to watch their child slowly deteriorate before their eyes. Many of my kind decide against procreating at all now, in case it happens to them. Over the last two hundred years, the chances of being born with Infadroniah have shot up to fifty per cent. With a flip of a coin, my kind is slowly becoming extinct. Humans have brought us hope. Hybrids are our future. It's the only plausible solution The West Haven Facility can find to our problem outside of cloning, which is a practice currently prohibited, the same as on Earth,' I conclude, hoping I've educated Ruby enough to do our plight justice.

Now that's off my chest, my muscles relax, and my heart slows to a steadier rhythm. I've offloaded so much information onto her, unburdening myself in the process. It's only fair to allow time for my words to soak in. I'm sure it's not easy to accept. It's not even easy to explain, and I've listened to guardians over the years try, with varying success. If Dawn and Ben can begin to accept it, then perhaps Ruby can, too. I need to believe she has it in her to forgive me.

'Hybrids? Are there any?' Ruby enquires, still sceptical.

'Yes, at present, there are five in existence. There were more in the past. They're the result of the four previous sims. Sasha's sister was a guardian in the second sim, and now she has a hybrid child called Darwin. That's why Sasha volunteered. She had her own baby once... a little girl—Raielle.' The ache in my chest intensifies. 'Rai didn't make it to her first birthday. A hybrid child is Sasha's only chance to be a mother again,' I disclose solemnly, and Ruby's expression softens somewhat. 'Adoption is very rare here. Not enough children are born, and the half that survives are usually cherished by their families.'

Ruby crosses her arms under her bust, and the way her breasts move under her grey sweatshirt raises my temperature again. *Fuck. Don't let your mind wander there, Logan. Not yet. You're nowhere near that place with her.* Though how I fucking miss being able to touch her, kiss her, grope her at night under the covers of my bed, wilfully ignoring the boundaries set. I'll be reprimanded for my wandering hands if Noah ever thinks to look through those more intimate moments. Before, I wouldn't have imagined he'd disrespect my privacy like that, but after what happened, he would be within his rights to. It's a good thing I encouraged Ruby to keep her clothes on when we were in bed together. Otherwise, there was a very real possibility that I would have made the mistake of taking things further.

Ruby's curt voice pulls me out of my impure thoughts. 'What's so great about a hybrid child?'

I yank on my trouser legs so the tightness around my crotch isn't as noticeable. 'From our analysis over the years, hybrids are immune to Infadroniah and many other diseases, including some from your planet. Influenza being one of them.'

She scoffs, disbelieving. 'Superhuman? Have they got their own comic book series yet?'

I breathe a laugh, relieved Ruby is herself enough to crack a joke. 'Yeah, Marvel will be making a couple hundred films about them soon,' I reply, but she doesn't laugh along. Instead, her mouth presses into a hard line.

Ruby flashes her eyebrows at me. 'So... the forest is the start of a breeding programme. Don't you think your methods of dating are a bit fucked up? Humans don't usually begin their relationships by abducting their partners, you know,' she remarks, continuing to mask her disgust with humour.

'What would you prefer? Being caged and inseminated as part of a series of cruel experiments? That's how things started when my arsehole of a grandfather, Creeden West, was in control of this facility. Luckily, when my father became director, he put in place some ground rules for experiments. He believes that humans deserve the right to choose, that insemination against their will is immoral and what you would call 'inhumane'. We may have to collect you first, without prior consent, but then the rest is up to you. We only guide decisions in a safe setting. We take people who are unhappy with their lives on Earth and present them with a new option: the possibility of becoming a part of something special—of falling in love,' I counter, not wanting her to think my kind are at all similar to the apathetic, probing monsters depicted in pop cu lture.

'You trick people into falling in love. That's not a choice,' Ruby snaps, her expression hardening.

'We may not have told you the complete truth but we were still ourselves in the sim; we were all connected to each other, we got to know one another, we grew together. Everything I told you about myself was true: about my mother's murder, the strained relationship I have with my father, and the fact that I love you. I *do* love you, Ruby. The whole thing wasn't some ploy to trick you into being a living incubator or anything like that. The sim is purely a safe environment for us to meet—as *equals*—to see where things could lead. It's not like I could just approach you on the street and casually bring up the fact that I'm from another planet in polite conversation. I had to earn your trust and you had to gain mine, too. I'm sorry that it had to be this way. I truly am. But it's the only safe way for us to introduce ourselves,' I say, more bluntly than I intended, but she remains stoic.

Even if Ruby doesn't accept anything else, I need her to know that I do love her and I regret having to deceive her, despite the necessity of it.

'Actually, thinking about it, there was one little lie about my mother: her name wasn't Hayley... it was Haven. I couldn't tell you that at the time, for obvious reasons,' I add, pulling at the collar of my white shirt. 'The West Haven Facility. The W.H.F. It's not as catchy as the H.I. Also, why did everyone lie about their names except you?'

The psychiatric team must have provided Ruby with our staff profiles already, where our full names and occupations are stated. 'It's not exactly a lie. They're nicknames. I call Alexel 'Alex', and I've known him since I was a toddler. Admittedly, his last name was also shortened. But that's only because Alexel Costellopearoh is a bit of a mouthful. My parents named me after one of the first humans they met: Johanna Logan. She was from London, too—a nurse. She was also one of the first of your kind to live in my world. Johanna stayed here for many years to teach my parents about your ways. She died before I was born, though.'

'Do you always snatch people from the UK?'

'The first link that was recorded—the one Aiddah fell into—apparently opened up somewhere in North Africa. The second opened up in England. Although now, we can open them up almost anywhere we want. My father prefers to pick candidates from the UK. He thinks British people are more open-minded and less confined by religious beliefs than most other countries nowadays. Plus, he says he likes your sense of humour and tea. A lot of my kind, especially in West Haven, speak English as a first language. Our own common tongue has faded in modern times, due to the ever-growing fascination with humans. Some have even adopted your different dialects. We have an obsession with your cultures and traditions. We even follow your fashion trends. Alex models the cheesy boy-band look rather well, I think.' I smile at her. She doesn't reciprocate.

'What do you call yourselves? What do you call this planet?' Ruby quizzes, trying and failing to hide her blatant interest.

My smile widens. 'This planet is called Sartah. The land we inhabit is Paleoguyah. We only have one main landmass here, unlike Earth. This facility is in a territory we call Polisto Norval. And my people are Suvians. Do you believe any of this or are you only humouring me?' I ask, hopeful.

'I haven't made my mind up yet. You should count that as a miracle because I was dead set on never believing anything that came out of your mouth again. But the technology here is so much more advanced. So... I guess it makes *some* sense,' Ruby allows, shrugging.

My heart leaps at that. 'I'm glad you're giving me the chance to explain. If you're willing, I can take you down to our labs to show you more? Before that, though, do you have any more questions regarding the sim?' I ask, struggling to keep my nervous excitement under control. She hasn't made her mind up yet. That means there's still a chance she'll accept this—accept *me*.

'If Suvians are humanity's ancestors, then I was right not to waste my time with religion. God obviously doesn't exist,' Ruby says, looking a little smug.

'Not necessarily. A lot of Suvians believe in a higher power and follow their own doctrines. I believe in something bigger than us sometimes, too. If there are things like rips in the universe—linking one world to another—then who knows what else is out there? Anything is possible, and not everything is within the scope of our understanding, either.'

'*I* believed in the impossible, when you said I was special. I wasn't, though, was I? I was only an easy target: alone, unloved,' Ruby expresses in a tight voice, talking to the wall, not me.

My stomach sinks, the progress I'm making seeming insignificant after that statement. 'You *are* special, Ruby. You're *very* special to me, and you were *very* special to *everyone* in that forest,' I maintain, my voice soft yet insistent. She shrugs half-heartedly, barely listening.

Just when I think Ruby won't respond, she mutters, 'Zoe would disagree with that.'

'Zoe was just jealous of you. She'll be leaving the facility soon, anyway.' I make sure to slip in this information so Ruby knows Zoe will no longer be around to cause issues. If Ruby *does* choose to stay, that is.

After that, Ruby continues to question me about some of my actions in the forest. Why I said certain things, why I acted the way I did, especially when it came to her and Charlie. Swallowing my pride, I admit that I was jealous of how easy their relationship appeared and how worried I was that she'd never open up to me. She then becomes rightfully angry that I already knew about her past and still pushed her to tell me. She assumes I was putting on a performance on the roof. But I assure her that wasn't the case at all. I was only craving a deeper connection with her—needing to hear her story in her own words.

Ruby also appears agitated over the fake wolf attack, which was the excuse I needed to pull myself out of the sim without suspicion. It was all so I could gather information from my father about the rebel.

'I know why you used wolves now: you knew they were the only thing that could scare me into returning to the cabin. You used my fear of dogs against me. The depth of your manipulation is astounding,' Ruby remarks, her tone frosted to mask her hurt.

'That wasn't my call, I swear. It was my father's,' I tell her, yet she doesn't seem to care for my excuses.

Ruby then goes on to ask about the others' motives—Sasha's, Freya's, and Alex's. And I try my best to explain from my perspective, though I encourage her to talk to them herself. She sneers at the idea.

Moving on, I inform her of the rebel's true identity—Stratton Drohgue—and that there are rebel groups, like Ascendant, fighting against the prospect of mating with humans. They class humans as our sub-species and believe they have a lesser cognitive capacity, and are therefore unworthy of our respect. The thought of our kind integrating with humans in any way disgusts them. This means the theory of cross-species breeding is something they vehemently oppose, to the point of violence.

The more I reveal, the more Ruby seems willing to communicate with me. She's gone from hardly listening and making sarcastic comments to showing genuine interest. I shouldn't raise my hopes too high as I know what she's like: her stubbornness will make it difficult for me to regain her trust. I'll have to fight to win back her affection. It won't be achieved overnight, that's for certain. It could take months, but I can be patient. That's what the trial run is for. If I can persuade her to make it to that stage, then she'll soon learn that she *can* trust me—that she *can* allow herself to love me.

I've viewed Ruby's chart results from before and after the sim terminated. They provide an abstract insight into a subject's mind and emotions. The results also show the depth of Ruby's connection to me specifically. On the last morning of the sim, after I spent the night tending to her needs post-strangulation, those levels were the highest we've ever recorded. And since she's woken up, they've only dipped slightly. I'm sure she still cares about me, deep down, and that she's only trying to fight it because she's afraid it was all a lie.

The next step is to show Ruby around the facility. My father, as well as the board, won't like it. Still, I made a promise and I want to show her that my word is my bond from now on. I'm determined not to break her trust again—whatever's left of it.

'Are you ready for the tour?' I ask, rising from my seat and offering her a hand.

Ruby glares at my open palm with distaste then stands without assistance. 'As long as I can see Charlie.'

Dropping my hand, I respond, 'I'll take you through the lab block first and then on to Charlie's cell.' Moving towards the door, I hesitate a step, then pivot back to her. 'Please don't try to run away or burn the place down or anything like that. I know it's deserved, but I promise you, it will be a wasted effort.'

'I'll try to be on my best behaviour. If I'm not on Earth then there's no point in attempting to escape, is there?' Ruby retorts, her tone full of bitterness.

'My father's going to kill me,' I mutter, placing my outstretched hand back on the door to open it for us.

I encourage Ruby to walk through the door first. She steps out into the hallway, surveying her new surroundings through wary eyes, as though she's afraid it's a trap meant to snap her spine in two.

Frowning, I say, 'You must at least know I would never hurt you, right?'

Ruby's head whips around, her suspicious gaze refocusing on me. 'I thought I knew that, but then you stabbed me in the heart.' Her face is as emotionless as her voice, though her eyes reflect my pain, and her disappointment in me is devastating. I can't decipher whether her statement was literal or had a deeper meaning. I don't think it matters.

Ruby turns her back on me, walking away. I follow behind her, my head bowed in shame, racked with remorse over my cowardly actions in those final regretful moments of our sim.

They will haunt me for the rest of my life, as will that look she just gave me.

Chapter 31

CLEAN SLATE

RUBY

With my mind still reeling, I concentrate on the sound of my steps: the little taps and squeaks these soft-soled plimsolls make on the polished marble floors. I wonder if these noises are only digital echoes inside of my head or if they *are* real now. I'm afraid I can't tell the difference anymore.

I was the first to wake from the forest simulation, lying in that capsule of machines, with the halo secured on my temples. Screaming my first conscious breath after death, I sat bolt upright and fought with the recovery team, struggling to escape their subduing grasp. They must have sedated me because the next thing I remember is waking in that fancy prison room, entangled in the disconcertingly soft sheets of the king-sized bed.

People I didn't recognise came in to talk to me; they said they were doctors. At that point, my mind was numb to my surroundings—my will to fight waning. Keeping all emotions locked away in the dark depths of my despair, I let them draw my blood and run tests on my body and mind. I didn't have to say a word because they used machines to determine my thoughts and feelings. I simply sat there in my wilful despondency, waiting for it to be over.

They told me things I had already guessed. Then they hit me with some good news: Charlie and Eli weren't dead, apparently. At first, I suspected it was another manipulation to trick me into communicating with them. So I continued to wallow in self-pity, but with a little hope warming and smoothing my sharpened edges. They *could* still be dead, and at times I wished I remained that way, too.

Freya, or *Freyessa*, whatever her name really is, paid me a visit this morning. She had the nerve to ask if I'll ever forgive them for what they've done. With my blank mask on, I pretended she wasn't there—that she was never there and that none of it was real.

None of *them* were real.

I can't believe Logan had the gall to show up. It took him a few days to pluck up the courage, mind you. Unfortunately, it's harder to pretend he doesn't exist.

His messy black hair is flat and straw-like; the shine of the ebony silk has dulled. His colourless eyes are fearful, like a child who's broken his mother's favourite vase. All of the intensity they used to hold has disappeared—the magnetism neutralised. His face is hollow and discoloured as if he hasn't been eating or sleeping. When he was peddling his various excuses to me, his body trembled. His once strong and sure hands were wavering. He was weak, and the cracks in his newly professional facade were glaringly obvious. He's not just an engineer as he told me: he's a 'Junior Director', whatever that means. All I knew before he revealed his colossal secret was that he was the boss's son. My kidnapper. The 'man' who haunted my dreams. The lover who quite literally cut up my heart. The *thing* I can't stop thinking about, no matter how hard I try.

I tried not to let Logan's presence affect me. I tried not to care at all—to pretend he wasn't really there—was *never* really there. I couldn't keep it up. My indifferent mask slipped a couple of times.

Also, to my surprise, I'm not afraid of him. I should be. He betrayed me. He killed me. And it turns out he's my stalker and kidnapper on top of that. And he's a fucking alien... *'technically'*.

Logan claims he's telling the truth now. To be fair, it's so outlandish and—under normal circumstances—unbelievable that I'm inclined to believe it. Who would think to make that shit up? And for what purpose? But I've been fooled by the ridiculous before, so my judgement can't be trusted. This could be another dream—another simulation designed to manipulate me. How will I ever be sure what's real again? Fearing my own thoughts are not my own anymore makes me want to shut my brain off completely. They could be monitoring them right now. How would I know?

Apparently, this place is The West Haven Facility, on a planet called Sartah, on a landmass called Paleoguyah, in a territory called Polisto Norval, with an alien race known as Suvians, who are actually human ancestors.

What the fuck?!

A rip in space and time is linking our two worlds. The first link used to inhabit, the second to extract. The first to give life to my planet, the second to take it. I was abducted to participate in a breeding programme—a sick and twisted *alien* experiment. *Participate*—like I had a choice. I was wrong and Zoe was right: choice is an illusion. Like most things. Including love. And there's no point in hoping for anything better.

I knew it was all too good to be true. I should have trusted my instincts, not my lonely, misguided heart.

They tell me I have choices—that I have a decision to make. I must either accept the next stage of the programme and agree to give this 'trial run' a chance—stay here and make peace with these human-like creatures and live amongst them for six months—or have all my memories of this experience wiped away, like a coffee stain on a glass table: never leaving a permanent ring, every drop ceasing to exist.

It would all be gone: everyone and everything from the forest, the good and the bad. Some of it I won't miss. I *want* to forget Sasha, Freya, Alex, and Zoe. I *want* to rewind to a time before I met *him*. Before he forced himself into my life—manipulating me, tricking me into having feelings for him. I *want* Logan to be wiped away, every word, every touch, and every kiss. Any remnant of those things will forever make me weak—make me crave them—crave *him*.

It's all or nothing now: all of him or none of him.

But If I do choose to forget, I'll also lose the others—Ben, Dawn, Eli, and Charlie.

Charlie—my best friend—will be expunged from my mind as though he never existed. If he ever *did* exist. I'm still not sure. But he'll be gone, nonetheless. My little lost boy, never to be found again. Can I give him up, too? The questions continue to circulate as I wander through these nondescript white corridors, with Logan shuffling behind me on our way to the lab block.

Logan said again that he loves me. Out of everything he's just told me, that's the most unbelievable. How could you do those things to the person you claim to love? I *am* alone. I *am* unloved. *That's* why he chose me. I was only an easy target to him.

Distracted by my muddle of thoughts, I don't realise I'm at the end of the corridor until a white wall is staring me in the face. Stepping back, I peer up at the digital sign detailing the various routes branching off ahead. One of them is marked 'West Wing Simulation Block'. Before I take the route, I glance back over my shoulder to check with Logan.

'Go ahead, it's all right. There aren't many people down here today,' Logan says, gesturing for me to carry on. He's letting me lead at my own pace. For some reason, his sudden consideration pisses me off further. It's another fucking lie. If he *was* considerate, he wouldn't have left me to rot in my cell for two days or done any of this in the first place.

When I don't make a move, Logan lifts a hand and I stiffen. Then he stiffens. His hand hangs in the air between us for a moment before he drops it to his side again, hurt written across his face. Did he think to guide me in? He knows better than to touch me. He's lost that privilege. He should have never had it.

'*People*? Hmm,' I scoff with dark amusement.

Not enjoying the flicker of pain in Logan's eyes as much as I expected, I quickly stride through the entrance to the next pristine, white corridor, full of more doors without handles. Along the way, Logan explains what's inside each of them.

The projector room: which contains the same insert machines the rebel used to code only his arm into the sim to drag me into the lake. Apparently, they should only be used to manipulate a digital environment in emergencies. Logan explains that they otherwise haven't been used for years as West Haven coders are becoming increasingly more competent at controlling the sims in real-time with the help of artificial intelligence.

The recovery rooms: which I never saw the inside of because I was heavily sedated. Logan tells me most of them are similar to a typical patient care lounge, with areas to relax while medical tests are analysed.

Also, there are two reflector rooms, although Logan doesn't offer a description for those. They're marked 'No Entry', anyway.

'At the end of this corridor is the main digital science lab for the sim block,' Logan mentions, still trailing a few paces behind. 'We also have labs in other wings of this facility. A biology one in the medical block. A weapons lab in the military block. The kids even have their own child-friendly one in the education block.'

The lab entrance scans us when we step up to it. Logan holds his palm up, pressing it against the flat grey surface of the metal door. It slides open after a brief pause, and then we enter.

It's a large, brightly-lit room full of computers and projections, similar to holograms. There are numerous workstations staffed by people in simple, slate-grey clothing, conducting what appear to be digital experiments. Some are wading through a simulated jungle, manipulating matter within using special gloves. Others are sitting at desks, coding. There's even one guy in a motion-capture suit, standing in front of a green screen.

'It looks like the inside of a VR headset,' I say before I can stop myself, and Logan laughs, nodding.

'Who do you think came up with that technology in the first place? My father slips our inventions into your world in dribs and drabs, so you're not left too far behind.' His smugness is all humour, but I glower at him anyway, wiping the smile off his face for spite.

The staff watch me curiously as I trudge through the lab with Logan by my side. I catch flashes of worry from them. Not hate or disgust, only concern. I don't know why they'd be scared of *me*. I'm not the one who steals people for weird experiments.

'Do you want to see how we synthesise certain types of food? We can grow crops within a day, and we produce synthetic meat, too. In West Haven, we live as vegans. Sartah does have a number of native species, although they look very different to the animals which have evolved on your planet. We have a small number of domesticated pets of our own. The most interesting is a... well, the easiest comparison is a giant fruit bat. We have four that live in the stables here. I could take you to meet them one day, if—if you want? Erm... Some Suvians would pay a high price for any living thing from your planet, even a cockroach. Alex has a cat. My father brought one back from Earth for his tenth birthday. The cat's called Fluffy, by the way, and she's remarkably still among the living,' Logan reels off quickly—he's rambling; he's nervous.

'Stop talking,' I insist flatly.

With a deflated sigh, Logan nods, disheartened. He'll receive no sympathy from me.

A moment later, three familiar faces enter the lab: Sasha, Alex, and behind him, Dawn.

Sweet, little, human Dawn; she's crossed to the dark side—accepted all of their bullshit without question. Between Ben, Eli, Charlie, her, and me, I knew she'd be the most likely to accept the trial run. I bet all Alex had to do was apologise. She probably forgave him without a second thought. She's too pure for this world, and our own for that matter. Maybe I should, but I don't think any less of her for it. If she's happy then who am I to judge?

It's then I remember that Alex is technically an alien and my judgmental side creeps back in to force a shudder down my spine. They're not human. *Logan* isn't human, and I nearly had sex with him. Well, in our digital bodies, anyway.

At the memory of our passion-filled moments, alone in our bedroom, I expect my gag reflex to react, but it doesn't. On the contrary, the only part of my body that's stimulated is the treacherous organ between my legs, a bolt of heat shooting there. For fuck's sake. It doesn't help that Logan was the one to stop us from taking things further. He wouldn't even let me grope him over his clothes, although he sometimes forgot himself and squeezed a bra-clad boob.

Earlier, Logan told me that he had to rein us in because there are strict rules regarding sexual contact with humans, even in the digital world, which state that it should only be conducted when both parties have informed consent. And the fact that I didn't know *what* he truly was isn't classed as informed to them. Thankfully.

When Logan mentioned that, it made me laugh. They have no problem with kidnapping and forcing us into a medically-induced coma to mess with our minds. But fucking us under false presences crosses a line for them? It *is* laughable.

When Dawn spots me, she squeals in delight. She must think I've also accepted my trial run, as I guess I wouldn't usually be allowed in here if I hadn't. Sasha's head turns in my direction and, as soon as her hazel eyes land on me, guilt floods them. Her whole expression tightens, contorts, then glistens with an instant sweat, her medium-brown skin losing its warm tone. She didn't expect to see me around this soon. That makes two of us.

Dawn skips over to me, and the impact of her embrace nearly knocks me off my feet. 'Ruby! Oh, I've missed you so much! I didn't think I'd ever see you again.' She's like an excited child, incredibly endearing, but I don't return her affection. Instead, I embrace the cold emptiness inside me, clinging to that numbness for dear life. I can't attach myself to anything here, even her.

After too many awkward seconds pass, Dawn lets go, stepping back. Her head tilts in confusion and she appears a little hurt by my apathy.

Alex slides Logan a perplexed look to match—a certain question unspoken in his rich brown eyes.

Logan scratches the back of his neck. It's his sign of discomfort. 'I'm showing Ruby around the lab and then I'm taking her to see Charlie. We've skipped a few stages,' he clarifies for them.

There's clear disappointment on each of their faces. *Hold onto the emptiness, Ruby. Stay numb, stay numb,* I drum into myself, to the place my heart once was, now aching.

Sasha aims a tentative smile my way, but my *dead-behind-the-eyes* stare targets her. I imagine they're dark pools of resentment as I glare at her, devoid of emotion. I terminate her smile with my indifference, and her face drops.

'Ruby, can I speak with you for a second? Please? Let me explain,' Sasha asks in a small, pleading voice as she attempts to pull me off to one side.

Without a word, I shrug Sasha off and stride past her, my eyes locked ahead. I don't glance back at any of them.

'Please, Ruby. I'm sorry!' Sasha calls before I dash through the next door.

Logan chases me out. 'Sasha really does care about you too, Ruby. She's the same person she was in the sim. The same friend. She used to watch your footage with me and tell me how much she admired you. How much she wanted a friend like you.'

'I want to see Charlie. *Now*,' I demand, my voice a low growl.

Rubbing a hand over his face, Logan exhales sharply, resigned. 'Okay, I'll take you to his cell.'

We drift down a few more corridors until we loop back around to the southwest wing and reach cell block two. This part of the facility is similar to the section I was kept in. It's like a posh hotel, with beige-panelled walls, gold and cream furniture, pretty pot plants, mini chandeliers, intricate ceiling roses, and various pretentious pieces of art hanging on the walls.

'Why is this block not as clinical and white as the others I've seen?' I ask, my curiosity winning out against my forced indifference.

'Warmer tones are more inviting. It's more human-like—familiar to you. We want you to feel comfortable,' Logan answers, plucking a ruby-red rose from a vase as he passes a side table. He hands it to me with a shy smile, testing the waters.

I glare down at the rose with distaste. 'Is this real?' I'm not sure what I'm asking. Is this rose real? Is this place real? Are *you* for real?

'It is. We have greenhouses full of Earthly trees and plants,' Logan replies, and from the look in his eyes, he knows I meant it in every way imaginable. Another small smile of his tries to brush past my defences.

Feeling spiteful, I drop the rose and crush it under my soft-soled plimsolls before I walk on, not looking back to witness the pain I know will be on his too-beautiful face.

'Why aren't there any windows in this place? Is it to prevent us from escaping?'

'No. There are no windows because this facility is built underground,' Logan mutters, his voice flatter now.

An underground lair on an alien planet; it sounds like I'm stuck in a bad Sci-Fi film.

We reach a black door, which has Charlie's three-dimensional picture projected onto the wall monitor beside it. Did my door have the same? I didn't look back to check when I walked out of my room. At the time, I was in a hurry to leave in case Logan changed his mind and trapped me back inside.

Logan, with a swift move of his hand, swipes away Charlie's picture, and another image pops up. It must be the view from the camera in his room because it looks exactly like my room. However, this one is empty.

A weight drops in my stomach. 'Where is he?' I demand from a confused-looking Logan.

Logan flicks through some digital files. 'Uh... he's not in there. I don't know.' A deep frown marks his face while he furiously searches the holographic system projected by the tiny wall monitor.

'What do you mean you don't know? Are you tricking me again? Is this another lie?! He's dead, isn't he? He really *did* die!' My voice grows louder with the drumming beats of my heart. Anger heats my face while fear pours ice down my spine.

My panic is contagious; Logan spins around to face me, his eyes wide and frantic. 'No, Ruby. He's alive, I promise you. I'm not lying!' He's too fucking close. The smoky, sandalwood smell of him invades my senses. Too real. Too familiar. I push him away, and even when there's space, I eat it up to push him again, his shoulder knocking against the beige panelling as I do so.

Seeing that I'm full of unpredictable rage, Logan attempts to calm me by gently holding onto my wrists so I can't swing at him. His palms burn through the material of the simple grey sweatshirt I'm wearing. All the while, his eyes pierce into mine, pleading with me to believe him. But I don't. I can't let myself. I won't allow it.

With my frenzy building like an uncontrolled fire, I struggle against Logan's grip. But instead of loosening his hold, he tightens it. A flare of panic has me trying to kick him away.

'Stop!' Logan orders, his face scrunching in pain when my foot connects with his shin. A second later, his arms are around me, his body pressing into mine so there's no space for me to use my feet as weapons again.

'Let go of me!' I shout in his face.

'I can't. I can't let you go.' His voice is desperate, cracking with emotion.

'Get off me! Liar! Liar! I fucking hate you!' I roar at Logan while his tears fall.

'You don't hate me. You don't,' he whispers, his breath catching in his throat.

I'm an inferno of hate. The feel of his warm body against mine is only feeding my flames of wrath. I want to burn everything that was *us* until it's only a pile of ash at my feet.

Going still, I bare my gritted teeth. 'I do. I can't stand to even look at you. You killed Eli. You killed Charlie. You killed *me*!' I scream the last line at Logan with every fibre of my being, throwing all my hate, all my fear, all my built-up rage at him, and he stands there, taking the full force of it.

Logan releases my arms so I can push him, so I can strike him. And I do. Across his face. Only once.

Logan stumbles back in shock, his face stained with tears, his body shaking, his chest heaving. My wild expression is reflected back to me in his blown-out pupils. It makes me pause. His expression is a devastating picture of heartbreak—of endless sorrow and despair.

Silence expands in the space between us. It's an all-consuming, tangible silence that seems infinite—a void—swallowing all hope. I think we both realise at this moment that there's no going back to how we were. I can't do it. It's impossible. I'll never be able to see past what happened—what he did. What he *is*. The person I thought I loved in the forest isn't him. The heart I was willing to give is broken beyond repair. And I think I just shattered his for good measure.

'That was entertaining. Hit him again,' a squeaky voice says from down the hall. We both turn to find it. Zoe is peeking around the corner, a malicious smile etched on her thin lips. 'Carry on, don't mind me,' she continues with mocking sweetness.

Stepping back from Logan, I catch my breath, while he does the same, wiping his face with the sleeve of his shirt. We avoid each other's gaze. In my periphery, I see that his cheek is red from my slap and a kernel of guilt settles in the pit of my stomach.

'What do you want, Zoe?' Logan growls at her when she approaches.

'You're not here to see Charles, are you?' She's still playing sweet; she has to be up to something.

'Do you know where he is?' Logan asks in a dry tone, not sparing her a glance.

'Yeah, I know where he is.' Smiling brightly, Zoe rocks on the balls of her feet like a child with an exciting secret to spill.

'Where then? Another cell? Recovery?' Logan is frustrated now—fists clenching, jaw tight.

'Nope, none of those.'

'Damn it, Zoe. Where is he?!' Logan snaps, making me flinch. He notices and immediately softens his stance, offering me an apologetic look.

Zoe's malicious grin returns. 'He's gone. Noah gave me the all-clear to slate him and throw him back to that godforsaken planet of rats. It's where they belong,' she delivers in a poisonous tone. Her eyes dart to mine. To measure my reaction, I suppose—to relish in my pain and to show her triumph.

Now, it's my turn to snap.

Seeing red, I dive onto Zoe in a flurry of fists—mine into her jaw, into her nose, and she returns one to my cheek. I hardly feel the impact of it as my adrenaline is in overdrive. The overwhelming pain of Charlie's absence is already enough for me. There's no room for more. Physical pain can no longer hurt me.

I'm wrestling with Zoe on the hard, varnished wood floor when Logan's arms loop around my waist; he lifts me off her like I weigh nothing. I kick out, screaming profanity at her. I'm like a wild animal and Logan's arms are my cage. They're not my safe haven like they once were.

Zoe staggers up, straightening herself out. Blood rushes from her nose. She pinches it between her fingers, stemming the flow. Even when I stop struggling, Logan doesn't release me. He drags me further back from Zoe, like he's afraid I'm preparing to launch myself at her again.

I am.

'You're a wild animal!' Zoe screeches at me, not daring to come closer. 'How can you love *that*, Logan? Why her?!'

'Go away, Zoe. *Leave*! Get the fuck out of here and never come back!' Logan commands, his voice colder and rougher than I've ever heard it.

'My pleasure,' Zoe grinds out before she spins on her heel and storms off, her hands cupping her bloody nose.

For a long, drawn-out minute, we stand there: Logan's body flush against my back, his arms keeping me contained—controlled—*steady*. Forgetting the hopeless void consuming us, I lean into his touch, my head resting against his shoulder, my eyes falling shut, our deeper breaths synchronising again. But as soon as his sweet-smelling breath warms the shell of my ear, and his tempting lips drag across to brush my cheekbone—angling for a kiss—I remember. I remember everything. So, before he can ensnare me, I tear myself out of his clutches. Immediately, the emptiness returns tenfold. Numbness engulfs me once more in its cold, dead flames.

My Peter Pan is forever lost. He has no memory of me—of our goodnight hugs, or secret agent meetings in the bathroom, or thimbles in the dark. It's all gone—*I'm* gone—deleted like I'm nothing more than a spelling mistake. I will never see his cute, boyish face again. Those warm hazel eyes that were forever smiling, and that cheeky grin you couldn't *not* like—*gone*. I will never see Charlie again. My only real friend has been snatched away from me. I'm worse than dead to him: I'm completely erased. Now, to him, I don't exist. The reality of it is unbearable.

'I want to go home,' I announce. There's no edge, no anger in my voice. I have nothing left to give.

With his head lowering in defeat, Logan murmurs, 'I know.'

'I don't want to remember any of this. Not the forest, not Sasha, or the others, not Charlie, and especially not you,' I declare, my tone retaining no malice. It's the most vulnerable I've been since I woke up here. I'm sure he can sense that as his breath puffs out of him, my honesty hitting hard. He knows he's my weakness, and moving forwards, I want to be strong.

'Okay.' Logan doesn't look at me. His face goes slack, like his brain has switched off. 'Follow me.' He walks past me, down another corridor to our right. I keep pace behind him.

A heavy fog descends, my senses dulling, my mind a haze of clouded thoughts. I can't see my way out of it.

So I let the fog claim me.

I give myself up to *it*, instead of to *him*.

We enter a dark room back in the west wing. It's small, or it feels smaller because of a bulky dentist-like chair in the middle of the room, facing a wall-mounted screen. Connected to the back of the chair is a movable computer screen. There's also a halo dangling off a hook at its side.

'Alex likes to call this place the clean slate room. This machine targets memories in order for them to be wiped from your mind. With the infilter on, I'll be able to target all the memories you have stored from the past two weeks and delete them. Once the procedure is complete, I'll arrange to send you back through a link to London with some new vague memories, so the absence of time won't be too jarring for you. We call this process slating. It's all standard practice when a subject rejects the trial run,' Logan states, like a doctor would to a patient—emotionless.

The whole thing sounds terrifying but I'm too far gone to care. 'Okay. Should I sit?' I ask, pointing to the imposing chair.

Logan nods solemnly. 'Get yourself comfortable. Then when you're ready, I'll attach the infilter.'

I sink down into the chair, reclining so I'm lying flat. I know I should be feeling tense or afraid, but the fog has me now. It's a safe, comforting blanket, like a protective layer—allowing me to hide away from my grief.

'Try not to move,' Logan instructs me before he fixes the halo—*infilter*—to sit at my temples. I feel its cool kiss, and then it fuses, the metal moulding to fit the shape of my head.

'Does the process hurt?' I enquire, still not afraid but curious.

'No. It won't hurt *you*,' Logan assures me, and I catch the slight emphasis on the last word.

Logan adjusts the computer screen, positioning it behind my headrest where he stands. When he places his palm on it, it hums to life. The screen on the wall lights up but remains blank—a dull grey.

After a minute, the halo begins to quiver. The vibrations continue to grow stronger, so I close my eyes, curling up into my brain fog where I'm safer.

'It's nearly ready. You won't stay awake. This is the last time you'll see this facility or have any memory of what's happened. It will all be wiped from your mind. You will never have to see me again, I promise. When you wake, you'll be back in your alleyway in London, like none of this ever happened,' Logan says, his throat thick. He's trying to hold his emotions at bay for me.

The last time I'll see this facility... the last time I'll see *him*. I have to know something first. 'Logan, why did you kill me?' I whisper, my eyelids too heavy to open. The vibrations tingle across my forehead. Frost seeps into my skin, liquifying and rippling through to my brain. The strange sensations make me shiver.

Logan sighs. 'I was weak. I couldn't see you in that much pain. And worse, I couldn't cope with my own,' he answers softly, melodically—a lullaby; a sombre lullaby, sung only to me. 'I'm truly sorry, Ruby.'

'I know.' My breaths are becoming shallow and rhythmic as the icy ripple turns into a wave, washing over me from head to toe. 'I forgive you, Logan,' I manage to breathe.

'If you remember one thing from this, remember that you're loved. I'll never stop. Even when I'm only an echo. Remember that.'

The fog gradually clears, and what waits for me on the other side is the star—my beacon. That pinprick of light draws me to it like a moth to a flame. The light glows brighter, bigger, wider—illuminating the night sky. There's no fog anymore. I'm free of it.

Before I fly away, I think I say, 'Goodnight, Logan.'

And his reply is a faint yet familiar murmur on a fresh spring breeze. I don't quite catch it in time, but I *feel* it resonating deeply.

The last thing I recall, before the light reaches me, is the tickle of tiny circles being drawn into my palm. It's comforting. It makes me smile.

Finally content, I drift off, the complete, fulfilling light a warm bath I'll happily drown in. And it's not long before all my worries wash away...

Epilogue

One Year Later - Ruby

I lift myself out of a haze of dreams, all too foggy to recall. Rubbing the sleep from my eyes, I smile lazily up at the sun warming my face. I forgot to shut the curtains again last night. The lure of twinkling stars always tempts me to leave them open, even when I slip into bed. Often, I find myself looking up into space, wondering what mysteries exist beyond those tiny beacons.

With a reluctant groan, I roll out of my comfy bed. No snoozing today. I can't be late for my first day as a supervisor. After I was told of my promotion on Friday, I rode the high all weekend.

It's been exhilarating but it still doesn't hold a candle to the morning my whole world changed, back when I was just a poor, vulnerable, homeless woman. The memory is still fresh and untainted; I remember dreaming of a faraway star before waking a little dazed, like I had been asleep for weeks. A bin had toppled over beside me, and a black backpack had fallen out of it onto my lap. That backpack changed my life. It *gave* me a life.

I opened the backpack to find ten grand in twenty-pound notes. Shocked, I burst into tears and laughed at the same time. After that,

I knew things would never be the same. Obviously, I kept the money. Whoever threw it away clearly didn't want it. Drug money, I suspected. Anyway, I saw it as a gift from the universe; a cosmic apology for screwing me over so many times. Even now, I feel no remorse for using it. It was better off in my pocket than a drug dealer's.

It afforded me a fresh start, with more options and better choices.

One of those choices was to leave London behind. It was too crowded, too busy, too expensive, and too alien for me moving forwards. It's not like I ever fit in there. I live in West Sussex now: in a quaint, country village. There are always birds singing in the trees, and small valleys to hike up in my spare time. It's full of friendly faces who wish me *good morning* when I pass by. I'm not invisible here. I've found a place I can call home.

Still, there seems to be something missing, like there's this hole in my chest I can't quite fill.

Singing along to Jake Bugg, I quickly apply some makeup and then straighten my hair. I throw on black trousers and my favourite shirt: the vintage cream one with pretty, pearl buttons. And, before I head out the door, I grab breakfast—a banana. I would usually make myself something like egg on toast, but I forgot to wash up the frying pan last night after dinner. It still has the remnants of the Spanish omelette I made; a small chunk of chorizo is stuck in grease, burnt around the edges. I'll clean it up after work.

Work. I don't think many people are as excited as I am about working. When I first landed a job in the garden centre, I wasn't sure I'd fit in. However, after a month or so of settling in, I started making friends and fully immersed myself in the role. Now, I'm the fucking *supervisor*. How did that happen? I hope I'm still able to tend to the plants, though. The rose bushes are my favourite. They were my mum's favourite, too.

My mum's smiling face appears in my mind's eye. I smile back at her. I hope she's proud of me, since I finally made it out of that muddy pit all on my own.

Distracted, I run right into a man in the hallway when I rush out my door. As I collide with him, I knock a box out of his hands. It crashes onto the floor, and some books and trinkets scatter.

'Oh, shit, I'm so sorry!' I say quickly, bending to scoop up his things. He does, too.

'No, it's completely my fault. I was lingering outside like some weird stalker, sorry,' the man responds, laughing lightly. 'For a minute, I forgot which flat was mine.'

We stand up at the same time and I finally take him in. The first thing I notice is his blue eyes—pale and gleaming, like crystal. His messy yet incredibly silky-looking coal-black hair contrasts with his creamy skin. The beauty of it—of *him*—is almost otherworldly. It's takes me too long to realise I'm staring, blatantly checking him out.

A little awkward laugh escapes me, and I blush when he smiles knowingly. 'I'm always in such a rush to get to work that I never pay enough attention,' I explain, fiddling with the strap of my satchel. 'I hope my clumsiness didn't cause any damage to your books. Or you, of course.'

The man chuckles. 'I think the only casualty was your banana,' he jokes, pointing to the squashed fruit under his box.

'Ah, I guess it's a better way to go than being nibbled on.'

He bursts out laughing, a cute dimple popping out on each cheek. I laugh along, warmth unfurling in my chest. Fuck, those dimples are cute. When the sound of our laughter tapers off, an inviting silence fills the space between us. And as soon as our eyes catch, my stomach flutters.

Flustered, I gesture to the piles of boxes by the door to the flat opposite me. 'Have you just moved in?'

'Yeah, I've moved from quite far away. I don't know this area well at all. I also don't know anyone here. I'm starting completely from scratch,' he tells me, shrugging a shoulder.

'I was where you are a year ago. It's scary, isn't it? But it was the best thing that ever happened to me,' I assure him.

'I hope it is for me, too.' This time, his gleaming eyes fix on mine, and for a split second, my knees weaken. The warm pull connecting us electrifies me. The heat from his gaze flushes down my neck and chest, settling low in my belly.

Luckily, before I make a complete fool of myself, I snap back to my senses. 'Well, I should head off. I'm always a little late for work but I don't want to take the piss today. Anyway, sorry again for knocking into you,' I mutter, going to leave.

'Hey, erm... what time do you finish work?'

Pausing on the stairs, I turn back to him. 'Six. Why?'

He shifts his weight between his feet, looking a little nervous. It's endearing. 'I was wondering, if you're free, whether you'd like to show me around? I've heard there are some good pubs nearby.' He flashes me a dimpled smirk. It's not cocky: it's flirtatious. It's the kind of fiendish smile which has my abdomen coiling in pleasure.

Blushing fiercely, I say more cooly than I feel, 'Okay, sure. Why not?'

This year has been one of the best of my life. I've found a place to call home, I have a job that I love, and I've even made some friends. Despite all that progress, there's still this tiny void in the back of my mind that sometimes pulses. Like it's calling out for something—someone. It wants to be filled.

I know something else which longs to be filled.

Oh, for fuck's sake, Ruby. Why did my mind go there? I'm such a perverted creep. This guy is doing funny things to my brain. Why do I like it?

'All right, then. I'll see you about six-ish. Have a good day at work,' he pronounces brightly, picking up his box of things.

Smiling, I give him a little wave before I move to continue down the stairs, but I hesitate, turning back to him once more. 'Wait, I didn't catch your name.'

He sets the box on top of the others before leaning across the bannister, reaching for me. 'Hi, I'm Logan.' He beams, offering me his hand to shake.

'Ruby,' I reply, taking his hand and that glimmer of hope.

STAY CONNECTED!

If you're eager to discuss *The Haven Ten* and its secrets, become a member of my spoiler-FILLED Facebook group here:

f facebook.com/groups/1169519154440078/

And here are the links to my spoiler-FREE socials:

♪ tiktok.com/@amberbayleyauthor

◎ https://instagram.com/amberbayleyauthor

The Haven Ten series will comprise six books in total. So far, four have been drafted to completion. The other two have intricate outlines.

Ruby's journey will continue in *The Haven Ten: Recollection*, releasing Spring 2024...

My next book, *Dangers Unclaimed*: a dark, why-choose Greek mythology retelling of King Minos/ Hades and Persephone, with *The Labyrinth* vibes, is scheduled for release November 2023.

Author's Note

Thank you from the bottom of my heart for giving this unknown indie author and this strange hybrid book a chance. I hope you enjoyed reading it as much as I enjoyed writing it.

The Haven Ten has been a decade in the making. Writing Ruby's unconventional journey of self-discovery and her exploration of friendship and love helped me through a difficult time in my life. It continues to help me still.

The idea clawed its way into my mind in the form of a nightmare in 2012. But it wasn't until 2013 that I started the first draft. I finished that draft in 2014. And in the years since, I've read over the words nearly a hundred times, closing plot holes, adding breadcrumbs, and developing the series as a whole, while also trying to teach myself to be a more competent writer (My D in English Literature at A-Level only got me so far.).

Out of all the characters I've written, Ruby holds a very special place in my heart. She's an extension of myself and many of her traits are my own—her overall appearance, her Jewish heritage, her ADHD, and her introverted nature and self-doubt and contempt. I also went through six months of homelessness at age fourteen with my mum and my younger sister. Although, luckily, we had family that helped us through that difficult time. A lot of people don't have that safety net.

In 2012, I worked with my local homelessness charity while making a short film with a friend to fundraise for them. We interviewed people who had formerly or were currently living on the streets. Some were even extras in the final scene. A few of their harrowing stories inspired the opening chapter of this book. I hope Ruby's inner thoughts gave you an insight into the harsh realities of homelessness and reminded you that anyone can fall on hard times, especially in the current climate. It's easy to judge from a place of privilege when you may not be aware of the intricacies of other people's lives and backgrounds.

I hope Ruby's story encourages you to be kinder and more mindful of those who are different to you. I also hope it inspires you to open yourself up to friendship and love, even when pain seems inevitable.

And finally, don't give up on yourselves. I nearly did, too many times, and even if this debut is a complete failure, the daily struggle will have been worth it.

Surviving the journey will be enough to make you proud, I promise.

This is the Samaritans website if you need to talk to someone:

https://www.samaritans.org

And this is the Crisis charity's website if you'd like more information on how you can help end homelessness:

https://www.crisis.org.uk

ACKNOWLEDGEMENTS

First and foremost, I want to thank *you*, the reader. I hope I haven't melted your brain and broken your heart too severely. If you ever decide to reread *The Haven Ten*, I've left little clues which will become clear once you know The Haven Ten's secret.

I also want to thank the BookTok community for your acceptance and encouragement. I wouldn't have had the confidence to self-publish without you bookish fiends and your willingness to embrace indie authors, like myself.

Thank you to Sophie Claypole, my friend and editor. Your eagerness to dive into this project was such a comfort and relief. Our trust in each other is so special, and I learnt a great deal while working with you. I hope to work with you again in future.

To my more recent beta readers and book besties: Vicky Seymour-Hunt and Morgan Koogle. Your support means the world to me. I lived for your real-time reactions and feedback. Not many people in my life took an interest in this book, and I was riddled with self-doubt over it. But your encouragement renewed my passion for this project. Also, Joyce Dunne: you're the best person to build someone up. I'm so grateful to have made such wonderful friends who lift me up every day.

A huge thank you to my little sister, Laura Bayley. You've always been the first person to read everything I write. Without you, I wouldn't have finished this book. You kept me writing chapter after chapter, book after book. You know the characters as well as I do, and I love you even more for that.

I also want to thank my friend, Stephanie Poole. You're the best cheerleader anyone could ask for. You read this book way back when it was a rough draft, and your support has never wavered. You've always encouraged me to go for it and I finally listened.

Thank you to my friend, Jade Parkes, for proofreading. Your sharp eyes really helped me out and your enthusiasm was infectious.

And to my partner, Russell Wood: your support has been emotional as well as financial. You're not much of a reader, but you still read this book and humbled me with your honest opinions. It also would have taken me much longer to publish if you hadn't loaned me the money for editing. I'm sorry you've had to suffer through endless days and late nights of me typing away while you shouldered the brunt of the household responsibilities. You enabled me to make use of my ADHD bouts of hyperfocus and encouraged me through my many down days when I thought I wasn't good enough to be a writer. I love you endlessly.

Lastly, I want to thank all the people in my life who have been there for me through the tough times. You've all helped me write and publish this book with your love and emotional support: especially my parents, John and Michelle, and my best friend Holly Sugden.

About the Author

Amber Bayley started writing screenplays in her teenage years, when she dreamed of becoming an actress and filmmaker, but writing books held a special storytelling magic.

Amber spends her time on the southeast coast of England, living with her partner, a mini dachshund called Hazel, and two needy cats, Rosie and Cleo.

When Amber isn't being a hyper-focused hermit—spending all of her free time reading and writing books—she's teaching herself digital art and travelling the world, one mini-break at a time.

Printed in Great Britain
by Amazon

27031313R00260